Faye Kellerman was born in St Louis, Missouri and graduated in Mathematics and Dentistry at UCLA. She began her career as a dentist but turned to writing after the birth of her eldest child in 1978. She has now completed seven novels featuring Detective Sergeant Peter Decker and Rina Lazarus and one historical mystery. In between writing, she tries to find the time to indulge in her two favorite hobbies, music and gardening. She has four children and lives with them and her husband, novelist and psychologist Jonathan Kellerman, in Los Angeles.

Sanctuary

Faye Kellerman

First published in Great Britain in 1994
by HEADLINE BOOK PUBLISHING

First published in paperback in 1995
by HEADLINE BOOK PUBLISHING

A HEADLINE FEATURE paperback

10 9 8 7 6 5 4 3 2

ISBN 0 7472 4702 1

Typeset by Keyboard Services, Luton, Beds

Printed and bound in Great Britain by
Cox & Wyman Ltd, Reading, Berks

HEADLINE BOOK PUBLISHING
A division of Hodder Headline PLC
338 Euston Road
London NW1 3BH

DEDICATION

As always with love and gratitude to my family

And a special thanks to Eli Benaron and Yehoshua Grossgold for giving me a wealth of information and for being such terrific tour guides

Part I
AMERICA

1

The call was a surprise; the reason behind it even more so. Though Rina had known Honey Klein née Hersh for years – the two girls had been classmates – she had never considered her a close friend. Their small Orthodox high school had had a student body of eighty-seven at the time of Rina's graduation: twenty-two seniors – twelve boys, ten girls. Rina had been friendly with all the girls. But as the years passed, the two women had crossed paths only sporadically; the chance meetings had held nothing beyond pleasantries. Honey had married young to an ultra-religious Chasidic diamond dealer. She had four kids. She seemed happy.

So when Honey asked if she and the kids might spend a week with Rina and her family in Los Angeles, Rina thought it strange. Her first thoughts were: Why me and why *here*?

Peter's ranch was located in the rural portion of the San Fernando Valley. The environs had wide streets and big commercial plots roomy enough for storage centers, wholesalers, and warehouses. Sure, the newer residential neighborhoods sprouted tract homes and apartment buildings, but there were still many ranches large enough to stable horses and livestock – parcels similar to Peter's homestead, *her* homestead now. The area was LA's last refuge of undeveloped scrubland, most of it hugging the timbered foothills of Angeles Crest National Park.

Rina knew Honey had closer friends residing in the heart of the Jewish communities – in the Fairfax area, Hancock Park, or the newer westside area of Beverlywood. Honey had girlfriends who owned homes within walking distance of the Orthodox synagogues, of the kosher restaurants and bakeries. No one deeply religious stayed at the Deckers' ranch because it was so isolated. But when Rina had mentioned the geography over the phone, Honey had brushed it off.

'So it's a little off the beaten track,' Honey stated. 'I figured it's about time I let the kids see the other side.'

'The other side?' Rina asked.

'You know . . . how the other half lives.'

'This isn't exactly a den of iniquity, Honey. I still cover my hair.'

'No, no!' Honey protested. 'I didn't mean that. I'm not criticizing you. Who am I to judge? By the other side, I meant the fun stuff – Universal Studios, Disneyland, Knott's Berry Farm, Grauman's Chinese Theater with the movie stars' footprints. Is that old relic still around?'

'It's called Mann's Chinese Theater now,' Rina said. 'You aren't planning to take the kids to the *movies*?'

'No,' Honey said. 'Just the outside of the building. And the sidewalks with the stars in them. They're still around, right?'

'Yes.'

'No, we're definitely not going to the movies,' Honey said, quickly. 'It would be too much for them. We don't have televisions here. We don't even have *phones* in the village. Well, that's not true. There are phones in the produce store, the butcher shop, and the bakery. For emergencies. But we don't have phones in the houses.'

Rina knew lots of religious people who didn't own television sets or go to the movies. She knew plenty of Orthodox adults who shied away from popular fiction and magazines like *Time* and *Newsweek*. The stories were too lurid, the pictures were prurient. But no phones in the houses was a first.

'Since when is it halachically forbidden to use a phone?' Rina stared at the receiver. 'Aren't you using one now?'

'I'm using the one at the bakery,' Honey said. 'I know it sounds like every year some group is trying to *outfrum* the other. That another group goes to more and more extremes to shut out the outside world. But the Rebbe's not trying to do that.'

The Rebbe, Rina thought quickly. *Which* Rebbe? Most people thought the Chasidim were one cohesive group. In fact, there were many Chasidic sects, each one interpreting the philosophy of the *Ba'al Shem Tov* a little bit differently.

'I'm sure you have your reasons, Honey. I don't mean to sound disparaging. Goodness knows most people think me strange, being as religious as I am. And poor Peter. The guys at the station house think he's gone nuts. Like you said, who am I to judge?'

'You have to understand the *Leibben* philosophy,' Honey said. 'Modern machines drive wedges between people.'

Leibben, Rina thought. That's right. Honey had married a *Leibbener* Chasid.

'Once you get used to *not* using a phone, it really is very *nice*,' Honey explained. 'We take walks in the park and schmooze. We have lots of afternoon get-togethers . . . tea parties. It's kind of . . . quaint.' Honey giggled. Rina remembered it as one of the nervous mannerisms Honey had developed after her mother died. 'Anyway, if putting us up is too much for you . . .'

'I'd love to see you, Honey, if I can arrange it. Things are a little hectic since the baby's—'

'You had a *baby*?' Honey gasped. 'That's so exciting! *When*?'

'Hannah's nine months old.'

'Oh, Rina, how *wonderful*! You finally got your little *girl*! You must be *thrilled*!'

'I'm very lucky.' Rina noticed her voice had dropped to a whisper. The birth had gone smoothly but there were complications afterward. Hannah would be Rina's last baby and not by choice. There was a long pause. Honey asked her if everything was okay.

'Just fine.' Rina tried to sound chipper. A strain since chipper wasn't part of her normal vocabulary.

Honey picked up the slack. 'So the boys must be big by now . . . teenagers.'

'Fourteen and eleven.'

'Isn't adolescence so *difficult*?'

Actually, Rina found the boys easier the older they got. But she answered, 'It can be trying.'

'Mendel's turned into a very quiet boy. He's lovely, but I can never tell what he's thinking. And Minda is so moody. Everything I say, she jumps down my throat. We all really *need* this vacation. So you think you can put us up?'

'I'm pretty sure I can, but I have to check with Peter.' Rina paused. 'Not that it's any of my business, Honey, but Gershon doesn't mind doing worldly things like going to Disneyland?'

Honey didn't answer. There was background chatter over the line.

'Hello?' Rina asked.

'Sorry, I was distracted,' Honey said. 'Gershon's not coming. He's in Israel. Didn't I mention that?'

It was Rina's turn to pause. 'I don't remember. Does he know of your plans to take them to Disneyland?'

'He didn't ask and I didn't say. All he knows is that I'm going back to Los Angeles to visit some old friends.'

'Very old,' Rina answered dryly.

'We're not exactly ready for the glue factory,' Honey said. 'Though sometimes it feels that way. Rina, it's been wonderful talking to you. Thanks so much for everything. And if it's too much trouble—'

'Not at all,' Rina said. 'I'll ask Peter and call you back.'

'Great. I'll give you the bakery's phone number. Just leave a message that you called and I'll ring you back.'

Honey gave her the number. Rina wrote it down.

'When exactly are you planning to come out, Honey?'

'Soon. In two days.'

'Two days?' Decker looked at his wife. 'She didn't give you much notice, did she?'

Rina spooned yogurt into Hannah's mouth. 'Not a lot.'

Decker sipped his coffee, then took a bite of his turkey sandwich. Watching Rina feed their daughter, he was grateful for the peaceful interlude. His new assignment at the Devonshire station took him farther from the ranch each morning. But work was still close enough to steal an occasional lunch at home. He sat contentedly, smiling as Hannah smeared coffee-colored goop over her mouth ... Rina was trying to keep her tidy but it was a losing battle – baby one, parent zero.

7

Decker's eyes swept over the cherrywood dining table. Crafted in his bachelor days, it was too small for the family, the surface scratched and gouged. But Rina could be hopelessly sentimental. She refused to part with his handiwork.

'Who is this Honey lady anyhow?' Decker said. 'I never heard you mention her name before.'

'That's because we weren't close.'

Decker finished half his sandwich. 'So what's she looking for? A free hotel?'

Rina wiped Hannah's mouth. 'I think there's more to it than that.'

'Such as?'

'Such as why didn't she call Evie Miller? She and Evie were as thick as thieves. If I were Evie, I'd be hurt.'

Hannah sprayed a mouthful of yogurt in Rina's direction. Without pausing, she threw back her head and chortled with delight.

'Very funny,' Rina said. But she was smiling herself. 'How come I can't get angry with you, Channelah?'

'Because I'm too cute, Mommie,' Decker answered.

Once again, Rina tried feeding Hannah, but the baby grabbed the spoon and started to bang it on her high chair tray. Rina leaned back in her chair. 'I don't know why she didn't call Evie.'

'Maybe she did. Maybe Evie doesn't want her. The woman sounds a little odd.'

'I wouldn't exactly say she was odd—'

'She doesn't own a telephone?'

'It's part of the ethos of the village.'

'The *village*?' Decker shook his head. 'What's wrong with living in a city or at least a *town*? Since when is upstate New York sixteenth-century Poland?'

'It's a psychological thing, Peter. Blocking out the outside world. Less distraction. Easier to learn Torah.'

'They sure don't mind asking for money from the outside world.'

'Everyone has to live, including scholars.'

'It's possible to work *and* learn. I don't believe in welfare for able bodies, Jews included.'

'The Leibben Chasidim are extreme,' Rina admitted. 'Their Rebbe has some very odd ideas about kabbalah and how it relates to the messiah and afterlife. It's considered very way out, not at all accepted belief.'

'Was Honey always fanatically religious?'

'Not at all. She grew up like me. Modern Orthodox. She had a big crush on John Travolta. I think she saw *Saturday Night Fever* ten times.'

Decker finished his sandwich and didn't say anything. Rina poured a half-dozen Cheerios on Hannah's high chair tray. The little girl dropped the spoon, stared at the Os, then carefully pinched one between her forefinger and thumb, successfully navigating it to her mouth.

Rina wiped the baby's plastic bib. 'You've got the cop look in your eyes, Peter. What is it?'

'What do you think she's really after?' Decker asked.

'An escape,' Rina said. 'But so what? You know how stultifying the religion can be at times.'

'Really now?'

Decker was impassive. Rina hit his good shoulder the one without the bullet wound. 'Why shouldn't Honey have an opportunity to cut loose?'

'You up for entertaining her?'

'Actually, Peter, I think it would be nice to have a little company. Someone to reminisce with.'

Decker smiled to himself. Could someone as young as

9

Rina actually reminisce? Because she was young – twelve years younger than he was. Something Decker didn't like to think about.

Rina liberated Hannah from the high chair and gave her to Decker. 'So what should I tell Honey? Should I give her the okay to come out?'

'It's up to you, darlin'. It's okay by me.'

Decker bounced Hannah on his knee. She was a good-sized baby – tall and long-limbed with red hair and pale skin just like him. But feature for feature, she looked like Rina, thank God. The baby gave him a drooling grin of six teeth, tiny fingers going straight for the mustache. With little hands on his mouth, Decker rotated his mustache to his daughter's glee.

He said, 'I'm just wondering how you get from John Travolta to no phones.'

'How d'you get from being a Southern Baptist to an Orthodox Jew, Peter – a much bigger transition. Life's just full of little mysteries.'

'I was running toward something, Rina. Mark my words. This woman's running *away* from something.'

'Agreed. So let her run here and I'll find out what it is.'

2

Nine months later and Decker still couldn't turn off the autopilot. Whenever he pulled out of his driveway, the unmarked strained to go east instead of west. He'd left behind a decade of memories at the Foothill substation – most of them good, some bad, and one overzealous chase-turned-political nightmare that would haunt the city for years to come. He had made few friends and missed few people. But habit was habit, and at times he felt nostalgic for the old country.

Exiting the 118, he made a quick series of turns until he was riding west on Devonshire. At this point, the wide, pine-lined boulevard was bordered by rows of small wood-sided ranch houses resting on patches of pale winter lawn. The driveways played host to older-model compacts and trucks as well as bikes and trikes. Most of the homes had attached two-car garages, ubiquitous mounted basketball hoops hanging above the parking structures.

Anywhere USA. The only hint of Southern California was the full-sized orange trees towering over the houses they framed. The street even held a couple citrus groves – remnants of LA's long-gone agricultural days.

Decker lowered the sun visor in the car, cutting the glare, and slipped on a pair of shades. He thought about his new job.

11

The transition had been easier than expected because Marge had come with him. Originally, Homicide at Devonshire had only one vacant slot. But with a little savvy, Decker had managed to stretch a single into a double. Given the profound need for LAPD to liberalize, the brass was quick to pick up on his drift. Yes, the carefully calculated decision to place Detective Dunn – i.e., Detective Dunn, the *woman* – in Homicide detail was politically correct. Still, the promotion had been just. Marge had the requisite experience, a keen mind, and lots of patience – a great combination for a murder investigator.

Cranking open the car window, Decker inhaled clean air, enjoying the smogless blue skies common during the cooler months. As he traveled west, the houses gave way to bigger buildings – apartment houses, factory showrooms, a medical plaza, and the ever-present shopping centers. Traffic was light, the area surrounded by foothills made green and lush from the recent rains. The mountains were the boundaries of LA City – to the north was the Santa Clarita Valley, to the west Simi Valley. Most of the hillside areas were still undeveloped plots or regional parkland, giving the San Fernando Valley plenty of breathing room.

Decker thought about his partner.

It was Marge's first time in Homicide and she was champing at the bit for a *real* case. All they'd gotten so far were two gang-related retaliations, a half dozen Saturday night party-hearty shootings, and some irate spouses with problem 'tudes toward their adulterous mates. Messiness with no brainwork.

But thems what it is.

Even if the cases were 'routine', it didn't mean the victims were any less dead. Marge had treated each assignment with impeccable sensitivity. But having spent some six professional years with the woman, Decker knew she wanted serious cerebral exercise. She wanted to *prove* herself.

Marge was around Rina's age – old enough to know the ropes but still full of the fire of youth. Marge was standing on the threshold of opportunity and was *bursting* to take a giant step forward.

They had been on Homicide detail for less than a year. Time was on her side.

Living in California earthquake country, Decker couldn't figure out why Devonshire, like most of LAPD's station houses, was made out of bricks. Maybe the architect wanted to impress upon the bad guys that the station was wolf-blowing durable and could double as a jail in a pinch. Or maybe the city had a sweetheart contract with a brickyard. Whatever the reason, Devonshire was like the rest of LA's station houses – a windowless masonry building adorned by an American flag. Except that this substation had the unique pleasure of being located next to power transmitters. Yes, a policeman's job was a dangerous one, but up to now, leukemia hadn't been a real concern.

What the hell. So he'd glow in the dark.

He drove the Plymouth to the back lot restricted to 'authorized personnel only', then saw Marge stalking through the parking area. She wore an olive car coat over khaki slacks, her arms folded across her chest. Her face, normally softened by doelike eyes, was stiff with tension. Decker honked, Marge looked up. Immediately, she shifted direction, tramped over to the Plymouth, and plopped down in the passenger's seat.

'Know what that Davidson asshole did?'

'What?'

'God, I hate that man. He treats me like a *peon*. While I realize I *am* a peon in this upper echelon of the boy's brigade, you'd at least think he could fake it better.'

'Are we talking in the car for a reason?'

Marge extracted a slip of paper from her purse. 'I've got to go calm down a hysterical woman who thinks Martians kidnapped her brother and his family. Believe it or not, Davidson has classified this as a possible homicide. You want to come with me?'

'What's the address?'

Marge handed him the paper. Decker looked at the numbers – Mountain View Estates. He did a three-point turn and pulled out of the lot.

'He gives me nothing but bullshit assignments, Pete,' Marge went on. 'He doesn't even *try* to hide it. He knows they're bullshit! He wants *me* to know they're bullshit, too! You know how he phrased this little jaunt? "Get this lady off our backs, Dunn. If something *important* comes up, I'll contact Pete and he'll fill you in." Can you *believe* that jerk? Not even a *pretense*.'

'Diplomacy isn't the Loo's strong suit.'

'The guy has a hard-on for me.'

'Yes, he does.'

Marge did a double-take. 'He does?'

'Yep.' Decker turned west onto Devonshire. 'Your appointment was shoved down his throat. He's resentful. But that's his problem.'

'But *I* gotta live with it.'

'So live with it.'

'That's your answer? Live with it?'

14

'Yep.' Decker headed toward the foothills. 'What's this assignment all about?'

Marge's jaw began to ache. She forcibly relaxed her mandible. 'Just what I said. We gotta make nice to some woman who's wondering why she hasn't heard from her brother.'

'How long has it been?'

'I don't know. At least twenty-four hours. The blues were out there yesterday. At the brother's house. No one was home but everything looked fine. Apparently that wasn't good enough. The lady's been calling nonstop, demanding some detectives.'

'Has she filed a Missing Persons?'

'I don't think so. It sounds like she wants reassurance more than anything. Someone to look around the house again and convince her that nothing terrible has happened.'

'What kind of family are we talking about?'

'Uh . . . wait a sec.' Marge pulled out her notebook. 'An Officer Mike Gerard interviewed her. Family consists of a mother, father, and two kids – boys. Teenagers specifically. My first thought was an impulsive vacation. But according to Gerard, the woman said no way.'

'That makes sense,' Decker said. 'It's in the middle of the school year. Weird time to take a vacation.'

'Or a great time,' Marge stated. 'Beat the crowds. I haven't talked to the woman directly. She's been persistent with the calls, a real pain in the ass.'

'What's her name?'

'Orit Bar Lulu. Bar Lulu is two words.'

'She's Israeli?'

'You got it. She's also a real estate agent.'

Decker said, 'Why does she think something happened to her brother and his family?'

'I don't know,' Marge said. 'Davidson dismissed me without many details. What do you mean, I should "*live with it*". Don't you think I should say anything?'

'You can do what you want. It's a free country.'

'You think I should just shut up and do nothing?'

'Let your *work* talk for you. You're a great detective, Marge. Eventually, you'll get a case that'll show off your balls. When you earn your stripes with Davidson, eventually he'll leave you be.'

'So the best I can hope for is a grudging acceptance?'

'I don't know Davidson any better than you do. Maybe he'll continue to be an asshole. Maybe he'll come around and turn out to be okay.'

'And in the meantime?'

'In the meantime, we do our job. Which means you've got to go out there and calm down an hysterical woman. Take my word for it, Margie. The assignment is no cakewalk.'

Mountain View Estates was a fifty-home development tucked into the Santa Susana pass, replete with communal tennis courts, pools, spas, and a gymnasium for homeowner exercise in inclement weather. Built in the profligate eighties, the customized tract houses, standing on third-of-an-acre lots, started at half a mil. Some of the houses had been originally priced upward of seven figures. But then the nineties hit, and with it a crash in California real estate prices. Decker had known a fair share of people who'd gotten into trouble by overextending themselves. With a sudden downturn in income coupled with a heavy mortgage, people were often forced to sell their bits of paradise at rock-bottom prices.

The given address put them curbside to a mock Tudor

roofed in genuine slate and faced with used brick and cross-hatched beams painted deep brown. The lawn was a rolling emerald wave breaking onto a shore of leafy ferns and leggy impatiens that would rebloom when the weather got warmer. The front door was wood-paneled and inlaid with stained glass. Decker parked the Plymouth, and he and Marge got out of the car. They began walking up the basketweave-brick pathway that led to the entrance.

Guarding the manor was a skinny woman with short black hair snipped close to the scalp. She wore a jewel-studded, oversized black T-shirt, black spandex leggings and backless heeled shoes, toenails polished fire-engine red just like her dragon-long fingernails. She had dark eyes and a dark complexion, her cheeks accented with blush. Half-dollar-sized gold earrings hung from her lobes. Decker wondered how a thin fold of skin could tolerate such weight. Her eyes became alive when she saw help had arrived. She tapped her watch.

'*Finally!*' She began rummaging through a floppy hand-bag as big as a carry-on suitcase. 'You want me to open the door for you? I don't want to go in the house again. To see it so empty . . . lifeless.' Her voice faded. 'You just tell me everything's okay, I leave you alone.'

She spoke with a heavy accent.

Marge looked at Decker. The woman suddenly became pale. 'You're the police, no?'

Marge took out her ID. 'Yes, ma'am, we are the police.'

'Orit, please. This is my brother's house. I haven't heard from him in going on two days.'

'What makes you think something's wrong?' Marge asked. 'Maybe he went on vacation.'

'Impossible,' Orit stated. 'Dalia works at my office; she

didn't say anything. The boys are in the middle of school. The school knows nothing. Besides, I come here yesterday. They are still getting the paper and their mail.' She craned her neck to look up at Decker. 'My brother's a diamond dealer. He deals in big stones and lots of cash. It's hard times. People do funny things. You never know. I'm worried about my brother.'

Marge and Decker exchanged glances, then pulled out their notebooks. Marge said, 'You think your brother might have been involved in something . . . illegal?'

Orit bristled. 'Impossible. My family has been in the diamond business for over a hundred years. Our family name is Yalom, which means diamond. My father taught us to cut diamonds before we could read. Arik wouldn't do shady busine s. But there are others who are maybe not honest.'

'Are you thinking about anyone specifically?' Decker said.

Orit bit a red bottom lip. 'No. No one particular. You go in, okay?'

Marge said, 'The officers who were out here yesterday said everything looked fine.'

Orit waved her hand in the air. 'I didn't like them – their attitudes. They looked unhappy to help me. Like why is this crazy foreigner wasting our time.'

'I'm sure that wasn't the case,' Marge said.

She shrugged. 'Fine. You can think what you want.'

'Did you tell the officers that your brother's a diamond dealer?' Decker asked.

'No. Why should I give personal information to people who sneer at me? You two at least take out notebooks and look like you're listening. You pretend good.'

Decker smiled. 'We're not pretending. We're here to

serve the community. When was the last time you heard from your brother?'

Orit said, 'Two days ago. I called police yesterday, then again today. I don't like this. I'm nervous.'

'Place seems pretty quiet,' Marge said. 'Family have any pets?'

'No. Arik doesn't like animals.' Orit sighed. 'Maybe I'm over-reacting. But this is crazy. Arik wouldn't leave without telling me. Dalia wouldn't leave without telling me. And the boys? Where are the boys? Why would they pull them out in the middle of the term and not tell me – even for a few days?'

'Do they go to the local high school?' Marge said.

'Yes. My daughter is in the same class as Dov. Gil is a grade older.'

'Have you asked your daughter about her cousins?' Marge asked.

'Yes, of course, what you think?' Orit shook her head. 'She knows nothing. Something's wrong.'

Decker slipped his notebook into his suit jacket, then ran his hand through ginger hair. 'Do you want to open the door for us?'

Again, Orit began hunting through her purse. 'Yes. I can wait out here?'

Marge said, 'You can wait out here.'

Orit pulled a key from her valise. 'Ah, here it is.' She snapped open the dead bolt and pushed the door wide open. 'Take your time and look around.' She gave them a wan smile. 'Please, tell me I am hysteria. Tell me I'm wrong.'

3

The first thing Marge noticed was how cold it was inside. Lots of stone and marble – elegant but not friendly. Footsteps echoed as she and Decker ambled around the massive two-story entry. The house appeared to be a center-hall plan – living room to the right, dining room to the left, and straight back was the family room. She stopped and peered upward at a coffered ceiling fifteen feet away.

'Pretty nifty spread. Guess diamonds are recession proof.'

'Guess so.'

'What do you think about Ms Bar Lulu?' Marge asked.

'She made me curious.'

'Me, too,' Marge said. 'Think she knows more than she's letting on?'

'Maybe.' Decker looked around. The place was massive, made even a person as big as he was feel small. First thing Decker noticed was an ornate, oversized mezuzah on the doorframe – a sterling-silver sculpture of vines and grape leaves and fruit. In his house, it would have looked grossly out of place. But here, it added to the splendor. Yet something about it disturbed Decker. He shrugged the feeling off.

'I'll take the downstairs, you take the upper story ...

stories. I thought I saw some dormer windows. Could be just a storage attic.'

'Or a place to stuff bodies,' Marge said. 'I'll holler if I notice something.'

'Ditto.'

Marge disappeared. Sketching the floor plan, Decker took in the entry area. It was big enough to be furnished – a large center table holding abstract sculpture, flanked by a couple of brocade wing chairs. Two open-shelf display cases sat against opposite walls. The one on the left, announcing the dining room, contained china plates on stands. The right sidewall held figurines and a bowl.

Decker studied the pieces in the case on the right wall. There were two multicolored porcelain fighting dogs, a set of cloisonné parrots, a set of aqua vases decorated with fire-breathing dragons, and a simple green bowl with a cracked glaze that probably cost a month's salary.

He stared at the pieces, eyeing them longer than he should have. The dogs were standing in a perfect line, the bright-colored glazes running into one another. The bowl was obviously the centerpiece of the cabinet. It took up a shelf by itself. The parrots looked very old; the blue enamel was dulled and drab. The vases were shaped like a thermometer bulb, dragons snarling as they encircled the bases and curled up the stems.

Interesting pieces, yet, again, something about them was off-kilter. The house was taking on the appearance of an Escher drawing – lots of steps leading nowhere. He exhaled forcibly, then shrugged it off and moved on. He walked through an arched doorway and stepped into the living room.

It was more a museum than a room in a house – cavernous, with a vaulted ceiling and a white marble floor covered at strategic spots with lush, floral area rugs. Artwork adorned apricot-colored walls that were topped with carved crown molding. The furniture was grand – giant sectional sofas holding tapestry pillows and throw covers. Lots of tables but no lamps on them. Decker looked up. Small, recessed lights were set into ceiling molding.

He began to jot down some notes.

Lots and *lots* of porcelain – vases and figurines sitting on tables, resting on the mantel and in a six-foot-long mirrored display cabinet. An expensive collection, yet the pieces didn't appear to be affixed to the surfaces. He wondered if the Yaloms had earthquake insurance.

He went on.

There was a semicircular outpouching off the living room. Decker stepped inside, turning on the light switch with a latex glove. A high-gloss wood-paneled space filled with books. The library. Neat . . . clean . . . nothing seemed out of order.

He reversed directions to examine the other side of the first floor. The dining room was designed on the same large scale as the living room. One entire wall was taken up by a breakfront that sparkled with china and crystal. Another wall was the backdrop for an antique clock.

Yalom seemed well heeled. Once, Decker would have assumed the man rich. But the last decade's pernicious policy of spend-now, pay-later made it hard to tell. Decker wondered how many of the items had been bought and paid for. He walked through the butler's pantry and into the kitchen.

It was bigger than Marge's apartment – a sterile expanse with white lacquer cabinets and dark granite counters. A booth was tucked into the corner. He ran a gloved finger over the surfaces. They seemed clean, at least devoid of blood.

Women are murdered in the bedroom, men in the kitchen.

Decker opened the cutlery and utensil drawers. Nothing seemed to be missing, the carving knives seemed to be complete.

Decker continued to open the kitchen cabinets. The couple was obviously Jewish, but they didn't appear to keep kosher. Decker found only one set of everyday dishes and one set of fancy china. He turned the plate over. Limoges – *tref* Limoges. For some stupid reason, he was bothered by Israelis not keeping the dietary laws, especially since they had a grandiose mezuzah in the entry hall.

He thought a moment, then looked at the kitchen doorframe. No mezuzah. That wasn't unusual. Only Orthodox homes seem to have mezuzahs on every doorframe.

Onward – through the kitchen into a utility bathroom and a service porch. The door leading out to the backyard was locked. He flipped the bolt and scanned the rear portion of the property. Most of it was taken up by pool and patio. A long strip of flowers against a stucco wall marked the end of the property. It didn't look large enough to bury bodies, but he'd check it out later.

Back inside into the family room. Like the library, it was wood paneled. But the room was lighter, the walls' picture frames fashioned from blond, burled maple. The furniture was casual, but expensive. There was a large leather sectional littered with patterned pillows and woolen throws; off to the side were suede game chairs around a green felt-top table. One wall was taken up by a floor-to-ceiling fireplace; opposite the hearth was a mirrored wet bar. The mirrored shelves held cut-glass crystal and a modern glass-sculptured menorah. Decker had to look twice but that's what it was. The two remaining walls were hung with family photos. Decker took a closer look at the snapshots.

The Yalom boys as babies, as toddlers, then as bar mitzvahs holding the Torah, with their prayer shawls draped over their shoulders. They were still prepubescent in the religious photos. A year later – in graduation pictures from junior high – the boys showed progression toward adolescence. The most recent pictures captured the boys doing sports – basketball and soccer for one, swimming for the other.

From Orit, Decker knew the boys were a year apart. But it was damn near impossible to tell which one was the elder from the photos. After studying the pictures for the longest time, he came to the conclusion that Gil was the swimmer, he had a small mole under his eye. Dov, according to Orit, was a year younger.

Handsome kids – muscular with curly black hair and dark eyes. They looked like their Dad. There were several family photos – a few formal eight-by-tens and one casual eleven-by-seventeen group picture. Dad and the boys were standing, dressed in T-shirts and denim. Seated in front of them was Mom, wearing a flowing, flowered dress and laced-up boots.

Mom.

She looked out of place – a different genetic strain, with light eyes, poker-straight auburn hair, and a peaches-and-cream complexion. Her expression was soft, the eyes seemed gentle. The body language of the photo showed the boys leaning toward her, not the father . . . whatever that meant. Kids usually felt closer to their mother.

He walked over to the wet bar and looked in the drawers.

Inside were bottle openers, ice tongs and pick, glass stirrers, plastic toothpicks, and an ice pick. Lo and behold, it *wasn't* covered in blood.

Decker tapped his pencil against his notebook. On a superficial level, everything seemed fine. He closed his notebook and went upstairs.

'Four bedrooms,' Marge said. 'Parents' room, guest room, and each of the boys had his own room.' She brushed her toe against the soft maroon carpeting of an upstairs circular landing. 'The boys shared a bathroom, the master bath is a marble palace.' She threw up her hands. 'I didn't grid-search the place, but I looked carefully. Nothing jumped out at me. How about you?'

'Nothing slapped me across the face, either,' Decker said. 'What about the attic?'

'Unfinished. Nothing up there except for furnace equipment. Did you take a peek under the house?'

'Just crawl space except for a small wine cellar which looked untouched.'

'No secret torture chamber?'

'Not that I could find.' Decker perused his notes. 'The garage had all three cars in it. I also looked around the yard, in the pool house, in the flower bed. Nothing.'

'I did find a few pieces of luggage,' Marge said. 'They don't have a perfectly matched set. There could be a piece missing and I wouldn't know. Clothes seem complete, but again – take a pair of pants out, who'd know the difference?'

'They're going to make this hard on us,' Decker said. 'I've got a couple of questions. This guy's supposed to be a big diamond dealer, right?'

'Right,' Marge said. 'You're wondering if there is a safe.

None that I could find. I looked in closets, behind pictures, underneath area rugs. I take it you came up dry as well. Otherwise you wouldn't be asking the question.'

'What a pro,' Decker said. 'No, I came up empty.'

'Nothing in the cellar?'

'Unless it's behind all those collectible bottles. I didn't pull them all out.'

'And I didn't look behind the furnace in the attic,' Marge reported. 'But I did check out the toilet tank – where druggies hide their stash. Nothing. Did you check the freezer?'

'Yep. There was food and ice – the H_2O kind.'

'Why don't we ask Sis about the safe? See what she has to say. What's the next question, Rabbi?'

'The guest bedroom upstairs. I did a quick search inside. There were no clothes in the closet or in the dresser. The bathroom was spotless – no toothpaste mucking up the counter or sink. It was also decorated with *guest* towels, not regular towels.'

Marge was puzzled. 'Guest towels generally go in the guest room.'

'That's the point,' Decker said. 'It is definitely a *guest* room.' He rolled his stiff, beefy shoulders. 'There was no maid's room downstairs, Margie. A house *this* big . . . think Mom cleans it by herself?'

Marge said, 'So the maid isn't a live-in. You want to know who she is.'

'It's always good to take a look at the staff.'

Marge's eyes lit up. 'You're thinking an inside job?'

'I'm just thinking out loud.'

Marge laughed. 'So I'm leaping to conclusions. It relieves the boredom. I'll go ask Sis to step inside now. You want to do the primary questioning?'

27

'You do it,' Decker said. 'It's officially your assignment.'
Marge paused, then shook her head.

'What?' Decker asked.

'There's something spooky about this case.'

'Agreed,' Decker said. 'We comb the house and everything looks in military order. There are clothes in the closet, food in the refrigerator, and three cars in the three-car garage. Everything's perfect except where are the people? It's as if the place had been nuked with a neutron bomb.' He paused. 'Ready to talk to the sister?'

Marge nodded. They walked down the stairs into the marble entry. Suddenly Decker placed a hand on Marge's shoulder, stopping her from opening the front door.

'Wait a second.' Decker crooked his finger, then pointed to the display cabinet. 'What is wrong with this picture?'

Marge stared at the case. 'What do you mean?'

'Something looks . . . out of place.'

Marge eyed the pieces up close, then took a step backward and studied the case. 'The shelves are open. Aren't most display cabinets enclosed?'

Decker said, 'Now that you mention it, that's a little weird, too. But that's not what's bothering me.'

Marge took another step forward and scanned the pieces one-by-one. The top glass shelf was host to two fighting dogs, the second one held a simple green bowl, the third had a set of metal parrots, and the bottom one gave support to two aquamarine vases with bas-relief dragons on them.

'Nothing looks broken.'

'Nope.'

'Strange dogs,' Marge commented. 'All those colors dripping into one another. And the aggressive pose. Their backs are arched and they're baring their teeth. They're disconcerting.'

28

Decker nodded. It *was* the dog statues. Something about them was *bugging* him. He zeroed in on the teeth. Each statue had four pronounced canine teeth – two uppers and two lowers, all of them perfectly pointed. Not a chip or a crack to be seen.

Marge brushed hair out of her eyes. 'You know, Pete, if I were displaying the dogs, I'd have them facing each other instead of lining them up tail-to-trunk, elephant style—'

'That's it,' Decker interrupted.

'*That's* what was bothering you?'

'On the nose,' Decker said.

'You're more of an aesthete than I gave you credit for.'

Decker laughed. 'You know *why* it looks off?'

Again, Marge looked at the pieces.

'It's the parrots, Marge,' Decker said. 'The parrots are facing each other. But the *dogs* aren't.'

Marge said, 'So what does that have to do with the price of eggs in Outer Mongolia?'

Decker shrugged. 'Maybe nothing. But I'll ask Sis about it anyway.'

'She'll know why the dogs aren't facing each other?'

'Maybe she helped Mom position the pieces,' Decker said 'Just *maybe* she knows how much eggs cost in Asia.'

4

As she tucked the phone receiver under her chin, Rina's attention was diverted by Hannah's babbling. She was sitting next to her baby, the two of them playing on a comforter spread out on the living-room floor. It was a busy blanket, toys sewn into the quilting – a mirror, a teething ring, several blocks that squeaked, and lots of fuzzy decals. But Hannah had grown tired of eliciting peeps from the bunny's tummy. She started to complain.

Of course, the phone rang. Rina made the big mistake of picking up the call. Hannah's vocalizing increased in volume and frequency every time Rina spoke into the mouthpiece. The baby soliloquy finally culminated in a loud, wet raspberry.

'Hold on, Honey.' Rina attempted to swipe Hannah's mouth. The baby protested with a shake of the head and a loud *ababababababa*.

Honey said, 'Should I call back later, Rina?'

'No, we're really fine. She's just expressing her opinion.'

'She sounds adorable,' Honey said. 'I love babies. I love children. I think it's the innocence. I should have had a dozen more.'

Honey sounded riddled with regret. So much so, Rina wondered why she didn't have a dozen more. Within their culture, it wasn't the least bit unusual to find families with

31

kids numbering in the double digits. It gave Rina pause for thought. Maybe something had prevented Honey from having more. Maybe they had a lot more in common than Rina had first thought.

'Just *enjoy* her,' Honey went on. 'I don't have to tell you this, but they do grow up so fast. One minute they're snuggle bunnies, the next minute, they're big boys who'll *maybe* give you a peck on the cheek on your birthday.' She giggled. 'At least I get a peck. I know quite a few women whose sons refuse to touch them.'

'That's ridiculous,' Rina said. '*Negiah* – men and women touching – doesn't apply to mothers and sons.'

'Of course it's ridiculous,' Honey said. 'So what else is new? The Rebbe is just floored by this extremism. Sure he doesn't like phones. But machines are one thing, love is another. *Love* is what's important. Love between Man and *Hashem*, between Man and Man, between Man and Woman – it's what makes the world such a beautiful place. Love is what distinguishes us from the animals.'

Rina looked at Ginger, the family Irish setter. The big, rust-colored animal was seated on the blanket as well, her snout nuzzling Hannah's leg. Rina didn't know a lot about dogs – she'd married Peter, she'd married his animals – but it seemed to her that Ginger had an infinite capacity to love. Rina had always felt that it was conscience and repentance that made man different from animals. But Honey sounded so sincere, and her thought was a nice one.

'Love is wonderful,' Rina said. 'We have wonderful families, *Baruch Hashem*.'

Rina heard a stretch of quiet. She could make out background noises, someone asking for a dozen poppy-seed bagels.

Honey said, 'Rina, thank you for getting back to me so fast. And thank you for putting us up. I can't tell you how excited I am to be actually going on vacation.'

'I'm glad, Honey.'

'Abababababbam,' Hannah shouted. 'Yeeeeeeee!'

Rina gave the baby a bottle. 'Do you want me to call the old gang for you?'

A pause. Then Honey said, 'Truthfully no. I just want an opportunity to spend some time with the kids away from people. That's why—' She stopped herself.

'That's why you called me,' Rina said. 'It's okay. I'm not offended. You want to relax away from everyone. The community has grown, Honey. It used to be we knew everyone who wore a yarmulke. Not so anymore. It's pretty easy to go about your business without someone bugging you. But I don't think it'll ever fully lose the provincialism. It's what makes us close. But we both know it can be a little restricting.'

'I just need a vacation.' Honey sounded desperate. 'You don't know what a *tova* you're doing. Thank you so much.'

'You're welcome.'

Hannah threw her bottle across the living room. Immediately, Ginger leaped to her feet to retrieve it. At first when Hannah had learned to toss items, Ginger would chase after them, then sit by them, crying until someone picked them up. Rina had since coaxed her into retrieving. Since Peter never hunted, it was nice that Ginger was finally allowed to do her genetically encoded job. The dog gave Hannah the bottle again, only to see the baby throw it in the other direction. Again, the setter was up on her feet. The dog loved the game.

Rina said, 'So, Honey, when exactly are you coming out?'

Honey clucked her tongue. 'Would tomorrow morning be too soon?'

Actually, it would be too soon. But there was something needy in Honey's voice. Rina said, 'Anytime you want.'

'Wonderful!'

Rina could almost see Honey's smile through the line.

'And don't you dare put yourself out,' Honey insisted. 'Just putting us up is *dayenu*. It's enough! I don't know the flight yet so I'll call you when we arrive in LA. If you're not home, don't worry. We'll wait at the airport. It's the first time the younger kids have flown, so they'll be very excited about everything.'

Rina said, 'I'll be sure to be home all morning.'

'Thanks, Rina,' Honey said. 'From the bottom of my heart, *thank you*.'

'A safe?' Orit looked surprised. 'Why would he have a safe? He keeps all his loose stones in the vault downtown.'

'Surely your sister-in-law has some nice pieces,' Marge said. 'Where does she keep them?'

'Downtown.' Orit walked around the entry hall, rubbing her arms. 'When she wants to wear a piece, she calls Arik up and asks him to bring it home. That's what I always do.'

Decker said, 'You keep pieces with him?'

Orit nodded. 'They're family pieces – for me, for my brother, too. If Dalia wants to wear it ... okay. Someday my daughter will wear them at her wedding, *ken yirbu*.'

As Orit smiled, webbing appeared at the corner of her eyes.

'My father is a very clever man. He managed to smuggle out of Europe some beautiful pieces. They are in the family for hundreds of years. What jewelry Papa didn't use to bribe the border guards, he swallowed stone by stone. On the boat, he had a very bad case of diarrhea.'

She laughed, but it was tinged with sadness.

'They almost didn't let him into Israel – it was British Palestine back then. But the British were as bad as the Germans. A stone here, a stone there, all of a sudden the guards changed Mendel Stein into Moshe Yalom. They gave him a new identity, a new passport, everything. That's why my father taught Arik and me to cut stones – a profession to carry on the back.'

Decker said, 'Let me ask you this, Orit. You call up your brother and ask him to bring home the piece you want to wear, right?'

'*Nachon,*' she answered. 'Correct.'

'So you go out for the evening, wearing the jewelry. Then you go back home, right?'

'Yes.'

'Where do you keep the piece until you give it back to your brother the following morning?'

Orit didn't answer.

Decker said, 'You're going to have to trust someone, Orit, if you want to get to the bottom of this.'

'You think something's wrong, don't you?'

'We're a little concerned,' Marge said.

Orit shrugged. 'On my dresser. If I want to hide it I don't put it in my safe.'

'So you *do* have a safe,' Marge said.

'Yes, but only for the robbers.'

Decker and Marge looked at each other.

'They know you're in diamonds, you have to give them something if they break in. Otherwise, they get mad. But you don't keep the good stuff there ... only junk.'

Again, Marge and Decker traded glances.

'I learned that from my father, too,' Orit said.

'What else did you learn from Dad?'

Orit hesitated, then spoke in a burst. 'Before my father got a vault at the diamond center in Tel Aviv, he had to keep lots of loose stones at home. He used to hide them in the toilet.'

Marge said, 'We checked.'

'You *did* ?' Orit was shocked.

'Drug dealers keep their goods in the water tank,' Decker explained. 'We also checked the freezer – another common spot. Nothing. Any other suggestions?'

Orit stared at them, then shook her head no.

Marge looked around. 'If I were diamonds, where would I be?'

Decker tapped his foot. Again his eyes went back to the mezuzah. Being new to the Jewish religion, Decker realized, was why it had taken him so long to see what was wrong. Outside-door mezuzahs were supposed to be posted on the *outside* of the door frame. This one was on the inside. Maybe because it was so fancy, they didn't want it sullied.

But then again.

Decker slipped on a latex glove. 'Detective Dunn, could you get me a screwdriver from the trunk of the car?'

'You got it, Sarge.'

'What you're going to do?' Orit asked.

'You stick around,' Decker answered. 'I want a family witness here in case we find the mother lode.'

'What do you mean – mother lode?'

'Cash, money . . . possibly diamonds.' Decker pointed to the mezuzah. 'There.'

'What?' Orit said. 'You're crazy. That's a religious article.'

'I know what a mezuzah is, Ms Bar Lulu. I also know where they are supposed to be posted. *Beytecha oovesha'arecha* – your houses and gates – on the *outside*.'

Orit stared at him. 'You speak Hebrew?'

'No, but I know the *Sh'ma*.'

'I knew I liked you.'

Marge came back in and handed Decker the screwdriver. Carefully, he unwound the top and bottom screws that affixed the scroll holder to the wall. They came out more easily than he had expected. He peered inside the hollow rut of the silver casing.

Empty – where was the parchment that contained the holy prayer?

Was there ever a parchment?

He showed the empty holder to Orit. 'Can I bag this for evidence?'

'Evidence of what?' Orit asked.

'I want to have this dusted for prints.'

'You think Arik kept money there?'

Marge asked, 'What do you think, Ms Bar Lulu?'

'I think it's funny the *Sh'ma*'s not there, yes. But Arik is not a religious man.'

'So why put up a mezuzah period?'

'Maybe for the boys.' Orit waved her hand. 'Yes, take it for evidence. As long as it comes back.'

'Ms Bar Lulu,' Decker said, 'does your sister-in-law have a maid?'

'Not now. Dalia had wonderful help for six years. Amelia went back to El Salvador a month ago. Dalia is still looking. She is very particular who is in her house.'

'So who's been cleaning the house?' Marge asked.

'My lady, Bonita, helps Dalia once a week. Not much to do except laundry. The boys do their own rooms. Bonita was going to come tomorrow. What do I tell her?'

Marge said, 'Tell her to hold off until we find out where the family is.'

'That's what I think, too.'

Decker said, 'Do you know anything about the porcelain dogs in the front entry hall?'

'Dogs? What dogs?'

Guess that answered that, Decker thought.

'You want to take dogs, too?'

Decker shook his head. 'Just the mezuzah. I'll need you to sign something that states we have your permission to take it,' Decker said. 'Make sure that everyone's satisfied that we did this by the book.'

'By the book?' Orit asked.

'That we acted kosher,' Decker said.

'Ah, *that* I understand.'

5

Sitting at the conference-sized dining table, Decker felt like a movie mogul. The tabletop was a slab of pink marble swirled with white and blue – no doubt some custom job out of an exotic quarry. Orit Bar Lulu was at his right; Marge sat across the rose-colored sea. Orit seemed scared. Their prolonged presence had justified her suspicions and that was not good news. Decker placed his notebook on the stone, wondering if he could write without scratching the surface. He gave Marge the go-ahead.

'I'd like to ask you a few questions, Ms Bar Lulu,' Marge said.

'Of course. Why else am I here?'

Marge cleared her throat. 'When was the last time you saw or heard from your brother?'

'Two days ago.' Orit sighed. 'We had lunch together – Arik came to the office – the real estate office where Dalia and I work.'

'The name?'

'Manor One Realty.'

Marge wrote it down. 'Anything special happen at lunch?'

'Not a thing. Everything was regular.'

'They didn't seem nervous? Excited maybe?'

39

'I saw nothing. Of course, I wasn't looking for something wrong, you know?'

Marge nodded. 'Then what happened?'

'What happened?' Orit shrugged. 'Nothing happened. We ate lunch, talked about the kids. Then Arik and Dalia left.'

'Together?'

'Yes. It was close to quitting time so she left with him. The next day Dalia didn't come to work. I didn't think anything about it. Real estate agents work from their homes all the time. So maybe she took the morning off. I called her in the afternoon to ask her to pick up Sharoni. No answer. I called two, three times maybe. No machine, nothing. I thought that was strange so I called my brother at work. His partner told me he didn't show up today – no explanation, nothing. Shaul was mad, I could tell. I didn't want to get Arik in trouble, so I made excuses.'

'What kind of excuses,' Marge said.

'Oh, the usual. Something came up . . . ehhhh, he must have something important to do. Shaul didn't like my excuses. He's very hard on Arik, but that's not new.'

'What do you mean, "Shaul's hard on Arik"?' Decker asked as he wrote.

'They're partners. But they are very different – fire and water.'

Marge caught Decker's eye. They'd go over that one later.

Orit didn't seem to notice. 'But just like life needs fire and water, they needed each other. So what if they don't get along?'

'They fought publicly?' Marge asked casually. 'Or was it more like a cold war?'

'Both.'

'What's the problem?'

Orit appeared to be thinking. 'Shaul's . . . slow, not slow, but . . .'

'Deliberate?' Decker tried.

'Exactly. Shaul's deliberate. Arik has creativity – all the ideas. Some work, some don't. The boys are a perfect mix for business, but they get on each other's nerves. Shaul's always mad at Arik for being careless. Arik's always mad at Shaul for slowing him down. But they don't give up each other. They're too smart for that.'

Decker didn't know if it was a language problem, but Orit's choice of words seemed telling. 'What do you mean by Arik being careless?'

Orit said, 'What do I mean?'

Marge picked up on Decker's drift. 'Is Arik careless with Shaul's money?'

Orit shook her head. 'I don't mean careless. It's a difference in personality. Arik wants to go, go, go. Shaul says, "Now, wait a minute." '

'Does Shaul have a last name?' Decker asked.

'Gold. Shaul Gold.'

'He didn't know where Arik was?'

'No,' Orit said. 'He was angry that Arik didn't come to work.'

Marge looked up from her pad. 'Shaul was mad at Arik?'

'Very mad,' Orit said. 'And that made me worried. Why didn't Arik show up? Despite what Shaul says, Arik is very responsible. I called the police. They send two men who looked at me like I'm crazy.'

Marge said, 'The policy is to wait twenty-four hours before reporting an adult missing.'

'This is not just an adult, this is a whole *family*.' Orit started to bite her nail, then stopped herself. 'When Sharoni – that's my daughter – she tells me the boys weren't in school, I start to get *real* nervous. That's when I called the police again and asked for someone else. You think there's something wrong, too, no?'

Decker said, 'It's unusual for a family to leave without notifying someone.'

Marge said, 'You haven't heard from your brother or sister-in-law in two days?'

'Or my nephews.' She shuddered. 'God only knows where they are.'

'What do you mean?' Decker asked.

Orit bit her lip. 'I mean if something happened to Arik, why take it out on the boys?'

'What could happen to Arik?' Marge said.

Orit looked over her shoulder, then leaned toward Marge. She was squirming, Decker noticed. As if the place was bugged. Maybe it was.

Or maybe she was squirming from guilt.

Orit said, 'Suppose someone wanted to rob my brother. You know, force him to go down to the vault in the Mart. Maybe they would take Dalia as hostile.'

'Hostage,' Decker corrected.

'Yes, hostage, I mean. So they take Dalia. But *why* take the boys? Why not just leave them in school and leave them alone?'

'Maybe they were home when it happened,' Marge said. 'Maybe they were witnesses.'

'But they're *boys*!'

Marge didn't answer. Orit threw up her hands. 'I'm sick with worry. Those boys are like my sons.' Suddenly, she sprang up and began to pace, chewing on a nail as red and lacquered as a candied apple.

Marge said, 'Have you asked Shaul if he's seen Arik?'

Orit turned to Marge. 'If he . . .' She punched her hand in her fist. 'No, he wouldn't. I talk crazy.'

'He wouldn't what?' Marge asked.

'If he hurt my brother, I'll kill him.' Orit nodded forcefully. 'I'll chop his head off.'

Again, Marge and Decker traded looks.

Marge said, 'Do you suspect Shaul has something to do with Arik's alleged disappearance?'

'Do I suspect?' Orit sighed. 'I don't know. They have been partners for years. But times change, people change. Diamonds is a moody business. You win big, you lose big. Shaul is very dark and moody. You will talk to him?'

'Definitely,' Marge said.

Decker said, 'Anyone else we should know about, Orit?'

Orit paused, then shook her head.

'I hate to have to ask you this, Ms Bar Lulu,' Marge said. 'But do you know if either your brother or sister-in-law was having an affair?'

Orit's eyes widened, then she clucked her tongue. 'Oh, you people are terrible.'

Marge and Decker said nothing.

Orit let go with a faint smile. 'Not that I know. Arik's a very handsome man. When we were little in Israel, he had many girls. I'm sure he could if he wants. But he is devoted to Dalia, takes good care of her.'

'That doesn't mean he can't have someone else.'

'Maybe. But I don't know if he does.'

Marge said, 'Do they have any close friends we should know about?'

'I'll get you a list of all their friends I know.'

'That would be helpful,' Decker said. 'Does Ms Yalom have family here?'

'All in Israel,' Orit said.

'And your parents live in Israel?' Decker said.

'Yes.'

'Have you called your parents—'

'They are not there,' Orit interrupted. 'I am sure.'

Decker paused. He didn't like her adamant tone of voice. Was she hiding something? He'd deal with it later. 'Do you have any other family in the States?'

Orit shook her head.

'Do you have an address and phone number for Shaul Gold?' Marge asked.

'Just the number downtown,' Orit said. 'At the Diamond Center. I give you my brother's work number. I don't know if Shaul's there or not.'

Marge said. 'We'll find him. Tell us a little about Dalia and the boys.'

'What's to tell? She's sweet. They are good kids.'

'You say the younger boy is friends with your daughter?'

'Yes. Dov and Sharoni are friends.'

'I'd like to talk to your daughter, Ms Bar Lulu,' Decker said.

'Of course,' Orit said. 'Go to the school. Talk to her now. Maybe she knows something I don't!'

Decker hung the mike back onto the car radio. 'Secretary says Gold's in a meeting and won't be back in the office until tomorrow morning.'

'A ruse?' Marge asked.

'Who knows?' Decker lowered the unmarked's visor, trying to block out the western sun. 'We'll find his home

44

number and try him tonight. If he split, we'll have either our first suspect or another victim.'

'What do you think about Gold and Yalom not getting along?' Marge asked. 'Think she's setting him up?'

'What do you think?'

'She seemed nervous.'

'Yes, she did. But her brother's missing.'

'You think she's clean?'

'I'm reserving judgment,' Decker said. 'Bar Lulu's right about one thing. The boys missing means something's wrong. Either the family took off in a hurry or someone herded them as a unit to parts unknown. We don't get any action on this by tomorrow, we may want to contact the media for help.'

'You're really bugged about the boys.'

Decker said, 'My sons are around the same age.'

Marge looked at him. 'You have kids about every age, don't you?'

'A young adult, two teens, and an infant. I'm raising my own grandchild.'

Marge smiled. 'Should we go back to the station and file for a full-blown MP case? Then we could come back and check out the neighbors. Find out what they've heard over the past couple of days. Or over the past couple of *years*. Maybe the neighbors, unlike Orit, were aware of something fishy. They pick up on things like that.' She paused. 'Except the ones that thought the serial killer was a nice, quiet guy.'

'Just a regular Joe except for the vats of hydrochloric acid kept in the basement.' Decker turned the unmarked onto Devonshire, headed toward the station house. 'We have enough of a case to ask Davidson for time to canvass the area, check out the parents' workplaces.'

Marge clapped her hands. 'Let's do it.'

Dispatcher's static was beaming through the squawk box. Decker tuned out the noise automatically *except* if the crime happened to go down near his location. Funny how the ear adjusts to what's important.

Marge said, 'The school's on the way back to the station. Want to stop by first?'

'Sure, why not?'

They rode a few minutes in silence.

'I'll do the talking with the administration there,' Marge said. 'That's okay, right?'

'It's your case.'

'You really see it that way?'

'That's the way Davidson saw it.'

'Davidson was giving me busywork.'

Decker said, 'He may have been giving you bullshit, but if it turns into something big, he won't take it away from you.'

'You don't think so?'

'Nope. Why risk a discrimination suit?'

'And if he *does* take it away from me?'

'Go to Strapp. I'll support you.'

Marge grinned. 'Really?'

Decker was insulted. 'What the hell do you think? Marge, you're letting your imagination drag you down. Stop thinking worst case scenarios and let's concentrate on the present. How old are the Yalom boys again?'

Marge paged through her notes, pleased by Decker's support. Okay, so she was getting on his nerves. So what? They were *partners*.

She paused.

Partners. Just like Yalom and Gold.

Decker was irked by Marge's silence. 'The *case*, Marge?'

'Yeah, sorry.' Quickly, she sifted through her notes. 'The boys ... are ... fifteen and sixteen. Gil's the older. Dov is in the class with Sharoni. How about if I take the administrators and the records, and you talk to the girl. You're better with teenagers, having raised one yourself.'

'Fine.'

'How's Cindy doing? Is she still interested in police work after the Bellson/Roberts affair?'

Decker felt his jaw tense and willed it to relax. ' 'Fraid so.'

'She'd make a good cop.'

'Bite your tongue, Dunn.'

Marge shrugged. 'We could use bright and brave women like her on the force.'

'She's too smart to be a cop.'

Marge glared at him. 'Thanks for the compliment, Deck.'

'Stop going testy on me.' Decker glared back. 'She's my kid, Marge. I want her safe, not battling gangs in the street.'

'It's her decision in the long run.'

'Right now, I'm still in the short run. My preference for her is a job that doesn't require expertise with a piece. You want to fuel up with some java before we hit high school?'

'No, I'm fine,' Marge said. 'You changed the subject away from Cindy, Pete.'

Decker grinned. 'My, you're astute. You must be a detective.'

Marge grinned back. '*Homicide*, baby. And don't you forget it!'

6

It surprised Decker that the Yaloms sent their children to public school. Although the West Valley didn't have a big white-flight problem, private schools still abounded, and folks with money took advantage of the fancier prep schools. Education was important in Judaism. But the Yaloms weren't religious, and perhaps, being immigrants, they didn't feel comfortable in a high-brow environment.

West Valley was a good school – an old-style public institution built at a time when land was cheap and so were construction costs. Like most of LA Unified, West Valley ran full, sometimes overfull. Classes were large and the teaching staff always needed more than the district was willing to pay for.

Just like Devonshire. The department gave them *nada*. Most of the furniture and electronics in the squad room were donated by the public. As a result, nothing matched. Every desk had a different configuration, every computer had a different keyboard setup. But no one cared as long as it worked. Thank God for community spirit. Without it, the Dees would still be communicating via tin cans and a string.

The school sprang up on the right side. Decker turned into a wide, open parking lot before pulling up to a loading zone at the side of the school. They got out, Marge sticking

49

the 'official police business' placard on the unmarked's windshield.

Inside, the central hallway was filled with students dressed in haphazard manner, and teachers dressed almost as casually. The corridors were old, but the floor gleamed and the walls were free of graffiti and that said a lot. They found the principal's office and presented their badges to the red-dressed secretary. She was young and black, her hair straightened and clipped short. She glanced at their shields, her eyes resting on the metal for only a moment before settling back onto her word processor. She was singularly unimpressed.

'Which one is it this time?'

Decker and Marge exchanged tired smiles. Police presence was sadly nothing new even in the supposedly *good* public schools.

'We're not arresting anyone,' Marge said. 'We just want information.'

The red-dressed woman looked up. 'About whom?'

'Gil and Dov Yalom,' Marge said. 'Any idea where they are?'

'Gil and Dov...' The secretary scratched her head. 'Names aren't familiar.' She pointed to two empty chairs. 'Have a seat and I'll see if Mr Maldenado's in.'

She disappeared behind a door and Marge and Decker sat down. A moment later, the door reopened and a bald-headed black man motioned them into his sparsely furnished office.

Everything about Maldenado was smooth – his head, his dark complexioned cheeks, even the backs of his hands. He was medium height and weight, his wireless glasses framing eyes that were hooded and tired. He motioned them to sit, then sank into a worn leather chair. In front of him were piles of charts and papers. Decker had a feeling the man hadn't seen his desktop in years.

Maldenado rubbed his eyes. 'Who did you say you wanted?'

Marge said, 'We're looking for Dov and Gil Yalom.'

'Dov and Gil?' Maldenado was surprised. 'They're good kids. What'd they do?'

'Nothing,' Marge said. 'They're missing. Any idea where they are?'

Maldenado hesitated. *'Missing?'*

'Their aunt called us,' Marge said. 'She can't seem to locate the family. We thought maybe you'd know something.'

'Me?'

'The school,' Decker clarified. 'Did the parents mention anything to the school about a winter vacation?'

'I wouldn't know,' Maldenado said. 'You'd have to check with records.'

'Maybe the boys talked to some school chums,' Marge said. 'Mind if Detective Sergeant Decker talks to their friends while I check records?'

'It's all right with me.' Maldenado leaned back in his chair. 'What exactly do you mean by missing?'

'Just that,' Marge said. 'We can't seem to find where the family went.'

'And the boys are missing, too?'

'Appears that way,' Decker said.

Maldenado looked upset. 'Ordinarily, I'd think of runaways even from nice families. But with both brothers *and* the parents being gone . . . I hope this resolves very soon.'

Marge said, 'That's why we're here.'

Decker started with Sharona Bar Lulu sitting in Geometry

I. It was her last class of the day – the last period of the day – and Geometry was a subject she shared with Dov Yalom. Maldenado gave Decker a note to present to the teacher, asking her to excuse Sharona – less intimidating than presenting a badge in front of forty hormonally erratic teens.

But Sharona was still wary when Decker pulled her out of class. They were in the outside hall, the girl as stiff as a board, Decker trying to appear casual by leaning against the wall. She stuck close to the classroom door, her eyes darting around the hallway, looking for passersby, looking for someone to take her away from the uncomfortable position. Decker showed her his credentials. The girl studied them but they did little to calm her.

'Did your eema tell you she called the police about your uncle, aunt, and cousins?'

Sharona jerked her head up. 'My *eema*?' In a soft voice, she said, 'Are you Jewish?'

'Yes, ma'am.' Decker pocketed his billfold. 'Your eema is worried about your uncle and his family. We're trying to locate them. Would you have any idea where they might be?'

The girl shook her head, eyes fixed on the notebook she was clutching. She had black, straight hair that hung down to her waist. A pelt just like Rina's. Except Rina was very fair. This one was dark-complexioned like her mama. She had expressive eyes topped by thick, inky lashes and brows.

Decker said, 'Frankly, I'm a little concerned about them, too. It's unusual to go off without letting *someone* know where you're going.'

Sharona just shrugged.

'Did Dov say anything to you about a vacation?'

'No. I already told my mother that I don't know where he

is.' She grew agitated. 'I don't know where anyone is, I swear.'

Decker stood motionless, then raised his eyes. 'You swear, huh?'

'What do you want from me?' The girl burst into tears.

Decker blew out air. 'Can we talk somewhere a little more private?'

Sharona took two steps backwards. '*Who* are you?'

She was clearly spooked. Decker said, 'Sharona, we can talk right here. Or if you'd prefer, I'll come to your home tonight and talk to you with your parents around—'

'No!'

Decker was surprised by the vehemence in her voice. 'No? Why not?'

'Just...' Sharona's voice had become tiny. 'Just because. Please don't make me talk in front of my parents. *Please!* I don't want anyone mad at me. I didn't know what...'

The girl appeared to be swaying. Decker gently took her arm and led the frail teen to an empty room. He placed her in a chair, then sat across from her, making sure the door was kept open. He took out his pad and a pencil. 'Sharona, it's important for you to tell me everything you know.'

Sharona's eyes went from her lap, to the door, to Decker, back to the door, then to the ceiling.

Decker said, 'You care about your cousins?'

The girl nodded.

'Talk to me.'

'He told me not to tell anyone.'

'Who? Dov or Gil?'

'Dov. Told me not to tell anyone he called.'

'When did he call?'

'Two days ago. Before Eema called the police.' She

glanced at Decker, then looked away. 'He said he was going away. He didn't say where. He sounded nervous. He told me not to tell anyone, *especially* Eema and Abba. I asked him if he was in trouble . . .'

Decker nodded encouragingly.

Sharona met his eyes. 'He hung up. That was it.'

'And you haven't heard from him since?'

'I swear I haven't.'

'Why didn't you tell your eema about the call after she called the police?'

'I don't know.' Her lip began to quiver. 'I was scared she'd get mad at me for not telling her sooner. And I kept expecting to hear from Dov. I didn't know Dov would be . . . I didn't know the whole family . . .'

'Yes?'

'I didn't think they were missing. I thought Dov had just had enough. I thought he just needed to get away from it all, you know?'

Decker said, 'No, I don't know. Please tell me.'

Sharona covered her face, then wiped her cheeks. 'My uncle's a diamond dealer. He's very rich. Did you see the house?'

Decker nodded.

'Isn't it humungous?'

Again, Decker nodded.

'Uncle Arik is really rich. I mean *really, really rich*! He made a fortune in diamonds during the eighties. Dov told me he made lots of his money selling big stones to the Japanese and the Chinese living in Hong Kong.'

'Dov seems to know a lot about the business.'

'He works there. *They* work there – both of them. My cousins . . . you'd think they'd be spoiled rotten, right?'

'Possibly.'

'Well, they're not, at all. They have to beg for everything they get. That's my uncle. Eema used to say he was the same way as a kid.'

'What does she mean by that?' Decker asked.

'I think she meant he was always a tightass—' Sharona blushed. 'I mean he was tight with a buck.'

'His kids resent him?'

The girl looked at her lap. 'It's not like my cousins don't believe in work. I believe in working, too. Everyone has to work to feel useful. My mom doesn't have to work but she does. Aunt Dalia certainly doesn't need to work, but she does. My uncle just overdoes it. Dov and Gil are carrying a full load at school, *plus* after-school sports and music lessons. Gil's a top swimmer. They're both good students. But that's not *enough*. Uncle Arik makes them go downtown two days a week and on the weekends to learn about the diamond business. I don't talk to Gil so much, but I know it's a big drain for Dov. He's very resentful.'

'How does he express his resentment?'

'Sulks. Escapes into his head. What can he do?'

'Escapes? You mean drugs?'

Sharona shrugged. 'Maybe a little pot. But mostly I meant escape by being spiritual. He used to be very religious. I think deep down he's still religious, but . . .'

Decker encouraged her to continue.

'Dov wanted to be more Orthodox . . . traditional.'

'I'm traditional, I understand.'

Sharona eyed him. 'You don't look Jewish, you know that?'

'So I've been told. Go on, Sharona. What happened to Dov's journey into religion?'

'Nothing, that was the problem. Uncle Arik is very anti-Orthodox. Dov wanted to try to keep kosher, but my uncle wouldn't do it. See, Uncle Arik wasn't simply ... disapproving. He was mean about it.'

'He made fun of Dov?'

'Exactly. Like his feelings weren't important.' Sharona shrugged. 'To Uncle, they weren't. He wanted his sons to be clones of himself.'

Good luck, Decker thought. 'What about Gil?'

'Gil is happy-go-lucky. He can fake things better.' The girl bit her nail. At that moment, she reminded Decker of her mother. Sharona looked up. 'I don't think Gil likes the business any more than Dov does.'

'Does Gil get along with your uncle?' Decker asked.

Sharona shrugged. 'My uncle gets on Gil's nerves, too.'

'Your uncle seems to get on a lot of people's nerves,' Decker remarked.

'You mean his partner, Mr Gold?'

Decker didn't say anything, surprised that the kid knew about the conflict.

Sharona said, 'Dov and I talk a lot. He said his father and Mr Gold were always yelling at each other. And you know what?'

'What?'

'Dov said that Mr Gold was right most of the time. Once Dov agreed with Mr Gold right in front of his father. His father had a cow. The last couple of months, Dov and his father were fighting all the time.'

'Gil, too?'

'Gil has a car,' Sharona said. 'Gil avoids fights by escaping – literally.'

'But Gil has to work in the business, right?'

'Like I said, Gil can fake it better. Dov has a harder time lying. I told you he's very spiritual.' Sharona took a deep breath. 'So when Dov called me ... I thought he was running away to find himself. I thought he had finally had enough of his father and couldn't take it anymore. I didn't dare tell Eema. But I guess I should have.' The teen's eyes watered. 'If something happened to them—'

'Don't torture yourself,' Decker said. 'They could be safe and sound somewhere. You thought you were keeping your cousin's secret. You couldn't have known that it might be something bigger.'

Tears flowed down the girl's cheeks. 'You think it might be something bigger?'

'Yes, I do,' Decker said.

'Like ... what?'

'I'm not sure yet. I need to ask you a few more questions. Tell me exactly what Dov said when he called.'

Sharona closed her eyes. 'Something like ... "Shar, I'm going away for a while." I asked him where he was going. He didn't answer. He just said he needed to get away. Then he made me swear I wouldn't tell anyone he called, especially Eema or Abba. Then I asked him if he was in trouble and he hung up.'

'Where did he call you?'

'On my phone.'

'Do you have a private line?'

The girl nodded.

'I'll need your phone bill. I'm going to have to tell your eema why I need it. Do you want to tell your eema about the conversation or should I?'

The girl blew out air, lifting bangs off her forehead. 'I'll tell her. We have to do this right away, don't we?'

'Yes, we do. I know Dov told you to keep this quiet. But I think he was really begging for help.'

'I sure hope you're right.' She looked upward. 'Because

I'm going to get grounded. I don't care. It's worth it if it'll help Dov.'

'It'll more than help, Sharona. Who knows? It could even save a life.'

7

At least the jerk was listening, Marge was forced to admit.
She and Decker were sitting across from the Loo in his
office. Old Thomas 'Tug' Davidson – once a Marine,
always a Marine – still wore his hair in a crew cut. The fifty-
five-year-old geezer didn't realize that crew cuts had come
full circle and were considered a *statement* by white boys
with 'tudes. Fashion didn't interest Davidson. He wore
black suits, white shirts, black ties, and oxfords as oversized as the same-named dictionary. Tug was built like a
barn – wide and strong. Marge felt he had probably
declared holy war on fat many years ago.

'Go over this one more time,' Davidson said.

Marge repeated the pertinent information. The family
had disappeared two days ago, the only hints of foul play a
one-minute phone call and an empty silver case that should
have held a prayer parchment. The Yaloms' sister had
called the police in a panic. When interviewed, she had
seemed on the level, but who knew?

'This guy, Yalom, is a diamond dealer?' Davidson
said.

'Yep,' Decker said. 'Does very well for himself judging
by the house. But to hear his niece talk, Yalom's a
tightwad. I was wondering why he didn't send his kids to
private school. Maybe he's too cheap.'

59

'Or maybe the niece is your average, bimbo teenaged girl with a big mouth.' Davidson said, 'The school doesn't know shit about the boys' whereabouts?'

'Not a thing,' Decker said. 'I interviewed quite a few of their chums. They seem in the dark as well.'

'Except for the niece who got a phone call,' Davidson said. 'Where was the booth?'

Decker said. 'About two miles from the house. It's a three-block shopping center. I have nothing definitive at this point. Tomorrow, I'd like to interview the store owners. It'll take time, but something might pan out.'

Davidson nodded, folding sausage-shaped fingers into fists. 'Tell me about this silver case.'

'It's a standard Jewish talisman, for lack of a better word,' Decker said. 'The one for the front door is always posted on the outside frame. The Yaloms had theirs posted on the inside—'

'Could be an oversight,' Davidson said.

'Not a chance,' Decker said. 'It would be like wearing your underpants on the outside. It was deliberate. I think it once held valuables – diamonds maybe.'

'Somebody took them,' Davidson said. 'A robbery?'

'Or a convenient source of cash if the family had to split suddenly,' Marge said. 'The sister said that was how her family dealt with the Nazis. The father paid off the border guards in stones.'

'An old habit that served them well in the past,' Decker said.

'What if it was a robbery?' Davidson asked. 'Hiding diamonds in a weird place like that. Looks to me like it would have to be an inside job. What kind of help do these people have?'

'We're working on finding the gardeners,' Marge said.

'Inside job might also be one of the kids,' Davidson said. 'Kid swipes the stones, then makes a panic call to his cousin. So what do we got so far?' Davidson held up his thick hand and began ticking off options. 'An inside robbery. A family on the lam. A Solomon thing. Or maybe even a Menendez thing. Any comments?'

Decker thought about Tug's observations. Menendez and Solomon. Two big cases. The Menendez brothers had shotgunned their parents to death. The Solomons had been a family that disappeared off the face of the earth. No bodies had ever been recovered – the case an open hole on the books.

Decker said, 'As far as we could tell, there was no killing done in the house. And all the cars were still in the garage—'

'Including the older boy's car, right?'

'Yes,' Marge said.

'What's his name?'

'The older boy?' Marge said. 'Gil. Dov's the younger one, the one who made the call to the cousin.'

'Okay, I got the names straight,' Davidson said. 'Back to the cars. If all the cars were in the garage, you've got to be thinking about a family abduction. Because if the boys lured the parents to a spot in order to whack them, a car would be missing.'

Marge said, 'Unless the boys returned the car to their house before disappearing.'

Davidson looked at her and squinted.

'Good point,' Decker said.

Davidson glared at him. 'I know it's a good point, Decker. You don't have to stroke her ego.'

Decker's voice was flat. 'I'm just a nice guy.'

Davidson looked disgusted. 'All right. So there's a chance the boys whacked the parents.'

'The bimbo cousin also mentioned the father argued with his sons,' Marge said. 'Especially the younger boy.'

Davidson squinted. 'I argued all the time with my old man. I never thought of whacking him.'

'Just presenting motive,' Marge said.

'And I'm saying what a prosecutor would be saying,' Davidson said. 'Kids and parents fight all the time. Most of us don't wind up murdering our parents.'

Nobody spoke, then Davidson said, 'Okay, it's a consideration. The boys whacked the parents or someone whacked the whole family. What about the family taking off for parts unknown?'

'We thought about that,' Marge said. 'We didn't find the passports. Of course, the search was superficial. Could be Yalom kept them in his vault.'

'Vault?'

Decker said, 'Yalom has a vault down at the Diamond Center.'

Davidson thought a moment. 'He keeps his passport in the vault?'

Decker shrugged. 'You know, Loo, even if we found passports it might not mean much. If Yalom suddenly went underground, he'd have to establish a new identity anyway. He wouldn't need his old passports.'

Davidson said, 'Why would he go underground?'

'Escape,' Marge said. 'Maybe one of his diamond deals turned sour.'

'Guy's a wily Israeli in a high-money business,' Davidson said. 'Maybe he knows things the Feds would be interested in.'

SANCTUARY

Marge said, 'He's running from the Feds?'

'Maybe he's working *for* the Feds,' Davidson said. 'Maybe the guy was forced to sign up for the Witness Protection Program and that's why the family just upped and disappeared.'

'I'll check it out.'

'Yeah, do that, Dunn,' Davidson said. 'Something's out of kilter here. Poke around the neighborhood. See if they noticed strange suits and ties coming in and out of the house.' He turned to Decker. 'Speaking of inside jobs, who's gonna do Yalom's partner?'

'Yo,' Decker said.

Davidson turned to Marge. 'So you're doing the paper on Yalom?'

'Yes.' Marge skimmed her notes. 'Social Security number, credit cards, tax ID numbers, bank statements and info, passport office.' She looked up. 'I'll also call the Feds.'

'So tell me about the partner, Decker,' Davidson said.

'Shaul Gold.' Decker recapped what he knew. 'I finally got hold of him. He seems cooperative. We've got a scheduled meeting with him tomorrow at eight in the morning.'

'He seem jumpy?'

'Surprised,' Decker said. ' "What do you mean my partner is missing?" That kind of thing. But he was cooperative.'

'How long has he known Yalom?'

Marge said, 'Sister says they've been partners for years. But they don't get along.'

Davidson squinted. 'So what? A lot of partners fight.'

Decker said, 'A lot of partners kill each other.'

'Not the whole family, Decker.'

63

'Except that we're talking about diamond dealers,' Marge said. 'Lots of money.'

Davidson scratched his head. 'Money. I take it the partner's another little, wily, shrewd Israeli?'

'Gold is Israeli,' Decker said. 'I don't know if he's wily, shrewd, or little.'

Davidson squinted. 'I was thinking the guy might be a flight risk.'

Decker threw up his hands. 'I can't find evidence to detain him.'

Marge said, 'We don't have a drop of blood, let alone a body.'

Davidson drummed his fingers. 'No justification for pulling him in. We'll have to take our chances. All right. Leave the partner until tomorrow.' The lieutenant took out a notebook. 'So this is what I got. Decker, you'll do the shopping mall and the partner. Dunn, you'll do paper and the neighborhood. This ... voodoo silver case has been turned in to forensics for printing. Anything else you got in mind?'

'Not at the moment,' Decker said.

'Keep me informed,' Davidson said.

'We thought we'd stop by the neighborhood tonight, sir,' Marge said. 'Before we go home.'

Davidson squinted at both of them. 'They musta whipped you two hard at Foothill, huh?'

'No, we're just bucking for overtime,' Decker grinned.

Davidson cracked a smile. 'You're barking up the wrong tree. You want money, get a law degree.'

'He's already a lawyer,' Marge said.

Davidson leaned back in his chair. 'No shit?'

'No shit,' Decker said.

'No wonder you're such a wiseass.' Davidson waved

them away. 'Do what you want, but forget about overtime. Jackass county keeps voting down police bonds, we'll be lucky if we draw our salaries.' He turned to Marge. 'You got a look on your face, Dunn. What is it?'

'Do you want us to contact the media for assistance?' Marge asked.

The lieutenant gave it some thought. 'Wait until you see what you've dug up. If you draw blanks, we'll contact the networks.'

'You got it.' Marge started to rise, then sat back down. 'Something else, Lieutenant?'

Davidson ran the palm of his hand across his crew cut. 'Nah, I'm through. Get out of here. Both of you.'

'Don't stroke her ego,' Marge fumed.

Decker sat down at his new desk recycled from a branch of the LA County Library that was shut down because of budget cuts. It was a gun-metal gray institutional number, but it had a kneehole large enough to accommodate his oversized legs, and two big file banks for case folders. Marge had a marred but functional oak desk donated by an office manager who had been forced to fire his secretary. The desks were placed front end to front end, which meant Decker and Marge sat across from each other.

Decker pulled out a manila folder and started a file on the Yaloms. 'At least he took us seriously, Marge.'

'He had to. The case warranted it.'

'That's for damn sure.' Decker started filling out the paperwork and handed forms over to Marge. 'I'll start a file on each of the boys; you do the parents. We'll Xerox all our papers and notes so we'll each have copies at our fingertips.'

'Rabbi Organized. How do you feel about your fellow countrymen disappearing?'

'You mean the Yaloms?'

Marge said, 'The little, wily, shrewd Israelis.'

Decker said, 'Why do I feel Old Tug has some preconceived notions about Jews and money.'

Marge said, 'Probably has notions about women and blacks and Hispanics—'

'Oh, don't start getting all pissy PC on me. I don't think Davidson's a racist. He probably hates everyone. Anyway, the Yaloms aren't my countrymen. I'm American, remember?'

'You don't feel any special twinge because they're Jewish?'

'Nah,' Decker smoothed his mustache and went back to writing. 'The only twinge I feel is for the boys.'

'If they're victims.'

'If they're victims,' Decker repeated.

Marge started filling out a Missing Persons form. 'I think you scored a notch on Davidson's belt.'

'By giving up law?' Decker continued to write. 'Yeah, I saw that, too.'

'Why did you give up law?'

''Cause I'm a gun-toting macho man and not a pussy wimp-ass in a designer suit.'

Marge laughed. 'The real reason?'

'I gave it up because Jan had forced me into it. She wanted me to take over Daddy's firm. Daddy did wills and trusts. It bored me to tears. I should have joined the District Attorney's Office.'

Marge smiled. 'Who knows? But for a slip of fate, you might even have been attorney general today.'

'I wouldn't have been nominated,' Decker said. 'I have balls.'

'Oh, don't start becoming a pig on me.'

'It's not a pig, it's sour grapes.' Decker smiled. 'S'right. I'll keep my balls and let your sex take on the Attorney General's Office.'

Marge lowered her voice artificially. 'See what a *broad* can do.'

Decker laughed without looking up from his desk.

Marge pulled out a sheet and started doing paper on Arik Yalom. She thought of the photos in the family room. A dark, muscular, handsome man with money. He had a lot going for him. What the hell happened?

She said, 'The case is getting . . . complicated.'

'Messy is the operative word,' Decker said.

'So many different angles of approach,' Marge said.

'So here's a chance for you to prove yourself. Just don't get bogged down with Davidson and his archaic attitudes. And let's try not to overdo it with the overtime. Sure, it's okay in the beginning for us to go the extra mile. But take it from me, Marge. Homicide detail will suck all the air from you if you let it. Don't get obsessed with your cases.'

'Why not? You get obsessed with your cases all the time.'

'No, I don't.' Decker went over the list of Yalom's friends one by one. Nine of them. It was going to take a while. He'd better call Rina, tell her to hold his supper. 'I don't get obsessed, Marge, I just do my job.'

8

'Peter's going to be late,' Rina said to her parents. 'He said to eat without him. You want to get the boys, Mama? I'll start serving supper.'

Magda Elias turned to her husband. Though she had lived in America for almost thirty years, she still spoke in an off-the-boat Hungarian accent. 'You get the boys, Stefan. I'll help Ginny with supper.'

The old man didn't answer.

'Stefan, do you hear me?'

'What? What?'

'Peter isn't going to make it for dinner, Papa,' Rina said. 'Can you call the boys to the table?'

Stefan slapped the paper down on the armrest and hoisted himself out of the living-room rocker. 'Everything's okay?'

'Everything's fine. He's just working on a new case.'

'What kind of a case?'

'A family disappeared. An Israeli diamond dealer.'

Her parents waited for more.

'That's all I know,' Rina said.

'Akiva's looking for a family?' Magda asked. 'I thought he was in murder now.'

'Maybe he thinks they were murdered, Mama.'

'Will he be home tonight, Ginny?' her father asked.

Rina smiled to herself. Her parents called her Regina – Ginny – which was her English name. And for some reason, they called Peter by his Hebrew name, Akiva. Maybe Peter sounded just too goyishe for them.

'Of course.' Rina turned to her mother. 'Do you want an apron? I don't think grease does well on silk.'

'This old thing?' Magda pinched the fabric of her blouse and let it drop.

Again, Rina held back a smile. It was a game with Mama. A way to amass compliments without looking needy. The woman was always dressed perfectly. Yet Mama had always been approachable even when Rina was a sticky-fingered child.

'Come into the kitchen,' Rina said. 'Let me get you an apron.'

'If you insist,' Magda said. 'Stefan, get the boys. Let's eat before the baby wakes up.'

Rina came back to the dining room, holding a baking dish filled with spinach lasagne. She placed it on a tile trivet, and a moment later, her sons shuffled into the dining room. They plopped themselves down on the chairs after ritually washing their hands and breaking bread. Their long legs sprawled under the table. Rina looked at their pants cuffs – short again. Each must have grown another inch in the past month. The boys were generally good-natured except when they were tired.

Which was all the time.

Between the pounds of homework the school loaded on and the hormones of burgeoning adolescence, they were a cranky lot. Thank God for Peter – a stolid island of refuge in a sea of emotional turmoil.

Sammy adjusted his yarmulke and poured himself a glass

of lemonade. 'Wow. Lasagne. Is it dairy, I hope? I don't want to be fleshig.'

'It's dairy,' Rina answered. 'Why don't you want to be fleshig?'

'I want to eat a milk-chocolate candy bar.'

That's a reason? Rina thought.

Magda brushed sandy-colored hair away from the boy's brown eyes. 'Think you would like to say hello to your omah?'

Sammy scooped up a double portion of lasagne and looked up at his grandmother. Her sentence came out 'Tink you vould like to say hello to your omah?'

'Hi, Omah.' He stuffed a forkful of lasagne in his mouth. 'Hi, Opah.'

'Hello, Shmuel,' Stefan said. 'How are you today?'

Sammy smiled through a mouthful of noodles. 'Okay.'

Stefan spooned a portion onto his younger grandson's plate. 'And how're you doing, Yonkie?'

The younger boy smiled, pushing black hair off his forehead. 'I'm doing okay. Thanks for the lasagne, Opah. Take some for yourself.'

'I will,' Stefan announced. 'I love lasagne.'

'He eats my lasagne like candy,' Magda said.

Rina brought in a salad. 'You make delicious lasagne, Mama.'

Magda blushed. 'I'm sure yours is twice as good.'

'I'm sure it isn't,' Rina said, smiling.

'Where's Dad?' Sammy poured salad dressing over a mound of lettuce. 'He's never home anymore.'

'Yes, he is, Sammy,' Rina said. 'He's on a new case. Whenever he starts a new case, he has to put in extra hours.'

'He works too hard,' Magda stated.

'He's on Homicide, Mama. It demands long hours.'

'How can he work with so many dead people?' Magda said.

Stefan said, 'He doesn't work with the dead people, Magda. Only the live ones.'

Rina laughed softly. Her father was serious. 'Have some green beans, Mama. They're Italian cut.'

'I'll take some green beans,' Jake said.

'Certainly,' Magda said. 'They're good for you.'

'Who was whacked?' Sammy asked.

'*Whacked?*' Rina said. 'Is that how they teach you to talk in yeshiva?'

'That's how Dad talks.'

'No, he doesn't.'

'Yes, he does,' Sammy insisted. 'He talks like that to Marge all the time. Just not to you.'

It was true. Rina said, 'No one was *murdered*. A family has disappeared.'

'Israeli diamond dealer,' Stefan said.

'Anyone we know?' Jake asked.

'I don't think so,' Rina answered.

'Isn't your friend who's coming out married to a diamond dealer?' Magda asked.

'Honey?' Rina said. 'Yes, she is.'

Sammy looked up from his plate. '*Who's* coming out?'

'An old friend of mine and her kids—'

'Great. I'm going to lose my room.'

'Hospitality is a mitzvah, Sammy,' Rina said. 'I'm sure they taught you about *hachnasat orchim* somewhere in your yeshiva education.'

'How long?' Sammy turned to his brother. 'Pass the beans, Yonkie.'

Jake gave his brother the bowl. 'They can have my room, Eema. I'll move into the attic.'

'You will not move into the attic. Your father hasn't put in the heater and we don't even have a decent staircase up there yet.'

'So I'll be careful and use double blankets. I like it up there. It's quiet and I have a view.'

'It's a perfect solution,' Sammy said. 'Please pass the lasagne, Omah.'

Magda placed another portion on her grandson's plate. 'Anyone else like as long as I got the spatula?'

'I'll take another piece,' Stefan said.

'You like the lasagne, Stefan?'

'It's good, but it isn't yours, Magda.' He winked at his daughter. 'No offense to you, Ginny.'

'None taken. I agree.'

Magda tried to hold back a smile and was unsuccessful.

'So how long is this *friend* coming out for?' Sammy said.

'I think she said a week.'

Magda said, 'She was a very strange girl growing up. Always very nervous.'

'She was okay,' Rina said.

'Meaning she's weird,' Sammy said.

'She's not weird,' Rina said.

Magda said, 'Didn't her mother pass away when she was young?'

Rina stared at her mother, then whispered yes. Magda instantly realized her faux pas and glanced at the boys. They were quiet. They had accepted Akiva as their father so completely, she had momentarily forgotten about Yitzchak. She clasped her shaking hands.

'I'm a stupid old woman,' she muttered behind tears.

'Oh, forget it, Omah,' Jake said, patting her hand. 'We love you.'

Sammy kissed his grandmother's cheek. It had become quite bony over the past year. Like always, Omah was decked out. 'Stop worrying, Omah. You can mention Abba here. We do it all the time. Even Dad talks about Abba.' He took the spatula out of her hand. 'Here. Take some more of Eema's lasagne. Even if it isn't as good as yours.'

Magda wiped her eyes. 'You are such good boys.' She suddenly stood and hugged her grandsons fiercely. 'I want you to know that I loved your abba.'

'Of course you did, Mama,' Rina said. 'Just enjoy the meal and relax.'

'It's just I get stupid with my words.' Magda sat down.

'Yitzchak is not insulted,' Stefan said. 'He knows we all loved him. Believe me, he knows. Now the important question. Who is Honey, Ginny? I don't remember her.'

'She had blond hair,' Magda said. 'Very nice hair. She married a very religious man, didn't she, Ginny?'

Rina nodded. 'A Leibbener Chasid.'

'Terrific.' Sammy's smile was snide. 'Another fringy Chasid.'

'Shmuel, show some tolerance,' Rina said.

'The Leibbeners are weird,' Sammy said. 'They don't use phones.'

'What you mean they don't use phones?' Stefan asked.

'Just that,' Sammy said.

'That's ridiculous.'

'I think it's true,' Rina said.

'Why?' Stefan asked.

'Because they're weird,' Sammy said.

Jake said, 'I really don't mind sleeping in the attic.'

'Is the baby crying?' Magda asked.

The room fell silent for a moment. Rina shrugged and went back to her lasagne.

'If your friend has a husband who is diamond dealer,' Stefan said, 'maybe he knows the family that disappeared.'

'What are you talking about, Stefan?' Magda asked.

'The case that Akiva's working on,' Stefan explained. 'The family that is missing.'

Rina said, 'I think there're a lot of diamond dealers in the country, Papa.'

Jake said, 'Why's she coming out with her kids?'

'You usually travel with your kids,' Rina said.

'In the middle of school?' Jake asked. 'Do they have vacation or something?'

'I don't know.' Rina paused. 'There's no holiday that I can think of right now.'

'So she's pulling them out of school?' Sammy grinned. 'Sounds like *my* kind of mother.'

'Just eat your lasagne, Shmuel, and stop opining.'

'Why does she come out now, Ginny?' Stefan asked.

Rina thought about that. It was a good question.

9

Marge opened the passenger door of the unmarked and slid in, kicking off her shoes.

'It's great to get off my feet.' She rubbed her toes.

'I drew blanks,' Decker said. 'Neighbors said the family seemed nice, but nothing beyond that. What about you? Did you get anything for your fallen arches?'

'Matter of fact, I did. The next-door neighbor...' Marge paged through her scribblings, 'Mindy Herrero ... she did say that there was a black Lexus parked outside during the day at least twice a week for years. This made me curious.'

'I'll bet.'

Marge smiled. 'Yaloms don't own a black Lexus. And neither does Orit Bar Lulu. But guess who does?'

'The partner – Shaul Gold.'

'Right on, Rabbi. He and Yalom may have hated each other, but Gold was here a lot. It could be that Gold and Mr Yalom were doing business at the house. Or it could be Gold and Mrs Yalom were doing monkey business. I saw the missus's photos in the family room. Dalia's a good-looking woman.'

'In a quiet, shy way.'

'It's the shy ones you have to watch.'

'Interesting,' Decker said. 'All right. Suppose Gold and

Dalia Yalom were having an affair. That still wouldn't explain why the whole family disappeared. If Gold wanted Arik out of the picture, only Arik would be gone.'

The car was quiet for a moment.

Marge said, 'Maybe he whacked the husband, then told Dalia to take the kids and run.'

'Then why would he stick around?'

Marge said, 'Somebody's got to earn a living.'

'And the kids?' Decker said.

'Hey, Sharona implied they hated the father. Good riddance to bad rubbish.'

'I don't like it, Marge.'

She paused. 'Okay, try this. Suppose Arik found out about the affair and went crazy. He killed his wife in a rage, then killed his kids, who weren't turning out like he had wanted, took his diamonds stashed in the silver case posted on the doorframe, and split the country. Maybe he even forged some documents and created himself a new identity. It could be another case of List.'

Decker thought about her theory. John List was a man who murdered his entire family and disappeared, taking on a new identity and eluding the police for about twenty years. He was finally caught after a nab-your-own-fugitive show aired the case on prime-time TV.

'It's possible,' Decker said. 'But we've got some major differences. First off, the bodies of List's wife, mother and children were found butchered inside the house, making him a prime suspect. Here we don't have bodies, only an entire family that vanished.'

'Maybe Daddy lured the crew somewhere into the boonies.'

'Except the cars are still in the garage.'

'So he rented a car.'

'Could be,' Decker said. 'You want to check out local rent-a-cars?'

'I'll put it on my list – no pun intended.' Marge wrote it down. 'What other differences do you see between this and the List case?'

Decker said, 'John List was swimming in debt. The house he had was big and expensive but empty, because he couldn't afford to furnish it. He claimed he had no way out. By all accounts so far, Yalom seems well heeled. He wouldn't have to murder to escape. He could have just taken the money and run.'

'Divorce is expensive,' Marge said. 'Yalom's got a rep as a tightwad. Just like *List*, I might add. What other differences do you see?'

'This probably isn't important,' Decker said, 'but I'll throw it out anyway. List had confessed his crimes to a minister, stating he felt that the murders were the only way to ensure his sinful wife and children's arrival in heaven.'

'Kill the body to save the soul,' Marge said.

'Exactly,' Decker said. 'Yalom isn't or wasn't a religious man.'

'So what's the point?'

'I'm not sure there is a point,' Decker said. 'Just that Arik seemed to disdain God. Dov was the spiritual one.'

'Maybe *he* was killing the body to save the soul,' Marge said. 'So we're back on the son or sons. Unfortunately, we still don't have a shred more of evidence.'

'No, we don't,' Decker said. 'But one thing at a time.'

It caught Rina's ear so she turned up her car radio. Top of the hour and the news station was presenting its feature stories – among them, something about a missing family. It had to be Peter's case. How many missing families could there be, even in a city as large as Los Angeles? Details would be given out soon, after the traffic report and a commercial for carefree aluminum siding.

She changed lanes and reduced the speedometer to fifty-five. It was smooth sailing this morning. Usually, the North Valley freeways were lightly traveled because the population in the Outback was less dense than in LA proper. She enjoyed the congestion-free asphalt, knowing cars would begin to back up as soon as she neared LAX.

Not to worry even if she did hit a jam. Honey didn't seem in a rush. Maybe she was just being polite, but Rina didn't think so.

Take your time, Rina. We're all so excited just to be somewhere new!

They're not exhausted?

Are you kidding! The kids are thrilled to be in a place so full of hustle and bustle – so full of life.

Honey's emotions sounded genuine and that made Rina introspect. Imagine being excited over an *airport*! She supposed it could hold a fascination for children – all the big jets flying up and down – but Honey herself sounded buoyant. Maybe she was just so happy to get away from her provincial existence, anything would be wonderful.

Take your time! Honey's voice had been full of melody. *We're in no hurry*.

Maybe it was time to stop and smell the jet fuel.

Hannah started to whimper. Rina gave her a bottle of apple juice. The baby drank greedily, hitting the bottle as she sucked.

Her analysis of Honey was cut short when the news item came back on the radio. Again, Rina had heard the word 'disappearance' but had missed the name of the family.

They lived in West Hills. A fancy private housing

development. Nothing seemed out of place. Confused and concerned neighbors. An interview with one of them. Police were asking the public's help.

The newscaster finally repeated the last name – Yalom. Yes, it was Peter's – and Marge's – case. She couldn't forget a name like Yalom. Rina had commented to Peter that Yahalom meant diamond in Hebrew.

There probably was a Stein somewhere in his family tree.

Peter had been amazed. *What's your secret, Sherlock?*

Stein means stone in German . . . Yiddish. It was probably Hebrasized when the family moved to Israel. They do that a lot.

Peter's expression was flat. *Maybe you should take the case? If you spoke to Bar Lulu in Hebrew, something sub rosa might come out.*

He hadn't elaborated. Rina was getting better at reading Peter. He'd been joking of course, but there had been a hint of truth behind his suggestion. She had responded lightly, said something about posing as an assistant if it would help. Peter had smoothed his mustache and said nothing. Meaning he hadn't ruled it out.

Not that she was anxious to get involved in Peter's work. Or any work for that matter. Rina was quite content to stay at home and take care of Hannah – her last baby. One swift cut from the surgeon's knife and she no longer could bear children.

How many times had she replayed the scene in her head? Yes, it had been an emergency. Yes, the doctor had been absolutely right. Yes, it had been the surgery versus her life. Everything had been handled letter perfect. She should feel grateful.

And she did.

But not all the time. At thirty-one, Rina had expected

and had wanted more children. She'd always felt that she was born to nurture. Unlike many women in this modern age, Rina considered childrearing a privilege and not a chore. Not that she didn't get mad at her kids, pound her head against the wall from time to time. But it was all in a day's work. There was no perfect way to raise children. Parenthood was filled with fuzzy borders and shades of gray. Some people were confused without a blueprint. Rina found the freedom exhilarating. Probably because she had worked so many years with numbers – first as a math teacher, then as a bookkeeper. Precision had made her a nervous wreck.

Rina had wanted lots of children. But that wasn't an option anymore. She was constantly telling herself not to dwell on the past. Anyway, raising kids was an occupation of planned obsolescence. They get big, they move on, they have their own lives. If you want lifelong, unconditional devotion, buy a dog.

Oh, stop brooding, she chastized herself. Enjoy your baby and your sons while they're home.

If only there was some way to harness her nurturance into a profession she could do at home. She had considered running a day-care center, but the required regulations and the insurance had turned it into a prohibitive proposal. Besides, with Hannah around, there might be too much opportunity for conflict. It might be hard for her to share her toys with the all-day interlopers. Hannah deserved to be queen for a good couple of years.

Rina switched the radio dial to an oldies station. As she tapped out rhythm on her steering wheel, she became philosophical. Something would come up.

There was enough luggage to sustain the Kleins for a year in deepest Africa. Thank God, Rina had remembered to bring the bungee cords. Honey was sheepish.

'I guess I didn't know what to pack so I packed everything.' Honey stuffed another suitcase into the hatch of the Volvo. 'If it's too much, I'll take some of the valises and follow you in a cab.'

'Cabs are expensive, Honey.' Rina hoisted a case on top of the car. 'I think we can make it if you don't mind squeezing. We'll have to double-belt, though. I'll keep the car seat up front.'

'Whatever is easiest,' Honey said. 'Mendie, help her with the suitcases. Rina, let him do it. He's a big boy.'

Mendel was thirteen – gangly and sullen. Rina waved him off as she secured the last of the batch to her car's roof. 'I think we're just about set.' She eyed the precarious cargo. 'I'll just take it slow and hope I don't get a ticket.'

Honey said, 'Isn't your husband a police officer?'

Rina eyed the load once more. 'Membership has its privileges, but I refuse to pull rank.' She smiled at the kids. 'I hope you don't mind being squashed for just a bit.'

The children were silent. Four of them – ages ranging from fifteen to five. Two boys with *payis*, dressed in black suits, white shirts, and big, black *kippot* that covered their scalp-shorn hair. The two girls had long plaits and wore long-sleeved, high-neck dresses over opaque tights. All of them were loaded down in heavy winter coats, sweating under their weight.

Guilt caused Rina's eyes to linger on their dress.

Two years ago, Rina had made a radical decision. She had pulled her boys out of the black-hat yeshiva of Ohavei Torah and shipped them off to a modern Orthodox yeshiva in North Hollywood. There, secular education was an important part of the curriculum, and college wasn't a dirty word. The boys were game, willing to give it a try since both were academically minded. But during the transition, whenever Rina closed her eyes, she saw Yitzchak's face. It was never a stern face – Yitzy was a gentleman and a gentle man. But it was a sad face.

She had changed since her first marriage, away from the insular black-hatted religious, toward the modern Orthodoxy she grew up with. Of course, she still covered her hair whenever she went out, but it was in a more modern way. Today, her head was topped with a knitted tam, her long black hair braided and tied into a knot. But the head covering didn't obliterate *all* her natural hair. The tam was not as kosher as the *shaytel* she used to wear.

Her eyes drifted to Honey and her *shaytel*. The wig was a good one – thick and multicolored and slightly waffled. Very natural looking. And it covered every inch of her hair.

Like the one Rina used to wear.

Both women were garbed in long-sleeved sweaters and over-the-knee skirts. Rina still refused to wear pants or go sleeveless. But she had changed. Her marriage to Peter had made her more modern, just as her marriage to Yitzchak had made her more Orthodox.

Honey took Rina's confused expression as a chance to make contact. She scooped up Rina's hands and swung them. It was an adolescent gesture and Rina was suddenly transported back to her teens. Honey still retained her girlish – almost boyish – figure. As thin and straight as a stick.

'Thanks for taking us in.'

'We'll have fun,' Rina said.

Honey's teal eyes beamed. 'Fun. I like that word.' She

turned to her kids, started to speak in Yiddish, then stopped herself with a giggle. 'I'm not used to speaking English. Come on, kids. Let's go.'

'They should probably take off their coats and lay them on their laps,' Rina suggested. 'It's going to be a tight fit as is.'

The children didn't move.

Honey said in English, 'You heard Mrs. Lazarus. Take off your coats.' She clapped. 'C'mon, people. Let's get this show on the road.'

Quickly, the kids obeyed.

Honey turned to Rina. 'It isn't Lazarus anymore, is it?'

'It's Decker.'

'Sorry.'

'Don't worry about it. Come on, troops. Pile in.'

Slowly, the kids inched toward her Volvo. The girls crowded together on the left, the boys leaned to the right. They looked stunned, in complete contrast to Honey, who seemed joyous. She cranked down the back seat window and peered out expectantly. Rina slid into the driver's seat and turned around to the back.

'Kids, you're going to have to put on your seat belts.'

They glanced at each other, dumbfounded.

Honey began hunting around. 'Seat belts. Like we wore in the airplane. They have them in cars.' She smiled at Rina. 'In the village, all we have is old jalopies for major hauling. We never use cars for traveling. Everything's in walking distance.' She reached over and pulled the harness belt. 'Come on, kids. Cooperate.'

Rina felt the kids weren't being stubborn. They were just confused. Buckling up took them another few minutes.

'Doesn't Gershon work in the city?' Rina asked.

'Of course. The village owns a bus,' Honey said. 'Several

85

buses. The men take the bus into the city. Gosh, you should see how they've altered it. It has tables and benches for learning, and a bookcase full of *sepharim*. I was shocked when I first saw it. A *bais midrash* on wheels. Now I'm used to it. The women have their own bus, too, but we don't use it very often. Everything we need is in the village. Good! We're all set, Rina.'

Rina started the engine and pulled out of the loading zone. Glancing in the rearview mirror, she noticed the kids were still huddled together. Honey was oblivious to their uneasiness. She was too busy looking out the window.

'Look out there, kinder! Winter back home and here everything's green. Can you imagine that? Do you know they can grow oranges and tangerines out here. They pick them right off the trees in their own backyard.'

Honey's youngest, a boy, said, 'We have trees in our backyard.'

'Not orange trees, Pessy,' the oldest girl said, derisively.

'Will you have some patience, Minda?' Honey scolded her. She smiled at Pessy. 'I'll show you the trees.' She spoke up to Rina. 'You still have orange trees here, don't you?'

'We have a whole citrus grove on our property,' Rina said. 'It's a ranch with horses and hay and a barn.'

Honey grinned. 'Oh, Pessy, trees, and horses and a barn! Like we see in the countryside. Isn't that *exciting*!'

The boy looked curious. 'Horses like cowboys ride?'

At least he knows about cowboys, Rina thought. She said, 'Yes, horses like the cowboys ride. My husband's a cowboy . . . of sorts.'

That was too much for Pessy. He knitted his brow and fell silent.

Honey said, 'I'm still amazed. When we left it was thirty

degrees outside. Our village was a carpet of snow and ice. Walking three blocks hurt your lungs. Then you get on a plane, five hours later, it's sunshine and greenery.'

'It's been raining,' Rina said. 'That's why it's so green. Anyone hungry?'

Honey began rooting through her handbag. 'I think I have a package of crackers.'

Rina laughed. 'I packed some fruit in a bag, Honey. It's under your feet. Help yourself.'

Honey retrieved the bag from under her seat and pulled out an apple. 'You thought of everything. Who wants?'

Pessy was about to pipe up when Mendel elbowed him in the ribs. The little boy sank back in the seat and was silent.

'Mendie, do you mind, please?' Honey spoke in Yiddish. 'Take it, Pessy. That's what it's here for.'

Slowly, little fingers extended toward Honey. She gave him the apple.

Mendel said, *'B'racha!'*

Pessy looked at Mendel, said a prayer, then took a bite of the apple. He told Rina thank you in English.

'You're welcome,' Rina answered.

'Anybody else want?' Honey asked.

Once again, the car fell silent. Rina hadn't heard boo out of the younger girl. She was fair like her mother, with a smattering of freckles on each cheek.

'Maybe later, Honey,' Rina said.

'Well, I'm going to have a tangerine. It looks good.'

Honey broke off a small bit of peel. 'Rina, I didn't officially introduce you to my kids, did I?'

'Not officially.'

Honey kissed her elder daughter's cheek. 'This is Minda. She's fifteen and beautiful—'

'*Mama!*' the girl whispered.

'Oh don't shush me. You are *beautiful*, right, Rina?'

'Right,' Rina answered.

The girl blushed, holding back a smile at the compliment.

'Mendel is my scholar. Contrary to what you might think, he does know how to smile.'

'Only if I'm forced,' Mendel said, dryly.

Rina laughed. 'You're going to get along with Shmuel just fine. What *mesechet* are you learning, Mendel?'

The boy paused, perplexed by Rina's interest in his studies. Girls just weren't supposed to be *aware* of these things. But he answered just to be polite.

'*Sukkos.*' Mendel paused. 'Do you have a *Shas* at your house?'

Rina let out a small laugh as she named the many Hebraic tomes in her library. 'We have a standard *Shas*, we have a *Steinzaltz Shas*. We have a *Shulchan Aruch, a Mishna Torah, Me'am Loez*, plus some others. Will that help you out?'

Mendel nodded, but didn't speak. Yet he seemed more relaxed. Perhaps he finally realized his mother wasn't taking him to Sodom and Gomorrah.

Honey said, 'See, Mendie, you've got nothing to worry about.' To Rina, she said, 'He's always afraid he'll fall behind in his *shiur*, so he studies and makes himself go ahead. Did I introduce you to my youngest daughter, Bryna, who is almost eight?'

'Hi, Bryna,' Rina said.

The girl smiled, showing missing side teeth.

'Are you excited about your vacation?'

The girl nodded.

'And you've met my sweetie pie, Pessy, who just turned five.' Honey clapped her hands. 'So what should we do first, children? How about the zoo? Is that far from where you live, Rina? We can take the bus.'

'I'll take you as soon as we unload all the luggage.'

Honey squeezed Bryna's shoulder. 'What do you think about that? Would you like to see *real* lions and tigers?'

Rina peeked in her rearview mirror. The girl seemed interested. Pessy could hardly contain his excitement.

'I wanna see them, Mama. Can I pet them?'

'You can't pet a lion, Pessy,' Minda said. 'Besides, they're in cages.'

'How do you know about a zoo?' Mendel asked.

'We once went to the Brooklyn zoo. We took a picnic lunch and spent the day in the park. Remember that, Mama?'

Honey nodded. 'Do you remember that, Bryna? You were about two.'

The younger girl shook her head.

Honey smiled. 'Wasn't that fun, Minda?'

'Actually, I felt sorry for the animals,' Minda said. 'All caged up.'

'The animals here aren't in cages,' Rina said.

Bryna's expression became petrified.

'They're in enclosures,' Rina said quickly. 'They can't get out and walk around. But they live in big open spaces that are supposed to be like the animal's natural habitat.'

Again, the car fell silent. Bryna whispered something in her mother's ear.

Honey smiled. 'How would you translate habitat?'

'The animal's natural home,' Rina said. 'It's a lovely park. You have to see it to appreciate it.'

'The lions can't get out?' Bryna said.

'No.'

'What happens if they do get out?'

'They just don't, Bryna.'

'But if they do?'

'They take a gun and shoot them, Bryna,' Minda said. 'And if you don't behave, they shoot you, too.'

'*Minda!*' Honey was exasperated. 'Your sister's talking stupid, Bryna. Don't pay attention to her.'

'I'll see the lions, Mama,' Pessy said, bravely.

Honey tousled his *kippah*. 'Isn't he a doll, Rina?'

'Yes.'

'Speaking of dolls, you have a really cute one in front.'

'I love her.'

'What's her name?'

'Channah,' Rina said, using her Hebrew name.

'Hello, Channaleh,' Honey cooed. 'You must be enjoying her so much.'

'Very much.'

'And your husband?'

'He's in seventh heaven.'

'He wasn't mad it wasn't a boy?'

'No, not at all.'

'That's nice. Some men are real strange that way.'

Rina didn't answer.

'Every child is a gift from *Hashem*,' Honey said.

'Absolutely.'

Honey scratched her wig. 'Boy, girl? Who cares?'

'I certainly don't.'

'Of course, husbands do like to learn with their sons. Gershon liked it when Pessy was born. Made a big deal about now having *mezuman*.'

Rina didn't answer. *Mezuman* – a quorum of three men – was needed to recite a special blessing before *Birkat HaMazon* the grace, after meals. When the boys got big, Gershon could now say the extra blessing each time he ate.

Rina said to Mendel, 'Your father must enjoy learning with you.'

Mendel didn't answer. His expression said it was none of her business. Honey hadn't noticed as she was back observing the scenery. Eyes focused out the window widened as the car passed an industrial park, its walkways and parking lots lined with palms. She took her younger children's hands. 'Those are palm trees, kids! Aren't they just majestic and beautiful. Don't you feel like you're in a tropical rain forest?'

Rina re-eyed the industrial park. It took a big stretch to imagine a tropical rain forest, but she said nothing. The kids were also quiet, perplexed by their mother's enthusiasm.

Honey laughed softly. 'I keep forgetting. They haven't grown up with TV and all those kinds of fun picture books. They have no idea what tropical means.'

10

The recent rains had not only greened the mountains but had washed the rankness from the streets of metro LA. As in most cities, the downtown area was hardly pastoral, but it wasn't as beaten as others Decker had seen. It was a mixture of gentrification and seediness, a city with an identity problem. Central LA played host to the seat of city government as well as a few fine hotels. In addition, the area had the old, established banking and law firms. But there was more to downtown than just maintaining the past.

Signs of urban renewal – the recently constructed, neon-green convention center, a top-of-the-line apartment city, a spanking new library. Like the phoenix, the building was resurrected from the ashes of the old one. Decker heard people talking about the city going down the tubes, yet he remained optimistic. Sure he'd seen the worst aspects of human nature. Yet he'd also seen plenty of everyday heroes – ordinary men and women who had risked their lives to help others. He wasn't just a fair-weather Angelino. He was in it for the long haul.

Today, Decker's spirits were high. It was the weather. The air was crisp, the sky as soft as cashmere, gauzed with filmy, mother-of-pearl clouds. Tall buildings were bronzed by the low sun, the beams bouncing off glass and metal.

The urban decay seemed softened as if photographed through a hairsprayed lens. There was a lot of foot traffic – the business suits, the immigrants, the homeless, the vendors – but it was flowing smoothly. A steady breeze rippled through the parade of clothing.

He negotiated the unmarked through a series of turns until he found the diamond center – a twenty-story monolith of granite near Sixth and Hill. Luck was with him and he found street parking. He eased the Plymouth curbside and shut off the motor, checking his notes before he went inside. Satisfied, he got out and walked through the center's doors.

The lobby, like the exterior, was fashioned from the same gray granite and presented as hard as a steel vault. The reception area was fronted by a mountainside of stone which held the building's directory. On either side were banks of elevators. Decker knew the unit number and pushed the button for the Otis special. The elevator soon opened and out came an array of foreign speech and Chasidic dress. His eyes followed the black robes of the ultra-Orthodox Jews and he almost missed the elevator.

He knew there were lots of Orthodox Jews in the diamond business. He also knew there were lots of secular Israelis like Yalom in the business as well. He wondered how they got along.

Then he wondered if there were other people besides Jews in the business at all.

He got off on the thirteenth floor, walked down a carpeted hall until he got to 1306. The door sign said YALOM AND GOLD, INC. The doorframe held a small, metal-cased mezuzah.

This mezuzah was on the outside doorframe. Yalom knew the difference.

Decker peered down the foyer. Lots of mezuzahs. And lots of closed-circuit cameras. He rang the buzzer to 1306. An accented female voice asked who was there. He answered and was allowed to pass through the portal.

Yalom and Gold, Inc. wasn't much for decorating. The reception area was basically a carpeted sally port – a passageway from the outside to the inner sanctum. A young, pretty receptionist sat behind a glass cage. She had a coffee-colored complexion set into drawn curtains of shiny, ebony hair. Brown eyes looked him over. Decker smiled and took out his identification.

'One minute,' she said, speaking through a voice amplifier. She picked up the phone. Her lips moved but Decker couldn't hear what she said. Holding the receiver up to her ear, she said, 'May I see your identification again, please?'

Decker took out his shield and accompanying card. The woman looked it over carefully. 'Mr Gold will be right with you.' She turned off her mike and went back to work.

No chitchat with this one. Decker looked around, feeling as if he were about to enter prison. Two more closed-circuit cameras were placed in the upper corners. He thought about waving, then nixed the idea. With no place to sit, he stood in place and rocked on his feet.

A minute later, a fifties-plus man came through the inner door, his appearance slightly unkempt – shirt wrinkled at the collar, tie askew, pants unpressed. He was balding, his salt-and-pepper hair combed to the side. Built solidly with a big chest and thick wrists, he looked like a man used to physical labor, uncomfortable in the black suit he was wearing. His eyes seemed sharp, his expression marked with suspicion. But he held out his hand in an effort to appear friendly. Decker took the proffered hand.

'All night I've been making phone calls.' The man also

had a thick accent. 'It's *meshuga*, Arik taking off like this. It doesn't make sense.'

'Shaul Gold?' Decker asked.

'Yes, yes, of course.' Gold was irritated. 'Who else would I be? Let's go in the office. Yochevet is trustworthy but she has a big mouth.'

'Not as big as yours,' the receptionist's amplified voice piped in.

Gold waved her off but she didn't seem offended.

Yochevet buzzed them through. Decker followed Gold down a short hallway into an office as bright as an atrium. Two walls of glass allowing a full view of the action from a thousand feet up. Not a place for an acrophobic. Or a claustrophobic.

Because the office was tiny.

It was set up like a lunch counter. Two stools sat tucked under a black Formica bartop. Gold pulled out a stool and motioned Decker to sit. He went around to the other side and sat as well, behind him a panoramic view of Pershing Square still under construction. At Gold's right was a brushed-steel vault. Above the safe were TV monitors showing the front entrance as well as the sally port. So far, the coast was clear. Between the TV monitors was a picture of the Lubavitcher Rebbe, recently deceased. He wore a black hat that covered his head and a full beard took up most of his face. But it was easy to see the great Rav was smiling in the photo – the kind, crinkly eyes.

Since Arik had been described as anti-religious, Decker wondered if the picture of the rabbi was Gold's doing. He didn't seem religious, though. He wasn't wearing a yarmulke.

Decker's eyes went back to the counter. On the top was a scale, a scoop, a jeweler's loupe and a two-by-two desk calendar, each square marked with appointments and obligations in multicolored inks and pencil. On the fifteenth, spilling over to the sixteenth, sat a heap of loose diamonds.

Decker kept his face flat, but was floored. Thousands of dollars of gems carelessly scattered on an old, marked-up calendar. Gold fingered them gently.

'I'll finish up later.' In one clean motion, Gold picked up the scoop and swooped the stones off the calendar. He stopped and studied Decker. 'Unless you're interested. I give you a good price.'

Decker smiled. 'Some other time.'

Gold said, 'Once a salesman...' He poured the diamonds into an envelope and stowed them behind the counter. His features weren't bad – light, gentle eyes softened a strong chin and a bulbous nose – the kind that comes from genes rather than booze. Gold rubbed his arms. 'Sure you're not interested? It's a new shipment.'

'Positive,' Decker said. 'Do you always leave your diamonds in the open like that?'

Gold's eyes met Decker's straight on. 'I have a gun under the counter. Someone starts something, I finish it. You want to see my license?'

'Not necessary.'

Gold said, 'Besides, you're the police. If you steal from me, you're in worse trouble than me.'

'How do you know I'm the police?'

'I saw your ID through the cameras when you showed it to Yochevet. If I don't like what I see, I don't buzz you in.' Gold rotated his neck and pointed to the TV monitors. 'We've got cameras and more cameras. On the outside, on the inside. The system works so you can't open the outside door and the inside door at the same time. For my protection. Still, everyone here walks around looking over their shoulder.'

'You've had incidents?'

'We've had robberies. Terrible.' Gold shook his head. 'One man was beaten so bad he almost died. Why you think I got a gun. Six years I spent in the Israeli army. One thing it does is make you comfortable with guns. That's a good thing. When you don't know what you're doing, that's when you screw up.'

'The old man who was beaten,' Decker said. 'Did they mug him in the hallway or come into his office?'

'In the hallway. But there have been muggings in both places.'

'Does Arik have a gun?' Decker asked.

'This is a shared office. We share the gun. So far, no need for it, *Baruch Hashem*.'

'Does Arik have a gun at home?'

Gold was quiet for a moment. 'No, I don't think so. He didn't want guns around the house because of the boys. Teenage boys can do some very dumb things.'

'His boys ever do anything real dumb?'

Gold shrugged. 'I suppose, yes. When I was a teenager, I did dumb things. I'm sure Arik did dumb things, too. That's why I'm nervous about him. He can be reckless.'

Decker took out his notebook. 'Anything different going on in his life as far as you could tell?'

'As far as I can tell, no.' Gold shook his head. 'Arik's Arik. Quick, sharp, fast-thinking, a big pain in the ass.' He ran his hand over his face. 'You want to ask me if he has enemies?'

'Does he?' Decker said.

'Arik has many people who hate him. Me? I can't stand the bastard. He's reckless, but he's also stingy. He hoards and hoards! I keep telling him we don't make money by keeping diamonds, only by selling. But I admit a good thing about Arik. He has a nose for top dollar. Like I say, he is very sharp. He knows when to buy, when to sell.'

'And what do you know?'

'I know *how* to sell,' Gold said. 'Arik and I are good for each other.'

Decker said, 'Are you also good for Mrs Yalom?'

Gold's eyes narrowed. 'You can explain that?'

'Mr Gold, why is your Lexus parked outside Yalom's house on an average of two days a week during daylight hours?'

Gold broke into laughter. 'You think something naughty is going on between me and Dalia? You have a very dirty mind, Sergeant.'

'Can you answer the question?'

'I'm doing business with my partner,' Gold said. '*Real* business.'

'You do business with Mr Yalom at his house?'

'All the time. Like you saw – about two, three days a week.'

'Then why bother with the office?'

'For the clients.'

Gold's face was unreadable. Decker didn't buy his story. 'Mrs Yalom doesn't get in your way?'

'Dalia works. Even if she's home, I rarely see her. We go into Arik's office, shut the door...' Gold shrugged. 'Certain things are better discussed away from Yochevet.'

'You're not worried about Dalia hearing things?'

Gold remained stone-faced. 'No.'

Six years in the Israeli army. Guy's a tough cookie. Decker said, 'And you haven't seen or heard from Mr Yalom in the past two days?'

99

'Nothing. I'm very concerned. Maybe he got too reckless.' Gold took out a pack of cigarettes. 'Do you mind?'

Decker shook his head.

'Yochie hates it.' Gold lit up. 'Says I smell up the office. That girl has a big mouth.'

'Why do you keep her?'

'Because she's good.'

Good in what capacity? Decker said, 'Tell me about Mr Yalom.'

'I told you all I know.'

'That Mr Yalom is stingy. How stingy could he be, living in a house like that?'

'That's for Dalia.' Gold blew out smoke. 'The house was bought with her money.'

Decker perked up. 'Dalia has money?'

Gold nodded. 'Her father is a very wealthy diamond dealer in Israel. When she met Arik, he was nothing but a poor stonecutter.'

'I thought his family had money . . . jewels smuggled out from Europe.'

'Yes, the Yalom family owns a few nice pieces of jewelry. But nothing compared to Mr Menkovitz.' Gold took a final puff of his smoke, then crushed the butt. 'It was Dalia's father who gave Arik money to invest in diamonds. She set him up.'

'Is it a sore spot with Mr Yalom?' Decker asked. 'His wife setting him up?'

'*Mah pitom?*' Gold said. 'Why should it be sore spot? Arik has done very well by himself.'

Decker said, 'But Dalia still has independent wealth?'

Gold said, 'Her father takes care of her.'

Decker now wondered if someone was out to get Dalia. Who would gain from her demise? First, Arik, then her sons. Maybe this was all some messy family affair. He said, 'I heard Arik didn't get along with his sons.'

Gold said, 'Where'd you hear that?'

'Is it true?'

Gold rubbed his chin. 'Does Arik fight with his boys? Of course he does. But that doesn't mean he doesn't love them.'

'What about Mrs Yalom? Does she fight with the boys?'

'Dalia? No.' Gold's face softened. 'Dalia doesn't fight with anyone. She is soft. Like her mother.'

'You know the family?'

'I knew them before Arik did. I'm old family friend. I grew up in the neighborhood. I baby-sat Dalia.'

'How'd she meet Arik?'

'Her father introduced them.'

'And you approved of the match?'

Gold studied Decker. 'What does my opinion matter? The family approved. Dalia approved. They get married. End of story.'

'But you're still in the picture.'

Gold smiled. 'Arik invited me in the business. I take opportunity. That is all, Mr Sergeant. That is all.'

Come back to that one, Decker thought. He said, 'I heard Arik fought a lot with Dov.'

'He can be hard on him, yes.'

'What about the older son?' Decker asked. 'How does Gil get along with his father?'

'Gil is easygoing. And he's no student. He knows eventually he'll have to come into the business. Arik knows it, too. He's not concerned with Gil. Dov is another story ... brighter. He has options. So he wants nothing to do with the business. That makes Arik feel bad. What does this have to do with the family missing?'

'I'm just wondering if the family didn't have one bad fight and things got out of hand.'

Gold genuinely looked horrified. 'You think one of the boys . . . not a chance in hell!'

Decker said nothing.

'I don't care what you've seen in your America.' He pointed to himself. '*I* know Arik's boys. They are good kids. It is impossible. Start thinking about other things because you are on the wrong side.'

The diamond dealer was vehement in his opinion. Was he doing it on purpose to bring attention to the boys? Take the search away from him? Decker started thinking. Who else might benefit from Yalom's demise? Perhaps Gold himself.

'Orit last saw her brother around two-thirty Friday afternoon,' Decker said. 'Did you see him after that?'

Gold thought a moment, then checked a desk calendar. 'Two-thirty Friday, I was just finishing up business with a client.' His finger scanned down the calendar. 'Last I saw Arik was maybe Friday morning around . . . ten.'

'You have no idea where the family might have gone?'

'None whatsoever. I don't mind telling you I'm scared for the family. People think they have plenty of money just lying around the house. What we have is inventory and investments, but burglar doesn't know that. He puts gun to your head anyway. Says open the vault. He doesn't see cash, he sees stones that are hard to fence.'

'I take it you've checked the vault?'

'As soon as you called and told me about the family is gone, I checked the common vault. Nothing is missing.'

'Does Arik have his own private inventory?'

'I think no.'

'You're sure?'

'Yes. We're partners.'

Decker smiled. 'You've never heard of partners cheating each other?'

Gold waved him off. 'That is not a problem, I promise you.'

Decker paused. 'You check up on him, don't you, Mr Gold.'

'Cheating is not a problem,' Gold stated once again.

'I'm just wondering if Mr Yalom has diamonds that are not part of your business partnership. Maybe diamonds acquired from Mrs Yalom's wealth.'

Gold shrugged, then lit another cigarette. 'Maybe. I never thought about that . . . but maybe.'

'The thought seems to bother you.'

Gold hid behind a cloud of nicotine. 'What do I care what Arik does with his money?'

Decker waved the smoke away from his face but didn't answer.

Gold put out the cigarette. 'Why do you ask about Arik's money?'

'If somebody robbed him, Mr Gold, I'm wondering what they would take from the house if the vault is here in the diamond center.'

'Maybe Arik has a safe at home. We're partners, but I don't know everything about his personal life.'

'How'd you two become partners?'

'He brought me into the business as a salesman. Arik is a terrible salesman.' Gold sat back in his chair. 'I can sell anything. Believe me, Mr Detective, I could have even sold you a diamond if I want. So it works well that Arik picks the diamonds and says when to sell. And I get the clients and match the stones to the clients. I just wish we could get *more* of the good stuff. It's not always easy to pick up stones

103

at the right price. They keep the quantity limited, you know.'

'Who does?'

'VerHauten. You know about them?'

'It's a South African diamond company, isn't it?'

'More than a company. VerHauten is a nation to itself.'

'Tell me about them.'

'What's to tell? They own eighty percent of the diamond mines. VerHauten mines a little more, they bring in more diamonds to sell and they make money. They mine less, they bring in less diamonds, the price of diamonds goes up, they make money, too. They not only own the mines, they own the distribution of the stones. *No one* can compete against them.'

Decker sensed that Gold was talking from a point of personal experience. 'You've tried competing with them?'

Gold burst into laughter. 'Me? I'm nothing. A glob of spit. I can't compete with VerHauten.' Again, he laughed. 'No, it's impossible even for the big dealers, let alone small potatoes like me and Arik. No one even tries.'

'You said they own eighty percent of the mines,' Decker said. 'Who owns the other twenty percent?'

'There are other mines – in Africa, in Canada, in Russia,' Gold said. 'Big mines in Russia in the north area. A region called Yakutia. They are government mines. The last I heard the Russian government was setting up a joint venture with VerHauten. It's a smart move. The Russians may be able to mine diamonds, but they can't distribute them without VerHauten's blessing.'

'Why not?'

'Where would they set up shop?'

'Why not in Russia?'

'The minute VerHauten finds out about competitors, they either buy them out or undersell them. They *own* the market. What does this have to do with Arik?'

Decker gave a noncommittal shrug. 'You said Arik was a hoarder. Maybe he was hoarding too much for VerHauten's liking.'

Gold grinned. 'You know how much inventory we have? Around two million. It seems like a big number, but no one can survive in this business if their inventory drops below five or six hundred thousand. You don't have stones on hand, buyers find other people. So we put money in stones. You know what VerHauten's worth?'

'More than two million,' Decker said, dryly.

'Try three to four *billion*. I don't think they lose sleep about Arik and me.'

Decker said, 'Still, two million dollars is well worth robbing for.'

'Except that nothing's missing in the vault.' Gold shook his head. 'It doesn't make sense.'

Decker said, 'Do you know of anyone who might want to shut you and Arik down?'

Gold took out another cigarette. 'That's what worries me. Arik can be reckless and rude in dealing with people. Maybe some dealers would like to shut us down. They know we have the good stones. Not good stones, great stones. I've made many good contacts over the years.'

Gold lit up his smoke.

'I've got to give Arik credit, too. He has a great eye for stones – cut and uncut. He can tell at a glance what the stone will look like when it's cut. All those years working as a stonecutter. He learned the trade from his father. Arik's taken me to Antwerp a few times. He looks at a diamond. To me, it doesn't look like much. He says, "Shaul, this is the one I want." Doesn't have to cut a window in it or anything.'

'Cut a window?'

'Cut a window,' Shaul repeated. 'Open the stone. VerHauten sets a certain price for the uncut stone. Nonnegotiable. But what they will let you do is open a small facet so you can look inside and see what you're buying before you buy it. Arik doesn't even need to do that. He can smell it.'

'Where is Antwerp?' Decker asked.

'Belgium. It's where VerHauten distributes its stones. Everyone big goes to Antwerp.'

'Why Antwerp?'

'Why do you go to the supermarket to buy milk? Because it's where diamonds are.'

Decker held back a smile. 'I meant why did VerHauten set up distribution there? Why not in South Africa?'

'VerHauten wants a center in Europe. And Belgium gives them easy laws.' Gold paused. 'Sometimes for a special client, Arik goes to Belgium and buys big uncut stones. Mostly we go to Israel and buy cut, mid-sized stones. More diamonds are cut in Israel than anywhere else in the world.'

Gold rested the cigarette in his ashtray.

'Still, I don't know anyone who would hurt Arik to put us out of business. This whole thing is very strange.'

Decker flipped the cover over his notepad. 'Yes, it is.'

Gold ran his hand over his face. 'Even with the gun, I'm worried. Because I don't know who this enemy is.' He looked at Decker. 'You keep looking for them?'

'For a while,' Decker said. 'But without a body, we can't justify looking for an extended period of time. The family may have taken off on their own accord.'

He stood and so did Gold. 'We'll keep in touch.'

Decker walked over to the door, then paused. 'Mr Gold, do you know where Yalom might keep his passport?'

Gold was quiet for a moment. 'No. Why?'

'If he took off for anywhere international, he'd need his passport.'

'I don't know about Arik's passport,' Gold said. 'Come. I'll walk you out.'

Decker realized that Gold was inching him down the hallway. Yalom's partner had been cooperative, even loquacious at times. But Decker couldn't shake the feeling that Gold was holding back. He spoke at length about VerHauten, but little about Arik and his *business* dealings.

They reentered the sally port. Yochie was about to buzz them out. She said, 'Uh-oh. You got company, Shaul.'

Decker looked at the outside TV monitor. A Chasid with a white beard. He was wearing a tall black hat and long black coat.

'*Shnorrers*,' Gold said with resignation. 'They don't leave me alone.'

'No, they don't,' Decker agreed.

Gold looked at him. 'You know about *shnorrers*?'

Decker nodded. Ostensibly, they collected money for worthy causes. Sometimes, the worthy causes were themselves. Since he had married Rina, they had invaded his house with outstretched hands, and always at inconvenient times. But Rina had a soft heart. She always gave them something.

Shaul said, 'Open the door, Yochie.'

She complied. The Chasid touched the mezuzah, kissed his hand, then walked inside. But Gold pushed him back out. Decker followed them into the hallway.

Gold said, 'Every day, it's someone else.'

The Chasid started a pitch in a foreign tongue.

'*Maspeek*.' Gold opened his wallet and took out a twenty. 'That's all I have. Go.'

The *shnorrer* didn't budge.

Gold showed the man his empty wallet. 'No more *kesef. Lech. Mayveen?*'

The *shnorrer* said, '*Ani mayveen.*' He looked at Decker.

Decker blew out air, then took out a twenty from his wallet and gave it to the man. The *shnorrer* pocketed the money, muttered some blessing, then moved onto the next mezuzah down the hallway.

11

Even though it was the job, Marge felt like a snoop. Decker had warned her about the feeling. True she had gone through other houses from the rafters to the baseboards, but in those cases, the occupants had been alive. Though Marge had no evidence that the Yaloms were dead, it didn't look good.

Though the paper still came and the mail was still being delivered, the only living things left in the Yalom place were houseplants.

So with key in hand, courtesy of Orit Bar Lulu, Marge plundered through items, bit by bit, with no one standing over her shoulder, nobody protesting her presence, or cussing her out.

They couldn't have just fallen off the planet!

Within three hours, she had amassed an abbreviated biography of the Yaloms' lives, had discovered private matter . . . secrets.

Dalia Yalom was on the pill and was a hidden lover of the soaps. To wit: magazines featuring daytime serials stowed in a hatbox, along with an autographed eight-by-ten glossy of a handsome but plastic man. Dalia's closets were well stocked although there wasn't an obscene amount of clothing for a woman of her means. But she did have odd tastes. A shoe collection made up from dozens of sneakers

– beaded ones, painted ones, embroidered ones. She had tennis shoes made of everything from buckskin to terry cloth, from silk to see-through plastic. A variation of the glass slipper.

Though Marge had sifted through the shoes, one by one, she had found nothing. Satisfying herself that the master bedroom was devoid of clues, she'd moved onto the boys' rooms.

She'd found Dov's small stash, not much more than a few measly crumbs of cannabis. Dov's escape from an overbearing father. She'd also discovered voluminous writings and stories crammed into three binders in the back of his closet. In light of what Decker had told her, Dov's stories about loneliness and alienation had come as no surprise.

What had surprised Marge had been the secret poetry of the *older* brother, Gil. Here was a sensitive soul. The writing was amateurish, excessive as only teens can be, but it was thoughtful. The older boy's poems spoke of *flowers budding in a mire of human greed*, of *good emanating from a cesspool of evil*, of *the birth of a child cradled from the ashes of the fire*. Marge wasn't quite sure to whom or what the kid had been referring, but the message seemed unusually positive for an adolescent.

Marge had looked and Marge had learned.

Decker fingered the Israeli passports with gloved hands. 'Where'd you find these?'

'In a billfold inside the Cross briefcase.' Marge pointed to a black-leather attaché with a gold clasp. 'I didn't even see this luggage set the first time around because the attic closet has such an odd shape.'

'The briefcase was hidden?'

'Not at all,' Marge said. 'I just didn't see it. I thought the closet door just led to finished attic space. At that point, the roof comes down at such a severe angle, you can't even stand up. So I just poked my head inside and saw the area was empty. It wasn't until the second time around that I actually ducked inside – at much expense to my back muscles – and saw the space was actually a closet that wraps around the house. There's this huge storage area on the other side containing the main family luggage. I'll show it to you if you want, but I've already been through it all. The rest of the valises were empty.'

Decker sorted through the papers inside the case – Xerox copies of birth certificates, Social Security cards, insurance cards, INS papers. He wondered where the originals were. If Yalom took the papers with him, why did he leave behind the passports?

Because the two passports he held were the originals. And they were up-to-date. He said, 'You didn't find the boys' passports?'

'Nope,' Marge said. 'And I looked. That could be significant. If the boys whacked the parents, maybe they took an international one-way flight.'

Decker thumbed through Yalom's passport – pages of stamped entries back into the States, Yalom's residing country. Then there were many other pages of foreign ink – Canada, Mexico, countries of Western and Eastern Europe including Russia, entries from the Far East, Latin America, and Africa. Lots from Africa – Egypt, South Africa, Kenya, Namibia, Liberia, Angola, Sudan, Ethiopia, Zaire, plus a host of other countries Decker didn't know existed.

Dalia's visa was simpler – stamps from Western Europe, Hong Kong, Japan, and the United States every time she reentered the country.

111

Marge said, 'Yalom was quite the Phileas Fogg.'

Decker said, 'You sound skeptical about something.'

'An Israeli going to Russia? I thought the Jews were leaving Russia for Israel.'

'Yalom's a diamond dealer,' Decker said. 'Russia has diamond mines.'

Marge paused. 'Oh.'

Decker said, 'What were you thinking about?'

'I don't know. Maybe Yalom was helping some of his countrymen get out of Russia ... something like that.'

Decker didn't answer.

'Farfetched, huh?'

'I wouldn't say that,' Decker said. 'You see a passport like this, you wonder what's going on.'

'I'm thinking the guy's an agent. Maybe that's why the family disappeared.' Marge took his passport and leafed through it. 'Lots of Third World countries.'

'I noticed.'

'Okay, so South Africa has diamond mines. His travels there make sense. But what's in Namibia or Angola?'

'Don't know.'

Marge handed the passport back to Decker. He flipped through the booklet again. Several entries for each African state he had visited. 'I don't even know why he'd even bother going to South Africa. From what Yalom's partner told me, VerHauten brings the uncut stones to market in Antwerp, Belgium. The cut stones are bought in Israel.' Decker recapped his conversation with Gold.

Marge said, 'So Yalom – even being a diamond dealer – really has no need to go anywhere except Antwerp and Israel.'

'If I understood Gold correctly, that's true.'

'And if Russia is only dealing with this VerHauten, what could Yalom possibly hope to gain by going to Russia?'

'Only thing that comes to me is maybe Yalom's talking to people sub rosa,' Decker said. 'Maybe he's making inroads that Gold doesn't know about.'

'He's double-dealing his partner?'

'It's been known to happen.'

'His partner finds out, gets mad, and whacks him?'

'It's been known to happen.'

'I still like the idea of him being an agent,' Marge announced. 'What else could explain all that traveling?'

Decker laughed softly.

'Go ahead,' Marge said, testily. 'Scoff.'

Decker smiled again. 'No, it's not that.' He glanced around the house. 'I'm just thinking that Mossad must pay pretty damn well.'

'Didn't you say the wife paid for the house?'

Decker nodded. 'I'll ask Gold about his partner's wanderlust.'

'Maybe they're in some kind of covert operation together, Pete,' Marge said. 'Maybe that's why they used to meet at Yalom's house instead of the office downtown.'

Decker remembered Gold not wanting to talk in front of the secretary. And when he asked about the meetings at the house, about Mrs Yalom.

Dalia is not a problem.

Yalom and Gold – agents.

Six years in the Israeli army. Makes you comfortable with guns.

Decker didn't know what comprised mandatory conscription for the Israeli army. He made a mental note to ask Rina. Then he laughed to himself, surprised by his runaway imagination.

'What's so funny?' Marge asked.

Decker said, 'Nothing really. Just thinking about the blanks in the case, how the mind fills in the blanks with foolishness. We should stick to what we know.'

'Which isn't much.'

'We know a family disappeared. Yet the house looks undisturbed to the eye. No signs of sudden packing, valuables in place.'

'So let's assume the family didn't take off on their own. Assume murder.'

'What would be the motivation for a murder?' Decker asked. 'No apparent robbery had taken place. By Gold's own account, no stones were missing from inventory.'

'That's why I like my spy theory. Someone wanted them out of the way for reasons other than money.'

Decker's head began to pound. 'Money could still be the motive.'

'What do you mean?'

'Marge, who would benefit from the parents missing?'

'The boys.'

'Right. And their passports *are* missing. Who else would benefit?'

'Possibly Orit. And maybe the partner, Gold, too.'

'Also consider this,' Decker said. 'We really don't know if the stones are missing. Could be Gold took the diamonds or Orit took the jewels. They could be telling us that nothing's missing, but in reality, they could have cashed out the goods.'

Marge was silent. Then she said, 'What we really need is an old-fashioned body.'

'It would help.' Decker rubbed his eyes with his bicep. 'I'm going over to that shopping center. Where Dov made

114

the phone call to Sharona. At least it puts him alive as of forty-eight hours ago.'

'I still like my spy thing,' Marge said.

Decker said, 'So do I.'

'You *do*?'

'Yeah. I'd love to get my hands on Gold's passport. See if it's as funny-looking as Yalom's. I wonder if we're getting in over our heads.' Decker smiled. 'Maybe I've read too many novels about Mossad.' Again, he waited a beat. 'Then again, Mossad agents did kill the wrong guy in Norway about a decade ago. Even spies make mistakes.'

Marge said, 'Hey, if you think this guy is into some kind of secret shit, I'm outta here. Cattle prods on the genitals is not my idea of a good time.'

Decker said, 'Let's not get carried away. But I am keeping an open mind. Though he downplays himself, Gold's no dummy. I wouldn't put anything past him.'

'Know what I *do* think?' Marge said.

'What?'

'I think it's time to get some lunch.'

Decker's house was eerily quiet except for the electronic chatter of a game-show host.

Rina *never* watched game shows.

A moment later, Ginger pranced out and jumped on Decker's chest, spraying a cloud of red fur and dander into his eyes.

'What's going on, girl?' Decker asked the Irish setter. 'Who's watching TV?'

The dog licked Decker's face. Decker shouted out 'Hello?' but there was no answer.

'Someone leave the TV on, girl?'

Decker stepped into the dining area and stopped in his

115

tracks. Seated around his homemade cherrywood table were four children who looked straight from the prairie. The two girls were garbed in high-necked dresses and opaque stockings; the boys had on black suits, white shirts, and hats. The eldest, who looked to be around Sammy's age, was reading a volume of Talmud. The other three kids were engaged with the TV. Upon Decker's entrance, their eyes went from the screen, to Decker, then back to the screen. The oldest boy looked up from his religious book, then quickly buried himself back in his study.

No one said anything. No one moved. Decker cleared his throat. 'You're the Klein kids?'

Silence except for the television. Finally, the older girl spoke, her eyes still on the TV monitor. 'Are we in your way?'

Decker hesitated. 'Uh, no. Not at all.'

The youngest, a boy, raised his head and caught Decker's eye. Shyly, he asked, 'Are you the cowboy?'

His sister elbowed the boy in the ribs.

'The cowboy,' Decker repeated. 'Well, I ride horses and wear a hat. So I guess some people would call me a cowboy. Anyone know where Mrs Decker is?'

Again, the elder girl piped up. 'She had a doctor's appointment with the baby that she forgot about. She'll be back soon. Then we're going to the zoo or something like that. Our mother told us to sit here and don't move a muscle. Are you sure we're not in your way? If we are, we can move.'

The kids didn't seem unduly nervous at being dropped into a foreign land. As a matter of fact, they seemed unusually trusting, a testament to their sheltered life.

'I'm positive you're not in my way.' Decker paused. 'Your mother went with Mrs Decker?'

The youngest boy said, 'She took a walk. She told us to sit here and not move.'

The older girl squinted at the TV, eyes a mixture of awe and cynicism. 'I don't understand what's going on.'

'Pardon?' Decker asked.

'In this game. I think if she guesses the price of the washing machine, she actually gets to *keep* it?'

Decker bit his mustache. 'Uh, yeah, I think that's how it works.'

The girl turned to him, her face full of confusion. 'It isn't a joke?'

'Uh . . . no, it's no joke.'

'That is *unbelievable*!' The girl said, 'You mean they just *give* that lady a washing machine?'

'If she wins, yes.'

'How can they *do* that!' the girl exclaimed. 'Why would they *give* away a washing machine? Isn't that *expensive*?'

'And the automobile,' the little boy chimed in. 'That's *real* ispensive!'

Decker paused. How do you explain the corporate world and prime-time advertising to kids who never owned TVs.

The girl still had her eyes glued to the monitor. 'How do you get to play that game? You got to give them money or something?'

'Minda!' the oldest boy rebuked her sharply. 'This is not our world!'

'Mendel, Mama could really use a new washing machine.'

'Then Papa will buy her one.'

'Yeah, sure. He never buys us anything.'

'Minda!' the boy scolded.

Minda fell silent. The little boy smiled at Decker. 'I saw the horses.'

Decker smiled back. 'Would you like to ride one?'

The boy's eyes grew big. 'Can I?'

'Pessy, wait for Mama,' the oldest boy said.

'Good idea,' Decker said, wondering where the hell Mama was. Instead he turned to Mendel and asked him what he was learning. The teenager shrugged, leaning over the volume of Talmud as if hiding his paper from a potential cheater.

Again, Decker bit his mustache. 'Anyone hungry?'

'We'll wait until our mother comes back,' Mendel said. 'But thank you anyway.'

Decker shuffled his feet. 'How long has your mother been gone, kids?'

Minda said, 'About half an hour. Before *Joker in the Deck* . . . will you look at *that*! She won a whole living room full of furniture! I can't *believe* it!'

Decker smiled tightly. 'Is anyone hungry?' He looked at the youngest. 'Are you hungry, Pessy?'

'He'll wait,' Mendel said.

'Don't be such a meanie, Mendel,' Minda said. 'Are you hungry, Pessy?'

The little boy looked at his brother. His brother nodded. Pessy said, 'I'm a little hungry.'

'I can fix you a sandwich,' Decker said. 'What would you like? Tuna? Egg salad? Peanut butter and jelly?'

'Peanut butter and jelly,' Pessy said. 'Please.'

'Coming right up.' Decker stood. 'How about you, Mendel? Anything?'

Mendel blushed. 'I'm okay.'

'You're sure?'

Minda said, 'Go ahead, Mendel. You already checked out the kitchen. It was fine.'

Mendel glared at his sister. Decker said, 'I'm glad you

118

checked out the kitchen. I want you kids to feel comfortable here.'

Minda said, 'Thank you very much. And thank you for letting us stay here. I've never seen a game like this in my life. It's *fascinating*!'

'It's *beetul Torah*,' Mendel said.

'Mendel, relax, okay?' Minda said. 'It's vacation!'

Decker smiled. 'I'll make you a sandwich, Pessy. Who else is hungry?'

Slowly, the younger girl raised her hand. Decker hadn't really noticed her before. She was so waifish, so thin, Decker wondered if she wasn't undernourished. Her name was Bryna. Not that she told Decker her name. Minda volunteered the information.

Mercifully, Decker heard a key inserting in the front lock. The door opened, Rina shouting out hello.

'We're in the dining room,' Decker shouted back.

Rina walked in, Hannah riding her hip. Decker smiled at his daughter, then relieved his wife of her sitting appendage.

'Hello, Hannah Rosie!' Decker lifted her into the air. 'How was your checkup?'

'She got a shot for hepatitis.'

'Oh.' Decker lowered her gently. 'What leg was it in?'

'Her right thigh. She has a high pain threshold. She couldn't decide if she should really cry or not. When she saw me smiling, she figured it was okay not to cry.' Rina looked at the children. 'Hi, kids. Where's your mother?'

'Out for a walk,' Minda said. 'Are we in your way?'

Pessy added, 'Mama told us not to move.'

Rina frowned. 'No, of course you're not in our way. What do you mean, she went out for a walk?'

Minda said, 'Just that she went out for a walk. She likes

to walk. I can't believe this show isn't a joke. Mrs Decker, how can they give away things like washing machines and furniture?'

'The show makes money on the commercials,' Rina answered.

'The commercials give the stuff away?'

Rina said, 'I'll sit down and explain it to you tonight, Minda.'

Decker forced out a smile. 'I was just about to make some peanut butter and jelly sandwiches. Why don't you come help me out, Rina?'

She followed him inside the kitchen. He closed the door and whispered, 'What the hell is going on? This woman drops her kids into a strange city, into a strange house, parks them in front of the TV, then goes out to take a *walk*? Is this logical, Rina?'

Rina was concerned. 'She wasn't here when you got home?'

'No, she wasn't.' Decker made a disgusted face. 'Poor kids. They're so lost. They don't even know what a *game show* is. They've got that beaten-down look ...' He paused. 'I wonder if she's abusing them?'

'Peter!'

'I've seen hundreds of abused kids, Rina. It's not an off-the-cuff diagnosis.'

Suddenly, Rina paled. 'Do you really think so professionally? Or are you just grumpy.'

Decker ran his hand down his face. 'I don't know. Maybe I'm just tired.'

No one spoke.

'What should I do?' Rina asked.

Decker said, 'Probably nothing you can do. If you confront her, she'd probably deny it and leave. End of case.

Reminds me of my days in Juvey. Nothing's worse than murder, but some things come close. Hell, I'm probably wrong. She might just be your average flakey Jake. Occupational hazard and all that jazz.'

'You sound very defeated, Peter. What happened?'

'Nothing. Probably my blood sugar's low.'

Rina said, 'I'll make some lunch. What would *you* like? Egg salad?'

'Fine.'

Hannah hit his chest and burped. Decker laughed. 'You want to go look at the horsies with me?'

Hannah grinned broadly.

'That's a good idea,' Rina said. 'Take her out to the horses.'

'Should I take the little boy, too? He seemed interested in them. He thinks I'm a cowboy.'

'You ride horses, you're a cowboy. Isn't Pessy sweet?'

'Yeah, he seems like a nice boy.' Decker shook his head. 'What?'

'The kids,' Decker said. 'Their behavior ... I don't know. They don't react like normal kids.'

'Peter, imagine if you lived most of your life in eighteenth-century Poland, then you were suddenly beamed into 1990s Los Angeles. They're in a time warp. They don't even know what tropical means.'

'Keep people locked up long enough, they become weird.'

'They're not locked up.'

'For all intents and purposes they are. These little religious sects are nothing but cults.'

'Except that Honey brought them out here.'

'Her rabbi would approve of this excursion?'

'The Leibbener Rebbe isn't David Koresh or Jim Jones,

121

Peter. He isn't apocalyptic. That isn't a Jewish concept.
The people are free to come and go as they please.'

'That's what they all say.'

'Goodness, you are such a *cynic*!'

'Of course I am. I deal with the dregs of society.' Decker
smiled at Hannah. 'We're going to see the horsies,
Mommie. I'll ask Pessy to come join us. If that's okay with
Mendel.'

'He's protective.'

'I guess I can understand that. Taking care of your
family.'

Rina frowned. 'I was listening to the news.'

'Why would you want to do that?'

'I heard about the missing family you're investigating.
How's it going?'

'It's not,' Decker said. 'Could be why I'm in such a bad
mood.' He turned to Hannah. 'Come on, puddin'. Let's go
see some horsies.'

Hannah flapped her arms excitedly.

Decker turned to Rina. 'This woman *is* coming back to
reclaim her kids, isn't she?'

'What do you mean?'

'You've never heard of the husband who goes out to buy
cigarettes and never returns?'

'Oh, Peter ... Honey would never ... I mean, I don't
think ...' Rina put her hand to her mouth, then dropped it.
'Sometimes I just can't read you. Are you serious?'

Decker was deadpan. 'What's four more kids? My life is
a mess anyway.'

Rina looked him in the eye, her own face just as serious.
'Life is tough, isn't it?'

They started laughing – a release for both of them.
Decker hated Missing Persons cases and this one was very

unusual – an entire family gone with only a phone call as a lead. Where was Dov now? he wondered.

He kissed Hannah on the crown of her head and swung her around. Again, the little girl flapped excitedly. Decker brought her over his shoulder and the baby nestled into his chest.

Ah, what couldn't be cured by a baby's hug.

12

What a difference a peanut butter and jelly sandwich made. The younger girl smiled and even talked. She said thank you to Decker, and when he offered to show her the horses, she actually looked at him before she averted her eyes. After urges from Minda, Bryna went with her younger brother, Pessy, to give the steeds some chow. She even gave the horses sugar cubes. Afterward, Decker gave her two glasses of milk and she drank them both.

Maybe she was undernourished.

Pessy squealed with delight as he related his tale of horses to brother Mendel. The teenager listened politely, then tousled Pessy's hair. Minda's attention was still fixed on the TV. This time she was watching a word game. She responded to the questions, smiling when she got the correct answers, but the competition didn't hold as much attraction for her as the prize shows. Decker checked the paper's TV guide, then changed the channel to *Wheel of Fortune*.

'You can win big things on this one,' Decker told her.

'As big as *The Price is Right*?'

'You bet.'

Minda nodded gravely.

Mendel went on with his learning.

And Honey still hadn't returned.

Finally, just as Decker was about to leave, a knock sounded at the front door. Decker opened it and knew something was wrong. The woman, who seemed light-complexioned to begin with, appeared pale and nervous, hands clasped tightly to one another. Still, she tried out a smile, her voice attempting to be upbeat.

'I'm Honey Klein. I hope my kids haven't been a bother.'

'No, they've been fine.' Decker felt a gush of relief as he stepped out of the way. 'Come in. Is everything okay?'

'Fine.' Honey bit her lip. 'I'm a little tired. Jet lag, I guess. Thank you very much for sharing your home with us. It's very special what you're doing.'

'It's our pleasure. Rina's in the kitchen.'

Decker started to walk and she followed. Not a bad-looking woman, if you like cute faces – small features and dimples in her cheeks. She had a nice figure, too. But her expression was full of anxiety. She saw her children gathered around the dining table and forced out another smile. 'Hi, kids.'

'Mama!' Pessy bounced out of his chair and began to jump as he talked. 'I got to feed the horses!'

'That's wonderful,' Honey said.

'They eat sugar.'

'They do?'

'Yes. Big sugar cubes. And carrots, too!'

'Really.'

'You want to feed the horses, Mama?'

'Yes, but later,' Honey said. 'Guess what, kids? I got us a car! Now we can go anywhere!'

Mendel said, 'I thought you said we weren't going to rent a car. That it was too expensive.'

Honey sneaked a sidelong glance at Decker and blushed.

'I changed my mind. Some things are just worth the cost. So we're mobile now. Let's just grab us some lunch and then we're off!'

'We had lunch, Mama,' Pessy said. 'Sandwiches. Peanut butter and jelly. And potato chips too!'

'Don't forget the carrot sticks,' Minda said.

'Yeah, and carrot sticks.'

'You all ate?'

'Each and every one of us,' Minda said.

Honey said, 'Bryna, did you eat?'

The girl nodded.

'You *did?*'

The girl nodded.

'*Really*, Bryna?'

'She had two glasses of milk, Mama,' Minda said.

Astounded, Honey looked at Decker. 'How'd you do it?'

'Must be vacation,' Decker said.

Honey's smile was genuine. 'Great. So I'll just grab something and then we can go to the zoo.'

'I'd rather watch TV,' Minda said. 'I can go to the zoo anytime. They're spinning this big wheel, Mama, and if it lands on the word "fur", they win a *mink coat*. It's not a joke. Come look.'

'*Beetul Torah*,' Mendel said. 'Stupidity! What would Papa say?'

'Papa isn't on vacation,' Minda snapped.

'Minda, Pessy really wanted to go to the zoo.'

'So go without me,' she said without anger. 'I'll be fine.'

Again, Honey blushed. 'The addictive powers of the boob tube. Gershon would be furious.' She shrugged. 'I guess a day of TV won't hurt.'

Decker wasn't about to offer an opinion. 'Come. I'll bring you to Rina.'

127

Honey followed him into the kitchen and closed the door behind them.

'*There* you are!' Rina said to Honey. She placed Hannah in her high chair and belted her in. 'I was getting worried about you.' She noticed Honey's tired face. 'Is everything okay?'

'I rented a car.'

'You did? *Why?*'

'I didn't want to bother you.'

'It's not a bother, Honey.'

Decker cleared his throat. 'I'd better be going.' He stared at Honey's eyes. Something was off. 'Are you sure everything's okay?'

Wearily, Honey sat down on a kitchen chair. 'Just the news, I suppose.'

'The *news*?' Rina said.

'Something about a family that disappeared. The father was a diamond dealer.'

No one spoke. Then Decker said, 'What about the family?'

'Gershon is a diamond dealer. I hear things like that, I get scared.'

Again, the room fell silent. Decker broke it. 'Why? Have there been incidents like that in New York?'

Honey's eyes went to her lap. 'Not a whole family disappearing, no. But we've had murders. It's a cash and carry business. Sometimes I worry.'

Decker sat down. 'The family that's missing? That's my case, Honey. Anything you might tell me is greatly appreciated.'

Rina cleared her throat. 'Honey's on vacation, Peter.'

Decker tapped his forehead. 'Anyone home in there? You're right. Scratch the question.'

'No, it's okay,' Honey said, quickly. 'What do you want to know?'

'Forget it, Honey,' Decker said. 'I don't know when to turn it off.'

Honey blurted out, 'I'm worried about Gershon. I'm . . .'

Her sentence trailed off. Decker urged her to continue.

Honey said, 'Just that he's been acting strange. Then I heard the news on the TV. No wonder we don't have television in the village. All it does is cause heartache.'

Decker waited a beat, then said, 'What does it have to do with Gershon?'

'Probably nothing,' Honey said. 'But when I heard this story, I went to call him. In Israel. I didn't want to worry the kids. That's why I told them I was taking a walk. I didn't want them to hear their neurotic mother talking about a disappearing family . . .'

She paused to catch her breath.

'He wasn't in, Rina. It's after ten p.m. in Israel. Where could he *be*?'

'Ten in the evening isn't really late for Israel,' Rina tried. 'People are just getting started—'

'It's late for Gershon. He's not the social type. Ordinarily, I wouldn't think a thing of it except that things have been . . . bizarre lately.'

Honey bit her thumbnail and stopped talking.

Decker said, 'What do you mean by bizarre?'

'This is so embarrassing,' Honey said.

Rina said, 'Honey, if you don't want to talk about it . . .'

Honey sighed. 'Just that . . . Gershon hasn't been well lately. He hasn't been sleeping well. Or eating well. He stopped bathing or changing his clothes. He walks around the neighborhood, talking to himself. Just ask anyone in the village. Even the Rav says there's something terribly wrong. But Gershon won't *talk* about it.'

Suddenly, Honey broke into tears. Decker and Rina exchanged quick looks as Honey sobbed into her hands. Decker found a tissue box and gave it to her.

'That's the real reason . . .' Honey pulled out a tissue. 'That's the real reason I'm here with the kids. I had to get them out of that environment! You see poor Bryna? She doesn't eat a thing. And Mendel used to be so outgoing and social. Now he's all quiet. We're all nervous wrecks!'

Hannah started to cry. Rina rescued her from the high chair.

'Now look what I've *done*,' Honey chided herself.

'Don't worry about it,' Rina said, bouncing Hannah on her hip.

Honey dabbed her eyes. 'This is terrible. Me bringing my problems to you.' She looked at Decker. 'I don't know if your case has anything to do with him, but I'll be happy to talk to you if you think it would help. It's the least I could do.'

Decker looked at Rina. She shrugged. He said, 'Tell me about the murders in New York.'

'Robberies. Mostly, they're robberies.' Honey took a deep breath. 'But once in a while . . .'

She stopped talking.

'What?' Decker said.

'You hear about people. About people overextending themselves. Making bad deals then owing money to the wrong people.'

'Who constitutes the wrong people?' Decker asked.

'Gangsters.'

'Do you think Gershon might be in this kind of trouble?'

'Maybe. He's been secretive about his business dealings.

He's always whispering into the business phone. And I know he gets hang-up calls.'

'How do you know if he doesn't tell you things?' Rina asked.

'I've lived with him long enough to know when he's in trouble!' Honey bit her thumbnail. 'He told me he had to make a sudden trip to Israel. Now I can't get hold of him. I have to wonder if he's running away from something ... hiding from someone.'

No one spoke for a moment.

Honey said, 'Perhaps I'm being overly dramatic.' Her face began to fall. 'Look, I need a few minutes to be alone. Please excuse me.'

She walked out of the kitchen. Decker looked at Rina. 'The woman is brittle. What I'm trying to figure out is how much of her story is bullshit.'

'You don't believe her?'

'Not completely, no.'

'Why not?'

'A cop's cynicism. I believe *she's* running away from something. And I don't think it's gangsters, I think it's domestic problems. Look, Honey lives in a small town, right?'

'Right.'

'Since she's staying in my house, I want to know what we're dealing with. I'm going to make a couple of calls to her village and ask about Gershon and her.'

'Let me do it, Peter. I know Yiddish. I'll try to call the Rav directly. I'm sure he knows everything that goes on.'

Decker thought a moment. 'You're right. You call. Find out about her situation. I'm not turning a blind eye to her problems, but I'm not about to step into the middle of a long-standing domestic battle. And if by some quirk, her gangster story is true, I'm not going to use my house as sanctuary from the mob, either.'

'Agreed.' Rina kissed Hannah. The baby held out her arms to Decker. 'You want to go to Daddy?'

Decker took the baby and let out a small laugh. 'Hey, Hannah Rose. How about a game of chess? I'll set up the pieces and you can throw them across the room.'

The baby grinned broadly. Decker smiled back. 'At least someone knows how to have fun.

According to cousin Sharona Bar Lulu's phone records, Dov Yalom had made a call at 6:55 to her number from a booth located in front of an ice cream store. The parlor was located in a block-long shopping center on Devonshire, about two miles from the Yalom house.

Decker started his search there. Three hours later, he ended his search there. He had come up with a big, fat goose egg. Nobody he had talked to had an inkling about the kid. He figured Dov made the call and ran.

Several theories, each one flawed.

One: The entire family was on the lam. Dov had momentarily escaped from them to make a farewell call to his cousin.

Then why would the parents' passports be left behind when the boys passports were missing?

Two: Dov and Gil were directly involved – as perpetrators – in their parents disappearances. They killed the parents and split. Dov made the farewell call before disappearing.

Then where did they do the killing? No evidence in the house. And where were the parents' bodies? Furthermore, why was Gil's car still in the garage if the boys had taken off in a hurry?

Three: Dov and Gil had *nothing* to do with their parents disappearance. But they knew something bad had happened to their parents. They were worried they might be the next victims. So they grabbed their passports and left, Dov making his final call before blending into the miasma.

Then why didn't they used Gil's car? And wouldn't they have *packed* something?

Four: Dov killed his brother *and* his parents. That would explain Gil's car in the garage. Dov wasn't old enough to drive.

But why would Gil's passport be missing, too? And wouldn't Dov have packed something or emptied out his bank account? He would have needed something to live on.

Five: Marge's spy theory. Someone whacked the entire family, parents first. The boys tried to escape, allowing Dov to make his call, but then they caught up with the boys and whacked them, too.

If this was the case, Decker would never find the bodies.

No bodies, no evidence.

If a homicide falls in the forest . . .

Tug Davidson sorted through the logs and reports.

'You got nothing unusual in the bank accounts.' He paged through the papers. 'Credit is fine, the Yaloms were current. Looks like the Jew knew how to hold a buck.'

Decker was impassive. Was Davidson riling him on purpose? Probably not. The statement was made too casually. He'd promised Marge he'd let her do the talking. She wanted it that way and he was happy to oblige her.

Davidson said, 'You got interviews with the neighbors and friends and schools.' He squinted as he read Marge's synopsis. 'The kids were in school the entire day?'

Marge said, 'Their last-period teachers had them marked as present.'

'When does school get out?'

'Three-ten.'

'And then they disappeared.'

'We can't trace their whereabouts after three-ten.'

'Did the older kid drive to school that day?'

'No one's sure,' Marge said. 'That's why I'd like a little more time—'

'To come up with more diddly-squat?' Davidson looked up from the notes and sat back in his seat. 'We need evidence of a crime. You got nothing so far.'

Marge was quiet.

Davidson said, 'Let me give you the lowdown, Dunn. Boys were in school. The parents had lunch with the sister. The wife . . . what's-her name?'

'Dalia,' Marge said.

'Yeah, Dalia. She didn't go back to her office after lunch, right?'

Marge nodded.

'Okay. She doesn't go back to her office, Yalom doesn't go back to his office. Lunch ended around what time . . .' He looked at the papers. 'Around two. So we lose track of the parents around two. We lose track of the boys around three-ten. Where would the family go? I vote home.'

Davidson waited for a comment. He got nothing so he went on.

'Say they all met at home around three-thirty. Then we don't hear from no one in the family. Except the younger kid, Dov, calls his cousin around five that same day. That was three days ago and you're still no closer to finding them.'

'That's one way to look at it,' Marge said.

'You got another way to look at it, Dunn? Show me your fancy footwork, huh?'

Decker couldn't control himself. 'Someone else might call it a comprehensive initial investigation.'

'Yeah, well, I ain't someone else and I call it shit.'

Marge said, 'My gut tells me something happened.'

'That's just great, Dunn. My gut tells me something happened, too. Problem is guts aren't admissible evidence to a grand jury. You don't even have a suspect, let alone a perp. You don't even know if you have a *crime*.'

'Whole families just don't disappear,' Marge said.

'Sure they do, Dunn,' Davidson said. 'It's called the Witness Protection Program. Did you get a good look at this guy's passport?' He thumbed through Yalom's official document. 'If the Feds have them stashed somewhere, you ain't going to find them.'

Marge said, 'Then why would the boys' passports be missing and the parents' passports be left behind?'

Davidson said, 'Parents had to stick around for the Feds to testify for something or other. But they shipped the kids off to Israel. How does that sound?'

'The sister has spoken to her parents in Israel,' Decker said. 'The boys aren't there.'

'If she's telling the truth,' Davidson said. 'You notice she's not bugging us like she was.'

'That's because we're *doing* something,' Decker said.

Davidson was quiet for a moment 'Look, we all know something isn't right. I vote spy.' He plopped Yalom's passport on the desk. 'Yalom's something covert. If the family's in hiding, we're not going to find any of them. Nor am I interested in finding them.'

'So you're saying we should fold our tents?' Marge said.

Davidson was quiet. Then he said, 'You can keep this in

the active files for a few more weeks. But don't spend all day on it.' He drummed his fingers on his desk. 'Take a couple hours a day, but no more. Unless, of course, something new pops up.'

Marge said, 'Sir, that sounds reasonable. But if it's all the same to you, if you could just give me another whole day—'

'And what do you think you'll accomplish in another day, Dunn?'

Marge fidgeted. 'I'd like another day to scour the house for possible crime evidence.'

'You already scoured the house. Another full day would just be a waste of department's time and money. It's time to move on to current affairs.'

Marge clenched her jaw, but said nothing. In vain, she waited for Decker to say something but he remained quiet. Did he actually agree with Davidson's assessment or was he just keeping his mouth shut? Damn, he was unreadable.

Davidson turned to Decker. 'You got a court appearance or something this afternoon?'

'The Williams shooting.'

'That was the Saturday night bar thing?'

'Yep.'

'Then I'll give this to Dunn.' Davidson took out a note and handed it to Marge. 'This came through dispatch 'bout fifteen minutes ago. You literally got the smoking gun.'

Marge unfolded the note and read the details. A shooting at a local college – a lover's quarrel in the science lab. The boyfriend knocked off his woman in front of twenty students. Blues already at the scene. A rookie could have taken this call. All she had to do was fill out the forms.

Marge pocketed the information and stood. 'I'll get right to it, sir.'

'Right attitude,' Davidson said. 'I like that. You're

learning. I know you want the Big One, Dunn. And you was hoping this Yalom thing was it. No harm in that. And maybe it taught you something in the process. You can't eat steak before you cut your teeth.'

Decker allowed himself a fleeting smile before his expression turned flat. But Davidson caught it. 'Did I say something funny, Decker?'

'Are you saying a more experienced person could have come up with more evidence in this case?'

'Yeah, maybe that's what I'm saying.'

'I'm experienced.'

'Obviously not as much as you think.'

Decker said nothing, his eyes still on Davidson. They were locked in an old-fashioned staring contest. G-rated wagging. Decker had an almost irresistible urge to make a funny face.

Finally, Davidson said, 'I'm pissing you off, Decker?'

'Nope. You're daring me. I like that even better.'

'I'm glad I'm making you happy. And if it motivates you to go out and solve this case . . . find some bodies, more power to you. But no more sucking on the department's tit, you hear? A couple of hours a day on it, the rest is your own time.'

Decker stood. 'Fair enough.' He held out his hand. Davidson stared at it for a moment, then took it.

13

Despite what was printed, Decker knew the LAPD wasn't vilified by all. Still, both he and Marge were pleasantly surprised by the amount of support given to Devonshire by the people it served. The squad room was made up almost entirely of community-donated items, from the furnishings to the high-tech hardware. Not to mention the push-button phones. Decker had used a rotary for years at Foothill.

The work space itself was generic LAPD squad room. The desks were grouped according to detail with Homicide located in the back adjacent to CAPS – Crimes Against Persons. The walls held the requisite blue file notebooks, the lockers, the division maps, and the emergency mobilization plans. But the Dees had done a little of their own homespun decorating. Decker's favorites were a poster of David Mamet's movie *Homicide*, and a large colored drawing of pigs wearing police hats as they snuffled for truffles.

Bending a gooseneck lamp over his notes, Decker sat at his desk, reviewing his court case, waiting to see if the analytical office in CAD – Crime Analysis Detail – could pull from the computer any prior family disappearances. He knew computer information could take a while. It depended on how the questions were phrased and entered, on who else was on-line. He probably wouldn't have answers before he left for court.

Not that Decker *had* to appear in court. Since the passage of prop 115, it was now permissible for uniformed officers to present the detective's evidence to the Grand jury, thus freeing up Dees to work in the field. But Decker preferred to state his own case if time permitted. Years of law school die hard.

Marge walked in and sat down at her desk across from Decker. He looked up and placed his briefs on his desk.

'How'd it go?'

Marge grimaced. 'What a waste! And I don't mean a waste of my time. I mean a waste of *human life*. Guy got pissed at his girlfriend so he shot her. Now he's all remorseful, bawling like a baby, hovering over the body. He was actually giving her CPR when the blues arrived, do you believe that? Like that's the treatment of choice for a thirty-two slug in the brain.'

'He was packing a thirty-two?'

'Pulled it out of his satchel.' Marge shook her head. 'They never learn.' She paused. 'Well, I did my job, made Tug happy. Can you *believe* him? Aren't you outraged about his blatant anti-Semitism?'

'Nah.'

Marge stared at her partner. 'How can you *not* be? Jews as spies. The way he says *your* people.'

'Doesn't bother me.'

'Just what *does* it take to rile you up?'

Decker thought a beat. 'If you were anti-Semitic, then I'd be outraged. We need to talk about Yalom.'

Marge stared at her wristwatch. 'Okay . . . go!'

'What are you doing?'

140

SANCTUARY

'We've got one hour, fifty-nine minutes, and fifty-six seconds left.'

Decker smiled. 'I'm leaving for court in a few minutes. Though I don't expect anything, I've spoken to CAD. See if they can come up with any past abductions that resemble the Yalom case.'

'What an idea. I'm sure there must be a slew of open files on family kidnappings.'

'You got a better approach, I'm all ears, Marge.'

Marge was quiet. 'Sorry. I'm just angry. Angry at what I just saw, angry at Davidson.' She turned to him. 'Aren't you pissed at him? He *dared* you.'

'I don't get pissed, I get even,' Decker said. 'Guy's going to eat his words with shit on top. What say you and I get together here around four o'clock and go over Yalom, bit by bit.'

'We've done that.'

'We might have missed something. Let's do it again.'

The notes and charts covered both desks. It had taken them over an hour to review, classify, sort and re-sort. At five, most of the other thirty-odd Devonshire detectives were calling it a day. At six-thirty, Davidson walked out of his office and over to their table. Old Tug had on his jacket and was carrying his briefcase. He looked embarrassed to be leaving before them.

He said, 'You're doing this to spite me.'

Decker threw a look to Marge that said, 'Let me take this one.' To Davidson, he said, 'Like I told you, I'm just doing my job.'

Davidson said, 'Don't you have a baby at home, Decker?'

'Yep. A little girl – a real cutie. She looks like her mom.'

141

'Don't you want to see her?'

Decker glanced up from his charts. 'If I didn't know better, I'd think you were sabotaging my efforts, Loo. Lucky for me, I know better.'

Davidson glared at him. Then his expression suddenly eased. 'We're on the same side, Decker. I'd like to find this family, too. I know something's hinky.'

Decker said nothing.

'Unfortunately, hinky's not enough.' Davidson shook his head. 'Look. I know you've had experience in Homicide. But I've had *more* experience. These kind of cases eat up hours and I can't afford to have two of my Dees punching in useless time, get it?'

'I get it.'

Davidson said, 'Of course, you and Marge find bodies ... *a* body – one's enough – now that's a different story. Then I can justify the hours.'

And then it dawned on Decker. Tug wasn't a bad man. Tug wasn't even a bad cop. Tug was just an administrator. The position had turned him into a bureaucrat. He was forced to evaluate cases in terms of hours clocked, and dollars and cents, instead of good guys versus bad guys.

Decker said, 'I see your position, Loo. That's why Marge and I are doing this on our own. Maybe we'll get lucky, maybe we won't. Anyway, it'll be our problem, not yours.'

Davidson evaluated Decker's words. 'Just don't wear yourselves out.' He paused. 'Good luck.'

'Thanks,' Decker said.

Davidson turned to Marge. 'Luck to you, too.'

Then he was out the door.

Marge was quiet. Then she said, 'God, he's a wily

bastard. Notice how he manipulated the whole thing. Like he was doing us a *big* favor by letting us work on this case on our *own* time.'

Decker said, 'Did I tell you I checked him out?'

'And?'

'People say he's a hardworking cop. Lots of folks had good things to say about him.'

'So what the hell happened?'

'What do you think? He got promoted. They cut off his balls and turned him into a pencil pusher. Now he's got to look at what's expedient rather than what's right. I think deep down inside he wants us to win. So let's find something and prove the motherfucker wrong.'

Marge sat down dejectedly. 'Find what? We've been over our notes a dozen times. Nothing's clicking.'

Decker sat next to her. 'We've got to start somewhere so let's start with the obvious. The boys' passports are gone, and the parents' passports are still here. How about we check out some airline schedules. International flights. Why else would the boys need their passports.'

Marge knew that could take *days* without the proper papers and warrants. But Pete was right. They had to start somewhere. 'What's Israel's official airline?'

'El Al,' Decker said. 'But lots of others fly to Israel as well.'

Marge looked at her watch. 'It's too late to call the corporate offices. We could go down to the airport and try their computers.'

'All right, let's do that. But before we do, let's get a time schedule for the boys.'

Marge nodded. 'If we heard from Dov around five from the shopping center, when do you figure the boys arrived at the airport?'

Decker was quiet for a moment. 'Margie, how did the boys *get* to the airport? Gil's car was in the garage.'

'You haven't heard of cabs or a bus?'

'But why not take the car? Gil was old enough to drive. Why didn't they just grab a car and hightail it off to the airport?'

'You're getting at something.'

Decker raised a finger in the air. 'The car was a marker. Gil and Dov didn't want to use it, because they didn't want to be followed. They didn't want anyone to know who they were and where they were going.'

Marge was silent.

'So the question is, how did they get to the airport?' Decker paused. 'Let's start with a simpler question. How'd they get to the *shopping center*? It's about a five-minute car ride, a twenty-minute bike ride, and about a forty-five-minute walk. Say they walked home from school around three-thirty. Next time we hear from them they're at the shopping center around five. Indicates to me, they walked.'

'Then what?'

'Then Dov made his phone call.'

'Then what?'

Decker rolled his tongue in his cheek. 'Then I don't know.'

The room fell quiet.

Decker said, 'Okay. Let's back it up. The boys get home at around three-thirty. Something's real wrong. They know they have to get out of the house. They have to ... hide out for some reason. What would they need to go underground?'

'Cash,' Marge said. 'They'd need cash.'

'Okay. That brings to mind the mezuzah case that was posted on the inside of the doorframe. It was empty. Yalom knew how to post mezuzah cases correctly. He posted it the right way in his office. So why post such a big, expensive-looking case on the wrong side of the doorframe only to leave it empty? Answer: Because normally it wasn't empty. I say it contained valuables – money, maybe stones.'

'Lam money,' Marge said. 'Arik Yalom knew he was doing funny business and kept quick cash in case he had to take off suddenly. Okay. Go on.'

Decker said, 'So the boys have their money. And they have their passports. They're prepared to split.'

Marge said, 'Except an hour and some odd later, Dov called his cousin from a *shopping center*. If I were on the run, I certainly wouldn't walk to a shopping mall and make a phone call. I'd go *directly* to the airport.'

'Agreed,' Decker said. 'So why *did* they bother stopping off at a shopping mall?'

'To buy clothes.'

'They could buy clothes with their money when they arrived at their appointed destination. Besides, you're on the run, you don't shop.'

'To buy airplane tickets.'

'They could buy tickets for cash at the airport.'

Marge looked at Decker. 'Okay, why did they bother stopping off at the shopping mall?'

Decker said, 'For transportation. They walked to the mall and found some other way to get to the airport from the shopping mall.'

Marge nodded. 'You mean like they caught a cab or took a bus from the shopping center. I can buy that.'

Again, the squad room became silent.

Marge said, 'It's going to take hours to check out all the bus schedules and taxicab fares.'

'This is true.'

'We might as well skip over the transportation and go directly to the airport terminals. I'm game if you are.'

Decker stood and stuck his notepad in his jacket. 'Let's go.'

Nightfall had brought another storm into the Southland. Between intermittent downpours, Decker and Marge walked from terminal to terminal, battling not only bureaucracy and security but dank air thick with humidity and jet fuel. The runways were awash with rain and grease forming a mirrored surface that reflected the jets like a bad Impressionist painting. After hours of questioning personnel and squinting at lists of passengers' names printed on dot-matrix computer readouts, Decker rubbed his eyes and decided to call it quits.

Which was fine with Marge. She'd been ready to fold up tents an hour ago. She looked at Decker. 'Now what?'

Decker checked his watch. A little after ten. 'Are you hungry?'

'Are you suggesting an airport coffee shop? Why don't we skip the middleman and just inject the ptomaine poisoning directly into our veins.'

Decker smiled. 'Grab a cup of coffee with me.'

'Axle grease.'

'But at least the water's boiled.'

Marge rolled her eyes as they trudged to the airport cafeteria. A few minutes later, they were sitting across the table from each other, perched on lemon-colored plastic chairs, sipping bitter coffee out of Styrofoam cups. The lighting was harsh and Decker's eyes were tired. He hoped the caffeine would fuel him up, keep him awake long enough to make the long drive home.

He said, 'Just because we couldn't find their names

doesn't mean they didn't leave the country. They could have taken a domestic carrier to some other location and left through another city.'

Marge said, 'Peter, even if you're right, it won't help us. Think of all the permutations we could have. All the different domestic airlines that fly into cities that have international flights to Israel. It will take weeks, even months, to go through the rosters. At this point, we'd be better off looking for bodies.'

Decker said, 'So let's start looking.'

Marge let out an incredulous laugh. 'You say the most outlandish things so casually.'

'What's outlandish about looking for bodies?'

Marge glared at him. 'Where do we start, Peter?'

'I don't know.' He shrugged. 'Near their house, I guess. It's not far from the mountain passes. Lots of dumping grounds. How about if you and I meet tomorrow morning before work and do a little hiking?'

'You're serious?'

'Absolutely,' Decker said. 'I'll bring Ginger. She's not a scent hound but she's got a good nose.'

Marge clucked her tongue. 'What the hell? I suppose I can use a little exercise. Because that's all we're going to get out of this excursion.'

'Maybe. Maybe not.'

'What time did you have in mind?'

'Around six.'

'Peter—'

'I walk Ginger around six. She's very alert in the early morning.'

'But I'm not.'

'Margie, combing the hillside means we're working real low to the ground. Ginger's real good at that.'

'All right.' Marge blew her bangs off her forehead. 'Pisser that we don't have the time to do both. That we have to do this with our *own* dogs, on our *own* time.' In a mocking voice she said, 'Because Tug can't justify department hours.'

Decker didn't respond.

'You're not pissed?' she asked.

'Nah.'

Marge watched as Decker smiled cryptically. She studied his face. 'It's a game with you, isn't it.'

'Homicide is never a game.'

'Bullshit, Peter. You *want* to do this on your own time. You're dying to prove the bastard wrong.'

'What's wrong with that?'

Marge thought a moment. 'Nothing.'

14

Decker finally pulled into his driveway a little after eleven. He was surprised to find Rina not only waiting up for him but still in her street clothes. He asked her if everything was all right.

'Fine,' she answered. 'We missed you.'

'I missed you, too. Everyone okay?'

'Dandy. Was it a fruitful night for you?'

'Not great. We've got one lead, Rina. A phone call made by one of the teenaged boys.'

'But that's a lot, Peter. At least you know the boy is still alive.'

Decker didn't answer. In fact, he didn't know if Dov was alive or dead. Dov had made a phone call three days ago. 'Why are you still up? You need your sleep.'

'I thought we might go out for a walk.'

Decker looked out his living-room picture window. It was pouring. 'I think the weather's a tad nasty.'

'Not up for a romantic walk in the rain?'

'What's on your mind, darlin'?'

Rina did a quick glance over her shoulder, her eyes brushing across the closed door to the guest room. She whispered, 'How about we talk in the barn? Just you and me and the horses.'

Decker was tired. His head and neck ached, his shoulders were stiff and his old bullet wound throbbed. Weather like this sure didn't help. But he tried to mask his weariness. 'Sure, let's go check on the horses and you tell me what's on your mind.'

Rina put on her slicker. Decker hadn't even taken his off. He slipped his arm around his wife, guided her through the kitchen, then opened the back door and a big, black umbrella. Huddled under a waterproof canopy with Ginger at their heels, they ran for the barn, their shoes muddied in the process. But once inside, the barn was warm and dry and smelled sweet from recently pitched hay. Decker turned on a hanging electric lantern which illuminated the ground with a halo of soft light. The horses were prone, surprised by the intrusion but not disturbed by it. Decker's favorite mare, Beatrice, whinnied softly, the stray cats purred. Ginger nestled next to the tabbies and lowered her head to the ground. Decker folded the umbrella and pointed to a clean pile of hay.

'After you, madam.'

Rina took off her coat and plunked down into the hay. Decker sat next to her. 'Well, it's different.'

'I think it's kind of romantic.'

'Ye olde variation of a roll in the hay,' Decker grinned. 'What is it you don't want Honey Klein to hear?'

'How did you know I wanted to talk about Honey?'

'Just call me Sherlock.' Decker pulled her down, then fell on top of her. 'The barn does have its merits, don't you think?'

Rina drew him into a kiss. 'The hay is scratchy.'

'No prob, Sugar, you can climb on top.'

Rina punched him lightly. Decker rolled her over until

she was on top of his stomach and brought her into his arms. She was tense. He eased his hold.

'Rina, I don't expect us to engage in fiery passion in a pile of hay. So just relax, okay? Tell me about Honey.'

A clap of thunder cracked through the sky. Rina startled, then cuddled deep into Peter's broad chest. At this moment, it was wonderful to be with someone so big and protective.

Decker held his wife, kissed her forehead. 'I hope Hannah doesn't wake up. Did you bring the intercom?'

'Oh, yeah.' Rina dragged her wet slicker forward, fished through the pockets and pulled out a hand-held intercom. She turned it on. 'So far so good. All quiet.'

'Tell me about Honey.'

'She finally convinced her kids to go to the zoo with her this afternoon. Convinced Minda and Mendel mainly. Mendel didn't want to leave his *sepharim*, Minda didn't want to leave the TV.'

'Aren't most game shows over by the afternoon?'

'Minda discovered the Home Shopping Network.'

'Uh oh.'

'Anyway, Honey did finally round them all up. I begged off, saying I wanted to watch Hannah because she just had her shots. It was the truth.'

'Go on.'

'I got through to Honey's village. It took me a while to get hold of the Rebbe because the only number I had was for the local bakery. The village doesn't have a lot of phones.'

'The Rebbe actually talked to you?'

'I claimed it was an emergency. And yes, he spoke with me. He took his time, too. He's very . . . otherworldly. As I spoke with him, I felt I was talking to someone who had a direct line to the heavens. I can understand why he has so many devotees. He's very charismatic.'

'What did he say about Honey?'

Rina looked pained.

'That bad?' Decker sat up, keeping Rina on his lap. 'What?'

'According to the Rebbe, Honey's assessment of her life was pretty accurate. Gershon was always a ... different type of man. Very devout. The type of guy who refused to sit during any portion of davening. You know how long the Sabbath prayers can be.'

He did know. Even for the most no-nonsense of *minyans* – prayer gatherings – it would take at least an hour, hour and a quarter to say all the required verses. If someone wanted to add cantorial singing, the service could easily be stretched to two or more hours.

He said, 'She isn't running away from a guy because of that, is she.'

'No. I'm just trying to give you some background.'

'Go on.'

Rina cleared her throat. 'Now I've known people who stand during the entire service. But Gershon went beyond that. On Shabbos, for instance, he'd attend both the early minyan and the regular minyan. And he'd stand through both of them.'

'Why?'

'I don't know. There is certainly no halachic basis for it. You don't get brownie points for saying the same prayers twice.'

'So the guy's a fanatic. Some people would call us fanatical.'

'There's more, Peter. About a year and a half ago, something very traumatic must have happened to Gershon.

Like Honey said, he won't speak about it, but it must have been pretty bad. Because he changed drastically. He was never a friendly sort of guy, but he'd say hello or *shalom aleichem*. He was polite. Abruptly, he stopped talking to people, Peter. He stopped caring about his appearance. He stopped bathing—'

'How would the Rebbe know about his bathing habits other than through Honey?'

'Because Gershon started wandering the streets at night, talking to himself.'

Decker made a face. 'Great. And we're letting these people stay in our house.'

'Can you let me finish, please?'

Decker smiled. 'Continue.'

'The Rebbe said that if anyone ran into him and asked him what he was doing all alone, talking to himself, he would say he was just trying to work things out. He was . . . coherent when you talked to him. But his behavior . . .' Rina bit her lip. 'No one, including Honey or the Rebbe, was sure what exactly he was trying to work out.'

'Does he hold down a job?'

'Yes, he's a diamond dealer—'

'That's right. And he's still functional as a diamond dealer?'

'Apparently,' Rina said. 'They're not millionaires, but the Rebbe says he does okay.'

'The Rebbe knows his income?'

'Gershon tithes twenty percent to charity. To the penny. He shows the Rebbe his tax statements, then makes out a check for twenty percent of the gross. By law, you only have to give away ten percent. But Gershon took it a step further. The Rebbe wouldn't tell me how much he makes of

153

course, but he did tell me that he makes money. That's not the problem.'

'It could be the problem if he owes money to the wrong people.'

Rina paused. 'I wouldn't know. The Rebbe didn't mention any threatening phone calls.'

'But Honey did.'

Rina nodded. 'Maybe it's true. Maybe it's on Gershon's mind. Or maybe it's all *in* his mind. There's more to my tale.' She sighed. 'About six months ago, he declared himself a Nazir.'

'What's a Nazir?'

'Remember Samson of Samson and Delilah fame? He was a Nazir. That's why his hair was so long. You've heard of Jesus of Nazareth?'

'Slightly.'

'Some say Jesus was a Nazir – a Nazirite I think they call it in English. If I remember correctly, Nazirites take this vow which is: They don't drink wine or alcohol, they don't shave or cut their hair, and they don't defile themselves by contacting dead bodies—'

Decker laughed.

'What?'

'I'm listening to you thinking: Hey, I could manage the alcohol and hair part, but I'm not so sure I could take that ban on dead bodies—'

'No joke. You couldn't do what you do and be a Nazir, Peter. You come into contact with dead bodies on a regular basis.'

Decker paused. She was absolutely right.

'The ban on dead bodies also means that Nazirites can't visit cemeteries or hospitals – anyplace where a person might have died.'

154

Decker held her at arm's length. 'This is for real?'

Rina nodded. 'Wait, it gets weirder. Gershon not only took the vows to be a Nazir, he separated from his wife.'

'Ah, so they *are* in the process of a divorce.'

'Oh no. I didn't mean that kind of separation. I meant a physical separation. The Rebbe wouldn't come out and say it, but I think he meant sex. I think Gershon refuses to have sex with his wife. Now, I'm no expert on Nazirites – you'll have to ask Rav Schulman for the specific details – but I never remember anything about Nazirites not being allowed to have sex with their wives.'

Decker stared at her. 'You know, I meet a lot of strange people in my line of work. But I do believe you've introduced me to the strangest.'

'Peter, it isn't funny. The Rebbe says that Honey is really suffering. She doesn't know why he's doing this to her – to himself. Because he refuses to talk to anyone.'

'Did she tell the Rebbe about the strange phone calls?'

Rina nodded.

'What'd the Master say?'

'The Rebbe said that they should be careful.'

'Profound.'

'Peter, I don't know what to do.'

'What to do?' Decker smiled. 'That part's easy. We're doing enough by letting this woman and her kids stay with us. We're not obliged to do anything more.'

'Peter, that sounds so cold.'

'I'm not saying kick her out. I'm just saying don't be her shrink, okay?'

Rina didn't answer.

Decker looked her in the eye. '*Okay*, Rina?'

'I shouldn't listen to her problems?'

'No, as a matter of fact, you shouldn't. She came out here

to be entertained, so entertain her. Take her to Disneyland or Universal Studios—'

'I'd rather listen to her problems. It's easier.'

Decker laughed, then lay back down in the hay. 'I don't mean to sound callous, Rina, but you've got your health and your family to think about. She sounds like bad news—'

'Troubled news.'

'It's not what you need right now. It's not what your kids need.'

'It's not what *you* need,' Rina said.

'You're right about that!' Decker said. 'I'm working on five simultaneous cases, one I'm doing on my own time. Because my own lieutenant can't justify my hours working on a scene with no bodies.'

'You can't go over his head?'

'No, no, no,' Decker said. 'No, you don't go over your Loo's head. Not without losing your own. LAPD is a military organization, honey. You either play by the rules or you're a very lonely person.'

'That's not fair.'

Decker laughed at her flat assessment. 'No, it's not. But thems the breaks. Anyway tomorrow at dawn, Marge and I are going for a walk in the mountain passes to hunt for bodies. All this and we're not even getting paid for the pleasure.'

Rina's watch suddenly beeped. 'Jeez, it's midnight. If you're going out at dawn, you need your *sleep*. Do you really have to get up so early?'

' 'Fraid so.'

'Then I'm sorry I kept you up so late.'

'Don't worry about it.' He pulled Rina on top of him. 'Of course, you can make it up to me.'

'Here?'

'The household is asleep and we have the intercom to Hannah's room. Why not?'

Rina laughed to herself. 'I don't know if I can do it in front of all the animals.'

Decker grinned. 'Just close your eyes, sugar. I guarantee you they won't mind a bit.'

'Your dog's driving me nuts,' Marge complained.

Decker adjusted his backpack. 'You're just sore because you forgot your hiking boots.'

'Hell with the boots. I need cleats, it's so damn muddy.'

'You'd make a poor foot soldier, Margie. Colonel Dunn wouldn't approve.'

'The word "approve" isn't in the Colonel's vocab list.'

Ginger turned in circles, sniffing each morsel of ground as if it were fine wine. They had been walking for over two hours in three different secluded areas, and still the Setter showed no signs of tiring. It was literally a field day for her.

Decker said, 'It's the rain. It brings up all sorts of interesting smells. It drives her nuts and she gets confused. You've got to remember their brains are about the size of a pea.'

'Really?'

'Maybe a large pea.'

Marge took out a plastic bag. 'Then maybe we should let her sniff the clothes again.'

Decker nodded. Marge gloved her hand, then took out Dalia Yalom's white blouse and bra along with Arik Yalom's pants and undershirt. 'Here, girl,' she said. 'You're not interested in every single turd that has ever been dropped. You're only interested in finding these people.'

157

Ginger raised her head, eyed Marge quizzically, then nosed the clothing. Once again, she was off. Decker had to trot to keep pace with her.

'Does she know what she's doing?' Marge asked, breathlessly.

Decker shrugged.

'Orit Bar Lulu is going to be pissed if we come back with nothing, especially after waking her up at five in the morning to get the clothes.'

'She'll just live with the pain.' Decker tugged gently on the leash. 'Slow down, girl. Give an old man a chance to enjoy the scenery.'

The mountainside was wet and soggy, the mud seeping out from under their shoes. The air was nippy and smoky with dew, but morning sunlight was beginning to filter through the fog. Decker had on a red-plaid flannel shirt, brown chino pants and an Englishman's cap given to him by his father-in-law, the expert on caps. *Maven* was the word Rina had used. Marge wore a cable-knit sweater under a down-filled vest, corduroy pants, and high-top sneakers. She hated jackets. They limited her mobility.

'You ever hunt when you were a kid?' she asked.

'Yep. Alligators and ducks.'

'That's right. You were born in Florida. Did you like it?'

'Florida's okay.'

'Not Florida, Pete. Did you like hunting?'

'I thought it was silly. Grown men getting up at four in the morning to hunker down in the trenches and quack aloud. Alligators are mean sons of bitches. Sneaky little suckers with eternal smiles. But the way they're slaughtered used to get to me. You can't shoot them outright because you'll ruin their hide. You've got to pith their brains out with a special type of blowgun.'

'Lovely. Further nauseate my queasy stomach.'

Ginger abruptly stopped, her posture freezing in the mist of the morning.

'She's found something?' Marge asked.

'I don't know.' Decker tugged on the leash. 'Come on, girl.'

Ginger refused to budge.

'Does she know what she's doing?' Marge asked again.

'I've never taught her how to hunt,' Decker said. 'But the instincts are there.' He lowered his backpack onto the wet ground. 'I trust her, Marge. I say we dig.'

Marge slipped her knapsack off her shoulders. 'At least we don't have to worry about destroying evidence. The rain helped us in that department. I sure hope your dog isn't smelling a dead possum or something.'

'It could be she is. Although she seemed to sniff the clothes with interest.' Decker smiled. 'Listen to me. I'm psychoanalyzing a dog.'

Marge opened her satchel and took out an array of tools. 'I always wanted to be an archaeologist.'

'Don't think you're going to find Cro-Magnon man here.'

'I'll settle for anything that doesn't move when I exhume it.'

Decker smiled, then lowered himself onto his knees, feeling the ground with a gloved hand. Within moments, he had sunk a couple of inches into the slime. He knee-walked backward until he felt the ground wasn't going to swallow him up. 'I think Ginger's on the money. Feel the ground right in front of me. See how soft and muddy it is compared to where I'm kneeling.'

'You're right.' Marge sighed. 'Dirt over here is much looser.'

'Like it was dug up and turned over and tamped back into place.'

'I didn't see a mound.'

'Rain could have evened out the topology. I'm telling you, this is turned-up soil. We've got a grave here.'

'Should we call in the experts?'

Decker said, 'Maybe we should try it ourselves first. Could be as innocuous as someone having a funeral for their pet.' Decker felt the ground again, trying to outline the perimeter by touch. Just by quick feel, the soft area seemed around four by four. Who knew how deep. Maybe someone buried a mastiff. 'Give me the trowel. I'll start out slowly.'

Marge handed him the trowel.

Carefully, Decker started unearthing the mud. As soon as he dug out earth, the depression filled with silted water. It was like digging sand at the seashore.

'I need a siphon.'

'I can get us some straws at the local Jack-in-the-Box.'

'Did we bring a hose?'

'No such luck.'

Decker tried to bail out water with his hands. 'I can't see a fucking thing.'

Marge pulled off his cap. 'Why don't you sacrifice this to the cause?'

Decker looked at her, at the cap. He took it and began scooping muddy water from his hole. He dug, he removed water, more water came to take its place. Twenty minutes later, sodden with sludge, he stopped.

'My hands are freezing. My fingers are numb.'

'My turn to slime fish.' Marge knelt and stuck her hands into the icy slosh. 'I feel something down there.'

'There're lots of rocks.'

160

'Yeah, maybe that's what they are. Give me the pail.'

Decker handed her the cap. She attempted to bail water from the hole. It was a losing proposition. Disgusted, she tossed the cap and dug blind. When she felt she had removed a substantial amount of mud, she lowered her arm into the quagmire of frosty, wet earth. Soon her shoulder was touching the ground. She fingered her way around, then tried to pull her arm out and was met with resistance – as if she were freeing an animal trapped in tar. She finally liberated her limb, wiggled her fingers. Her sweater sleeve was encased in brown slime. 'Something is definitely down there.'

'More than rocks?'

'More than rocks. Jesus, my arm's frozen solid.'

'Move it around,' Decker said. 'Does it feel like dog bones or cat bones or . . . what?'

Marge attempted to wipe the mud from her forearm. She had a pained look on her face. 'I wouldn't swear to it, but I think I just shook hands with someone.'

15

Davidson scratched his nose. 'Looks like you found a body. At this point, I'm sure you'll take any corpse you can get.'

Marge looked at him. Now *how* do you respond to that? She said nothing, regarding the two lab men who were unearthing the contents from the makeshift grave. One wore a yellow slicker, the other chose a full black raincoat that Dracula could have used in a pinch. Both of the garments were caked with mud.

She lifted her eyes to the surrounding areas. The mist had evaporated but the sky was still gray. Now and then the sun appeared in a cameo role, but it added little light and warmth. Three police dogs were sniffing out the mountainside. Ginger hadn't liked the interlopers, had barked furiously and distracted the professionally trained canines from doing their jobs. Or so had complained their handlers. Decker had been forced to take her home, but not before recommending Ginger be cited for fine police work.

It was after eleven in the morning, Davidson having taken three and a half hours to get all the papers in order. Marge still felt Tug was a schmuck, but at least he was responsive, immediately assigning Decker and her to the case and allotting them the needed hours. Davidson watched the lab men dig.

163

'Don't envy their job.'

'Don't I know it,' Marge said. 'Mud's not only messy but was cold as ice. Freezes your fingers.'

'I thought women liked mud facials.'

'You're a funny one, Loo.'

Davidson actually twitched the corners of his mouth. Marge felt that was as close to a smile as he was ever going to give.

Davidson said, 'Good work, Dunn. You got your case, you got your time. Probably worth a few frozen nails for that.'

Marge said, 'What's a few frostbitten fingers between friends?'

Davidson looked her over. 'You think I'm a son of a bitch, Dunn? I can live with that. Besides, look how it got you going. Think you would have been motivated like this if I woulda patted your hand and said, "Take your time"?'

She didn't answer.

Davidson scratched his nose again. 'I got my stripes. Keep going like this, maybe it'll be your turn.'

Marge nodded, turned away, then broke into a soft smile. Damn it, they *did* do a good job! She took in a deep breath and put her hands in her pocket. Orit Bar Lulu was coming their way, her footing less than steady. She stopped and checked her watch.

'It's been over an hour,' she snapped to Davidson.

'We're moving as fast as we can, Mrs Bar Lulu. You can't rush these things.'

'You're driving me crazy.' She pointed to the grave. 'How long does it take to dig someone up? Give me a shovel. I'll do it in ten minutes.'

'It's not the unearthing, Mrs Bar Lulu,' Marge said. 'We

164

don't want to harm the body. I don't think you want that, either.'

'We're moving as fast as we can, ma'am.' Davidson looked around. 'Detective Dunn, you keep an eye on the lab men. I've got a few calls to make.'

Marge nodded and he left. Bastard probably wanted to get warm because it was *cold* outside. The yellow-slickered lab man raised his head. 'We got most of the mud off. Do you want to take a look, Mrs Bar Lulu?'

Orit glanced at Marge. As she stepped forward, she lost her balance. Marge caught her. She called out to the mountainside. 'Sergeant Decker, we're ready for an ID.'

Decker pivoted around and jogged over to Marge. He saw how she was supporting Orit. He flanked the Israeli woman on the other side and offered her an arm. Orit was white as she grabbed his wrist.

'First, I nag you to hurry up . . . then I don't know if I can even do it.' Tears formed in her eyes. 'Let's go.'

'You want a few minutes to catch your breath?' Decker asked.

'No, I'm ready,' Orit said. 'Let's get it over with.'

Slowly, they approached the body, Orit's eyes bobbing in their sockets.

'I've got you,' Marge said. 'Just take your time.'

Orit looked at them for moral support, her head lolling from one side to the other. Decker patted her shoulder. 'Take your time. If you feel sick, let us know.'

Orit nodded, then forced herself to study the face. A moment later, she jerked her head up, took a step backward, then gulped in a lungful of fresh air. Decker grabbed her arm.

'Are you okay?'

Orit's face was ashen, her voice a whisper. 'It's . . .

Dalia.' She teetered on her feet. 'I don't feel too good.' She burst into tears. 'I want to go home.'

Marge said, 'I'll take you to one of the squad cars.'

'I can't go home!'

'Of course you can,' Marge said, gently. 'But let us drive you. Can I call your husband for you?'

Orit nodded, allowing herself to be led by Marge to a heated black-and-white.

Decker stared at the grave, at a petite form outlined in mud. The face had been wiped but was still streaked with gook. Yet Decker could tell it had been a gentle face. Anger drove a blush to his cheeks. He choked it back and spoke to the lab men. 'Anything else buried under her?'

'We can't tell until we lift the body,' the black-coated man responded. 'We're waiting for the police photographer.'

'He should be here in a minute.'

Davidson was coming toward him, his stride quick and precise. 'Your wife's on the line,' he said. 'Your kids are fine, but she needs to talk to you. She says it's an emergency.'

'What kind of emergency?'

Davidson shrugged ignorance.

Decker felt his heart race as he ran over to the Plymouth. Was it his mother? His father? His brother? Randy was in vice – narcotics, mainly. He'd been shot three times by three separate dealers. Decker grabbed the mike from his radio. 'What is it?'

'Peter, everyone's healthy.'

Rina's voice was tense, but the words were all he needed. He heard himself taking a deep breath.

'It's not us, Peter, it's Honey Klein,' Rina said. 'It's Honey's husband. I just got a call from someone in the Manhattan Police Department,' Rina said. 'Gershon was found dead in his office at the diamond center. He'd been shot, stuffed into a closet—'

'Good God!'

'Peter, I don't know what to do!' She began to cry. 'I'm panicked!'

'Where are Honey and the kids now?'

'They left the house about two and a half hours ago to go sightseeing.'

'Where were they headed?'

'I don't *know*! She didn't tell me. I don't know what I'm going to tell her—'

'I'll handle it,' Decker said. 'You don't have *any* idea where they are?'

Rina paused. 'She said something about going to the old Grauman's Chinese Theater when I first spoke to her. But she said nothing to me about it this morning. Just that she was going sightseeing.'

Decker thought back to Gershon's strange phone calls, Honey's talk about gangsters. Not knowing any details, it was safer to be cautious. 'Rina, I'm going to send a squad car over to the house. I'll have the police wait outside until I can get over there. Don't answer the door and don't let anyone – and I mean *anyone* – in until I figure out what's going on. I may take a little time to come. We just dug up Dalia Yalom—'

'Peter, you don't have to—'

'I want to, okay?'

'Thanks.' Rina's voice was small. 'I'm scared.'

'I know, sweetheart. I'll be there in a jiffy.'

'I love you, Peter.'

'Love you too.' Decker paused. 'Rina, do you know where Honey got her rental car?'

'I think from the place on Foothill. Tour-Time Rentals. Does that sound right?'

'It sounds right. Just stay put. Keep the doors locked and don't open them for anyone. I have to make a few phone calls. I'll call you back in about fifteen minutes.'

He hung up the mike and called Foothill substation. Tim Calais's unit was the closest to the house. He was happy to help out a former Foothill member. Besides, Decker was sure Tim had heard about Rina's beauty. After thanking Calais, Decker cut the line, then put in a call to the dispatch operator, asking to be connected with Tour-Time Rentals. As he waited, Decker suddenly realized he was standing outside of the car. He sat down in the driver's seat and closed the door. Davidson came over to the unmarked, bent over, and peered through the open window. 'Everything okay?'

Decker covered the mike. 'We have some houseguests. The woman's husband, a diamond dealer, was just found murdered in Manhattan.'

'Jesus!' Davidson squinted. 'You just say the guy was a *diamond dealer*?'

'Yep.'

'Any relation to our case?'

'Who knows?' Over the radio, Decker heard a perky lady say, 'Tour-Time, this is Nancy speaking.'

'Nancy, this is Detective Sergeant Peter Decker of the Los Angeles Police.' He gave her all the requisite ID. 'I have an emergency situation here. I have to get hold of a woman who rented one of your cars. And I don't know where she is. Are your cars equipped with a location tracking system like the Lo-jack?'

'Yes, they are.'

'The woman's name is Honey Klein. I need you to activate her car's system for me.'

'One moment.'

Decker waited nervously. Davidson said, 'You trying to track this lady down?'

'Better I tell her than my wife.'

Davidson nodded and started to walk away. He turned around and shouted, 'You find her, ask her if she knows this Yalom character.'

Decker shouted back he would. A minute later, a less-than-perky Nancy came back on the line. 'We have no record of a rental to a woman of that name. Are you sure she rented from us?'

Shit, Decker thought. No, he wasn't sure. 'She may have rented using an assumed name—'

'We ask for ID.'

'She may have assumed ID.'

Nancy was silent. Decker said, 'She was a pretty, thin, blonde woman. She rented the car yesterday around . . . maybe twelve, one p.m.'

'I wasn't here yesterday.'

'The car she rented was an ice-blue Aerostar van.'

'Well, we do rent Aerostars. One moment.' Nancy checked and reported back five minutes later. 'I do have records of a rental of a blue Aerostar yesterday at twelve forty-five. The identification we have belongs to a woman named Barbara Hersh.'

He said, 'That might be the one. Can you activate the system on that car?'

'Yes.'

'How long will it take you to trace it?'

'About fifteen minutes to a half hour. I'll call you back, Detective.'

'I'm in the field, Nancy. I'll be hard to reach. If I don't hear from you, I'll call you back.' Decker cut the line and waited. Five minutes later, one of the dogs started barking furiously. The handler yelled out, 'Lieutenant, I think we found another one!'

Decker came out of the car. He met Davidson. The Loo said, 'You hear that?'

'Yep.' Decker stuffed his hands in his pockets.

'How far is this spot from the Yalom development?'

'About a twenty-minute, half-hour walk.'

'And you hit it the first time out?'

'This was the third mountain pass Marge and I checked out,' Decker said. 'Perseverance pays off.'

'Tenacious suckers, you two are.' Davidson looked over the mountain. 'Maybe the family took a walk and the boys popped them here. You got lucky 'cause the rains washed away the trail. It's probably the husband. We'll need another ID.'

Tug turned to the squad car where Orit Bar Lulu was resting.

'How's she holding up?'

'I'll think she'll be okay. Marge has been talking to her for a while.'

'Yeah, that's what the females are good for. Talking to the other females.' Davidson rubbed his hands together. 'How's your home emergency. Your wife sounded shaky.'

'Under control.'

Davidson nodded and left to check out the newest discovery. Decker went back to the car and called Rina.

'He's outside,' she said. 'Officer Tim Calais?'

'That's the one.' He checked his watch. 'Are you feeling better?'

'I'm nervous Honey is going to walk in any minute. Peter, what do I *say* to her?'

'I'll be home soon. Don't say anything until I get there.'

'Okay. I love you.'

'I love you, too.' He hung up and checked his watch. Fifteen minutes had passed. He'd try his luck and call back Tour-Time. 'Nancy, this is Detective Sergeant Decker—'

'We found the car, Detective.' Nancy's voice was nervous. 'It's on the Santa Monica Freeway.'

Decker took out a pencil and his notepad. 'The number ten freeway ... Okay. Is the car heading west or east?'

'It's not heading anywhere. It isn't moving.'

Decker paused. 'It's on the shoulder?'

'Yes, it appears to be on the westbound shoulder, stationed right before the 405 off ramp south.'

The off ramp to the airport, Decker thought.

'We're sending someone from the company out to investigate,' Nancy said. 'We've also placed a call to the Highway Patrol. It could be she just had engine problems or tire trouble...' Her voice faded. 'Maybe you'd like to call the Highway Patrol personally.'

'No problem.' Decker hung up, then asked the RTO to be connected with the CHiPs unit closest to the Aerostar. Again, that took some time. Five minutes later, Rachel Parks identified herself to Decker.

'I'm at the site.' She sounded tense. 'I don't know what you're working on, but maybe you should come down here. The car has two flat tires, but no visible puncture wounds. Something's screwy.'

'Anyone inside?'

'No, Sergeant. No one's inside.'

171

'Is the car locked?'

'Nope.'

'Officer Parks, could you just take a peek inside the interior and tell me if something looks funny.'

'Hold on, Sergeant.' Rachel returned a minute later. 'Nothing immediate. I take it you don't want me poking around, messing up your evidence. You want to come down before the rental company picks up the car?'

'Yeah, I'll be down.'

'I'll be waiting.' Patrol Officer Parks hung up.

From the outside, he heard one of the lab men shouting. 'Another one – male. Gun shot wound in the gut.'

Decker joined Davidson at the mountainside. The Loo said, 'As soon as Bar Lulu makes the ID, I'll put out an APB for the boys. I'll also have a couple of uniforms check out the airlines. Free you and Dunn up for the major investigation.'

Decker nodded, staring at the lab men who were gingerly scraping mud off the buried corpse. 'This is going to take a while.'

'You got a plane to catch?' the Loo asked.

Decker recapped his conversation with Rina and with Rachel Parks.

Davidson said, 'It's West LA's problem, Decker.'

'Not when it affects my wife.' Decker kept his voice even. 'Loo, the lady's got four kids, they were staying at my house. Now, I don't care under whose jurisdiction it technically falls, *I'm* going out there.'

Davidson stared at the chilled ground and rubbed his hands together. 'Body'll keep. Be back in an hour.'

Decker nodded. 'See you in an hour.'

16

Decker reflected: A twenty-minute ride from the corpses to his ranch – a sobering thought. He welcomed the sight of Tim Calais's patrol car parked in front of the house, thanking Tim for coming through and offering to return the favor, if needed, in the future. When Decker opened the front door, he found Rina in the living room, pacing, Hannah bouncing on Mommie's hip. In front of the fireplace was a suitcase. Decker kissed Rina, then took Hannah and gave her several smooches on her cheek. The baby took the assaults with stoicism, then patted Daddy's chest. Decker's eyes traveled back to the luggage.

'Planning an impromptu vacation?'

'I'm very good at reading your tone of voice,' Rina said. 'You're going to suggest we spend the night at my parents' house.'

'Very good.'

'I'm willing to go. But what do I do with Honey and her family? I can't just desert them.'

'I don't think you're going to be hearing from them.' Decker told her about the abandoned van. 'An HP officer is waiting for me. But I wanted to get my family squared away first.'

Rina's face was frightened. 'Abandoned ... they just

173

upped and left . . . or was it an abduction . . . like the case you're working on?'

'Rina, I don't know,' he said, nervously. Then he remembered he was holding Hannah. He didn't want her to absorb his tension. He spoke calmly, 'Do you know if Honey's luggage is still in the house?'

'I haven't checked.'

'I'll do it.' Decker kissed his wife's cheek, then walked into the guest room.

It was as neat as an army barracks – two twin beds and four cots, all of them made up. The Kleins' suitcases were still in the room. They were closed and stacked in the corner. Decker switched Hannah to his other arm, went over to the valises and opened up the top piece. It seemed to belong to Minda, judging by the size of the dresses. The clothes inside were jumbled. He opened the second suitcase – Pessy's. Again, the apparel was messy.

That made Decker feel better. Honey didn't seem to care about her kids' packing habits. She was just trying to keep the room neat for *them*. Decker closed the second suitcase.

'How you doing, Muffin?' Decker said to Hannah. 'Putting up with crazy Dad?'

The baby smiled. Decker tickled her tummy. 'Let's see what's in the bathroom, okay?'

Again the baby smiled. Decker smiled back. 'My, but you're agreeable. Are you sure you're a member of this family?'

He went inside the bathroom. The towels were neatly hung, the vanity to the sink was clean, five toothbrushes standing in the borrowed glass cup.

Decker leaned against the wall. Toothbrushes still in the bathroom, suitcases still stuffed with clothing. His stomach was tight. Rina interrupted his thoughts.

'The suitcases are here. They were planning on coming back. Peter, this is *sickening*!'

'Yes, it is. But worrying about them isn't constructive. Honey Klein said her husband might have been involved with the wrong people. You're right. I want all of you out of here for the night. Better to be paranoid than sorry. Can you get the boys after school?'

'Of course.'

'Then let's go.' Decker started to pick up a suitcase, then noticed Rina hadn't moved. 'Are you all right?'

'Peter, I don't mind being exiled to my parents as a precaution, but it's disruptive for the boys. I took the liberty of calling Rav Schulman. He said he would watch the boys for a couple of days. I think they might be better off at the yeshiva.'

Decker frowned. 'Rina, we just pulled them out of the yeshiva. You think it's smart to send them back?'

'Just for a couple of days.' She clasped her hands together. 'I'm still ambivalent. I spent almost eight years of my life at *Ohavei Torah*. I'm very attached to it – to the Rav. And he's so attached to the boys. I feel obligated to keep up contact for the boys' sakes.'

Decker blew out air. Moving the boys from the ultra-orthodox yeshiva to a more modern Orthodox school had been a mutual decision. But he knew Rina had guilt pangs. Though she didn't say it, Decker knew his wife was trying to preserve the memory of her late husband for their sons. And that was admirable. Decker also knew that if something ever happened to him, Hannah would know who her father was. And in police work, who knew what could happen?

'Fine,' he said. 'Send the boys over there for a couple of days. Actually, it's a good idea. They'll be safe, they'll have fun visiting their old friends. Now if you'll kindly take Hannah, I can load up the Volvo in one trip.'

Rina took the baby back. 'Will you be sleeping here or at my parents' tonight?'

Decker picked up the suitcases. 'Somehow I'll make it back over the hill. I always enjoy visiting the other half.'

Rina smiled. Her parents weren't made of money, but they did live in the posh area of Beverly Hills. Their home was an old ranch house placed on a block made busy by renovators and contractors. The house next door to them had been redone recently. The modern monolith of ten thousand square feet looked as oversized for the lot as a dowager in a bikini.

They stepped outside, Decker locking the door. Rina said, 'Peter, I was so flustered this morning, I forgot to write down the name of the New York detective who called me about Gershon Klein's murder.' She reached in her baby bag and pulled out a slip of paper. 'But he gave me the precinct's phone number. Here.'

Decker pocketed the paper. 'I'll take care of it.'

'Is it my imagination or do I seem to rope you into doing a lot of unofficial overtime.'

Decker gave her shoulder a slight squeeze. 'Don't worry about it.'

'It's the kids—'

'I know, sweetheart. I'm concerned for *all* of them. So far, we have a stalled van with a couple of flats. For all we know, it may be simple car problems.'

'And you think that's a real possibility.'

Decker didn't answer. Instead he opened the door. 'You're all set.' He took Hannah from Rina. 'I'll put her in her car seat. Are you sure you don't want me to pick up the boys and run them over to the yeshiva?'

'It's not a problem for me, Peter. I'm sure you have enough to do without worrying about carpooling.'

True enough, Decker thought. He was a busy man, having people both dead and alive vying for his attention.

Through the mike, Decker heard Marge's dulcet tones.

'*Where in the* hell *did you disappear to!?*'

'Tug didn't tell you?'

'Squat.'

Decker explained Rina's phone call, then a quieter Marge said, 'Jesus, that's *terrible*! No sign of the kids?'

'I just got off the line with Highway Patrol Officer Rachel Parks – who's pissed as hell that I'm taking so long to get there. I lied and told her I got stuck in a traffic jam. Anyway, so far no one's reclaimed the vehicle. I'm on my way there now. What's going down on your side?'

'Well, we got what we were looking for – two positive IDs – Arik and Dalia Yalom. I thought I'd feel excited about the progress. Instead, I feel wrenched. That's why I'm so pissed at you. I've got no one but Tug to talk to and he's about as helpful as a hangnail.'

'How's Orit Bar Lulu holding up?'

'She's in awful shape, Pete. I rang up her husband, told him to come down and pick up his wife. The lady's absolutely torn up. I also told him to call her doctor. She was sitting in the squad car, shaking, trying to get down some soda. Then she got nervous and tried to stand. She passed out. Luckily, I caught her.'

'Call an ambulance.'

'I did. Davidson thought that was a peachy idea because – and I quote – "The last thing this department needs is another wrongful death suit." Old Tug's a sensitive soul.'

'Has the coroner arrived yet?'

'Yeah. It's Chuck Kann. He's moving slowly. Someone blasted a hole in Dalia's chest. It's going to take a while to clean her up and assess the damage. It appears to be a shotgun, or some heavy-duty automatic. Chuck hasn't started on Arik yet.'

There was silence over the line. Marge asked Decker what he was thinking.

'We've got a big hole in the chest, ergo, a big weapon. If we're figuring that the boys popped the parents, could you picture them leading Mom and Dad up to the mountain-side, swinging shotguns at their sides? Hunting's not allowed up there. Don't you think the parents might have been a little suspicious?'

'Maybe they were sawed-off numbers and the boys stuffed them in their jackets.' Marge paused. 'Or with their tennis gear. I found tennis rackets at the house, and there are public courts on the other side of the hill.'

Decker said, 'Okay, suppose they could hide sawed-off shotguns in their gear bag. What if the weapon turns out to be an automatic? I haven't seen a hell of a lot of small AK47s.' Decker sat up in the driver's seat. 'Or small *Uzis!*'

Marge sounded excited. 'Aren't Uzis given out to soldiers in the Israeli army?'

'I don't know if they're standard issue, but I think a lot of Israeli soldiers own them.'

'Yalom must have been in the army. Aren't all Israelis inducted?'

Decker said, 'Damn, I meant to ask Rina about that.'

'You did?'

'I wanted to ask her how long the required tour was for an Israeli soldier. Because Yalom's partner, Shaul Gold, spent six years in the Israeli army.'

'This is very interesting,' Marge said. 'Maybe we ask Gold the question in person. See how he reacts. Unless you think he might be a flight risk.'

'Of course, he's a flight risk. He's got another country to flee to.' Decker thought a moment. 'I checked him out. Superficially, he doesn't have a motive. He appears to be in good shape financially. He's not like Yalom, but he's got money in the bank, gems in his vault, and good credit. But at the moment, he's a suspect.'

'I'll call him,' Marge said. 'Even if he's clean, he's going to find out that his partner was murdered. It might as well come from us.'

'Good point,' Decker said. 'We'll go over there together and break the news. See how he reacts. Although I don't suspect he'll freak. Gold seems . . . controlled.'

'When did you want to do this?'

'As soon as I'm done with HP Officer Parks. How about in an hour, hour and a half?'

'Fine. Meet me back at the crime scene.' She paused. 'Pete, you did say your houseguest's husband was a diamond dealer?'

'Yes, I did say that. And yes, he was a diamond dealer. No, Marge, I don't know if there's any connection between his murder and our case. But I'll look into it.'

Marge said, 'Why should I bother talking to you when you can talk for both of us?'

She cut the line. Decker hung up the mike.

Touchy, touchy, touchy!

No problem finding the car. The off-balanced Aerostar looked like an iceberg floating in a sea of concrete. Decker pulled the unmarked behind the HP cruiser and got out. Rachel Parks was a compact brunette with short, curly hair and gray eyes. She had to crane her neck to make eye contact with Decker. 'Traffic bad?'

'Yeah, sorry I'm late. I appreciate you waiting. Anything I should know before I check out the van?'

Rachel said, 'I've made a couple of preliminary contacts. The HP and Triple A have no record of any distress calls coming through the nearest call boxes. I've also had time to phone the closest service station. I figured maybe the lady called from there. Nothing so far. What's going on?'

Decker recapped the details, then they both went back to work. Rachel began making inquiries from her car radio, Decker slipped on latex gloves, readying himself to tackle the van forensically.

He opened the driver's door. The van had seated seven – two captain seats up front, a bench seat for two in the middle, and a bench seat for three in the back. There were lots of cup holders and most of them were filled with boxes of kosher fruitade. There were a few kosher candy wrappers littering the seats and floors.

Pulling up cushions, he searched underneath the seats – clean and crumbless unlike most family cars. The floor carpet was also free from dirt and food. The rental places must vacuum them carefully.

On to the glove compartment. Then the console between the two captain seats, then the door consoles. He looked inside the roof-mounted sunglass case. He ran his hands inside the pockets lining the back of the captain seats. He flipped visors, he opened vanity mirrors and ashtrays and panels that held electrical wiring. Nothing.

He stepped outside the car, looked under the hood. In the radiator, in the oil tank. He went over to the back of the van and opened the hatch – empty except for a deflated spare tire mounted on the side.

Disgusted and disappointed, he began to grid-sweep the immediate area around the van. The wind swept lots of garbage along the sides of the freeway. Decker meticulously searched through the trash but still came up dry.

A tow truck was approaching westbound. It slowed, its front bumper announcing that SHIT HAPPENS. It stopped in front of the tipped van and pulled onto the shoulder of the freeway. The driver got out – a skinny kid with lots of moles, wearing a ponytail and an ear-ring. He released the cable pulley from the tail of the truck. Decker came over to him and the kid took a step backward. Being big, Decker was conscious of the way he made most men feel. Some deferred, others got belligerent. This guy was a deferrer. The nametag on his shirt said Rich in red scroll.

Decker held up his hands – a gesture he did on purpose to help guys like this relax. 'Who told you to tow the truck?'

The kid looked down. 'My boss. If there's a problem, I'll wait.'

'You work for the rental company, Rich?'

'Yes, sir. My boss told me the HP called and told them to get the van off the freeway.'

Officer Rachel Parks walked over and joined them. 'No leads,' she reported. 'We all done here?'

'I suppose so.' Decker turned to Rich. 'You get a lot of abandoned rentals?'

'Yep, but they're usually not left on a freeway.' Rich picked at his ear. 'You see, people'll rent the car under a false name and ID. Then, you see, they'll use the car for a day or two. Then they'll just leave the suckers flat, you see. Use the car without paying . . . or even use the car for like a robbery or a drug deal. Lots of drug dealers use rented cars to transport their shit – er, stuff. I once towed this bitchen

Porsche. Man, it had more residue powder than Mammoth after a ten-foot snowfall.'

Rachel turned to Decker, 'Does this woman have a criminal record?'

Decker said, 'I didn't think so.'

Rich said, 'So I can take the car, now?'

Decker nodded.

Rich looked at the lopsided van. 'I'll just hook it on up and inflate the tires. Easier than changing them.'

'Do me a favor, Rich. Check out the tires when you get the van back to the rental lot. I want to know what caused them to go flat.' Decker heard his name being patched over the unmarked's radio. 'Excuse me.' He picked up the mike. It was Marge.

'I need you, pronto. I just got a call from Orit Bar Lulu. Her husband was driving her home from the hospital. They stopped by the Yaloms' house. Why she wanted to do that is anyone's guess. But the upshot is, the place was ransacked.'

'Good grief!'

'Someone was looking for something, Pete. Maybe the junior Yaloms are still in town. Maybe it was Gold.'

'Are any cars missing?'

'That I don't know. I'd go right now, but one of us should stick around for Chuck's info on the bodies.'

'I'll go,' Decker said. 'I'm done here anyway.' He told her the situation.

'Weird,' she said. 'We've got two cases of two murdered diamond dealers. Makes you think of some kind of B-movie plot – some cursed stone.'

Decker laughed, but it was a weary one. 'I'll meet you at the house.'

'Talk to you later.' She hung up. Decker got out of the

unmarked, just as Rich had finished hooking up the Aerostar.

'I'm all set,' he announced.

Rachel gave Decker a wave. 'Good luck.'

'Thanks,' Decker watched the cruiser speed off, then watched the truck and the van-in-tow ease into the flow of traffic. He looked at the shoulder where the van had been. All that remained of Honey Klein and her family was skidmarks on the pavement.

17

Rina should be at her parents' by now and Decker was ten minutes away. Picking up his radio mike, he called Marge.

'Are the uniforms still at the Yalom house?'

'Yes, of course. They're waiting for you. What's wrong? You can't make it?'

'No, I'll be there. I just wanted to make sure the place was secure. It may take me a while. There's lots of traffic.'

'Where are you?'

'Still on the freeway. I've just finished with Honey Klein's abandoned van. Nothing jumped out at me, but I don't like it, Marge. Technically, it's West LA's case. But personally, it's *mine*.'

'But you *are* going to call West LA, right?'

'Of course, just as soon as I get off the horn with you. What's happening over there?'

'Kann is done with Dalia. Davidson brought in four guys to help me comb the hills. Nobody's optimistic because of the rains. We're concentrating around the base of the mountain. Maybe something washed down. When do you think you'll make it to the Yaloms' place?'

'Maybe an hour.'

'Then check in with me when you're there.'

'Talk to you later.'

Decker broke the line with Marge and asked to be

patched through to West LA. A Missing Persons case could be assigned to different details depending on the circumstances. If kids were involved including teenage runaways, the file might go to Juvenile. If something nefarious was suspected, it could be routed into Homicide. Decker had to think about murder as an option considering the circumstances in New York.

West LA desk answered and Decker asked for Homicide. He spoke to a Detective Sturgis. As he related the details, he heard Sturgis groan. Everyone hated Missing Persons cases, especially when children were involved.

Decker pulled off the 10 Freeway at Robertson and headed north. 'I've checked out the van thoroughly. As soon as I get back to my station house, I'll write you up a formal report and fax it to you. I'll go through the lady's luggage as soon as I get home.'

'She's still got her luggage at your place?'

'Yep. So either she left in a hurry or she wasn't planning to leave at all. There's not a lot for you to do at the moment. I just wanted to report the incident in case you found bodies.'

'You have some pictures you can fax me?'

'Not at the moment.' Decker gave Sturgis a physical description of the Kleins. 'They're ultra-Orthodox Jews. Their dress is pretty distinctive, should be pretty easy to spot if they're wandering around lost.'

'And the lady and her kids were staying at your house?'

'Yeah, I'm Orthodox. Not like them but – not important.'

'Not important,' Sturgis said. 'I'll do a couple of passes through the area.'

' 'Preciate it.'

'Are you going to call Manhattan?'

'If that's all right with you?'

186

'It's all right with me. It's even all right with me if you want the entire case. The lady you described sounds like a wacko. You want to know my opinion of the situation?'

'You think she arranged her vacation around a hit on the husband. The thought crossed my mind, but I don't think that's the case. But if I'm wrong, the woman's a psycho with balls. Of all the friends she could have visited, she opted for the one whose husband's a homicide cop.'

'Psychos love to play games.'

'She wants to mess with my head, I can take it,' Decker said. 'But not when there are kids involved.'

Sturgis said, 'I hear you. Call me in a couple of hours. We'll swap notes.'

Decker thanked him and hung up. His mind was on work, but his heart was on Rina. This time emotions ruled.

The flats of Beverly Hills, known as BH 90210, described a three-square-mile area where teardowns started at close to a million. Some of the houses were magnificent, others were so embarrassingly ordinary, Decker wondered what was the deal. The city itself had its own police force, its own mayor, its own fire department and its own school system which was thriving because of a high residential and business tax base. The streets were well maintained – void of potholes – and tree-lined, the luxurious arbors being the pride of the city. Palm Drive hosted jacarandas, Maple was shaded by the boughs of camphor trees, but Elm, lo and behold, was flanked with elm trees.

The Eliases lived on Camden Drive in a three-bedroom, three-bathroom house that came with a pool but no jacuzzi. A big minus for resale value, a real estate broker once told them. But the location was excellent and Rina's parents, who had bought in twenty-five years ago, had netted a fine chunk of equity in their now pricey home. He parked the Plymouth under a magnolia tree and walked on a brick pathway up to the front door. Rina answered his knock. She brought her hand to her chest.

'It's bad news about Honey?'

'It's no news.'

Rina stepped aside to let him in. She looked pained. 'Nothing at all?'

Decker shook his head. He looped his arm around his wife and they walked into the yellow-tiled kitchen. It was large in absolute terms, but gnat-sized by neighborhood standards which were: If the kitchen floor space couldn't accommodate a full-sized catering truck and its crew, it was time to remodel.

'Where's Hannah?' Decker asked.

'My parents took her and Ginger to the park. I think they could tell I was nervous. I wanted to be alone. Something's terribly wrong.'

Again, Decker let go with a forced smile. 'Hey, knowing your wacky friend, she and her kids could show up any time.'

'You're not optimistic.'

Decker didn't answer. Instead he hugged her. 'I love you. I just stopped by to tell you that.'

'You're worried.'

'Concerned.'

Rina looked at her husband. 'Honey said that Gershon had gone to Israel. But he was found murdered in New York.'

'Obviously, he didn't go,' Decker said. 'Either he lied to Honey about going. Or Honey lied to us.'

SANCTUARY

'Peter, what could she gain by lying to us?'

'If she was involved with his murder, she'd lie to throw us off track.'

'Peter, *why* would she be involved in his murder?'

'I'm not saying she is. I'm just speculating. By her own admission, she said the guy was acting weird. Maybe she was afraid of him.'

'So she'd divorce him, not kill him.'

'Correct me if I'm wrong, but isn't divorce in that community like a big scarlet letter?'

'Not as big as murder.'

'All I'm saying, Rina, is that *if* she was involved, it would make sense for her to disappear, right?'

'That's a *big* leap.'

'Maybe. But I've got to consider it. Especially since Honey was using an alias.'

'She was?'

'Barbara Hersh. Any idea why Honey might use that name?'

Rina raised her eyebrows. 'I don't know why she would use Barbara. Hersh is Honey's maiden name.'

Decker nodded. 'I should have thought of that.'

'Peter, maybe Honey's using an alias because she's scared that the people who murdered Gershon might come after her. Remember she spoke of strange phone calls.'

'Could have been a front.'

'Or maybe she was telling the truth. Maybe she bolted with the children.'

'Then why come out here, Rina? Why not leave immediately. And why did she use an alias yesterday *before* Gershon was murdered.'

'Maybe she realized that Gershon was in *deep, deep* trouble. Maybe she decided that LA wasn't far enough of an escape. So she went to Israel. Lots of places for her to hide there. All the black areas. Doesn't that make sense?'

'Black areas?' Decker asked.

Rina smiled. 'A semantic misinterpretation. Not black as in Afro-American, black as in *black hat* – the ultra-religious area. The Black Hatters – the *Charedim* – must make up at least a third of Jerusalem – *Sanhedria. The Ramot. Har Nof. Sha'arey Chesid. Mea Shaárim* ... now that's a *good* place to hide. The name literally means a hundred gates. It's a labyrinth. Like a lot of Jerusalem, it's filled with passageways and walls and gates that lead nowhere. The entire city was built on top of a dozen previous civilizations. So there's a lot of underground structures – tunnels, viaducts, passage ways. It's a perfect place to take refuge.'

Decker gave Rina's words pause for thought. And here he was, searching for not one, but *two* separate groups of people who might have desired sanctuary in the Holy Land. His brain was scrambled. Man, he was tired.

'I've got to get back to work. I just wanted to check in on you, tell you I love you. Hug the boys and kiss Hannah for me.' His smile widened. 'And even kiss your mom for me.'

Rina hit his shoulder – the one without the bullet wound. 'You take care of yourself. I love you, too.'

Decker started for the door, then turned around. 'Rina, how many years is an Israeli required to serve in the army?'

'That's a non sequitur.'

'Detectives are full of them. It's part of our clever interviewing technique. Do you know the answer to my question?'

'Active duty is three years for men, two for women. Then there's *meluim* – reserved duties – a month or two out of the year.'

'For how long?'

'Until you stop breathing.' Rina smiled. 'I'm not sure. Once you're too old for *meluim*, you do civil duty – *haggah*. Does that help?'

'Yes, it helps a great deal. I have come to the conclusion that though I've studied a great deal of Judaism, I know nothing about Israelis – or Israel. Maybe you can show me the ropes one day.'

'You mean *go* to Israel?' Rina brightened. 'Peter, what a wonderful thought!'

Decker smiled but felt uncomfortable. Rina was thinking vacation. Unfortunately, he was thinking work. He wondered if one day wasn't close at hand.

Marge ducked under the yellow crime-scene ribbon that fronted the Yaloms' mock Tudor estate. With a gloved hand, she opened the front door and stepped inside the enormous entry hall.

'Yo!' She called out. 'Anyone here?'

'Upstairs,' Decker answered.

She walked a few steps, peered into the living room, and halted in her tracks.

A hurricane had come through. Furniture had been overturned, cushions slashed and ripped apart. Glass cabinets had been knocked over, glittering shards sprayed over the floor, creating an obstacle course. Some of the display pieces had been broken, others were still whole, resting on their bases on the floor. Marge figured Pete must have uprighted them.

She called out again. 'You want me to come up?'

'Hold on,' Decker yelled. 'I'll come down.'

He stood from a crouched position, his knees cracking as he rose. He and the Tin Man – they needed oil. He popped

off his gloves, slipped his notebook inside his jacket and
gave a final glance to the Yaloms' bedroom. Someone had
tossed the place with serious intent. Nothing had been
overlooked or cast aside. This kind of damage took time –
several hours at least. Decker wondered if the someone –
or someones – had found what he/they were looking for.

Marge was waiting for him in the entry, her tapping foot
sending out echoes against the marble floor. She said, 'See
what happens when the maid doesn't show?'

Decker gave her a warm smile. She was upset, trying to
hide her feelings with macho humor. 'You all right?'

'Me? I'm fine. Why do you ask?'

'Just being polite. Frankly, I don't give a shit how you
feel.'

Marge burst into cathartic laughter. 'How long have you
been here, big guy?'

'Over two hours.'

'And the upstairs is as bad as the living room?'

'The whole house is trashed. No wonder Orit went nuts
when she saw this.'

'How's she doing?' Marge asked.

Decker ran his hand over his face. 'Lousy. Tell you the
truth, I've had better days myself.'

'Any news with your houseguests?'

'I just called back West LA. The case was given to a D-3
named Sturgis. He's working with me at my request.'

'As if you don't have enough to do?'

'Yeah, that probably wasn't a smart move. But I keep
seeing those children, thinking about their dead father in
Manhattan.' Decker threw up his hands. 'You know me.
I'm a sucker for kids.'

Marge pushed wisps of blond hair out of her eyes. 'At
least Davidson'll give you time to look for the Kleins. He

thinks there's a connection – the big Jewish conspiracy. They control the media, you know.'

Decker was silent.

'It was a joke, Pete.'

'I'm just wondering if there isn't a connection. It does seem like a mother coincidence.' He looked at Marge. 'So what big-ticket item do you have that you didn't want to discuss over the lines.'

'It's that obvious?'

'Yep. What's up?'

Marge held a safe-deposit-box key with a gloved hand. 'Kann found it inside of Arik, in a place where the sun don't shine. The key could be what the ransacking was all about.'

'It was stuck up his ass?'

'You've got it.'

'Kann checked out the remaining orifices?'

'Yes, he did. Nothing.'

'He check out Dalia as well?'

'Of course. Nothing. When I left Kann had bagged the bodies and was off to the morgue. Photographers left about a half hour ago. Uniforms have cordoned off the area, but we'll probably take down the ribbons in a day or two. Our search was disappointing because of the rains . . . except for the key.'

Decker said, 'Have you found a bank to match it?'

'I'm one step ahead of you,' Marge gloated. 'Orit gave me the name of Yalom's accountant. From him, I found out that Yalom has accounts at six banks. I called all six institutions. Yalom has safe-deposit boxes at three of the six banks. Davidson's pulling the papers for inspection. Trouble is, once he announces the Yaloms as dead, the IRS will step in and freeze the boxes. It's quite a paper chase for Old Tug, but I gotta hand it to him. He's actually acting like a cop. A racist, sexist cop, but I'd rather have that instead of a bureaucrat. I think the corpses lit a fire under his butt.'

'When will the papers be ready?'

'Hopefully in an hour, maybe a little longer.' Marge looked around. 'What's the story here?'

'Doesn't appear to be a burglary. They left behind valuables including money. Maybe they were looking for specific items like the jewels and diamonds that were stored in Yalom's vault at the LA diamond center.'

'They were looking for this.' Marge held up the safe deposit-box key.

'Possibly,' Decker said. 'Or possibly they were looking for the Yaloms' passports.'

Marge looked surprised. 'Who would toss the place like this just to steal dead people's passports?'

'Someone who didn't want it known that Arik traveled to strange places,' Decker said. 'If Arik had been working for some covert organization, his passport would have been a concise record of his assignments.'

'Good point. Guy certainly went to some weird places.' Marge paused. 'Didn't you say he was in the Israeli army for six years? Or was that the partner, Gold?'

'It was Gold. Speaking of which, we should talk to Shaul immediately ... let him know what happened to his partner.'

'If he doesn't know already.'

'Yeah, you're right about that. He's a prime suspect until we know otherwise.'

'He *and* the boys are prime suspects.'

'The boys ...' Decker thought a moment. 'No, I haven't given up on the boys. I'll ask Davidson to assign a couple of men to follow up on the airlines. Also, someone should check out cabs and bus schedules. But first things first.

Since we can't follow up on the safe-deposit-box key until we've got our papers, let's pay Gold a visit and see what he has to say about his partner's murder.'

'What do we do with the house?'

'Seal it off and hope nobody trespasses,' Decker said. 'You coming with me?'

'I'm coming with you.'

18

'No one's picking up the phone,' Marge said. 'I've got Gold's home number. Should I try him there?'

Decker said, 'How far are we from his condo?'

'About fifteen minutes away.'

'I vote for spontaneity. It's in Encino, right?'

'Off Ventura Boulevard.' Marge gave him the exact address.

The numbers corresponded to several new, Mediterranean-style security buildings, all of them three stories, plastered in pink and framed with apricot cornerstones. The condos stretched a block and were fronted by a green lawn. Specimen trees and big bushes had been brought in to give the neophyte development some maturity. But it was a weak cosmetic job, like putting lipstick on a baby. The place seemed to be built on a large chunk of land judging by the number of tennis-court lights in the background.

Decker wasn't sure which building housed Gold, so he parked in the middle lot in a visitor's space. He and Marge got out of the Plymouth and started walking on meandering brick pathways toward the building on the right.

Marge said, 'Gold and Yalom are . . . *were* partners. But Gold lives here and Yalom lives in a mansion.'

'Arik was the senior partner,' Decker said. 'Gold told me that. And you're forgetting Dalia's independent money.'

197

'Still, there's quite a discrepancy.'

Decker said, 'This seems like a nifty place for a bachelor. Betcha there're lots of hot tubs and exercise rooms – a good set up for meeting women.'

Marge thought about that. She could afford a small house, but chose to keep her apartment. Although she was private, she liked the idea of having people close at hand. She turned to Decker. 'So why didn't you move to a condo after your divorce?'

'I had Cindy. When she came to visit me, I wanted her to have a home.' Decker consulted the paper. 'I think Gold lives on the third floor. It's a security building. We'll have to be buzzed in. You want to do the talking?'

'You met him before, you do the talking.'

Decker found the directory and pressed the red button corresponding to Gold's name. A few moments later, a deep voice spoke slurred, incoherent words over the squawk box.

Decker said, 'Police, Mr Gold. Can we come in and talk to you for a moment.'

A pause, then a loud buzzer rang in Decker's ears. They pushed in the double glass doors and stepped inside an atrium filled with potted ficus and ferns. Against the back wall were the elevators. They took one to the third floor. Gold was standing in the hallway, blocking his front door. As they approached, both noticed he was unkempt – unshaven with his shirt-tail hanging out of baggy pants. He was holding a half-filled glass and reeked of strong whisky.

'Was he like this before?' Marge whispered.

'Nope. He knows what happened.'

'Wonder what else he knows,' Marge spoke through the corner of her mouth. 'If you want to be the tough one, I'll be all tea and sympathy.'

Decker nodded. He stopped at Gold's door and held out his hand. The Israeli took it, then dropped it. Like holding a dead fish. And just a day ago, it had been a vise grip.

Decker said, 'You must know about your partner and his wife. I'm sorry.'

Gold's lost eyes went from Decker, to Marge, then back to Decker. Though swarthy, his complexion was pale underneath a stubble of black beard. His hands were trembling. Standing in front of the doorway, he continued to stare blankly at them.

Decker said, 'Can we come in, Mr Gold?'

The Israeli hesitated, then backed up into the interior of his condo. Marge and Decker stepped inside.

No one spoke. Finally, Gold motioned them forward. They followed him into the living room. Decker looked around.

It was spacious – high vaulted ceilings, white crown moldings, light floors, and lots of light from french doors that led to a plant-covered terrace. The furniture was alabaster white and over-stuffed, accented with throws and blankets that looked to be hand-made. The walls were cream-colored, striped with floor-to-ceiling shelving. The display cases were filled with antiquities and primitive sculptures, each piece accompanied by a small card on a stand that gave a description of the work. Decker studied the visuals for a moment.

So that's where his money went.

His eyes returned to Gold, who pointed to the living-room sofa. Decker and Marge walked over to the couch but nobody sat down.

Decker said, 'You've got a bulge under your shirt-tail, Mr Gold. You're carrying a gun. Would you mind taking it out and slowly laying it on the coffee table?'

Gold's eyes narrowed. He put down his drink. 'I tell you I know how to use it.'

'That's what I'm afraid of, Mr Gold. You're drinking, you've got a gun. That's not a good combination.'

'Drink and shoot,' Gold said. 'That is your cowboy films.' He broke into an exaggerated American accent. 'I give you to the count of three, partner.'

'Please remove the weapon,' Marge said.

Gold's eyes hardened further. 'Since when is law that I can't have a nip and carry a gun in my own house.'

Decker said nothing. Abruptly, Gold reached for his weapon, holding the semi-automatic by the butt, then gently placed it on the coffee table. 'Better?'

'Much,' Marge said. 'Thank you.'

They sat down.

Decker said, 'If I just found out my partner and his wife had been murdered, I'd be nervous, too.'

'Who are you nervous about?' Marge asked.

Gold focused in on her. 'Who's this lady?'

'I'm Detective Dunn.' Marge showed Gold her ID. 'Detective Sergeant Decker and I have been assigned to investigate the murders of your partner and his wife.'

Gold pressed his lips together and said nothing.

'I'm very sorry about your loss,' Marge said. 'Who broke the news to you? Orit?'

'Yoni, I think.'

'Husband,' Marge whispered to Decker.

'Maybe it was Orit . . .'

Gold rubbed his forehead, then positioned himself on the couch opposite Decker and Marge. 'I don't know who'd do such terrible thing.'

Marge said, 'No idea?'

'No.'

Decker said, 'You know we're going to have to question you.'

Gold looked up, then down. Burying his head in his hands, he broke into deep, dry sobs. It took him a minute to calm himself. He said, 'I'm sorry. You want something to drink?'

Marge said, 'No thank you.'

'Do you mind if I get something to drink?'

Decker said, 'Would you mind if I unloaded your weapon?'

Gold picked up his glass, then put it back down. 'You don't trust me?' He waved him off. 'I was in the army – *tzalaf* – how you say . . . the one with binocular . . . scope . . . who shoots.'

'Sniper?' Decker said.

'Yes, sniper.' He pointed to Decker. 'With scope, I shoot a nail from five kilometers away. I was in four wars – '56, '67, '73 and '81. I did three years in '56, three in '67. In '67 war, I was in Golan Heights. The Syrians shooting down on us, picking us off like video game. We send up fourteen tanks, one comes back. I say *maspeek! Enough!* I crawl on my hands and knees to top of mountains. I climb up tree. Next thing bastards know, I pick *them* off.'

He sighted down an imaginary scope and pulled a finger trigger.

'Pop . . . pop . . . pop.' He blew on his finger. 'Anyone fucks on me, I can take care of myself.'

Decker said, 'Can I unload your gun?'

He rubbed his forehead. 'Sure. Take the clip out. I don't care.'

Decker did just that, laid them both on the coffee table. 'Was Arik also a sniper in the army?'

'Arik was in tanks. Dalia did office work.' A slight smile

201

formed on Gold's lips. 'She did filing papers. Nothing important. But she was proud to be in uniform.' His lower lip trembled. 'So Arik and Dalia come to America for the good life.' Gold slapped his hands together. 'Pow, it's over. What a *bastard*, God is!'

Marge said, 'And you have no idea who would do this to Arik and Dalia?'

'No idea.' Gold swayed as he sat, then homed in on Marge. He pointed to her. 'If you lived in Israel, you know you would be in army. They take women in Israeli army. Not like in America.'

Marge nodded.

'I bet you'd make a good soldier.' Gold made a muscle. 'You look strong.'

Marge smiled.

Decker said, 'You want to tell me what you were doing around two-thirty Friday afternoon?'

'I already tell you, I was at my office, seeing client.'

'You didn't give me his or her name.'

'I know I don't. My business is private for my clients' protection. You need to know anything, get papers from a judge. Then I have no choice. But if you want. I take lie test for you. That doesn't hurt my business.'

'Maybe we'll set a lie-detector test up,' Decker said. 'I understand you were close to Arik's younger son, Dov.'

Gold rubbed his face. 'You have not found the boys.'

'Not so far,' Marge said.

Decker stood up and sat next to Gold. The Israeli's frame, muscular and compact just a few days ago, now seemed flaccid and droopy. 'Any idea where they might be, Mr Gold?'

'Why would I know?'

Marge said, 'They never called you for help?'

Gold whispered, 'No, they never call me.'

Decker said, 'I understand Dov and his father had been fighting a lot.'

Gold stared at him. 'You think they hurt their parents? You are wrong. *Goyishe mishugas*.'

Gentile craziness, Decker translated in his head. He didn't bother to inform Gold that there had been a West LA case years ago where two sons had been charged with murdering their parents as they came home from Yom Kippur services.

'Sure, they fight with Arik,' Gold said. 'But they don't kill him. They certainly don't hurt their mother. They would never, ever hurt their mother. No, that is not why they are missing. They are missing because they are scared.'

'Who scared them?' Marge said.

'If I know that answer, I would tell it to you first thing.' Gold tried to sip from his empty glass. 'I don't know who scared them. If I know, I kill him. End of problem.'

Decker and Marge exchanged glances. Decker said, 'Arik did a lot of traveling, didn't he.'

'Yes, of course.'

'I'm not just talking about Antwerp and Israel, Mr Gold, I'm talking about Russia, Zambia, South Africa, Angola, Mozambique—'

'That's long ago travel,' Gold grunted.

'According to his passport it was recent,' Marge said.

Gold sat up, drool dripping from the corner of his mouth. He wiped it with the back of his hand. 'You say Arik went to Africa *recent*?'

'According to Arik's passport, he went to Angola as recently as a month ago—'

'You have Arik's *passport*?'

Marge nodded.

203

Gold didn't speak for a moment. Something in his eyes went dead. 'Where else do you say he goes?'

'Russia, Zambia, South Africa, Mozambique. Other places that I don't remember.'

The room fell quiet. Gold reached in his pocket and pulled out a pack of cigarettes. He lit up his smoke with a steady hand. Arik's travelogue had seemed to sober him up. He said, 'I don't know why Arik would go to Africa.'

'You must have been there lots of times yourself.' Decker pointed to the wall. 'You have some beautiful primitive pieces.'

Gold's eyes went to his artwork. 'Yes, I've been to Africa.' He blew out a plume of smoke. 'But I don't know why Arik would go there *now*. Bastard doesn't collect art. Wouldn't know beauty if it bit him in the ass.'

Marge and Decker swapped raised eyebrows.

Decker said, 'What did you mean when you said that Arik would go to Africa *now*? Had Arik gone in the past?'

'Many times.'

'For what?'

'To squander money.'

Decker looked at Marge. She picked up the ball.

'How did he squander money?' she asked.

'He invested in crazy schemes. Arik got scrambled brains. He thought he could be the next VerHauten. He took his wife's money and flushed it down the toilet. I think he got it out of his system. But maybe not, the crazy bastard.'

Gold sat back in his couch.

'What? You think I kill him because I call him a bastard. He is a bastard. Bastard to me, bastard to his kids, bastard to his wife, spending *her* money like it's his.'

Decker noticed his eyes were dilated. Could be from the booze, could be he was lying. 'Why would Arik have gone to

Russia? Does it have anything to do with the diamond mines there?'

Gold stared at Decker. 'Maybe he goes to the diamond mines and buys stones. If he did, he don't tell me.'

'Has Arik been an honest partner to you, Mr Gold?' Marge asked.

'Honest when it counts?'

'What does that mean?' Marge asked.

'It means *I* was never cheated.'

Decker waited for more. When nothing came, he said, 'Why do you think he didn't tell you about his travels to Africa? Do you think he was investing in schemes again?'

'Not with business money. I keep watch on that.' Gold flicked his wrist and checked the time. 'I call Orit. Maybe she knows when the funeral is.' He looked up. 'Or maybe you know?'

'We haven't released the bodies yet, Mr Gold.'

'Then I wait until she calls me. It's terrible what happened, terrible for Dalia. She really was a lovely woman.' He took a deep puff of his cigarette and blew out a cloud of poison. Decker squirmed in the smoke. Going on four years and the lust for nicotine had yet to leave his bloodstream.

'You liked Dalia,' he said.

Gold said, 'I know her many, many years back in Israel. Many, many, many...' He took another drag off his cigarette. Marge brushed away the smoke, but Decker inhaled deeply.

'You were jealous when she married Arik?' he asked.

'No, I was not jealous.' Gold's lip quivered. 'What difference it make? She's...'

Marge looked at the Israeli. His eyes were wet. She thought about Arik's travels which he apparently kept secret from his partner. Then she thought about Gold's car parked outside the Yalom house. Just who was screwing whom.

Finally, Marge said, 'You were close to Dalia.'

Gold snapped his head up. 'Yes. As friends. I already explain that to your partner.'

Decker said, 'Mr Gold, are you angry that your partner traveled to Africa—'

'Yes, I'm pissed off,' Gold broke in. 'I have to wonder what Arik was doing there? Was I being cheated? He also took money for travel. I thought he goes to Israel or Antwerp. Now I think he takes a safari vacation on my money.'

Decker said, 'Except his wife didn't go with him.'

'That means nothing,' Gold said. 'He left her alone many times.'

'Was Arik Yalom having an affair, Mr Gold?'

Gold paused, then said, 'Dalia suspected, yes. I tell you we were good friends.'

Decker said, 'She ever mention a name?'

'No. Dalia is a lady.'

Marge said, 'And you don't know where Arik's sons are?'

'No, Detective, I don't know.' Gold pursed his lips. 'Maybe I make it easy for you. Maybe I find them for you.'

Decker stared at him. 'Keep out of police business, Mr Gold.'

'Ah, but the boys are my business.' Gold's smile became cryptic. 'I am honest when I say I don't know where the boys are. But I tell you this much.' He picked up his semi-automatic and shoved the clip into the release catch. 'When I find them, I am prepared.'

19

In all the years Rina had lived at Ohavei Torah, she had never seen the *Bais Midrash* devoid of students. As a young widow, she had had many sleepless nights, praying for her departed husband's soul as well as some personal peace of mind. When prayer had failed – as it often had done in the early days – she had bolted out of bed into the cool night air to take aimless walks and clear her mind. Several times her journeys had led her over to the study hall. Inside, she had always found a few of the truly dedicated poring over volumes from the many religious tomes that lined the room. Though women were not forbidden to enter, Rina had always felt that there were unspoken restrictions. She had never gone inside the study hall to learn – even at dinnertime when the *Bais Midrash* was quiet and peaceful as it was right now.

Her sons had no such qualms. Suitcases in hand, they marched into the room, each one headed for a different bookcase. Sammy scanned the volumes of the *Mishna Torah* authored by the Rambam. Yonkie went straight for a set of *Shas* – the Talmud.

Rina watched her sons from the doorway. Sammy was actually more tall than big, but his shoulders were starting to widen, his musculature beginning to fill out. Rina

207

thought him objectively *very* handsome. A mop of sandy-colored hair surrounded an unusually clear, adolescent complexion napped by peach fuzz. His eyes were dark and alert, and though his teeth were encased in braces, she could make out the future man in the teenager's face.

Jakie was still a boy. He had just started his growth spurt, but his arms and legs continued to be thin and bony. His complexion was baby-smooth peaches-and-cream; his blue eyes held a mischievous sparkle.

Both of her sons wore untucked, long-sleeved white shirts that fell over dark pants. Their feet were protected by high tops. Neither was wearing a hat, which immediately marked them as visitors rather than live-in students.

Rina felt a presence behind her. She turned to see Rav Schulman walking down the hallway some fifty feet away. He was walking by himself – a rarity – and headed toward the *Bais Midrash*. Right on time. Rina straightened her spine and, without thinking, cast her eyes downward. Some habits were impossible to break.

A twinkle in his eye, he nodded to her as he entered the study hall, and she nodded back. It wasn't that he was ignoring her. He didn't want to embarrass her by being overly solicitous. The students in the room immediately stood upon the old man's arrival and the great Rav motioned them to sit back down. He crooked a finger at Sammy, then at Yonkie. The two boys came over, their heads lowered, hands straight down at their sides.

Stroking his long, white beard, Schulman welcomed them with a warm smile. Rina always felt his kind expression combined with crinkly, alert eyes opened up the Rosh Yeshiva's face, made him seem younger than his eighty years. Yet he was an old man now. His spine was bent, his fingers, once long and graceful, were now spindly and misshapen. But the great Rav still had spark left in his earthly body. As usual, he was dressed immaculately – a dark suit, starched white shirt, and shiny black oxfords. A new, stylish homburg covered his snowy hair.

Sammy stood up straight, then realized his shirttail was untucked. Quickly he remedied the situation only to realize he wasn't wearing his hat.

'I left my hat at home, Rav,' he said, softly.

'Is your head cold, Shmuel?'

Sammy stifled a smile. 'No, Rav. I just...'

Schulman placed his hands on Sammy's shoulders. 'You've grown into nearly a young man, Shmuli. If you'd like to wear a hat, I'm sure I have something to fit you at home.'

'Thank you, Rav.'

'You're welcome.' He turned his eyes to Jacob. 'And you too, have grown, young man. It's so good to see you both developing and in good health.' He placed his right hand over Shmuel's head, his left over Jacob's. Closing his eyes, he said a prayer for their well-being.

Afterward, Schulman opened his eyes and smiled. 'So what are you two learning. Yonkie first.'

'*Baba Kama*.'

'That is a difficult *masechet* for sixth grade.' Schulman tousled the boy's hair. 'It is a difficult *masechet* for any grade. I am happy your new school is challenging your mind. Now you, Shmuel. How is school taxing your gray matter.'

Sammy lowered his eyes. 'We're learning *Makkot* and ... *Baba Bastra*. We just started *Baba Bastra*.'

'A good choice. I miss you both but I can see you two are in able hands.' He turned to Rina, then turned back to her sons. 'I'm sure your eema made sure of that.'

Both boys nodded. The Rosh Yeshiva looked around the *Bais Midrash*, always interested in who was learning when it wasn't required.

'You boys seem anxious to learn. It restores my faith in the school you attend. But even scholars must have food in their stomachs. Go into the dining room and have some dinner. If you two have eaten, go anyway and catch up with old friends.'

Sammy and Jacob exchanged looks.

'Go, go!' Schulman shooed them away. 'You'll have plenty of time to learn tomorrow.'

Sammy said, 'Should we take our suitcases, Rav?'

The Rosh Yeshiva nodded. 'Come to my house after dinner and we'll do a little head-sizing, then a little Gemara. I'll see you both later.'

The boys picked up their suitcases and scampered off, calling out a bye to Rina. She waved her fingers at them.

Rav Schulman motioned Rina to come walk with him. She waited for him to leave the room and start walking, but kept a few paces behind him. Schulman stopped and beckoned her forward. Quickly, Rina took a place by his side. They walked down a long hallway of the building until they found the door leading to the grounds.

The yeshiva had been built into the valley's mountainside, and the perimeter of the school was still marked with much of the original terrain – rocky terraces naturally landscaped with wild vegetation and flowers. The grounds themselves had been bulldozed and leveled for the buildings. The dozen or so structures were separated by rolling lawns scored with cement pathways. Rina walked with the Rav in silence as they headed toward a grouping of private houses.

Rav Schulman and his wife lived in the largest house in

the tract. Not because his ego demanded it – although that would have been fitting – but because the couple was always entertaining guests. Sammy and Jacob were just two of the many people who revolved through the Schulmans' doors. The house had six bedrooms upstairs and a downstairs with no living room or den. Most of the bottom level space had been converted to a communal dining room dressed with long, linen-covered tables. What space was left had been allocated for a kitchen, a service bathroom, and the Rav's study.

The old man swung open an unlocked door and waved Rina inside. As she came in, the smell of homemade chicken soup opened her nostrils. Schulman sniffed deeply.

'Smells good.'

'Very,' Rina answered. 'The Rebbitzen is a wonderful cook.'

'I have been truly blessed. Not only is the Rebbitzen an *eshet chayil*, but a superb chef, *Baruch Hashem*. Me? Maybe I can boil an egg.'

The old man took a seat at one of the dining tables, keeping the front door wide open. In Jewish law, it was forbidden for a man and women who weren't married to each other to be alone in a closed room. From the Rav's action, Rina surmised that no one else was home.

Schulman folded his hands and set them on the table, inviting Rina to sit across from him. He said, 'As I recall, Rina Miriam, you were quite a cook yourself.'

'With time, I improved.' She smiled. 'The first time you and the Rebbitzen ate over our house, Rav Schulman, I burned the roast.'

'I don't remember that.'

'I do very much. All of us ate leather that night. I should have brought in take-out and made wallets out of the meat.'

'And what did Yitzchak say to you after the meal was over?'

'He told me I prepared a lovely meal and that the roast was delicious.'

Schulman smiled sadly. 'He was a good boy, my Yitzchak, *alav shalom*. I miss him still.'

Rina nodded but said nothing.

'Akiva is a good boy as well. Different those two, but similar in character. Both were endowed with a strong moral fiber.' He smiled again. 'And with a strong love for you.'

'I've been very fortunate, *Baruch Hashem*.'

'Tell me how my Akiva is doing? As tormented as ever?'

Rina let go with a small smile. 'He works hard.'

'That disappearing Israeli family ... that is Akiva's assignment?'

'Yes, Rav.'

'And have they found any trace of the family yet?'

Rina lowered her eyes. 'I think they found the parents ... their bodies this morning.'

The old man winced. 'Ah, such a terrible, terrible thing. Akiva must be very upset.'

'He says it's his job – Homicide. I don't see how a person can ever get used to such horror, but I'm not a cop.'

'I see I have upset you by asking about the case. I am sorry.'

'No, no, Rav, not at all. I ... I mean, I am upset ... but ...' She stopped talking.

Schulman said, 'I have made time for you, Rina Miriam. Tell me about your houseguests.'

In a gust of breath, Rina unburdened herself, starting

with the phone call from Honey, ending with the murder of her husband and the abandoned van. By the time she was done, tears had formed pools in her eyes.

'I'm scared for Honey, Rav, but it's the children ... I can't get those faces out of my head. I should have paid more attention to Honey's concerns. I should have traveled with her—'

'And if something nefarious had happened to you, would you have felt better being a victim?'

Rina didn't speak.

'I've been a victim, Rina Miriam. Though it is not an easy task, it is better to deal with survivor's guilt.'

Tears ran down her cheeks. She brushed them away. 'I suppose I should have told you the detailed story in the beginning. I just didn't know how to tell you everything over the phone.'

The old man was silent, reflecting upon Rina's story. 'Tell me again about Gershon Klein. His attempt to become a Nazir.'

Rina told him as much as she could remember about her conversation with the Leibbener Rebbe. 'It was very nice that he spoke to me. Very kind. But . . .'

'Yes?'

'I don't know how to say this without sounding disrespectful.'

'So you now have made your disclaimer. Speak your mind freely.'

Rina smiled and looked down. 'I had the feeling he wasn't telling me everything. Then again, why should he? He doesn't know me at all. Why should he trust me when something so grave has happened?'

Schulman said, 'Perhaps I should intercede on your behalf.'

213

'You mean call him for me? Rav, I would never ask you to do that.'

'You didn't ask, I volunteered. I will assist you if you think it would be helpful.'

'Yes, I think that would be extremely helpful,' Rina said. 'The Rebbe was very nice to me, but I'm sure he would be more open . . . as one Rav to another.'

'If our differences don't get in our way.' The old man grinned. 'The Leibbener Rebbe is a Chasid. And I'm a Litvak. That can be *fireworks*!' Schulman held up a finger. 'But for the common good of your houseguest and her young children, I'm sure we can be civil to one another.' The old man stroked his beard. 'I, too, am very concerned for the children.'

Rina blinked hard.

'How are you feeling, Rina Miriam?'

'Fine, Rav, thank you.'

The old man nodded, not pressing Rina to talk about herself and her recent hysterectomy. Right now, she was too concerned about her houseguests. 'I'm glad you're feeling well.'

Schulman stood and so did Rina.

'I will call the Leibbener Rebbe and ask about Gershon Klein and his family. Then I will report back to you and Akiva all that he tells me.' The old man shrugged. 'It may have nothing to do with their mysterious disappearance, but at least you may learn something about your houseguests.'

'Thank you, Rav Schulman. And thank you for taking in the boys. I'm sure they'll enjoy their stay here very much.'

'And I will enjoy having them.'

'They were very happy here at the yeshiva, Rav Schulman.

I want you to know that. It was my decision – mine and Akiva's – to take them out and put them in a more modern school.'

The Rosh Yeshiva's eyes turned crinkly. 'That being the case, let them learn here to their hearts' content. And you can go to college in their places.'

The title of assistant bank manager belonged to a young Hispanic woman named Marie Santiago who wore a key-ring bracelet on her wrist. She stood at a long marble counter topped with a computer and a phone, and shuffled through official papers. Then she looked at her wristwatch.

'It's almost closing time.'

Decker's eyes went to the wall clock – four-thirty p.m. 'Still got a half hour.'

Marie was not easily swayed. 'We're supposed to put a hold on the boxes for the IRS.'

'You can freeze the assets,' Marge said. 'We don't want to take them, just have a look at them.'

'I'll have to stay with you as a witness.' Marie attempted meaningful eye contact. 'To make sure that nothing's tampered with. This procedure is still very irregular.'

Marge said, 'Yes, I'm sure most of your clients don't wind up victims of double homicides.'

Marie winced.

Decker asked, 'Did you know the Yaloms personally?'

'I wasn't their personal banker, no. But I knew them by name.'

'Who used the box more?' Marge asked. 'Him or her?'

'Him,' Marie said. 'Mr Yalom. She used it rarely, if at all. But I knew her from the teller lines. Often she'd ask if we could process out-of-state checks for immediate clearance.'

'And?' Marge asked.

215

'We complied. Their assets were very good and we considered them valued clients.'

'What country were the checks from?' Decker asked.

'I don't remember.'

'How about Israel?' Decker stated.

'Yes, I think they were from Israel.' Marie bit her lip. 'This is just awful!'

'Yes it is,' Decker said. 'Thanks, Marie. Can you pull Mr Yalom's safe-deposit-box signature card for me now?'

Marie liberated her key ring from her wrist and opened a drawer. 'I can't believe . . . it's just terri— ah, here's the signature card.'

Marie informed them that they'd have to sign in for the record. After the bank's files appeared to be in proper order – approved by two of Marie's superiors – she finally escorted the detectives into the vault, closing the metal grate behind them. It wasn't the biggest vault Decker had ever seen, but it contained twenty or thirty oversized boxes. Marie pointed to an eight-by-ten box on the top row. Marge handed Marie the key found on Arik's body. The bank manager had to stretch to reach the door to the box, her skirt riding up on her rear. Even on her tiptoes, she barely managed to insert both keys in the slots. She lowered her heels to the ground and pulled down her skirt.

'Ah, I remember this one now. My aerobic body stretch.'

'Would you like some help?' Marge asked.

'I can manage, thank you.' Again, on her tiptoes, Marie managed to rotate both keys at the same time. The door opened.

Decker grinned and so did Marge. She whispered that sometimes you get lucky. Again Marie stretched, attempting to retrieve the box.

'Why don't you let me get it down, Marie. I'm a bit taller.' Decker raised a gorilla arm and, with one hand, brought the box down, hefting its contents.

'Heavy?' Marge asked.

'Not too bad.' Decker handed it to her.

Marie opened the vault grate. 'Let's go to a room. Someone is waiting to enter the vault and can't as long as we're here.'

She took them into a six-foot-square private room, a fan kicking in when Marie closed the door and turned on the light. It contained a built-in desk and acoustical ceiling tiles for noise absorption. Marge put the box down and opened the lid.

Stuffed with papers – piles crammed upon piles. Marge pulled a wad off the top, unfolded the first piece of paper and smoothed its wrinkled body out on the desk.

Correspondence – the letterhead stating it was from The VerHauten Company, INC. Dated over two years ago. Marge read the contents, Decker peering over her shoulder.

Dear Mr Yalom:

Kindly note that all future correspondence shall be conducted through our attorneys: Kronig and Dekker, Inc. Any further inquiries or business you may have with The VerHauten Company should be forwarded to them.

Sincerely,
Kate Milligan
Senior Vice-President.
Overseas Marketing and Sales

'I like the name of the law firm,' Marge said.

Decker smiled. 'Yeah, Dekker spelled with double K is a Dutch name.'

'Who's VerHauten?' Marge asked.

'The largest diamond company in the world. About four billion's worth of assets.'

Marie whistled. Decker had forgotten about her. He held up a stack of rumpled papers. 'You know, Marie, to go through this mess thoroughly . . .' He plopped the papers on the built-in desk. 'It's going to take an awfully long time.'

'I've been instructed to wait with you.'

'I bet your boss said wait *for* us, not wait *with* us.' Decker gave her a big smile. 'I can't imagine they'd want to tie up your valuable time, having you just sit back and twiddle your thumbs.'

'Yeah, they know how long a proper investigation can take,' Marge chimed in. 'It's hours of tedium and you know how these corporate types can be. Time is money.'

Decker opened the door. 'We'll call you when we're done. Thanks for all your help.'

With a dubious look, Marie didn't budge.

Decker let out a small laugh and held out his hands. 'Hey, you can stay if you want. I, for one, certainly don't object to the scenery.'

Marie lowered her head and stifled a smile. 'I think I'm being conned.'

'By *moi*?' Decker said. 'Heaven forbid.' He bowed and showed her the door. 'Thanks for your cooperation.'

Marie paused, shook her head, then left with a smile on her face.

Marge whispered, 'If some guy pulled an *aw shucks* stunt like that on me, I'd pop him.'

'Dunn, you would have made a piss-poor Southern

218

belle.' Decker examined the next bit of mail. 'Take a look at this, Margie. VerHauten again.'

Dated before the first piece of correspondence, the letter was single-spaced, the language and legalese complex and long-winded. Decker read it to himself. Marge scanned it silently as well, then began reading snippets out loud.

'Disputed certificate of ownership . . . unauthorized land parcels . . . international trade violations . . .' Marge raised a brow. 'Looks like our boy Yalom was taking on the big boys.'

'To hear Gold talk, Yalom couldn't compete. But damned if he couldn't threaten.'

'And *without* benefit of an attorney.'

'That's not as unusual as you think.'

'What do you mean?'

'There is a certain tiny percentage of the population that thrives on sticking it to major corporations. They usually file the motions themselves and become real gnats . . . gadflies. They wear the corporations down. Often the companies will settle just to get these nutcases off their backs.'

'You think Yalom was a nutcase?'

'From what we've heard, Yalom sounded like a pretty independent thinker. I can see him trying to handle something by himself. What I can't understand is why a VerHauten representative answered Yalom personally in the first place. Someone should have smelled *problem* with a capital P. The complaint should have immediately gone to the corporation's lawyers.'

'You're the attorney,' Marge said. 'Use your three years of night school and tell us why.'

Decker smiled. 'Offhand, I'd say someone was attempting to manage Yalom with kid gloves. They didn't want the lawyers involved right away because they didn't want him to freak.'

'Meaning Yalom probably had something the corporation wanted. And VerHauten was attempting to keep the guy calm until they could figure out how to get it.'

Decker nodded. 'You just summed up my thoughts.'

'So what was VerHauten after?'

Decker shrugged. 'Let's keep reading.'

Marge said, 'Whatever it was, according to this letter, VerHauten eventually did hand the problem over to its lawyers. I wonder if eventually Yalom engaged an attorney of his own.'

Decker took out another piece of paper from the stack and unfolded it – a preprinted certificate. It looked to be a deed of trust for land in Angola. He showed it to Marge.

She said, 'VerHauten wrote about "unauthorized land parcels." This could be the disputed certificate of ownership.'

'It could be one of many.'

'So Yalom was still investing in Africa. Do you have any idea where Angola is in relationship to South Africa?'

'Northwest,' Decker said. 'The two countries are separated by Botswana and Namibia. I looked at a map of Africa after you found Yalom's passport.'

'Does Angola have diamond mines?'

'I don't know,' Decker said. 'But the countries are contiguous. They probably have similar terrain.'

Marge said, 'Maybe Yalom was cutting some sort of side deal with VerHauten, leaving Gold out on ice. That's why Gold freaked when he found out about Yalom's passport.'

'But the letters were hostile. If there ever was a deal, something soured pretty quickly.'

They both were silent.

Marge said, 'I brought some yellow stick 'ems. Why don't we tag the papers we've gone through.'

Decker said, 'Good idea. I'll take a pile. You take a pile. We'll write notes, then compare when we're done.' He fished out a handful of papers.

Marge pulled out her notebook. 'I know this sounds farfetched, but do you think that the boys *might* be in Africa?'

'I suppose it's a remote possibility.' He sorted through some papers. 'After we found the bodies, Davidson assigned a crew to check out the airlines, the cabs, and the buses ... free up our time to investigate the murders. I hope they find something soon. I know we haven't ruled out the boys as suspects. But finding stuff like this ... reading Yalom's hostility and threats ...'

'Guy probably made lots of enemies,' Marge said.

'I'm sure.' Decker paused. 'If only Arik Yalom had been killed, I wouldn't be as worried about the kids. But someone also popped Dalia. If someone blew away one innocent bystander, are the boys far behind?'

'If they're even still alive.'

'A sobering thought.' Decker picked up another batch of correspondence. 'One thing at a time.'

He returned his attention to the paperwork. Lots of letters, lots of angry correspondence between Yalom and VerHauten, between Yalom and VerHauten's lawyers. Decker never did discover an attorney for Yalom.

There were also lots of stock certificates: Consolidated Gems, Southwest Mines, West African Consolidated. Yalom's stocks added up to thousands of shares in each company. Decker read on. He eventually found a letter to Yalom from Southwest Mines.

The company was announcing bankruptcy.

Digging deeper, Decker found another round of angry letters from Yalom to VerHauten – Yalom accusing VerHauten of illegal stock manipulation. Still no indication that Yalom ever hired an attorney to represent him.

Decker kept reading and hunting.

Marge said, 'Look at this, Pete. A whole stack of land deeds in Angola, Mozambique, and Namibia.'

Decker looked at them. They were dated two years ago. 'I wonder if they're still valid.'

Marge said, 'I wonder if they were ever valid.' She kept reading. More letters – the gist of the irate exchange had to do with who officially owned stock and land in Angola, Mozambique, Namibia, Zambia, and Botswana.

He and Marge had scratched the surface of about half the contents of the box when they heard a knock. Marge muttered some obscenity, then opened the cubicle door. A Suit-and-Tie was looking at her. He broke into a venal smile.

'You two aren't supposed to be here unsupervised.' He wagged his finger. 'I'm not pleased about that at all. I have a good mind to call your captain.'

Marge and Decker said nothing. Finally Marge said, 'We're just working away, sir.'

Suit-and-Tie pursed his lips. 'Well, that's good to hear. Always like it when my tax dollar is well spent.' He let out a forced laugh. He was in his fifties – a big man with a big gut. When he laughed, his belly jiggled. 'Chuck Holmes – senior vice president. I hope that as the chief representative of World First Savings and Loan, I've been of service to you.'

'Yes, you have,' Marge said. *Fucker had no choice with our papers*. 'Thank you very much.'

'No thanks is necessary.' Holmes held out his hand as if

warding off demons. 'I like to do my job, I like to help our boys in blue. And I know Marie likes to help, too. But sending her away.' He clucked his tongue. 'That's going a little too far.'

Decker didn't answer. Holmes suddenly became magnanimous. 'Well, no harm done, I guess. I'm afraid you're going to have to stop anyway. It's closing time.'

'We're not done,' Marge said.

Holmes flipped his wrist and looked at his timepiece. 'Sorry, but I have to close the vault by a certain hour or bells go off. I hope you two found *something* that'll elucidate this terrible, terrible incident. The Yaloms were very valued customers.'

Decker asked, 'How much time do we have left?'

'About two minutes. Just enough time for you to put everything back in the box.'

Marge said, 'How about if we come back first thing tomorrow morning. Say around eight?'

Holmes gave them a small smile that said no can do. 'Sorry, Detective. I've already bent the rules once, giving you access to the box before contacting the IRS. Can't do that again. I'm going to have to key the box until the tax man gives me an okay to open it.'

'We'll clean up,' Marge said. 'Afterward, do you have a minute to talk to us about the Yaloms?'

Holmes managed to smile and frown at the same time. 'Sorry, but I'm a little pressed right now.'

'Of course,' Marge said. 'So I'll just schedule the meeting tomorrow morning . . .' She looked up and smiled. 'Let's make it eight before the bank opens. I'll even bring the doughnuts and coffee, Mr Holmes. Can't beat that.'

The senior veep didn't speak. Finally, he said, 'I suppose I can afford a *few* minutes tomorrow morning. But right now I really am pressed for time. Please clean up quickly so I can lock the vault.'

'You bet,' Marge said.

After the vice president left, Decker said, 'Spiffy how you trapped him into an appointment, Margie. I like that doughnuts and coffee addition.'

Marge smiled. 'See that guy's gut? You work on the weaknesses.'

Decker burst into laughter, cramming papers back into the box. He was just about to close the lid, then paused, looking at the top certificate. Southwest Mines. A land deed for acreage in Angola. Decker pulled it from the box, folded it into a tiny, thick square and stuffed it in his underwear.

Marge raised her eyebrows. 'What do you think you're doing, Rabbi?'

'Old Chuck is doing his job. But I'm doing *mine*.'

'Pete—'

Holmes knocked, then walked through the cubicle door. He smiled at the detectives. 'All done?'

Decker spread out his arms and smiled back. 'All done.'

20

The Rosh Yeshiva invited Rina to sit in the chair opposite the desk. Unlike his study in the yeshiva, the home office was smaller and plainer. It was walled in bookshelves, filled with *sepharim* – religious books. His desk was an old one and Rina suspected it had sentimental value. It was scarred, carved mahogany, its top covered with books and writing material. The only concession made to ornamentation was an old-fashioned sterling inkwell and a set of fountain pens encased in semiprecious stone – malachite, lapis, tigereye, and garnet. He kept the door ajar, but not wide open as he had done earlier in the afternoon.

Rina was exhausted. After she had dropped the boys off at the yeshiva, she had raced back to her parents' house to put Hannah to bed. Once the baby had fallen asleep, she had made another trek out to the yeshiva to say goodnight to the boys *and* to talk to the Rav about Honey. She must have put another hundred miles on her aged Volvo. But Rina felt she had no choice. *Her* family was safe and sound. How could she sleep soundly when Honey and her children were missing? Where were they now?

Rabbi Schulman went over to a shelf and pulled out a bottle of schnapps. 'An old man must do many things to keep a sound mind.' He smiled, but Rina felt he looked troubled. She said nothing, biding her time until Schulman finished his drink.

Finally, the old man put down his shot glass and sat down at his desk chair. He stroked his beard. 'I spoke to the Leibbener Rebbe. I'm afraid I have nothing elucidating to add.'

Rina waited. Schulman took his time.

'Of course, the Rebbe is shocked and saddened by Gershon Klein's untimely and violent death. And he is very upset about the disappearances of Honey and her children. However, he is also concerned for your family's welfare, Rina Miriam. He wishes no hurt or harm to come to any of you.'

'He thinks we might be in danger?'

'If you investigate Honey's disappearance, yes, he feels you may be endangering not only Honey and her children, but you and your family.'

'Why?'

'I'm not certain. But for your protection, he has recommended that the matter be left up to the police in New York. That neither you – nor Akiva – conduct any independent investigation.'

It took a moment for Rina to digest what Schulman had told her. 'He doesn't want Akiva to at least *look* for the family?'

'It appears that way.'

'That doesn't make any sense.'

Schulman raised his eyes. Rina caught it. 'You're as puzzled by his request as I am.'

'Indeed, I am, Rina Miriam.' Schulman took a moment to choose his words. 'Though you did not hire me to be Akiva's advocate, I took the liberty of extolling your husband's exceptional talents as a policeman. The Rebbe still held firm to his request. Let Manhattan worry about Gershon's death.'

'But what about Honey – and the *children*?'

The old man sighed, his shoulders hunched by the burden of life. 'The Rebbe . . . seemed to feel . . . that they are best left in the hands of *Hashem*.'

There was a moment of silence.

'I don't understand,' Rina whispered. 'Does he mean that they're . . . dead or that they're okay.'

The Rav began to curl the tip of his beard around his index finger. 'Again, I'm not certain. Perhaps I should recall our conversation for you. According to the Leibbener Rebbe, Gershon had been a troubled man for many months. His business had been flagging for over two years. The Rebbe felt Gershon may have become involved with unscrupulous people.'

Rina thought of the phone calls Honey had reported. 'Who?'

'He wouldn't say.'

'Did the Rebbe tell the police that?' Rina asked.

'He has been in close contact with the Manhattan police.' The Rav continued to curl his beard. 'Though he said nothing overt, the Rebbe . . . suggested that Honey and the children, after hearing about the death of Gershon, might have disappeared to *escape*, not because of foul play.'

'But how could she have known about her husband's death before I did?'

'The Rebbe felt that Honey might have come to you because she *knew* something was amiss.'

'Honey knew that something was going to happen to her husband? So why didn't she get him help?'

'Perhaps she tried. But Gershon was troubled, Rina

227

FAYE KELLERMAN

Miriam. It could be he refused help for himself, but sent his family away.'

'So that's why Honey came out here?' Rina made a face. 'To escape Gershon's enemies?'

'You seem skeptical.'

'It just seems illogical.'

'Perhaps not, Rina. It might be Honey sought you and Akiva out because she felt Akiva could protect her family.'

'It didn't help. Her van was found abandoned.'

Again, the room became still.

Finally Rav Schulman said, 'Didn't you tell me that the van was rented under a false name?'

Rina nodded.

'Then perhaps the Leibbener Rebbe is correct. If Honey had been acutely aware of her husband's nefarious associates, it would have made sense for her to use a false name. And it would have made sense to hide herself and her children after she'd heard of her husband's demise. If we find them, Rina Miriam, we may be doing more harm than good. We could be leaving a trail for the gangsters to follow.'

Rina shook her head in confusion.

Schulman said, 'I know what preys on your mind, Rina Miriam. What if they aren't in hiding? What if they were abducted? Should we not intervene just to be certain?'

'Exactly.'

'I don't have a satisfactory answer for you. I'm simply interpreting the Leibbener Rebbe's wishes.'

'And he wants us to let sleeping dogs lie.'

'Apparently.'

'And what do you think, Rav Schulman?'

The old man appeared very thoughtful. 'Personally, I am concerned for the children. Yet, there was . . . *something* in the Leibbener Rebbe's voice that told me the kids were safe.'

Rina thought about that. The Rosh Yeshiva's intuition was not to be taken lightly. 'Rav, maybe Honey and the kids have returned to the village. Maybe the Rebbe is hiding them until Gershon's murder has been solved.'

Schulman paused. 'I don't think so. If only because Manhattan police have been investigating the village extensively, have been knocking on doors and questioning the people. Yet you bring up a very important question. If they are hiding for fear of their lives, and they couldn't go home, where would they go?'

'Well, she took them here,' Rina said. 'Maybe it wasn't far enough away. Maybe she took the plunge and went to Israel.'

'My thoughts exactly.'

'But what if the Rebbe's *wrong*, Rav Schulman. What if they're waiting for somebody to save them? I can't get the faces of the children out of my mind.'

Schulman looked pained. 'Yes, the children come first. As this is not a halachic issue, I am no *maven*. So I suggest we apprise Akiva of the situation, of our concern for Honey and her family, and let the expert decide.'

'*Shit!*' Decker rubbed his face with scratchy palms. 'I *forgot* to call Manhattan. God, at forty-three, I'm going *senile*.'

'It's called preoccupation with a double homicide,' Rina said.

Decker sank down on the guest bed. It was after eleven and the rest of the household was asleep. He was weary, hungry, and mad at himself for not calling New York earlier. Both cases were weighing heavily on his mind, because both cases involved missing kids. He wondered if, by working the two cases simultaneously, he was doing justice to either case. Probably not.

Rina bit her nail. 'Can't you call New York now? Police stations are open all the time.'

'Not the Detective Bureau. Everyone wants a gold shield because the hours are good.'

'Maybe someone's working overtime, Peter. Maybe someone out there is as dedicated as you.'

'Yeah, that's me. Supercop.' He rubbed his eyes. 'What the hey. I'll give it a whirl.'

He picked up the phone and punched in the numbers. The phone rang and rang and rang and finally the line was answered by a man calling himself Romero. Decker introduced himself officially and asked for a Detective Dintz.

'Dintz went home hours ago. You know what time it is here?'

'Close to two in the morning.'

'The man can add. Nah, nobody's here except me. I'm here because I just got divorced and I'm drowning my sorrows in my job.'

'It doesn't work.'

'You're right about that. It only makes you more pissed at her. Whatdaya want with Dintz?'

Decker updated Romero.

'Yeah, Klein's the diamond dealer. I know the case.'

'What's the scoop?'

'Nuttin' so far. But Klein was in a high-cash business. Plus, he was also a member of that weird cult.'

'By cult you mean the Leibbener Rebbe?'

'Yeah, that weird place upstate – Leibbentown. You ever been there?'

'Nope.'

'You ever been to Plymouth Rock, how the guides dress up like Pilgrims and act like they was on the *Mayflower*?'

'Haven't had the pleasure,' Decker said.

'It's the same at Leibbentown. They dress up like they're livin' in an old Polish village. Only they ain't doing it for a skit. It's their life. Now I work Manhattan, I used to work Brooklyn. I'm used to your garden-variety Chasid. But these guys are beyond that.'

Decker noticed how Romero had pronounced Chasid, gutturalizing the Ch.

'This woman,' Romero said. 'The wife who was staying with you. She seem normal?'

'I'm no psychiatrist.'

'Meaning she was a psycho, too.'

'I'm not a psychiatrist,' Decker repeated.

'So the family was staying with you when the old man was popped.'

'Yep.'

'And then they disappeared?'

'That's a fact.'

'Something's off.'

'That's a fact, too.'

'Lemme call up Larry for you. Even if it is two in the morning, I think he'd want to hear about this.'

' 'Preciate it.'

Romero said, 'Yeah, Larry would definitely want to hear about this. Let me see if I got all your numbers right.' He repeated Decker's phone numbers over the line.

'You got it.' Decker hung up and turned to Rina. 'He described the Leibbener village to me as a cult. From what I've heard, I think that's an accurate description.'

'It's not coercive.'

'That doesn't mean it isn't dangerous.'

'So just what are you saying, Peter?' Rina said, angrily. 'You think the murder was an inside job?'

'I'm not saying anything because I don't know anything.' Decker paused. 'I'll tell you what I do know. If this Rebbe cared about Honey, he wouldn't be telling me to back off.'

'He's concerned for our welfare.'

'You know, Rav Schulman is a very wise man. He said Honey Klein isn't a halachic issue. It's a *police* matter. He's right.'

Reluctantly, Rina nodded in agreement. The phone rang. Decker picked it up.

'This is Detective Dintz,' a low voice announced. 'I'm looking for a Sergeant Decker.'

'You found him.'

'Man, I wish you'd called earlier. I got all my notes in my desk.'

'Wish I could have. I'm on a double homicide out here.'

'Yeah, a diamond dealer and his wife. It was on the news. You think there's a connection between them and Klein?'

'So far the only connection I've found is me.' Decker brought him up-to-date on thc Kleins – the abandoned car on the shoulder of the freeway, Honey's claim about receiving crazy calls, Gershon Klein's strange behavior.

Dintz listened without interruption. When Decker was through, he said, 'So first you found two Israeli stiffs. Now the Klein family has disappeared. And you don't think there's a connection?'

'If I find one, you'll be the first to know,' Decker said. 'Right now we're still trying to determine if the Klein family is in hiding or if they were abducted.'

'And you're assigned to investigate Klein's disappearance?'

'Yes. Can you tell me something about Gershon Klein's

murder? Something that might help me figure out what happened to the wife and kids?'

'All I got so far was a prelim on the coroner's report. Klein was shot, but that wasn't the cause of death.'

'What was?'

'Drowning.'

21

Lying in bed, Rina had the book in front of her, but had read the same page for the last fifteen minutes. Peter was still on the phone, saying a lot of uh-huhs, and taking a lot of notes. She was dying to look over his shoulder, but didn't. Finally, he ended the conversation with a 'thanks a heap, I'll call you tomorrow' then hung up the receiver. He plopped down on the bed. Rina put down her book and waited.

Peter stared at the ceiling, then at her. 'How about a two-minute recap?'

'That should tide me over, thanks.'

'The official cause of death was drowning. So why was Gershon Klein shot in the head?'

'A coverup.'

'You're good,' Decker said. 'Dintz, the detective assigned to the case, is working on the assumption that the shooting was done afterward – to throw the police off track.'

'The ploy obviously didn't work.'

'Autopsies don't lie, and all homicide victims are autopsied. Death by drowning is a very easy thing to spot.'

'I'm confused,' Rina said. 'Are you saying that Gershon was drowned on purpose. Then someone shot him to make it look like a normal murder.' She frowned. 'Normal murder. Now there's a contradiction in terms.'

'It looks that way.' Decker rubbed his eyes. 'Seems to me, we're working with amateurs instead of professional hit men.'

'What kind of amateurs?'

'Could be anyone – disgruntled friends ... family ... wife that's pissed because her husband won't make love to her anymore.'

'You mean Honey?' Rina shook her head. 'I don't believe it! I refuse to believe that. Beside, Honey's what? ... five four. Gershon was a lot bigger than that.'

Good point, Decker thought. Man, he was tired. His brain waves were close to flatlining. 'I need some sleep.'

Rina leaned over and kissed him. 'You're going to keep working on the case, aren't you?'

'Yep,' Decker said. 'I don't care what her Rebbe says. Something's rotten in the state of New York.'

'He seemed genuinely concerned about Honey's safety, leery about the family's whereabouts. He seemed to feel you could be endangering them.'

'And just *what* is he basing his thoughts on, Rina?'

She shrugged.

'You know what I think?'

'He's holding back.'

'Bingo, you win the Thanksgiving turkey. Either he knows something bad or he's protecting somebody.'

'Honey?'

'Maybe Honey. Maybe someone in the community. Maybe even himself.'

Rina stared at her husband incredulously. 'Are you *actually* saying that the Rebbe had something to do with Gershon's murder?'

'I'm saying I have a trained nose and, baby, I smell a rat.' He turned away from her. 'Let's go to bed.'

Rina waited a beat, then shut the lights off.

At his desk at seven the next morning, the first thing Decker did was call up West LA. His intentions were to leave a recorded message for Detective Sturgis, the one who had been assigned to Honey's abandoned van. But to Decker's surprise, Sturgis was in.

Decker filled him in. 'Anything new I should know about?'

'Not on my end.' Sturgis paused. 'What's your make on the drowning?'

'Someone was working the guy over and didn't want to leave marks. You know. Dunking his head in the toilet. Meanwhile, the wife was conveniently out of town. It could have been mob. But it sure could have been an arrangement made by the wife. But if she actually arranged the water torture, what was she trying to gain? To get any kind of renumeration like an insurance policy, her husband would have to kick.'

'He did kick.'

'A messy way to arrange a hit, don't you think? Especially if you're going to shoot him anyway. No, I'm thinking something got bungled. They were working him over but he wasn't supposed to die.'

'Or could be someone *meant* to drown him. The head shot was done to confuse us. Which is precisely what it's doing. Has anyone checked out the insurance policies?'

'Dintz from Manhattan said there's none to speak of. But Gershon Klein was a diamond dealer. I'm sure he has some fancy stones in inventory.'

Sturgis said, 'You want to know my take? She ripped off her husband, hired thugs to pop him, cashed out her stones here, then went underground.'

'But, Sturgis, she didn't go underground. She came out *here*, to LA with her family.'

'To throw everyone off track before she made her big escape.'

'She's religious. She'd have a hard time hiding.'

'Unless she decided to become un-religious.'

Decker thought about that. Honey was a religious woman swathed in clothing and custom – a lady who covered her hair practically all of her adult life. To change her appearance all she'd have to do would be take off her wig, put on some tight jeans, and eat *tref*. No one would recognize her.

'You still here?' Sturgis asked.

'Yeah, sorry. I was just thinking about what you said. If Honey decided to become un-religious, she could hide very easily. But, no pun intended, old habits die hard. If Honey chose to remain Orthodox, a religious lady just doesn't have too many hiding spots in *this* country. I think there is a very real possibility that the lady bolted to Israel.'

Sturgis paused. 'Yeah, could be. You know anything about Israel?'

'I've heard there are lots of religious people in certain areas. Lots of places to hide. Honey and her family could easily fade into the miasma.'

'That being the case, nobody's going to find her.'

'*We're* not going to find her, that's true. But an insider probably could.'

'You've got someone in mind?'

'I have only one international informant on Israel, Sturgis. But she's doozy.'

Marge raised her eyebrows and drank lukewarm coffee

from a Styrofoam cup. 'Just like Chucky the Clown to keep us waiting.'

'Be charitable, Dunn. It isn't even eight yet.'

Marge grumped, set the cup on a side table, and took in the office – nice but it wasn't overdone. An institutional desk, a leather couch, a couple of glass and chrome side tables, and one picture window with a smoggy view of the SF Valley. The bookshelves were filled with folders and binders. A moment later, Chucky graced them with his presence. He was dressed in a conservative-cut blue suit, white shirt, and hand-painted tie – doves and swans in brilliant colors. Must be how bankers let their hair down, Marge thought. She stood and held out her hand. Holmes took hers first, then Decker's.

'Thanks for making time for us,' Marge said, returning to her seat.

'As long as you're brief.' Holmes sat in his black leather desk chair and rubbed his forehead. 'I've got the IRS breathing down my neck, angry that this wasn't reported yesterday. I told them you had the paperwork but that didn't seem to mollify them. They're out for me now. I can just *feel* it.' He looked up at Marge and Decker, eyes ablaze. 'Just *who* do they think they are?'

The room was silent for a moment. Holmes cleared his throat. 'Yes, well . . . the Yaloms were valued clients. I do want to help you – as long as you're quick about it.'

Decker got comfortable in his seat. 'Mr Holmes, I'm sure you know that money is always considered a prime motive for murder. Tell me everything you know about the Yaloms. I want to know what they had . . . what someone could have been after.'

Holmes's eyes went upward. 'The bank holds the mortgage on his home. We also hold a note for a loan totaling three quarters of a million dollars. He was timely with his payments.'

Decker said, 'Is the loan secured or unsecured?'

Holmes winced. 'Unsecured.'

'So you must know something about Mr Yalom's assets,' Marge said.

'I felt . . .' Holmes squirmed. 'I felt comfortable loaning him the money.'

'You arranged the loan personally?' Marge asked.

'Yes.'

'Tell me what you know about Mr Yalom's investments.'

Holmes hesitated. 'I know there's no confidentiality with the dead, Detectives. Especially murder victims. But, like I told the department yesterday when the detective called, I still feel . . . unloyal talking about Mr Yalom's affairs, even to policemen.'

Like I told the department yesterday? Decker pulled out his notebook and scanned through the pages. Who the hell did Holmes talk to? 'Mr Holmes, do you remember whom at the department you spoke to yesterday?'

Holmes made a quizzical face. 'Detective Misheria or Mishtara, or Mistara. He had a broad Texas accent. He didn't speak to you?'

Decker shook his head. 'No, we . . . must have missed each other.'

'I didn't talk to him for very long. I was very busy. But I did let the authorities into the box. Anyway, it wasn't the appropriate time to start talking about Arik Yalom's foreign investments.'

Again, Marge and Decker passed meaningful glances. 'Well, maybe you can help us out now,' he said, 'Who handled Mr Yalom's overseas operations?'

Holmes snorted. 'I wouldn't exactly call them operations.'

'More like risky business ventures,' Marge broke in.

Holmes pursed his lips. 'Ah ... you must have seen all
the certificates in his safe-deposit box. Yes, he had invested
in quite a few speculative ventures.'

'Your idea?' Marge asked.

'Of course not! We're in the business of keeping money,
not losing it. I was quite blunt with Arik. I told him –
straight out. But Arik had his own mind when it came to
business.'

Marge said, 'Did Mr Yalom have success with any of his
mining investments?'

Holmes chuckled. 'Success is a state of mind.'

'Meaning?'

'He felt he was successful.'

'What about you?' Decker asked.

'Sergeant, I could have doubled that man's portfolio with
my eyes closed. The typical balance we're currently
recommending is twenty percent cash, ten percent debits,
seventy percent equities. It's not fancy, it's not exotic. But
it is prudent. Arik wanted big time.'

'Did he get big time?' Marge asked.

'Not to my knowledge. Not only were his cash reserves
depleted from a high inventory in stones, but any profits
he made from his legitimate business went toward venture capital in his Africa scheme. I'm not saying there
isn't money to be made from alluvial mining of Angola
beds. There are stones to be found. But it's iffy at
best, and you know the political situation in Africa
right now – volatile with a capital V. Mr Yalom would
have done much better with a simple, conservative
approach.'

241

Marge said, 'Especially with the lock VerHauten has on the diamond industry.'

Holmes folded his hands across his stomach. 'Exactly.'

Decker said, 'Mr Yalom seems to have gone head to head with VerHauten.'

Holmes said nothing.

Marge said, 'Or don't you know about his correspondence with them.'

'I know Arik had certain ideas about VerHauten. A lot of people do.'

'Do you want to elaborate?'

'What can I say?' Holmes clapped his hands. 'He claimed he had inside support from the company. Either he was lying or something went bad. Because the relationship turned hostile and he went after VerHauten. Like a gnat going against a lion. Sooner or later, a quick swat was bound to squish him.'

'Arik was squished?' Marge said.

Again, Holmes chuckled. 'VerHauten simply has the resources, and they don't appreciate being bad-mouthed. You can't buck city hall.' He paused. 'Perhaps I should paraphrase that. You can't buck two hundred years of experience and four billion dollars in assets.'

Decker closed the driver's door to the Plymouth, slipped the key in the ignition, but didn't start the car. 'Someone should inform Shaul Gold that it's against the law to impersonate a police officer.'

Marge said, 'You think it was Gold?'

'I know it was Gold. He used his cowboy accent.'

'The case has been high-profile, Pete,' Marge said. 'It could have been a lackey for VerHauten. Perhaps they had a vested interest in seeing Yalom and his wife . . . terminated.'

'They're a multibillion-dollar company. Why would they bother with small potatoes like Yalom? No, VerHauten didn't call. Gold did. He knows Arik's been doing some funny business in Africa. He's tracking down our leads. He's traveling the same road we are. In this case, he questioned Holmes *before* we did. I don't like that, Margie. He's fouling up our element of surprise. The man needs a few guidelines.'

'Should we pay him a visit?'

Decker nodded and called up his number from the car radio. The phone rang and rang. Cutting the line, Decker tried him at the office. Again, no one picked up. He slammed down the mike. 'Now what?'

Marge said, 'I like your truism about money as a motive for murder. There was a lot of angry correspondence exchanged between Yalom and VerHauten. Let's pay the giant a visit. I'm sure they have a local office.'

'And do what?' Decker answered.

'Wing a line of questioning. Find out why the letters turned so hostile.'

'Marge, I'm sure Yalom was hostile so VerHauten answered him aggressively. I'm sure VerHauten couldn't give a solitary hoot about Yalom.'

'They obviously cared enough to correspond with him over several years.'

Decker thought about that. He reached into his pocket and took out the stock ownership pilfered from the safe-deposit box – Southwest Mines. He showed it to Marge. 'We could use this as an entrée maybe. Say we're investigating the company. Wondered if they had any information on it.'

'Good idea.'

Decker paged through his notes. 'A woman by the name of Kate Milligan signed this letter to Yalom – Damn. The letter was postmarked from Belgium.'

'VerHauten must have a local listing somewhere near the diamond center.'

Decker tried LA information. Nothing for VerHauten. He tried three other directories, the results equally frustrating. Then he tried New York City for a listing in Manhattan.

Zip.

He slammed down the phone. 'What's going *on* here! A multibillion-dollar company and I can't find a fucking listing for them.'

'They probably have some weird subsidiary name.'

Decker rubbed his face. 'Now what?'

Marge shrugged helplessly. 'Anything new on the Yalom boys?'

'They're still checking out terminals. Thank God for computers. Without them, the task would be unthinkable. You want to call up some airports ourselves?'

'No, I'm still curious about VerHauten,' Marge said. 'Why don't we go back down to the diamond center and grab ourselves a random dealer. Someone over there has *got* to know something about VerHauten.'

Decker thought a moment, then started the motor, pointing the unmarked for downtown LA.

22

Unsure how to start, Decker took out his shield and flashed it to the first Chasid he saw. The man was five ten, his face hidden behind a thick pelt of beard and side-curls. He wore the requisite uniform – black suit, white shirt, and black hat. His tzitzit – prayer fringes – were peeking out from under his shirt. He fingered them vigorously as he eyed the gold badge.

Decker said, 'Excuse me, I'm looking for the offices of VerHauten Corporation. I was told they are located around here, but I can't seem to find them in any building directory.'

The religious man was confused. 'VerHauten corporate headquarters is in South Africa.'

'How about their local subsidiary offices?' Marge said.

Again, the man squinted. 'They don't have any offices here.'

'Maybe they're not listed under the name VerHauten. Some sort of satellite office, perhaps.'

The Chasid shrugged. 'Nothing I'm aware of.' He turned and spoke to another of his ilk, the two men dressed identically. 'Eli, do you know if VerHauten has a local office here?'

'In LA?' Eli shook his head. 'I don't think so.'

A thirtysomething blond man in a black suit and tie

interjected himself into the conversation. 'You're looking for VerHauten?'

'Yes,' Marge answered.

'The actual corporation?'

'Try South Africa,' another businessman shouted out.

Decker noticed they were attracting a crowd. The blond man stuck out his hand and said, 'Ronnie Guttenburg. Why don't you come up to my office?'

Decker eyed Marge, then said thanks. Guttenburg led them into the express elevator that took them up thirty-five flights in fifteen seconds. They got out and went with Guttenburg into a small office, not unlike Yalom's place. The layout was almost identical – an anteroom, a hallway, then the office. Guttenburg's lair was furnished in warm woods and oiled leather, but it wasn't overdone. He pointed to two plush chairs and Decker and Marge sat. Guttenburg took a seat behind his desk.

'You're the police?'

Marge and Decker nodded.

'Can you tell me anything about Arik Yalom's murder?'

Decker took out a notebook. 'Why are you asking me about Yalom's murder?'

'Because you're the police and I'm scared. I knew Arik only slightly. But that's not the point.' Guttenburg tightened his jaw. 'Diamonds are risky business. Every time you hear about something like this, it scares the wits out of you. And his wife, too. Did Yalom have children?'

'Yes, he did,' Decker said. 'They're missing.'

'Missing?' Guttenburg frowned. 'You mean someone kidnapped them?'

Marge said, 'We're not sure.'

Guttenburg said, 'Why are you asking about VerHauten?'

Marge said, 'Because we can't find a listing in the phone book.'

'That's because they have no US offices. They're considered a monopoly, and as such, they're not allowed to do business in the US. We have antitrust laws here.'

The room was quiet for a moment.

Marge took out her notebook and raised her eyebrows. 'You're telling us they don't do business with the US?'

'No, I'm telling you they can't set up shop here. But they do *plenty* of business in the US. We'd all be out on our asses if VerHauten didn't exist.'

Guttenburg folded his hands and placed them on his desk.

'It's Sherman Anti-Trust Act technicalities. It's stupid and inefficient. The upshot is American cutters and sellers are forced to shell out money in travel to get our stones overseas.'

'From Antwerp?' Decker took out his notepad.

'Personally, I go to Tel Aviv to buy my stones. But VerHauten deals with Antwerp. VerHauten *is* Antwerp.'

Guttenburg smiled.

'I exaggerate, but only a little. VerHauten may be barred from our soil, but they still control us lock, stock, and barrel.'

'Why do you go to Tel Aviv?' Marge asked.

'I'm not big enough to warrant a box from VerHauten directly, so Antwerp isn't really suited to my needs.'

'A box?' Marge asked.

'The big guys – the real, real big guys – get their stones directly from the South African mines, the diamond pipes. The giants send in their orders, and twice a year they get their boxes of diamonds from VerHauten directly. The company tries hard to satisfy their customers, but even the big players are forced to buy stones they really don't want.'

'Forced to buy stones?' Marge looked up from her notes. 'What do you mean?'

'You either take all – no questions asked – or you get none, meaning you're relegated back to the secondary market.'

Decker said, 'The boxes are nonnegotiable?'

'Precisely. The only questions you can ask concern things like grading – quality, color, things like that. Even so, VerHauten has the final decision. In this business, they are God.'

'What constitutes being a really, really big guy?' Marge asked.

'How about Sir Maxwell Ogdenbaum.'

Maxwell Ogdenbaum. For fifty years his name had been associated with the jewels of kings and sultans. Glitter and glitz. Decker remembered reading about a tiara designed for some sultan's wife. The price tag was about the cost of Hawaii.

'Yep, Sir Max is definitely a big player,' Guttenburg said. 'If you're approved, by appointment only. Getting a box from VerHauten is like getting a seat on the stock market. You've got to earn it and be big enough to afford it. Which leaves ninety-nine point nine percent of small players out of the first string. However, second-string players like me are vast and many.'

Decker said, 'So a company like VerHauten wouldn't even bother working directly with men like you or Arik Yalom.'

'You're getting the picture.'

'Yet Arik used to travel to Antwerp.'

'That would make sense. There's a huge secondary

market over there. For my needs, Tel Aviv is better.'

'Mr Guttenburg, what would it indicate to you, if a man like Arik Yalom had an ongoing correspondence with a vice president from VerHauten?'

Guttenburg paused. 'What do you mean by ongoing correspondence?'

'Have you ever heard of a woman named Kate Milligan?'

'Everyone knows who Kate Milligan is. She was director of marketing and sales for VerHauten . . . used to work out of Belgium.' Guttenburg brushed sandy hair out of his milky-blue eyes. 'She corresponded with Arik?'

'That would be unusual?' Decker asked.

'Very.'

Again, the room fell silent.

Guttenburg said, 'This is all very interesting.'

Decker said, 'Tell me about it.'

'Kate Milligan is a dynamo – a highly esteemed international lawyer. That's how she originally came to VerHauten. But she was so sharp, they moved her into marketing and sales. Anyway, she passed the American bar here and in New York some time ago. Then suddenly, about a year ago, she opened up her own firm – a multinational law corporation. Its LA branch is just down the street.'

'She left VerHauten?' Marge said.

'Yes. It surprised everyone.'

'Is VerHauten using her offices as a front for their business?'

'No, they couldn't get away with that,' Guttenburg said. 'Milligan deals in international business law. You know, she helps foreign investors wade through the mountains of red tape to set up business here. No, her practice is her own. But I wouldn't be surprised if a lot of her practice was dedicated to finding a way to get VerHauten into the American market legally.'

Decker asked, 'Are they bankrolling her?'

'Let's just say rumor has it that they have a great deal of confidence in Kate Milligan.'

Marge said, 'The parting was very amicable.'

'More than amicable. VerHauten and Ms Milligan are on the very best terms.'

Marge cupped her brow with extended fingers, protecting her eyes from the onslaught of the midmorning sun. 'You've got to ask yourself why a top dog like Milligan would bother with Yalom. The answer is, he had something she wanted. But I can't think that his stockholdings would be anything worth screaming about. Hell, if they were truly valuable, seems to me the easiest thing would be for VerHauten to buy the guy out.'

Decker said, 'Agreed. Something else is at stake. You want to pay an impromptu visit to Ms Milligan?'

'What are the chances that she'll be in or that she'll see us if she's in?'

'Her offices are only a few blocks away. Let's go for it.'

Marge shrugged. 'You're the veteran.'

Decker looked at the street signs. 'This way. Let's walk. The weather's nice.'

Ten minutes later, Decker was standing in front of a waffled monolith of chrome and glass that reflected the glare of sunlight. He shielded his eyes and rolled his shoulder.

'Your bullet wound acting up?'

'Just when the weather's been damp.' He smoothed back his hair. 'Let's do it.'

They went into a sunlit lobby, taking another express elevator. Decker felt his stomach lurch with each stop until they exited onto the twenty-third floor. Steel doors opened and they stepped into a paneled lobby. The entrance to the inner sanctum was blocked by a twenty-foot walnut desk manned by a pair of headphoned receptionists – one blonde, one brunette. The blonde had on a short-sleeved teal-blue dress; the dark-haired lass wore a tomato-red suit. Across the satin-smooth paneled barrier bronze capital letters spelled out MILLIGAN AND ASSOCIATES. The left side of the lobby held a six-foot leather couch; on the right were two wingback club chairs, between them a table holding several copies of the day's *Wall Street Journal*. Decker approached the desk, attracting the attention of the blonde receptionist. She smiled at him, but continued talking into her headphones. A moment later, she gave them her full attention.

'May I help you?'

Her voice was delicate, shaded with a South African accent. Decker said, 'Kate Milligan, please.'

The blonde furrowed her brow. 'And your name?'

'We don't have an appointment.' Marge took out her badge. It attracted attention not only from the blonde but from the brunette as well.

The brunette said, 'What's this all about, Mae?'

Mae answered, 'I don't know.'

The phone rang. The brunette answered, 'Milligan and Associates. This is Ellen. How may I direct your call?'

Mae said, 'So Ms Milligan isn't expecting you?'

Decker smiled. 'Just tell her the police are here.'

Mae seemed mired in indecision.

Decker said, 'Why don't you pick up your phone and call her?'

Mae seemed impressed by Decker's solution. She pushed buttons on a switchboard, then turned her back. Neither Marge nor Decker could hear what she was saying. Then she swiveled back to face them. 'May I have the nature of your business?'

Marge said, 'Personal.'

Once again, Mae turned her back. Then she hung up the phone. 'Ms Milligan's secretary is contacting her. Why don't you have a seat for a few moments?'

The moments stretched to minutes, then to a half hour. Just as Decker was about to get up, Mae smiled at him. 'That was Ms Milligan's secretary. He said that she'll be down in a few moments.'

This time the moments were really moments. A woman appeared, and instantly, Decker felt his heart lurch in his chest. He cursed himself for reacting like a man first, a cop second. But he just couldn't help himself. He stood, focusing on her face, trying to observe without staring.

Goddamn Guttenburg for not warning him.

She was beautiful – tall and lithe with skin as smooth as buffed bronze. Her bone structure was flawless, her eyes clearwater blue. Her hair was a wavy perm of copper-colored tresses. She wore a tailored ivory suit with a lace camisole peeking between the lapels. Her perfume was light with a floral hint. Decker's eyes went from Milligan's face to the shield in his hands.

'Ms Milligan?' He showed her his shield. 'Detective Sergeant Peter Decker from the Los Angeles Police Department. This is Detective Dunn. We'd like to have a word with you.'

Milligan stared at the badge, then at Decker. 'What's this about?'

Of course, her voice had to be husky.

'Arik Yalom,' Marge said.

'Oh, not *him*!' She became cross, her South African accent pronounced with her anger. 'I can't actually believe he's sicced the police on me! I resent having to deal with such rot! While I have nothing but admiration for law and order, I am very busy. You may feel free to take any official matters up with my personal lawyers. Their offices are on the floor above. I'll even have Ellen ring them up for you.'

'Can we just have a few minutes of your time, Ms Milligan?' Decker said. 'I promise we'll be brief.'

Milligan's eyes met his. They were exquisite but unreadable. 'All right. Come.'

She turned on her heels, expecting to be followed. Decker looked at Marge, who rolled her eyes. They walked behind Milligan's long legs, her heels clackety-clacking on the hallway's floor. Up yet another two flights in an elevator. Decker never thought of himself as claustrophobic, but he felt a sweat coming on.

Maybe it was the woman.

Milligan turned into her executive secretary's office, waltzing past the young man's desk. She led them into a grand-sized room sporting a panoramic view of downtown LA.

Decker's sweat had turned suddenly cold. Maybe that was the office – all chrome and glass and ultra-modern with wall art that didn't believe in anything representational. Expensive though. Big canvasses and big names, the most notable being the dripping style of Jackson Pollock. Sunlight streamed in through the windows, but instead of providing warmth and softening, it only added heat and glare. About as inviting as the spotlight on an operating table.

253

'Have a seat,' Milligan said.

But she remained standing by her desk – an enormous high-polished piece of granite rock. Behind the desk was a floor-to-ceiling bookcase. The top half held law books – American law, South African law, English law and international law. The lower half was dedicated to books on economics. Books by John Maynard Keynes and Milton Friedman. There was one full row of books on the post-World War II economies of Germany and Japan.

Immediately, the phone rang. Milligan told her secretary to hold all calls and slammed the receiver down.

'He sees I'm leading two people into my office, you'd think he'd know better than to ring a call through.' Milligan shook her head. 'But he's loyal. Followed me from VerHauten. I suppose you can't put a price tag on allegiance.' Absently, she leafed through a folder that was lying on her desk. 'You said you'd be brief. I'm already behind schedule.'

She'd pronounced the last word *sheduel*.

Decker pocketed his shield. He sat on a black leather couch big enough to accommodate his frame. Marge sat next to him, spine ramrod straight. They both were intimidated by the wealth, the power. A big no-no for a detective, but sometimes it couldn't be helped.

Decker said, 'Thanks for your time, Ms Milligan—'

'You may skip the pleasantries.'

There was an awkward moment of silence. The rudeness kicked in his professionalism.

He stood. 'Okay, ma'am. Then just tell me why a multibillion-dollar company like VerHauten felt threatened by Arik Yalom's meager holding in African diamond mines.'

Milligan's eyes became hot blue flames.

Decker smiled. 'You can start anytime you want, Ms Milligan.'

A slow smile spread across Milligan's lips. She leaned against her desk, placing a hand on her jutting hip. 'Are you serious?'

Decker said, 'Yes.'

Milligan straightened her spine, crossing her arms in front of her chest. 'I don't answer absurdities.'

'We have records of your correspondence with Mr Yalom,' Marge added.

'Then you have records of a deranged man sending VerHauten his incoherent ramblings.'

'Why'd you bother answering them?' Decker asked.

'VerHauten answers all its correspondence, deranged or otherwise.'

'That's not what I asked, Ms Milligan,' Decker said. 'I asked why you, *personally*, bothered answering them.'

'His correspondence was sent to my division—'

'And you answer *all* correspondence directed to your division?'

Milligan bit a coral, bee-stung lower lip, but her eyes never wavered from his face. Decker had faced many an ice-water-veined felon, but her stare went right through his spine. He dropped his voice a notch.

'When you surmised the nature of his business, why didn't you immediately forward his letters to VerHauten's attorneys? Correct me if I'm wrong, but you had already been moved out of the legal department by then.'

'You seem to know a great deal about me.' Milligan let her arms drop at her sides. 'Why the interest?'

'I'm interested specifically in your business with Arik Yalom. When you realized that Yalom was a quote-unquote deranged man, why didn't you forward his correspondence to VerHauten's attorneys.'

'Because they are busy individuals, not to be bothered by cranks and fools.'

'VerHauten's attorneys are on retainers and are paid handsomely to deal with cranks and fools. I would think *you*, on the other hand, a one-of-a-kind, highly valued employee, would have better ways to spend your time.'

Marge found her voice and broke in. 'Look, Ms Milligan, Sergeant Decker and I are working very hard, trying to investigate this double homicide. We're not out to give anyone grief. So let's work together.'

'If for no other reason than you'll get rid of us faster,' Decker added.

No one spoke for a moment. Then Decker noticed that Milligan seemed frozen in position. He said, 'You didn't know?'

Milligan stiffly shook her head.

Decker said, 'Arik Yalom and his wife, Dalia, were found murdered a couple of days ago.'

Marge said, 'It was extensively covered on television and in the newspapers. I'm surprised you didn't hear—'

'*When* was this?'

'It was two days ago,' Decker said. 'We've started going through Mr Yalom's affairs and found your letters. Tell me about them. What was Yalom onto?'

'Nothing as far as I could ascertain. Nothing that anyone would want to ... murder for. My God, that's ... this is surreal.'

Decker said, 'Mr Yalom had some holdings in African diamond mines. What do you know about them?'

Milligan dropped into her desk chair and stared out the window.

Decker said, 'Are you all right, Ms Milligan? Do you need some water?'

'Nothing,' she whispered.

They gave her a minute to get over the shock. Then Marge said, 'Beautiful view. Especially on a bright, sunny day like today.'

Milligan continued looking out the window. 'I hadn't heard about Yalom. I've been rather preoccupied with my own affairs. This seems very tragic.'

'Yes, ma'am,' Decker said.

'So why are you interviewing me?'

Marge said, 'You two exchanged angry letters. You want to tell us about them?'

'What is there to tell? The man was delusional.'

'How so?' Decker asked.

Milligan said, 'Allegedly, he owned land that was supposedly rich in diamonds. He wanted a joint venture with VerHauten and they weren't interested. Mr Yalom wouldn't take no for an answer.' She looked down. 'I can't believe someone actually *murdered* him.'

'And his wife,' Marge said. 'Do you know if he was involved with anyone – business or otherwise?'

'I only know he wasn't involved with VerHauten,' Milligan took her eyes from the window. 'I don't know anything about the man except that he had grandiose ideas.' She stood. 'Anything else?'

'Ms Milligan, why did you deal directly with Mr Yalom?'

'A grave error on my part.' She laughed but it lacked mirth. 'I answered Arik's correspondence directly because the man had a sterling reputation as a player in the secondary market. As a top employee of VerHauten, I was very conscientious about the company's image. They don't look kindly on top-rated dealers bad-mouthing the company. They try to appease before setting on their barristers.'

'A billion-dollar company like VerHauten actually gives a hoot about one lone salesman?' Marge asked.

'Yes. Despite what you've heard, VerHauten is very much a family business.'

'Mr VerHauten is personally involved in the day-to-day activities?' Marge asked.

'VerHauten's the company's name,' Decker said. 'Thaddeus Whitman is the chairman of the board. Sir Thaddeus Whitman, isn't it?'

Again, Milligan bit her lip. 'Very good. Sir Thaddeus is VerHauten. And he doesn't like slights, no matter who gives them.' She leaned forward and rested her elbows on the desk. 'These people are very ... gossipy. Very clannish.'

These people. Meaning *Jews*? Because most diamond dealers were Jews. Decker asked, 'Which people?'

Milligan's eyes went to his face. They betrayed nothing. 'Diamond dealers are a very closed-minded lot. But they're jolly good at what they do. No one's debating that, least of all Sir Thaddeus. The company needs them to process and sell its raw stones through America. Not that VerHauten puts up with renegades. But Yalom's reputation, according to the IADD and word of mouth, was beyond reproach.'

'What's the IADD?' Marge asked.

'International Association of Diamond Dealers.' Milligan looked absently at her desktop. 'VerHauten had had direct dealings with Yalom in the past with no problems.'

'Overseas dealings?'

'Pardon?'

Decker said, 'VerHauten isn't allowed to do business in the States, correct?'

'Yes, correct.'

'So their dealings with Yalom. They were overseas dealings?'

'Of course.'

Marge asked, 'What kind of dealings? I thought he wasn't considered a major player. He didn't warrant a box, did he?'

'Of course not!' Milligan smiled. 'You two have done some homework.'

Decker said, 'So as a buyer, Yalom was small.'

'As a buyer, Yalom was a flea,' Milligan stated. 'But as a cutter . . . he was on our list.'

'List?' Marge asked.

'Every so often VerHauten unearths a particular stone with the potential to become a world treasure – *if* it's cut correctly. It takes a very special cutter to look inside the stone—'

'Cut a window?' Decker said.

Milligan smiled. 'Yes, Sergeant. They cut a window to try to determine how the grain runs. But that's not enough – not nearly enough. Computer enhancement helps, but it still boils down to human experience, judgment, and just plain talent. One wrong move and a stone can be shattered. VerHauten has a list of pre-approved exceptional cutters and Arik was on that list. He had done fine – exceptionally fine – work in the past. That's why we . . . that's why *I* was taken aback by the vehemence of Yalom's accusations. I'd maintained good relationships with the man, found him quite sane actually.'

Marge said, 'And you're telling us that VerHauten

wasn't interested in Yalom's land and mining company holdings?'

'It was an interesting moment of diversion,' Milligan said, casually. 'VerHauten is very much aware of the Angola problem. It's an annoyance, but they've been dealing with it for years.'

Decker said, 'Tell me about the Angola problem.'

'It's complicated.'

'Let me make a stab at summing up the problem,' Decker said. 'Angola has land that's diamond-rich, thereby presenting VerHauten with unwanted competition.'

Milligan seemed to be choosing her words. 'There has been some free flow of loose stones from the alluvial riverbeds. But the company has adjusted itself to the situation.'

Marge said, 'Why doesn't VerHauten with its billions in assets just buy up the land?'

'Because most of the land produces boart – industrial diamonds – about two dollars a carat on a good day. Yes, there's money to be made in boart. But at the time I was with VerHauten, they chose to concentrate on gem-quality stones. From VerHauten's perspective, it was easier to buy up the few expensive diamonds the lands produced than to mine the stones themselves.'

'But that swells up VerHauten's inventory, doesn't it?' Decker said.

Milligan pursed her lips. 'Have a side interest in business, do you, Sergeant?'

Decker said nothing.

Milligan said, 'Suffice it to say VerHauten knows what it's doing. It has been around a long time. If Sir Thaddeus says Angola's not worth the bother, it isn't.'

Marge said, 'And Yalom's holdings weren't attractive to VerHauten?'

Milligan started rummaging through papers. 'His alleged interests held *no* interest at the prices he wanted.'

Decker said, 'Why the word *alleged* when talking about Yalom's land holdings?'

'VerHauten had some doubt as to Yalom's claims of ownership. Another reason we didn't want to deal with him.'

'Doubt of ownership based on what?'

'Based on sources.'

'What sources?' Marge said.

'That's VerHauten's affair.'

Decker said, 'Why'd VerHauten try to negotiate with Yalom if you felt he didn't own the land you were negotiating for?'

Milligan's cheeks took on a blush. 'I have been quite patient with you. And I really am very busy. As a matter of fact, I am no longer even associated with VerHauten. So you really should be taking matters up with their barristers.' She walked over to the exit and opened the door. 'Good day.'

Marge exchanged glances with Decker. 'You don't know anybody who'd want Yalom dead?'

'The man was rude and abrasive. No doubt he made enemies.' She nibbled her thumbnail. 'But I know of no one personally who'd want him dead,' Milligan gave him a patronizing look. 'I've given you quite a bit of time. Can we wrap this up?'

Decker said, 'I think we're about done. If I have more questions, I can call you at your office, right?'

'Certainly.'

'You'll be in town?'

'Yes, yes. But please don't call arbitrarily. I have a big case coming up. I'll need to concentrate and I find this very distracting. *If* you have questions, leave them with my secretary. I'll get back to you.'

Decker smiled boyishly. 'Sounds like a Hollywood line. I'll get back to you.'

'Good-bye, Detective.'

Both Marge and Decker stood. Then, as an after-thought, Marge said, 'What do you think of Yalom's partner, Ms Milligan? Did you or anyone else at VerHauten ever deal with him?'

A spark passed through Milligan's eyes, disappearing as fast as it ignited. 'Yalom's partner? Arik doesn't have a partner.'

The room grew quiet.

Marge stuck her hands in her pocket. 'Interesting.'

Milligan stated, 'Yalom never negotiated in the name of any partnership. Are you sure your information is correct?'

Decker shrugged.

'You're not aware of Yalom having a partner?' Marge asked.

'That's what I said,' Milligan answered. 'Unless you're referring to Arik's bald-headed, obnoxious salesman. What was his name again?'

Decker and Marge were silent.

'It was Gold, wasn't it?' Milligan said.

Lady, you know damn well it's Gold.

'Gold told you he was Arik's partner?' Milligan laughed. 'Rather slipshod on your part to believe him.'

Decker stood. 'Thank you for your time. I think we're done for now.'

'You're welcome.' Milligan smiled. 'Did Mr Gold actually tell you he was Yalom's partner?'

Decker said, 'Yes, he did.'

'And you believed him?'

'Everyone we've talked to, including Mr Yalom's sister, had told us that Mr Gold was Mr Yalom's partner. Obviously Mr Yalom told you something different.'

'Is that important to you, Ms Milligan?' Marge asked.

Milligan's face was flat. 'Of mild interest. I always wonder what makes people deceitful.'

Decker smiled. 'Ms Milligan, it's what keeps my partner and me in business.'

23

Slipping on his shades, Decker said, 'Two things stick out in my mind. One: Why did Milligan act so weird when we mentioned Gold—?'

'Yeah, something was off. Her voice cracked, the smile got hard.'

'But her eyes never wavered. You notice that?'

'Sure did,' Marge said. 'Probably something she learned in CEO school – the same one that teaches "Never let them see you sweat."'

Decker smiled. 'The disparaging way she talked about Gold. And for no apparent reason.'

'So right away, being of perverted mind, we start thinking that Milligan and Gold are up to something.'

'The thought crossed my mind.' Decker walked slowly. 'The other thing that bothered me was this: Why would Milligan be dealing with someone like Arik Yalom even if he was a top cutter. Milligan was in charge of marketing, not manufacturing.'

'I know how your mind works,' Marge said. 'You're thinking that maybe she had no choice. Yalom was blackmailing her.'

'Something.' Decker thought a moment. 'The letters Milligan and Yalom exchanged. The veiled threats in them. Actually not so veiled in the later correspondence.'

Marge said, 'To me, they sounded just like Milligan described them. Like the ravings of a lunatic.'

'So assume he was a lunatic. Why would Milligan deal with a lunatic?'

'She stopped dealing with him, Pete.'

'Or maybe she dealt with him in the ultimate way. She had him popped.' Decker paused. 'I know, I know. Big leap. I'm stretching from here to China, looking for something that isn't there. Probably VerHauten told her to deal with Yalom because they needed him as a cutter.'

'Besides, why would Yalom blackmail Milligan?'

'I've got an answer for that. Yalom wanted an in to VerHauten to hawk his mining stocks and land and Milligan was his ticket.'

Marge pushed hair off her forehead. 'I like that.'

Decker licked his index finger and sliced air, making an imaginary tally mark. 'If you assume Milligan in the role of blackmailee, it makes sense why she answered Yalom directly. You don't go to the boss if you have a personal problem. You keep everything hush-hush and attempt to take care of it yourself.'

'But, Pete, she eventually did forward the letters to VerHauten's attorneys.'

'Yeah, she did.' Decker shrugged. 'So I'm off base. Not the first time.'

They walked into the darkened labyrinth of the underground parking lot. After the requisite minute needed for orientation, they found the unmarked. Marge took the wheel, Decker rode shotgun.

Marge said, 'What I want to know is, what's with Shaul Gold? His partner's dead and he's nowhere to be found. Last we saw and heard of him, he was half drunk with a loaded gun, planning to rescue the boys.'

'You forgot impersonating a police officer,' Decker said.

'What's his role in all of this? Then we mentioned him to Milligan, and she went all hinky. Maybe we weren't off base. Maybe Gold and Milligan are in on something together.'

'In on what?'

'I don't know.' Marge thought for a moment. 'Let's go back to your blackmail thing, Pete. Say Yalom was blackmailing Milligan. Say he had something really big on her. If Milligan was going to hire out to pop Yalom, who better to do the job than Gold? He didn't like his partner—'

'Gold has an alibi.'

Marge said, 'Gold can also bribe. The man had also been a sniper in the Israeli army. We both know that a sniper's just a sanctioned murderer anyway.'

'That's a shitty thing to say,' Decker blurted out. 'What the hell do you know about wartime rules anyway?'

The car grew cold and quiet.

Marge stumbled until she found some words. 'Look, if I hit a nerve, I'm sorry. I'm just trying to solve a case, okay?'

Decker ran his hands over his face. 'Sorry.' He clapped his hands. 'You're right. We're working on a case here. Go on.'

'Where was I?' Marge asked softly. 'I lost my train of thought.'

Decker said, 'You were thinking that Milligan hired Gold to blow Yalom away.'

'When you state it like that, it sounds ridiculous. I was just talking theoretically.'

'Theory's all we have,' Decker said quietly.

Marge drove a minute, then said, 'You want some coffee, Pete?'

'I'd love some.'

'Shall we live dangerously and try out for the corner coffee vendor?'

'I'm game. Just don't get me anything designer.'

'I know, I know. Black coffee—'

'*Plain* black coffee. Nothing with a lemon peel in it.'

Marge let out a small laugh, pulled over, and parked the car. She got out and a minute later brought back two steaming paper cups to the Plymouth. They drank in silence. Decker broke it.

'Sorry I jumped on you, Margie.'

'No prob.' She looked down, then back at Decker. 'You want to talk to me about it, Rabbi?'

'Talk to you about what?'

'About what pushed your button.'

'No, not particularly.'

Marge broke into laughter and so did Decker. He said, 'I'm fucked up. End of story. Back to the case, Margie. Assume that Milligan had been dealing with Yalom because he was blackmailing her.'

'A logical leap, but okay. Assume blackmail. What could Yalom have had on Milligan?'

No one spoke.

'The hard part, huh?' Marge smiled. 'If he was black-mailing her, the woman would have to have a past. How about she was a hooker?'

Decker shook his head.

Marge pursed her lips. 'Yeah, she's too pretty and too smart. We need something classier, huh? She was a call girl – an expensive call girl.'

Again, Decker shook his head.

Marge said, 'Okay, forget hooker. How about ... she has a record.'

'Seems to me a company like VerHauten would scrutinize its top employees. A rap sheet would be an easy thing to check out.'

'Not if she was a juvenile at the time and the records had been sealed.

'Assuming the South African legal system is the same as ours.'

Marge made a face. 'You're right. I don't know if they're comparable.'

Decker said, 'I don't know if she's even South African. She could be English or Australian or Rhodesian. Only it's not Rhodesia anymore.'

'What's it called now?'

'Uh ... Rhodesia's Zimbabwe, I think.'

'So she could be Zimbabwean,' Marge said. 'Pete, I don't know *anything* about the Zimbabwean legal system.'

They both laughed. Marge said, 'The fact still remains that she could have been a former felon – juvenile or otherwise.'

'And you don't think a giant like VerHauten would have found out about that?'

'Well then, how about this, Pete?' Marge said, testily. 'How about you suggest some theories and I'll shoot them down?'

'Fair enough. Okay. We have a beautiful, brilliant lady who worked for one of the biggest, wealthiest, most powerful monopolies in the world. If she had a skeleton, what would it be?'

Decker tapped his foot.

'A reformed hooker just wouldn't have made it up the ladder that far. That only happens in Hollywood. And a felon wouldn't have made it that big, either. Former felons don't become high-powered, seven-figure-a-year corporate lawyers. They become screenwriters.'

Marge erupted into laughter. 'No, former *cops* become screenwriters.'

'Or even novelists if they're talented.' Decker smiled. 'So what could put a woman like Milligan under?'

Marge said, 'VerHauten is a bastion of conservatism. How about if she was illegitimate?'

Decker paused. 'That's not bad.'

'You like that?'

'It's a start. She could have come from trash and she's trying to hide her roots. But then again, I venture to say VerHauten would have done an extensive background check on her – who her family was, where she went to school, things like that. If she came from poor stock, they would have found out about it.'

The car was quiet.

Decker said, 'You know, I'm thinking like a white, American male. Milligan's a white, rich, South African female—'

'With an emphasis on the rich part. You see her suit? A Cesucci. Musta cost two grand if it was a penny.'

'I didn't even notice.'

'See, the ordinary Joe Blow isn't supposed to notice. Then it wouldn't be classy. It's strictly for the upper crust to notice.'

'So my roots are showing,' Decker said. 'Margie, what would be a big no-no for a rich, white, educated, established, South African female?'

'Having an affair with a black.' She looked at Decker. He was grinning. She said, 'Even if it was true, how would Yalom have found out about it? Yalom and *not* VerHauten.'

'Good question,' Decker admitted. 'The only thing I can think of is ... God, how do I say this without feeding stereotypes and prejudice.'

'Spit it out.'

'The Jewish diamond network.'

Marge laughed. 'Too much talking to Tug.'

Decker smiled. 'Remember the way Milligan spoke about the diamond cutters ... described them as gossipy and *clannish*. I think she was referring to the Jews, Marge. Because the Jews are primo diamond cutters. And just maybe she was talking from experience. Maybe one of them saw and heard something. And Yalom was a greedy bastard who took advantage of the situation.'

Marge said, 'So say we're right. Say somewhere in Milligan's past she had a torrid affair with a black. Does that kind of thing make a difference in this day and age?'

'Not if you're an ordinary Jane. But if you're a South African working for a white, conservative company like VerHauten, I think it could make a hell of a difference.'

'Yeah, VerHauten is an entity unto itself,' Marge said. 'As long as we're spinning fairy tales, let's take it a step farther. Assume Milligan wanted Yalom out of the way for good. I still think Gold would make the perfect triggerman.'

'Why would Milligan hire Gold to pop Yalom? Wouldn't she be worried that now he'd become a problem, too? Take on where Yalom left off?'

'But Gold wouldn't be a problem now. He's figuratively in bed with Milligan.'

Decker thought about that. 'So let me play Devil's

271

advocate. Why would Gold have bitten the hand that fed him?'

'Because he was sick of playing the supporting role, sick of Arik being the big man on campus.'

'Gold had amassed a mighty fine African art collection by being number two.'

'So Gold was an ingrate. It's been known to happen. Anyway, this was Gold's big chance. Once he got rid of Arik, he got not only the business but the wife. Remember the Lexus parked outside the house every week.'

'Dalia was killed along with her husband, Marge.'

Marge frowned. 'Yeah, you're right. That was stupid. Okay, so maybe the Lexus being parked outside the house was just Gold and Yalom doing business. So just assume Gold popped Yalom to get him out of the way. Dalia was the side dish – got eaten in the process. It still makes sense. Gold got the business and Milligan got her little blackmail problem solved.'

'And Gold was the hit man?'

'He was a former sniper, he knew guns. Furthermore, Arik and Dalia *trusted* him. Who better to lead the Yaloms under false pretenses to an isolated spot on the mountain?'

That was true enough. Decker ran his fingers through his hair. What she said did make sense. Maybe he just didn't want to see Gold as a murderous thug. Not with the way Gold spoke about Dalia. Yet Decker had known many murderers to express regret over their actions.

He said, 'If that's the case, if it's played out like that, we've got a *big* problem, Marge.'

'Yeah, I know. It's called evidence.'

'No, it's called the *boys*,' Decker said. 'What about Yalom's sons? They made an escape. They must have known what was going on. Suppose they knew Gold was the triggerman. What do you think's going to happen to them?'

No one spoke.

Marge said, 'Well, we know the boys ran for it. Hopefully, they escaped.'

'To where?'

'Well, if I was a teenager and needed to escape, I'd find a faraway place with some relatives.'

'And for the Yalom boys, what place is that?' Decker asked.

'Israel,' Marge stated.

'And that's *exactly* what I'm afraid of. Gold came out and said he was going to look for the boys—'

'He was drunk.'

'Maybe not so drunk as he appeared. If Gold had anything to do with his partner's death, we're in trouble. Because we now have the boys in Israel on *Gold's turf*. If what we're saying is true, they're worse off *there* than they are *here*.'

'There's logic to that.' Marge sighed. 'We need to find the boys before Gold finds them.'

'Let's try the sister Orit again,' Decker said. 'If the boys are staying with relatives, she'll know about it.'

'She already told us she doesn't know where they are.'

'You know me, Marge. I don't take no for an answer.'

Wearing a long black skirt and a glitter-splattered, over-sized sweater, Orit paced her living room and smoked up a nicotine fog.

'You don't solve my brother's murder. You don't solve nothing. All you do is accuse. I tell you once, I tell you again. I don't know about the boys.'

Sitting on the edge of a velvet sofa, Decker had his

notebook out, but the pages were empty. Marge sat next to him.

'You're sure they're not staying with your parents in Israel?' Marge tapped her pen against her notebook. Her pages were also devoid of writing. 'Because if they are, they could be in danger.'

'Yes, Ms Detective, you told me that. And I tell you they're *not* with my parents. Please don't call them. They've gone through enough. Please. Just leave them alone.'

Decker said, 'Ms Bar Lulu, we're trying to help—'

'You want to help, leave them alone. They are in anguish now. I go to them as soon as *you* people release the bodies for burial. How long does that take, for Godsakes?'

'The bodies were just discovered a few days ago—'

'Ach, you people have no feelings. I wait and wait and wait and I can't bury my family. I have to go to Israel with the bodies for *shiva* – for mourning. Do you *understand*?'

'I know what *shiva* is,' Decker said.

'That's right. You're Jewish. So you know how important burial is.'

Decker nodded.

Orit's voice dropped. 'My brother ... he and Dalia would want to be buried in Israel. All Jews should be buried in Israel.' She inhaled a mouthful of smoke and blew it out in one big gust. '*I* help you any way I can. Just leave my parents alone.'

No one spoke for a moment. Then Decker said, 'They know something, don't they?'

Orit shook her head. 'Leave them alone.'

'Orit,' Decker said softly. 'I'm trying to help. I'm trying to ...' He stood, walked over to her, and put a hand on her shoulder. The gesture made her stiffen. He immediately backed off.

'You're a tough lady, you know that?'

'You live in a country with all its life wars, you'd be tough. Lucky for you Americans, war is something that always happens on other people's land.'

Again, the room was quiet. Orit turned and pointed to Decker. 'You have the look. You were in the Gulf War?'

Decker shook his head. 'Vietnam.'

'Ah, that's right. I forgot about that. A fiasco that wasn't ours.' She regarded Decker. 'The same look as my husband. In the eyes. I trust someone with that look. You've been to hell and back, *nachon*?'

'*Nachon*,' Decker answered.

Orit paused. 'You want to help the boys. I don't know where they are. But I say to you this. If they are with my parents, my parents aren't telling me.'

Decker gave Marge a sidelong glance. 'You think your parents are trying to protect the boys?'

'Their son and daughter-in-law was murdered. You tell me the boys are running, afraid for their lives. So what do you think?' Orit threw her cigarette down and crushed it with a high heel. 'If the boys are with them, yes, they are protective. Anyway, they don't tell me anything. Maybe they don't want me to know. Maybe they think I be scared, scared for my kids. But between my husband and me, we'll be okay. I was in the army, too, you know,'

'What was your assignment?' Decker said.

'Desk job,' Orit said. 'But I went through basic training. I know how to use an Uzi. Someone makes the wrong move here, I'll blow the head off.'

Marge and Decker traded looks. Decker said, 'And you're positive you don't know where your nephews are?'

275

'You give me a *chumash*, I put my hand on it and make a *shevuah*, Mr Sergeant. You know what a *shevuah* is?'

'An oath,' Decker said.

Orit nodded. 'Yes, an oath. I make an oath on my Bible. You don't believe me, give me a Bible.'

'I believe you,' Decker said. 'I believe you because I think you really care about your nephews.'

Orit's lower lip quivered. 'Of course I care about my nephews. I love them.' Tears streamed down her cheeks, dragging with them rills of mascara. 'They are my family. I don't have much family. I only had my brother and . . .'

She dropped into a chair and cried bitterly. Decker waited her out until she wiped dark streaks off her cheeks with her fingertips. Orit said, 'Why don't you go to Israel? Who knows what you'll find?'

There was a long pause. Marge finally said, 'Are you saying your nephews are there?'

'I'm saying *nothing* about the boys. I say everyone goes to Israel to try to find something. Maybe you go to try to find God. Everyone else tries, why not you? If you don't find God, maybe you find my nephews. Now please leave me alone. I'd like to find some *shalom* now.'

24

Hannah was a wonderful baby; she liked her playpen. The boys had never tolerated the confinement for more than five, ten minutes at most. Then they got restless. Not so with Hannah. She was content, sitting in her little space, playing with her busy box or fingering her roly-poly ball that jingled every time she gave it a shove. Once in a while, the baby looked up expectantly at Rina, waiting for Mama to give her a smile. Rina would comply and heap on the praise. Then the baby would go back to work. Hannah's willingness to busy herself for up to an hour gave Rina a freedom she never knew existed with babies.

Needing a little more time today, Rina opened up a box filled with colorful plastic blocks. She poured them into the playpen and watched Hannah's eyes go wide. Little fingers reached for multihued squares, cylinders, and triangles. Hannah was a child learning how to manipulate her world. Rina took advantage of her daughter's rapt attention and ran to the bedroom closet. Standing on a footstool, she reached up and swung down a suitcase from the highest shelf.

This was something she just *had* to do. As long as those kids were missing, Rina couldn't find peace.

It had been the Rebbe's reluctance that had spurred Rina

forward. His reticence had been her personal invitation to check out the village. Why else hadn't he wanted help from Peter? If he was hiding Honey and the children, what had Honey done to need a city of refuge?

But try as she might, Rina just couldn't believe Honey had anything to do with her husband's death. When in doubt, do it yourself.

Peter was going to give her grief. He would argue that it would be too much work for her mother to take care of Hannah. Her mother wasn't young anymore. Hannah needed someone with energy to watch her.

Rina would counter by saying it would be for only three days and two nights. She had hired Nora, Hannah's former baby nurse. Nora was happy to help out while she was gone. They both knew how capable Nora was. And Hannah loved her dearly. The topper was that Rina's mother and Nora got along just great.

Peter would complain about the cost. Rina would counter by saying she'd found an extremely cheap standby coast-to-coast flight. She'd be staying with relatives in New York so lodging wouldn't cost a penny. And Jonathan, an old friend and Peter's newly discovered half brother, had agreed to let her borrow his car. So she had cheap transportation to travel upstate to the Leibbener village.

Peter would say it was dangerous.

Rina would introduce the argument that Jonathan had offered to come with her if she felt she needed protection.

Enlisting Jonathan's aid could potentially make Peter angry at his younger half brother. The last thing Rina wanted to do was create friction between the two men. Their relationship was fragile as well as recent. Jonathan's mother was Peter's biological mother, who had given him up for adoption. Peter held no malice against the woman –

she had been a teenager when Peter was born – but their relationship was strained at best. Peter did get along well with two of his half brothers.

And Rina was taking a chance by asking Jonathan for help.

But this was something she just *had* to do. For the sake of the children.

She put the suitcase on the bed and checked on Hannah. The baby was banging two plastic triangles together.

Rina opened up her drawers and began to pack.

Tug Davidson had turned florid. 'You want the department to allocate money to go *where*?'

'Israel,' Decker replied calmly. 'It's a very small country in Asia—'

'I know where Israel is, Decker. Don't wiseass me. The answer is no.'

Davidson looked down at his desk and began to busy himself in paperwork. Decker and Marge didn't move. His eyes returned to their faces. 'The "no" was the signal for both of you to leave.'

'Lieutenant, we might have two dead teenaged boys on our hands if we don't go,' Marge said.

'For all you two know, we may have two dead teenaged boys right now.'

'And for all we know, they may be alive,' Marge said.

'And for all we know, Dunn, they may have popped the parents.'

'All the more reason for us to find them,' Decker said. 'If they turn out to be our prime suspects, we should have them extradited to stand trial.'

'You make perfect sense except you don't know where

the hell the kids are. Then you come to me with this half-assed theory about Shaul Gold being a hit man. If you suspected him in the first place, you should have brought him in for questioning.'

'We didn't have any reason to do it back then,' Marge stated.

'And you don't have any reason to do it now,' Tug answered. 'Get me some concrete evidence as to the whereabouts of the boys, then we can talk.'

'The boys are in Israel,' Decker stated.

'Show me the plane tickets, Decker.'

'We haven't been able to locate any yet—'

'Or maybe never,' Davidson said.

Decker said, 'I think they went through Canada. I think that's why we haven't been able to trace the tickets. There's a large Jewish community in Toronto—'

'Find me plane tickets and then we'll talk.'

'It may be too late by then.'

'Decker, is my hearing going bad or something? Didn't you tell me that the sister specifically told you that she didn't know where the boys were?'

'In a way that specifically told us the boys were in Israel,' Marge said.

'So now you mind-read, Dunn?'

Decker was growing frustrated. 'Look, if it's a matter of money—'

'It's a *big* matter of money,' Davidson said. 'And it's a matter of time, too. I don't like pulling two seasoned detectives off the field.'

Marge was sure she'd heard right. He had said two *seasoned detectives* – *two* detectives – as in plural. The son of a bitch considered her seasoned. He was actually giving them a backhanded compliment. She looked at

Decker to see what his reaction was. All she saw was frustration.

Decker said, 'Look, Loo, *I'll* pay for my own transportation—'

'What is it with you?' Davidson interrupted. 'You suddenly want to make a pilgrimage to the Holy Land for a holiday or something?'

Decker kept his mouth in check. 'Lieutenant, Gold said he was looking for the boys. All I want to do is *find* them before he does. That's it. Find the boys and bring them back to America.'

'And you're willing to pay for it out of your own pocket?'

'Yes, I'm willing to pay for it out of my own pocket. I'll take a no-frills fare and travel with livestock. I'll do it because I want to find the boys. But I also expect to be *reimbursed* by the department if my trip solves this case.'

'With a *big* emphasis on the *if*,' Davidson said. 'Meanwhile, you still haven't figured out the problem of your time loss.'

Decker told himself to unclench his jaw before he spoke. 'I'll be *working* on a homicide case, Lieutenant. I won't be sightseeing.'

'It still amounts to me losing two homicide detectives from the field.'

'I'll stay behind,' Marge volunteered. 'There's still plenty to do here in LA.'

'Yeah, it's called solving the case.' Davidson waved her off. 'Okay, so you're not the problem now. *He* is.' He stared at Decker. 'So what exactly do you think you can accomplish over there, Decker? Think you can just waltz into Israeli police headquarters and start coordinating an investigation in a foreign country? By your *own* admission, you don't know a rat's crap about Israel. Do you even speak the language over there? What the hell is the language over there? It ain't English, I bet.'

'It's Hebrew,' Decker said.

'Yeah, that's right,' Davidson said. 'They speak Hebrew. Do you speak Hebrew, Decker?'

The room fell quiet.

'Terrific, Sergeant. You're going to solve a major homicide case in a foreign country using sign language. Get out of here and do something useful.'

Decker felt a giant headache coming on. His old bullet wound started to throb. He squeezed his eyes shut, then opened them. He hated fudging, but what option did he have. 'I've already got that worked out.'

Davidson glared at him. '*What* worked out?'

Decker sat back in his chair as if he had triumphed. 'The contacts, Lieutenant. I'm already set up with all the major police departments in all the major cities. I've even got myself a top-notch interpreter – an American who moved to Israel when she was . . . eighteen. So I'm all set. All I need is your go-ahead.'

Tug's glare grew icier. Decker sneaked a glance at Marge. She was trying to stifle a smile.

'You set this up already?' Davidson asked.

'Just being thorough, Loo. And thoughtful. Didn't want to burden our department with details I could handle.'

Davidson squinted. 'Who's your contact, Decker?'

'Yaacov Cohen,' Decker said, glibly. Meanwhile, he thanked God for Jack Cohen, his ex-father-in-law. Without him, he wouldn't have been able to think up a Jewish name on the spot.

Davidson said, 'I thought you said your interpreter was a woman.'

'You asked for my contact. I thought you wanted the

name of the guy at Police Headquarters. My interpreter's name is Rina.'

Marge bit her lip to keep from laughing.

'Rina?' Davidson said to himself. He threw Decker a sarcastic smile. 'Same name as your wife?'

'Yeah, same name as my wife. It's a common name over there.'

'What a coincidence.'

'Life's full of them.'

Davidson rubbed his forehead.

Decker said, 'Just give me a week. Two at the outside.'

'How much vacation time do you have accrued?'

Decker spoke slowly and emphatically. 'This shouldn't come out of my vacation time because I'm *not* taking a vacation.'

Tug smiled genuinely. Decker knew the game was finally over, the shithead. Putting them through the wringer and for what? But that was the way it was going to be with this one.

'All right, all right,' Davidson said. 'I won't dock you time. One week on *our* time, *you* pay for your own transportation – both in the air and on the ground. And you pay for your own accommodations—'

'To be reimbursed by the depart—'

'Yeah, yeah. I'll agree to that. If your jaunt leads to solving this case, you'll get your money back. Just keep receipts, including how much it cost you to set things up with the Jews. I know that didn't come cheap.'

Though boiling inside, Decker put on a grin. 'Don't worry about that, Loo. I got a bargain. Remember, I'm Jewish, too.'

Davidson was about to agree, then looked at Decker and realized he shouldn't say anything. Tug thought he detected

a hint of sarcasm but not enough to call him on. He looked
at his detectives without affect. Calmly, he said, 'You got
what you wanted. Now get out of here and go be useful.'

Just as the door opened, Rina had stuffed the last of her
clothing into the suitcase. Quickly, she closed the valise
and attempted to snap it shut, but it was too full. From the
living room, she heard Peter cooing to the baby. Then he
called her name out loud.

'In the bedroom,' she answered. 'Wait, I'll come out to
you.'

She sat on the suitcase, trying to secure the latches
without making noise. But it was too late. Peter was
standing in the doorway, holding Hannah. The baby had
her head against his chest. He stared at the suitcase, then
his eyes went back to Rina.

'Well, you're certainly fast when motivated,' he said.

Rina looked at him, but didn't answer.

Decker kissed Hannah's cheek. 'Go to Mama, so Daddy
can get going.' He handed the baby to Rina and swung
down the matching suitcase. Canvas – nice and light. 'You
know where the passports are?'

Rina paused, then said, 'Of course I know where the
passports are.'

'Excuse me.' Decker went to his closet and pulled out a
couple of suits. Slightly out of style, but the fabric packed
well. 'I didn't for a moment doubt your competency. I was
just asking a question for information.' He pulled out a
couple of ties. 'These go with the suits? I want to look
professional but not like a stiff.'

Rina didn't answer. Decker regarded his wife's confused
face.

'I'm not posing for *Vogue*, Rina. I just want an opinion.'

Rina remained silent.

Decker said, 'Are we on the same planet here?'

'Peter, what's going on?'

'What do you mean?'

'Why are you packing?'

'Because I can't travel wearing just a suit on my back.' Decker stood, legs apart, hands on his hips. Cop's stance, Rina thought. He said, 'We're missing some vital connecting sentence, aren't we?'

'I believe so.'

Decker said, 'I called you about a half hour ago. Left a long, involved message on the machine about our going to Israel. Any of this sound familiar?'

'I haven't picked up messages from the machine today.'

'So . . .' Decker let out a deep breath. 'So you have no idea what I'm referring to, right?'

'Right.'

'So the obvious question for me is . . . why are *you* packing your clothes? I know the marriage has had a few rough spots, but . . .'

Rina laughed. 'I'm going to New York.'

'Why? Somebody die suddenly?'

'God forbid, no! I'm going to visit Honey Klein's village. This is something I just *have* to do, Peter. So don't try to stop me. Something strange is going on—'

'Hold on!' Decker held out the palms of his hands.

'I've got to see for myself—'

'Wait, wait, wait!' Decker started to talk, but laughed again. 'You're packing to go to New York?'

'Yes. And I'm going. I've spent two hours making arrangements—'

'I'll write you up as a contact and get you reimbursed.'

'What are you talking about?'

285

Decker said, 'How about we strike a deal? On our way *back* from Israel, we'll stop in New York. I may even be able to swing reimbursement for that if Davidson will buy my looking into Honey Klein's disappearance. But I wouldn't count on it.'

He was talking more to himself than to her. Rina said, 'Peter, why are we going to Israel?'

'To look for the Yalom boys.'

'They're there?'

'Well, darlin', that's what we're going to find out.'

'*We?*'

'I need you, baby. I'm winging this on spit and prayer and I'll drown without something to hold on to.'

He sat on the edge of the bed and explained the situation to her. When he was done, Rina said, 'You have no contacts with the police?'

'Not a one.'

'And you have no idea where the boys are?'

'I have addresses of relatives on both Arik's and Dalia's sides and a lot of creativity. That's about it.'

'Can I see the addresses?'

He took out his notebook, flipped through the pages, and handed her the numbers. After a moment, he said, 'The areas are familiar to you?'

'Rahavia's in Jerusalem. That's no problem. Ramat Aviv is a suburb of Tel Aviv. I don't know Tel Aviv all that well, but I can find my way around with a good map.'

Decker waited a beat. 'Rina, the diamond center is in Tel Aviv, right?'

'Yes. The Bursa is in Ramat Gan, I believe.'

'The Bursa is the diamond center?'

'Yes. The Bursa is the diamond center.'

'Is that far from Ramat Aviv?'

286

'No. Not at all.'

'Is it open to the public?'

'I don't think so. I think there are a few shops around the place where you can pick up some goodies.'

'I'm not interested in shopping, I'm interested in talking to people. How would you get into this Bursa?'

'I haven't the faintest idea.'

'Then how do you know it's not open to the public?'

'I just know.'

Decker held his head. 'Mr Quixotic. Just call me Don.'

'You need to get into the Bursa?'

'I need *everything*. Davidson gave me a week to find the boys in Israel. I told him I had police contacts when in fact I have nothing. I also told him I had a translator named Rina. I hope I have that.'

'Of *course* I'll help you.' She placed the baby on the floor and sat on the bed beside him. Hannah busied herself with the fringes on the bedspread. 'I was only planning to be gone for two nights because of the baby—'

'Oh shit! Just forget it. Hannah comes first.'

'Peter, we'll all manage for a week,' Rina said. 'I just have to make some calls. And don't worry. Israel's a very small country. Don't worry. I'll get you contacts.'

He looked at her with amazement. 'You can find me *police* contacts?'

'I know quite a few people, honey. I'll swing something. As a matter of fact, I had a friend whose brother was with the Jerusalem police. We even went over to his house for Shabbat once. I remember we all walked to the Old City that afternoon, *davened maariv* at the *kotel*, and watched the sun set, the stones of the wall turning fiery gold.'

Decker hesitated, then said, 'Who's we?'

Rina suddenly blushed. The room fell quiet except for Hannah's babbling. Decker took his wife's hand. 'This trip, Rina. Is it the first time you've been back since Yitzchak passed away?'

Slowly, she shook her head. Her voice was soft. 'I've been back since. Right before I returned to Los Angeles, before I returned to you . . . I took a quick trip there with his parents. To visit the cemetery.'

'You never told me.'

'I thought it would have upset you.' She studied her husband's eyes. 'Would I have been right?'

Decker blew out air. 'Yes, honestly . . . it would have upset me – back then. But it wouldn't upset me now. If you want, we can visit his grave together. Least I could do for you . . . for the beautiful sons he produced.'

'He's buried in Bnei Brak. That's right outside Tel Aviv. Are you sure you'll be okay with it?'

'I'll be fine. I hope the boys . . .' He laughed to himself. 'What a can of worms. You want to tell them or should I?'

'I'll handle it. I'm sure you have enough on your mind right now.' Rina stood. 'You finish packing and look after Hannah while I find the passports.'

'You made arrangements for Hannah?'

'Yes. I thought I was going to New York. I had it all worked out. Nora, the baby nurse, agreed to look after her—'

'I liked Nora. You got her back?'

'For three days. But I don't think she'd mind staying a week. My parents also agreed to stay in and look after the boys.'

Decker swooped up Hannah and threw her up in the air.

The baby howled with delight. He held the baby to his breast and nodded to his wife. 'Thank you, Rina.'

'You're welcome, honey. And by the way, the ties go perfectly with the suits.'

Part II
ISRAEL

25

After twenty-six hours of flight, they were greeted by quite a welcoming committee. Unfortunately, none of the crowd was for them. Decker was amazed by the number of people stuffed into the miserly allotment of outdoor space, making it that much harder for him to move their luggage cart. He knew Lod was an international airport but it had more of the feel of an airstrip. Someone bumped hard into his cart, almost toppled it over. But Decker was quick and prevented the spill. In fairness to the woman, she did help him upright the cart, but then she left without a word of explanation.

'Excuse me!' Decker muttered under his breath.

Rina smiled, 'Reminds me of the classic joke.'

'Which is?'

'It's long. I'll tell you another time when we're not so tired. Suffice it to say we're in a Levantine country. Remember that. It'll take you a long way.'

Sleep-deprived with a monster-sized headache, Decker was cranky. And still wobbly on his legs, having been compressed for over a day in an airplane filled to capacity. Lots of families and lots of howling babies. Plus, there had been a troop of Jewish Argentinian teenagers with beat-up guitars, who had never heard that hootenannies had gone out of style along with Nehru jackets and beaded

293

headbands. The music never stopped. When he finally did manage to fall into a restless, sweaty sleep, some unknown Chasid woke him up and asked him if he would please make a *minyan* – a quorum of ten men needed to recite public prayer. It took all his control not to deck the guy. Rina had said it was because he'd been wearing a *kippah* – a yarmulke.

Decker's response to that? Why hadn't she warned him. She had known the ropes. He was a stranger in a strange land. Not that he hadn't been in exotic locales around the world, but it had always been with the army, with other men – rather *boys* – who had been as confused as he.

But at this moment – at five p.m. Israeli time, as he lugged a cart through foreign-tongued people, he felt truly the *ger*. *Ger* had come to mean convert, but it also meant stranger. Never had he felt more *gerish* in his life.

The rental-car signs were in English as well as Hebrew. It made him feel a little more comfortable. He pushed the recalcitrant cart toward the brightly lit cubicles. At least the weather was accommodating – slightly overcast skies, but mild. They had landed in daylight. Just a half hour later it was dusk approaching dark with a vengeance.

He said, 'They don't have much of a twilight, do they?'

Rina said, 'We're in a different part of the world. But rental cars are the same throughout.' She pulled out a paper contract from her oversized purse. 'Wait here. I'll get us our car.'

Decker followed her into the tiny office anyway. He needn't have bothered. He couldn't understand a word she was saying. The man behind the desk was short, squat, bald, and very dark. He nodded as Rina spoke. Then he screamed 'Yossi' into an intercom.

Decker said, 'Everything okay, Rina?'

'Hunky-dory. He's calling Yossi. Yossi's going to take us to the car lot.'

'Where's Yossi?'

'That's what we're trying to figure out.'

Decker said, 'By the way, do you know where I could get a gun?'

At the mention of the word *gun*, the rental-car man jerked his head up and stared at Decker with suspicious eyes. Rina quickly said some mollifying words. Decker caught one of them – *mishtarah*. Rina turned to him.

'Will you please be careful? Most people understand English – at least enough to know what a *gun* is.'

'I thought there was a peace process going on.'

'There's a process going on. Peace is a relative term. What is the significance of arming yourself? Are you anticipating something you haven't communicated to me?'

'Are you deliberately using obtuse words to obfuscate our receptionist?'

'Exactly.'

'Then we shall converse on the said subject later. What does *mishtarah* mean?'

'Police. Why?'

'Someone in LA has been going around impersonating a police officer,' Decker said. 'He calls himself Detective Mishtarah.'

'An Israeli,' Rina said.

'Gold,' Decker answered.

And Rina remembered why they were there. Two boys were missing and Shaul Gold was looking for them. At the moment, Peter didn't know if Gold was a redeemer or a murderer. She suddenly realized what it meant to Peter to be without his Beretta.

'I'll find you some armament.'

'Something so I don't feel so vulnerable.'

'Ah,' Rina said. 'It looks like Yossi has arrived.'

'Mazel tov,' Decker said. 'Let's get out of here.'

The car was a Subaru and Decker was the sardine. He drove, knees to the wheel, while Rina navigated. The night was moonless, the expressway poorly lit, and Decker had to strain his eyes to make sure he was in the correct lane. At least the roads were in good shape – better infrastructure than LA. The airport was a hop from the city of Tel Aviv.

'Which exit do I take?'

'I'm not sure. Take any of them and I'll ask directions. The hotel's on the main drag near the ocean – HaYarkon. We'll find it eventually.'

Decker complied, took the first exit into the city, and drove a few blocks only to find himself smack in the middle of a slum. Streetlights were few, garbage was plentiful, and the neighborhood obviously didn't believe in street signs.

He looked around. Old tenement houses were zigzagged by thin fire-escape staircases. The construction was cheap, stucco buildings with tiny windows. No longer exhausted, he realized his system had turned into its fight-or-flight mode.

'I don't like this.'

Rina said, 'Why don't you pull over and I'll ask directions from those guys over there?'

'Are you nuts?'

'What's the problem?'

'Do you know *where* we are?'

'No, Peter,' Rina said, testily. 'If I knew where I was, I'd get us to the hotel.' She rolled down the window and yelled out a *s'lichah* – an 'excuse me'. Punks began approaching the car. They wore tight jeans, open-necked shirts under leather jackets, and gold glimmered around their necks. Decker pressed metal to the floor of the car, flattening Rina against the back of the passenger seat as he peeled out.

'Are you crazy?' she screamed.

Decker drove a few blocks, then pulled the car over. 'Why in God's good green earth are you asking assholes for directions? You might as well put a sign around your neck, saying, "I'm a stupid tourist. Mug me."'

'What are you *talking* about?'

Decker looked at his wife. She was confused, making him confused by her lack of understanding. Up to this point, Decker had never thought of his wife as *that* naive. Now he realized how trusting she was and it scared him. He took a deep breath.

'Sweetheart, we're in the middle of a slum. And those boys whom you were about to ask for directions? They are what we call in the business scumbags—'

'Peter—'

'Honey, they'd sooner rape you than help you.'

'This isn't a slum. It's the heart of Tel Aviv.' Rina looked around 'Probably a working-class area. Those kids were just your average Israelis out for a good time—'

'I'll bet—'

'We're not in America, Peter. While I'd place money that the boys weren't rocket scientists, I'd also place money that they weren't rapists. Repeat after me: We're in a Levantine countr—'

'Rina, I know *scumbags* when I see them.'

'All right. If no one was looking, maybe they'd break into the car and steal the radio. They'd figure it's just a rental car anyway, right?'

'Rina!'

'I'm just trying to explain the mentality.'

'You don't have to tell me about people, all right?' He started the car. 'Doesn't the country believe in street signs?'

'Everything's done with landmarks. You go to the market, turn left until you reach the post office, turn right, go straight until you reach Dovid's cleaners—'

'I don't know what possessed me to think I could handle an investigation here,' Decker groused. 'Can't you tell me where I am?'

'Haven't the foggiest notion,' Rina said.

He drove a few blocks in darkness. A haze began to settle over the streets. Just what he needed to further confuse whatever meager sanity he had left. He spied another group of kids walking, but at least this one had two girls among three scumbags.

'Can I try them?' Rina said. 'They have girls.'

'Ever see the damage that female gang members have done?'

'We're *not* in America, Peter!'

'What if you're wrong? What if they try to rob us. I don't have my gun.'

'I'm not wrong,' Rina said, forcefully. 'Pull over, please.'

Decker pulled over. 'At least you said please.'

As soon as the car stopped, Rina opened the door and jumped out of the car, speed-walking her way to the pack. Decker bolted from the rental and caught up with her. He took her arm, but they both kept walking.

He whispered, 'We're going to have to have a serious talk.'

'When we're not sleep deprived,' Rina whispered back. She pulled away from Decker as she yelled out another *s'lichah* to the group. They stopped walking and Rina went over to them, showed them her map, and spoke. They answered back en masse, a few studying the map, one of them pointing one way, two pointing in another direction. Decker couldn't understand how any of them heard a damn thing because they were all talking at once. Finally, the whole group headed toward Peter.

Rina said, 'They said it would be easier if they just rode along with us.'

'There're five of them,' Decker said.

A boy with dark curly hair and a wispy mustache answered in broken English. 'The girls sit on us.'

Involuntarily, Decker smiled at his misuse of the language. Under his breath, he said, 'In your dreams, kiddo.' Out loud he said to Rina, 'What are they doing? Bumming a ride?'

'Yes, I believe that's exactly what they're doing.'

Decker rolled his eyes. Up close, the kids looked less fearsome – like kids. They must have been around fifteen, sixteen. He waved his hands forward. 'Come on.'

Excitedly, the kids piled into the backseat of the rented Subaru – boys sprawling their spindly, adolescent legs, girls giggling on their laps. Decker started the car. Three spoke at once, using their hands as well as words.

'You go straight,' Rina announced.

'For how long?'

Rina asked, then answered back. 'Just go straight.'

Decker threw up his hands and drove.

'Where you from?' asked a girl in English. She was pretty

299

– black hair, hazel eyes, and dimples. She had a cherubic face.

'Los Angeles,' Decker answered back.

'Ah, Disneyland!' she said, with admiration. 'I . . . was . . . in . . . Orlito . . .' She knitted her brow. 'Orlatto . . .'

'Orlando,' Decker filled in.

'*Cain!* Orlando!' The girl beamed at being understood. 'That is Disney . . . world.'

Decker said, 'I grew up near there.'

The girl nodded. 'You . . . livid in Orlando?'

Decker smiled. 'Yes. I lived near Orlando.'

'You go to Disneyworld?'

This time, Decker laughed. 'It wasn't around when I grew up.' He turned to his wife. 'Will you please translate this?'

'She likes speaking English to you.'

A boy shouted something out.

Rina said, 'Slow. You turn right at that gray building.'

Decker complied.

And so it went. The girl with the dimples practicing her English, the rest of the crew talking and shouting out directions at various intervals. Decker drove until he found himself looking out at a black expanse melding into a black horizon of nothingness. The Mediterranean Sea.

The boardwalk was teeming with people. The kids asked to be let out near a hot dog vendor, pointing them toward the Malon Melech HaYam – the King of the Sea Hotel – a couple of blocks away. They left, the girl saying thank you in English.

The car was silent for a moment. Then Decker said, 'Don't say it.'

'Say what?'

'I was wrong.' Decker shrugged. 'They were nice kids

just playing a little dress-up. I need some adjustment time, that's all.'

'Couple of hours and you'll be thinking like a native.'

He shook his head in wonderment. 'I can't believe we just picked up five teenagers and allowed them to ride with us in our car. If my daughter did that, I'd kill her. I also can't believe that the kids *willingly* came into the car without a drop of fear.' He looked at Rina. 'What *happened* to America?'

Rina smiled sadly. 'The Jews in Israel, for all that's written about the conflicts among them, are basically a homogeneous population. Just like everyone in Japan is basically Japanese. America is heterogeneous – many cultures, and lots of communication problems. But it also has the creativity and tolerance brought about by cultures residing side by side.'

'Israel has diverse cultures.'

'You mean the Arabs here? The Israelis and Arabs don't *mix*. That's why they're carving out their own state.' Rina sighed. 'Maybe they'll come to some kind of cold peace. But I'm not holding my breath.'

'Hope springs eternal.'

'I suppose,' Rina said. 'South Africa just crowned its first Black Miss South Africa. Ten years ago that would have been unheard of. I guess things can change ... at least superficially enough to satisfy political ambitions.'

Immediately, Decker thought about Kate Milligan. He wondered if he and Marge were right about her. If she had dared to love a black ... saw his plight. Maybe it had touched a rebellious spirit in her.

Milligan's face appeared to him with clarity. Young and beautiful, she was a brilliant attorney at the top of her career. She was a woman with a mission. Decker mused about the nature of her mission as he started the car and drove to the hotel.

In the daylight, the Tel Aviv apartments didn't look any less slummy and the neighborhood didn't look any less poor. The sun only highlighted the defects. Decker saw the years of wear on the buildings – the crumbling plaster, the two-tone patch-up jobs, the lines of drying laundry strung from window to window. Though the main roads of the city were smooth, many of the side lanes were dirt ruts. He clucked his tongue.

'What's wrong?' Rina asked.

'The way the news reports Israel . . . it makes it seem like it's this big fat cat of a country preying on its impoverished neighbors. I don't know . . . it looks so poor itself.'

'It certainly isn't a fat cat,' Rina said. 'But it's not poor. You're just thinking like an American. I'll bet almost every apartment here has a color TV and a VCR.'

'So do ghetto kids.'

She turned to him. 'Even though the area where the Yaloms live is solidly middle class by Israeli standards, don't expect too much.'

Decker said, 'I'm just wondering, where are the homes and the yards and the playsets?'

'City living means apartment living – like Manhattan. There's not enough room for anything else. There are parks . . . not Central Park, but little corner places. If you want real countryside, Israel has plenty of farms or *moshavs* – collective farms. You miss your horses, Peter. I'll find some for you.'

'Are you being sarcastic at ten in the morning?'

Rina smiled. 'I think of it as acculturating you.'

'You're making fun of me. Like I'm this big, dumb goy who doesn't know shit from shinola—'

'You're not dumb and you're not a goy—'

'I need you for this assignment, Rina. I'm the first one to say that. Can we have a cooperative, respectful working relationship?'

Rina took his hand. 'I'm sorry, Peter. I know you're dealing with something very serious.'

The car grew quiet. Decker said, 'I liked the breakfast buffet the hotel gave us this morning. You can eat enough to get by for the entire day.' He smiled. 'Even if you don't surreptitiously wrap rolls with tissues and hide them in your purse.'

Rina sighed. 'Now who's mocking?'

'Why do they *do* that?'

'*They?*'

'I mean the tourists—'

'You mean the *Jewish* tourists.'

'I've never seen anything like it,' Decker exclaimed. 'You know, Israel may not be fancy, but it isn't shtetl Poland. The country's not going to run out of food. Not to mention the fact that the nefarious roll stuffer could afford to lose a few pounds.'

'It just gets thrown out anyway.'

'It's uncouth.'

Rina smiled. 'It's déclassé, I agree, but what the heck. They're paying for the food, they might as well eat it.'

'Eating it is one thing. You can eat all you want on the premises. But filling your purse with fruit and rolls and pats of butter—'

Rina began to laugh. 'We only saw one lady who did that.'

FAYE KELLERMAN

'Then she put in a carton of yogurt . . .' Decker smiled. 'That was just out of line.'

They both started laughing. Decker finally said, 'Thanks for coming.'

'It's my pleasure. I know you're going to be working the whole time, but I do hope you get a little chance to at least . . . soak up some atmosphere.'

Atmosphere, he thought. Then he said, 'It's weird. I feel like I'm in a foreign country. But I don't feel I'm in a *religious* foreign country. Nothing Jewish except the Hebrew.'

Rina said, 'If you get a chance to see the Bursa, you'll realize it's a Jewish country. From what I hear, it's replete with Chasidic Jews.'

'There were lots of Chasidic Jews in the LA diamond mart, too.' He bit his mustache. 'Maybe I'm not explaining myself right. This just doesn't feel that much different from a working-class area in LA.'

'Wait until you get to Jerusalem. Then tell me if you feel the same way.'

Decker drove a few more blocks, following Rina's directions. The area seemed to have turned nicer. The apartment buildings weren't necessarily newer, but they seemed more solidly built. They were fashioned from ocher-colored limestone, held bigger windows, and had patios landscaped with potted trees and flowers. The main road was wide and divided, and had visible street signs. Directions to various cities were posted at the main intersections.

'Where are we now?'

'Ramat Aviv.'

'It's a wealthier area.'

'You can tell.'

304

'I'm learning. Are we near the Yaloms' address?'

'Not too far.'

They passed a complex of big buildings floating in seas of emerald green lawn. Across from the buildings was a series of parking lots.

'University?' Decker asked.

'Museums.'

'Ahhhh. Are the museums good?'

'The Museum of the Diaspora is outstanding.'

'Is that where the Dead Sea Scrolls are?'

'No, that's in Jerusalem. At the Shrine of the Book. You have an interest in biblical archaeology?'

'Just a curiosity. Too bad I won't see any of it.'

Rina looked at him. He wasn't being flip, he was disappointed. She took his hand and kissed it. 'Next time. Under better circumstances.'

Decker heard himself answer with an amen.

26

A house of sadness. Black cloth had been draped over the mirrors, the paintings, and the TV. The cushions from the sofa had been removed, exposing the couch's gauzy underlining. Decker knew that with the cushions gone, the sofa was permitted to be used as seating for the Jewish mourners.

But Moshe Yalom still opted for the floor. He was a thin man, perhaps in his early seventies, clean-shaven with curly, gray hair atop a long saggy face. A man beaten by life, but not defeated by it. There was still obstinacy in his milky blue eyes. His wife, Tziril, seemed younger. Proportionately, she was heavier than her husband, more meat on the bones, but her doughy flesh was pale. She wore a loose smock and her hair was covered by a scarf.

Rina had made the appointment with Tziril. She had commented that Mrs Yalom had sounded amazed by the request, as if it had never occurred to her that America – a foreign country ten thousand miles away – was actually *pursuing* an investigation of her son's murder.

Decker studied the woman as she spoke to Rina. Rina reported that she and Peter should sit in the chairs, they weren't in mourning. Tziril talked some more. Rina translated: They had started the process of *shiva* – the

307

seven days of intense mourning – earlier than Jewish law required. Technically, *shiva* should take place only after burial. But both Tziril and her husband had felt it was ridiculous to hold off. Who knew when their son would be brought home?

Tziril spoke once more, then disappeared inside a cubby off the living room. Her husband stood up slowly and paddled down a long hallway.

'Where's everybody going?' Decker whispered.

'I don't know where Mr Yalom's going,' Rina said. 'Mrs Yalom went to get us some tea. She asked and I didn't want to refuse her hospitality. It seemed important to her.'

'Absolutely.' He looked around the living room. 'If it helps her relax . . .'

The apartment was small, the living room paced off around ten by thirteen. But it seemed larger because it had double glass doors that led to a generous wraparound porch. It was screened and held all-weather furniture – a dining-room table and chairs, an outdoor sofa and coffee table, a rocker in the corner. There were two potted citrus trees that were starting to bloom, the flowers emitting a lemony smell. The porch doors were open and allowed a fair amount of circulation. Otherwise, a room this compact would get stuffy in no time.

Decker looked down. The floors were made out of some kind of crushed rock tile, like nothing he'd seen in America. Rina sat in one of the many folding chairs that had been crammed into the room. Decker had counted twenty of them. He sat beside his wife.

'Did they hold a meeting here or something?'

'The chairs are for the morning and evening *minyans*,' Rina explained. 'The father isn't allowed to leave the house. So the men come to him and say services here. So he can say *kaddish* . . . for his son.' She looked down, her eyes moist. 'This isn't the natural order of things.'

'No, it's not.'

Slowly, Mr Yalom paddled back into the living room and lowered himself onto a pillow resting on the floor. The old man hadn't paid them much attention. Decker felt that if it had been up to the father, they wouldn't have been granted an interview.

Tziril came back, holding a tray filled with four tea glasses resting in sterling cup holders. She went through the ritual pouring, setting down a glass on the floor for her husband. A few minutes of sipping and it seemed to Decker they were as comfortable as they were going to get. He took out his notepad. Tziril's eyes went to the pad, then to Decker's face.

She said in accented English, 'What do you want to know?'

'You speak English,' Decker said.

Tziril nodded. 'In gymnasium, we learn English almost as soon as we learn German. When we came to Israel . . . it was then Palestine . . . I say to my uncle, the British are in control, why cannot they speak English over here? But I learned Hebrew.'

'You speak well,' Decker said.

'You are kind,' Tziril answered. 'In Europe, you must learn other languages because countries are so close.' She sat back in her chair. 'Your wife . . . speaked . . . spoke . . to me in Hebrew, so I answer her in Hebrew. But I remember my English a little.'

'Tell me if you have problems understanding my questions.'

Tziril nodded.

'And tell your husband he can talk, too.'

Moshe looked up and spoke in Hebrew. Decker glanced at Rina and waited.

'He said he has nothing to offer, but *you* have a lot of explaining to do.'

The old man spoke again. Tziril shushed him, but Rina translated anyway.

'He wants to know what's holding up the body?'

'Don't pay him attention,' Tziril said.

'No!' the old man replied. 'You *pay* me attention!'

Decker said, 'Tell him I'm sorry. We're moving as quickly as we can but America has a terrible bureaucracy.'

Rina translated. The old man responded.

'He said it couldn't possibly be as bad as Israel's and even Israel has the decency to release a body for burial.'

Decker said, 'Tell him I hope it's soon.'

Moshe Yalom snorted and spoke under his breath. Rina couldn't make out his words. It didn't matter. Decker caught the essence by the tone of voice.

He said, 'Mrs Yalom, I wish I spoke Hebrew. Then I could tell you in your language – your *lashon* – how sorry I am.'

Tziril's eyes met his. She didn't speak, she didn't cry. Then she said, 'Thank you for . . .' She shook her head and muttered in Hebrew. 'I don't know the word in English.'

'Sympathies,' Rina translated.

'Thank you for sympathies,' Tziril completed her sentence.

'They are heartfelt.' Decker put his hand to his chest. '*Lev.*'

'I understand,' Tziril said.

'I am in charge of your son's investigation, Mrs Yalom,'

310

Decker said. 'I have reason to believe...' He stopped himself. Stop sounding like TV and get to the point. 'Your grandsons are missing. Do you know where they are?'

Tziril didn't answer.

'Do you understand my question?'

'Yes, I understand.'

'I need to find them, Mrs Yalom,' Decker said. 'I think they could be in danger.'

Tziril looked up, then down. 'I don't know where they are. *Emes*, I don't know.'

Decker studied her face. 'But they were here, weren't they?'

Again, the woman's eyes scanned the room until they glided across her husband's face. He moved his brows almost imperceptibly.

Decker said, 'I came a long way, Mrs Yalom, just to warn ... to help the boys.'

'They are ...'

Decker waited on the edge of his folding chair. But Tziril was silent. He said, 'I *really, really* do think that something bad could happen to them. I *need* to find them. Do you understand what I'm saying?'

'They are ... here ... somewhere ... in Israel. But I don't know where.'

Moshe Yalom snorted again. As much as Decker wanted to explain that he was on their side, he didn't have time. To Tziril he said, 'Can you take a guess and tell me where they *might* be?'

Tziril looked confused. Rina translated.

'I don't have guess,' Tziril said.

Decker bit back frustration. 'But they *were* here. In this house.'

'They were never here,' Tziril insisted.

The old man said, 'No, boys not here. Why you say boys dangerous here in Israel? Boys dangerous in *America*. Everytink dangerous in America.' He picked up his glass of tea and muttered. Decker made out the words Sodom and Gomorrah.

Tziril said, 'I don't know where are my grandsons.'

'Then how do you know they're in Israel?' Decker pressed.

Tziril held her throat. Decker remembered Orit making the same gesture. She blurted out, 'They called me. To tell me . . .' Tears began to pour down her cheeks. She started speaking Hebrew through choked sobs. Rina listened, nodding at intervals.

Decker waited, restrained himself from tapping his pencil against his pad. Finally, Rina spoke. 'They called the house a couple of days after the . . . the murder.'

Decker started writing. 'Go on.'

'They said they were very frightened. They said they had to go into hiding, that people were after them.'

'Which people?' Decker asked.

'They didn't say,' Tziril responded. 'I asked but they don't tell me.'

Rina went on. 'They told Mrs Yalom that policemen might come and ask them – the grandparents – questions. Lots and lots of questions.'

Decker wrote, then looked up. 'Ask her . . . as diplomatically as possible . . . whether . . .' He leaned back in his chair and ran his hand over his face. 'I'm attempting to inquire as to *why* the boys were perturbed.'

'You want to know, did they do it or didn't they?' Rina said.

'Exactly. It's possible she's going to mistake my professional intentions for something nefarious and accusatory.'

'I'm sorry, I don't understand,' Tziril said.

Decker paused. Honesty is the best policy ... sometimes. He turned to Tziril. 'I'm sorry, but I have to ask you unpleasant questions.'

'*Ani mayveenah* – I understand. What?'

'Did they say *why* they were scared? Why the police might come and ask you two questions?'

Tziril said, 'You be scared, too, if your parents were killed.'

'Yes, I'd be scared,' Decker said. 'Especially if I killed them.'

Tziril's mouth dropped open.

'I'm sorry, but I need to ask—'

'You are a terrible, terrible man!' The old woman stood up from the uncushioned couch and wagged her finger, drool escaping from the corner of her mouth. 'You should be shamed. You ... you ...'

Rina spoke quickly in Hebrew. Whatever she said seemed to have a palliative effect. Tziril, though fuming, nodded briskly. After a minute of silence, she turned to Decker. 'I am sorry.'

'It's all right. I underst—'

'You're not terrible man. But your job makes you ask terrible questions.'

Decker agreed with her.

Tziril looked him in the eye. 'They were scared because someone killed their parents. They were scared for theirselfs.'

'They said specifically that someone else killed their parents?'

Tziril spoke in Hebrew. Rina said, 'She said they sounded too frightened to make much sense.'

Tziril spoke again.

313

'She – Mrs Yalom – asked the boys where they were. They wouldn't say.'

'Which one did she talk to?' Decker asked.

'Both,' Tziril answered. 'They talk to me for five minutes maybe. They told me they are alive and in Israel. I tried to find out where are they. But they spoke too fast. They said they will call me later. But they don't . . . didn't.' The tears came back. 'I'm very frightened. Maybe something happened to them.'

Decker said, 'Has anyone else been here? Anyone else asked you questions about your grandsons?'

'No. Just you. I only said I would talk to you because Oritie said you were working hard. She said I need to answer your questions. If she didn't tell me, I would not talk to you. My grandsons were very frightened. I don't know who I trust.'

'You're very smart,' Decker said. 'So you haven't talked to anyone?'

'Just you.'

'And the boys didn't say where they were?'

Tziril shook her head. 'I wish I just knew they were live. If I *knew*, I wouldn't . . .' She bit her knuckle and wiped away tears.

Decker said, 'We're on the same side, Mrs Yalom. We want the same things.'

Again, she held her hand to her throat.

Decker said, 'So the boys spoke to you for only a few minutes. They told you that someone was after them. They told you they came to Israel to hide.'

Tziril nodded.

'But you don't know where they would go to hide.'

Again, Tziril nodded. Mr Yalom finally spoke up. He let go with rapid Hebrew to his wife in a rough tone of voice.

314

She waved him off. The old man got disgusted and walked off. Decker waited for Rina to translate, but it was Tziril who spoke.

'He's very mad that I talk to you. He thinks maybe you want to kill the boys.'

'Didn't your daughter explain me to him?'

'He says, how do we know you are the man that Orit said is all right?'

'Would you like me to speak to your daughter right now? I'll be happy to pay for the call.'

'It's night in America. Anyway, I trust you. How much big, very tall policeman with red hair can they be?'

Decker smiled. He was about to speak directly to Tziril, then changed his mind and spoke to Rina. 'Tell her as clearly and as emphatically as you can that I am *legitimate*. I will show her all my identification if she wants it and give her all the proper phone numbers. But frankly, Rina, I'm very concerned that *other* people may come and try to talk to her.'

'Gold specifically?'

'Exactly.'

'I'm sure she knows Gold. If he comes around here asking questions, she's not going to view him as a threat. Are you going to bring him up?'

'I'm going to have to bring him up.'

Tziril said, 'I'm sorry. You speak too fast.'

Rina translated Peter's words, Tziril nodding very seriously. Rina said, 'Do you want me to mention Gold to her?'

Decker said, 'Mrs Yalom, what do you know about your son's business partner?'

'Shaul?' Tziril scratched her arm. 'Shaul called me right

after ... to send sympathies. We speak ... spoke ... for a long time. He was very hysterical. He loved Arik—'

She stopped herself.

'That isn't the truth. No, he didn't love Arik. He loved *Dalia*. He was an old, old friend of Dalia.'

'They grew up in the same neighborhood,' Decker said.

'Yes. They were good friends even though Shaul is maybe fifteen years older than Dalia. It was Dalia that made Arik give a job to Shaul. When they go ... went to America, Shaul went with them.'

'They weren't boyfriend and girlfriend before Arik met Dalia?'

'I think no. Dalia was young when she married Arik, maybe nineteen. Dalia's father is very proper. I don't think he'd allow Dalia to date a man so much older.'

Decker didn't talk for a moment. Shaul Gold was certainly no stud but there was something manly about him. Maybe he'd been forbidden fruit to Dalia for years.

Then the little girl grew up.

That could certainly explain the Lexus parked outside the Yalom house. Were these murders brought about by a lovers' triangle?

He pondered the situation:

Could be Arik shot his wife, Gold shot Arik. Then Gold dragged them both up to the mountains to bury them.

Could be Arik and Dalia decided to reconcile, Gold getting the shaft yet another time. Gold couldn't take the rejection and shot them both.

Dalia finally got up the gumption to leave Arik. An argument ensued. Arik shot his wife. Gold burst in and shot Arik.

Or: Argument ensued. Arik shot his wife, then felt remorse and killed himself. Gold burst in but too late.

Just *what ifs*.

But then why would the boys need to escape from America if the murders were the result of a messy real-life soap opera. Decker noticed he'd been silent for a long time. 'So you know Shaul Gold very well?'

'Not well,' Tziril said. 'But I know him.'

'If he comes here, *don't tell him anything*!' Decker turned to Rina. 'Can you translate that? I want to make sure she understands that completely.'

'I understand. Why you don't want me talking to Shaul?'

To Rina, Decker said, 'Will you explain to her about Gold impersonating a police officer, falsifying his identity to ask questions. Tell her he is interfering with my investigation and that could endanger her grandsons.'

Rina translated as best she could. Tziril looked surprised and worried. 'That is . . . not the Shaul I know. He is not unhonest like that. He is always honest. Even Arik say he is honest.' She appeared thoughtful. 'Arik and Shaul never liked each other. I think Shaul was . . .'

'Jealous?' Decker tried.

'Yes, he was jealous.'

'But you just told me you didn't think they were boyfriend and girlfriend.'

'That doesn't mean that Shaul didn't have eyes. And Arik was jealous, too. Dalia married Arik. But she still made Arik take Shaul into the business.'

'Why did Arik do it?'

'He loved Dalia . . . and it was her father's business. Whatever Dalia wants . . .' She shook her head. 'Shaul knew *nothing* about diamonds.'

'And Arik?'

'Arik was born in the business. Our last name means diamonds. My husband's family are in business for many, many years. Many *dorot*.'

'Generations,' Rina said.

'Yes, generations. We are in the diamond business for generations. Shaul?' She wiped her empty hands together in an exaggerated motion. 'Nothing.'

'But Arik took Shaul into your family business?'

'Into her father's business, yes. Until he made enough to make his own business. Moshe, my husband, was a good cutter. But Arik ... he is the best. Dalia's father was very...' She waved her hands, trying to think of the word.

'Impressed,' Decker guessed.

'*Oy vay*, was he impressed! He had never see a cutter as good as Arik. He make *sure* that Arik and Dalia meet.'

'Dalia's father was a diamond cutter, too?'

'No, *dealer*. Joseph Menkovitz is still very *big* dealer here. He's very rich. Arik did not like Dalia when he first met her. He said she was very spoiled. I say the girl is young. Give her time. And he did and he fell in love.'

Tziril grew thoughtful.

'Still, it was not easy for my son to please a rich girl. Dalia grew up in Rahavia . . . in a very big house. *Two* stories with a *garden*. Dalia likes big houses. You see their house in America?'

Decker nodded.

'Like a castle. It is only missing the water that goes around it.'

'The moat,' Decker said.

'Yes, the moat,' Tziril agreed. 'They have a castle for two kids.' She waved a hand into the air. 'But Dalia wanted a big house, so she gets it. It was her father's doing. The only child, the father never learns to say no. Her father is quite old now . . . in his late eighties. But he is still strong. He's at the Bursa every single day. He drove himself until he turned eighty. Now someone drives him. Every day he is in his office.'

'Even now when he's sitting *shiva*?'

Tziril was quiet for a moment. 'I don't think he will sit *shiva*. Joseph isn't a religious man. Anat is sitting *shiva*. Yesterday, I talked to Anat. Every day, we talk. Every day, we cry. Every day, we wait for our children.'

She burst into tears. Rina went over and put her arm around the old woman. Tziril leaned her head into Rina's shoulder and wept for a long time.

'The old man has no heart,' Tziril stated angrily. 'Only work, work, work.'

'Maybe that's how he copes with the pain,' Rina suggested.

'Maybe,' Tziril said in a cracked voice. 'Ah, that's just men!'

It was an indictment, Decker felt, she had uttered many times in the past. 'So he's probably at the Bursa right now?'

'Yes, probably.'

'That's close to here?'

'If you have a car.'

'I have a car. Can you have your husband call him up? I'd like to visit him there—'

'Only members are invited into Bursa.'

'There's no way to get me temporary privileges?'

Tziril looked puzzled. Rina translated.

The old woman said, 'I don't know much about Bursa. My husband would know more.'

'I'd really like to talk to Mr Menkovitz, now.'

'Why? You think my grandsons are with him?'

Decker stared at her. 'Are they?'

Tziril put her hand to her chest. 'I don't think so. Anat told me . . .'

She let her words hang in the air.

'Anat told you what? That the boys might stay with her?'

'No. But maybe she got a quick phone call, too. The boys are not with her. That I know. Because she is worried about them, too.'

Decker rubbed his eyes. The jet lag was doing funny things to his head. 'Still, I'd like to meet Mr Menkovitz. He might have some things to tell me about Shaul Gold. After all, you did say that Dalia and Shaul were old friends. Can you ask your husband to arrange something?'

'Maybe he could. But he won't. He's a mule.'

'Tell him his grandsons' *lives* may depend on it.' He turned to Rina. 'Can you please translate the gravity of that statement?'

'I understand you, Mr Decker.' Wearily, Tziril stood. '*Rega.*' She paddled down the hall.

'What did she say?'

'She said wait.'

Tziril returned a minute later. 'Moshe said only relatives can come into the Bursa—'

'So say I'm a relative—'

'*Rega, rega . . .*' Tziril said. 'Moshe will do anything that will help the boys. He will take you there.'

'Today?'

'Yes. He's getting dressed. It will take a few minutes.'

Decker gave his hands a clap. 'Thank you.'

'Mr Decker, there are rules. You must say you are his son-in-law.'

'That's not a problem.'

'And you must not talk to anyone on the floor. *No one!* Nothing until he gets you alone in Joseph's office.'

'That's not a problem, either.'

'You must bring your passport.'

'I have it with me.' He patted his jacket.

'And your wife must come, too.'

Decker paused. 'That's fine. He needs her to translate and so do I.'

'This is true but not the reason he wants her. My husband says he likes her much better than he likes you.'

27

Rina drove, Yalom sat in the front passenger's seat, allowing Decker to take surreptitious notes in the back. Not that there was anything worth recording. No conversation to speak of. Finally, Yalom mumbled something to Rina.

She said, 'He wants to know how his daughter, Orit, is doing.'

'Tell him she seems to be in good health.'

The old man nodded and spoke to Rina.

'Did you meet his grandchildren?'

'Just his granddaughter, Sharona,' Decker said. 'She seemed very nice. Very bright. I liked her a lot.'

Mr Yalom grunted out, 'Pretty, no?'

'Beautiful,' Decker said. '*Yef . . . yaffa meod*.' He turned to Rina. 'Did I get that right?'

'Perfect.'

The car returned to its silent state. A moment later, Yalom indicated something by a point of the finger. Rina got off the *ayalon* on the Rekevet exit. The old man directed her into a series of turns that put them on a gravel and dirt pay lot. No parking spaces had been marked but the cars, mostly subcompacts, that occupied the lot were spaced in an orderly fashion. The parking area bordered a busy tree-lined boulevard. Across the roadway stood three

ultra-modern granite and glass skyscrapers jutting out from
what looked like a strip mall. Decker looked out the rear
window. Behind the lot was a nest of square patched-up
apartment houses, laundry hanging from the windows. No
sense of a neighborhood. Nothing matched – Tijuana
meets Century City.

Rina shut off the motor and they got out of the car. The
boulevard was more of a highway with cars racing at high
speeds in both directions. The nearest intersection with a
traffic light was a blip in the distance. Yalom rooted along a
wire fence that acted as a barrier between the lot and the
boulevard until he found a hole. He squeezed through it,
then stood in the street and watched cars speed by.

'We're going to cut across?' Decker asked Rina.

Rina said, 'I'm just following the leader.'

Traffic finally cleared on one side. The old man dashed
across with surprising speed. Decker and Rina followed
until the trio took temporary refuge on the boulevard's
divider – a concrete island in a sea of blurred metal and
smoky exhaust.

Decker said, 'You know, if this was America, we'd all get
a ticket.'

Rina said, 'I know. LA's really big on jaywalking.'

'That's because people get killed jaywalking.' A truck
shot past, blowing wind through Decker's hair and almost
knocking Rina off her feet. He said, 'This is crazy.'

The old man shouted a 'go' in English. All three of them
tore across.

'See?' Rina said. 'We made it.'

Decker ran his fingers through his hair and didn't
answer. Yalom motioned them forward, his gait slowing to
that of an old man. He led them up a series of museum-
sized granite steps while speaking to Rina. She translated.

'There are three major buildings in the diamond center. The Maccabee is where the Bursa is. It's also where Joseph Menkovitz keeps his private office.' She paused and listened to Yalom's words. 'Even though the bigger dealers have offices now, they still do lots of trading in the Bursa itself. It makes excitement.'

'Makes excitement?' Decker asked.

Rina shrugged. The old man spoke and Rina clarified. 'The Bursa is for everyone. Those that have private offices, those that don't. If you're a member of the Bursa, even if you don't have an office, you can rent a locker and trade on the floor with everyone else. When you trade in the Bursa, it makes excitement.' She paused. 'I think he means the Bursa generates excitement because it's out in the open. I guess we'll understand when we see it.'

The lobby to the Maccabee building was compartmentalized – trisected and encased in thick glass. Yalom went into the right-hand section, through steel revolving doors into a small sally port filled with people. Decker's first impression: He was in line to the betting cage at the track. The windows up front were marked BUYERS/TENANTS. Yalom stood in the back of an undisciplined squiggle of human flesh; Decker and Rina fell in behind him.

Decker looked around. To the right was another set of steel revolving doors that led to a main lobby of the building. Security was visible at every turn of the head – in the sally port, in the lobbies, behind the windows. He must have spotted dozens of men and women dressed in gray shirts, blue ties, and dark blue pants.

The line inched forward, people nudging Decker in the back. In his experience, crowds brought tension. Strangely, no one seemed irritated. Here was humanity in all shapes,

325

sizes, and religious inclinations stuffed into a small area and no one was grousing.

They finally made it to the front. Four security guards manned the window behind bullet-proof glass. Three of the watchdogs were seated; one male was standing behind the others, either overseeing them or kibitzing. Yalom got up to the window and spoke his case, the guard nodding and looking Decker and Rina over as the old man explained what he wanted.

'Passports, please,' she said.

Decker took them out of his jacket, then reluctantly forfeited them to the guard. She opened them, but her eyes weren't on the ID. Instead, she seemed to be listening to the goings-on at the line next to hers. Then she butted into the conversation, arguing with her colleague who was dealing with a woman and a small child.

'What's going on?' Decker asked Rina. 'What's she doing?'

Rina smiled wearily. 'She's getting distracted is what she's doing. There seems to be a *sh'aylah* about kids under twelve needing a passport.'

'A *sh'aylah*?'

'A question.'

'Oh. A *shylah*!' Decker said, pronouncing it as if he were in the yeshiva.

Rina smiled. 'Yes, a *shylah*.'

Finally, the guard deigned to look at the passports placed in her hands. She studied them, then punched something into a computer. Mr Yalom spoke to Rina.

She said, 'They're issuing us badges and ID cards.'

A minute later, Yalom handed them two plastic cards and they were allowed to enter the main lobby. A thick fog of people scurried across white and gray marble floors. To the left was a bank of lockers; straight ahead were the elevators. They squeezed into the first car and rode up one floor. To Decker's surprise, everyone got out. Yalom took them into a second elevator and pushed the fifteenth-floor button.

Decker said to Rina, 'What was that all about?'

Yalom seemed to understand the question. He talked to Rina in Hebrew.

Rina said, 'The first elevator goes only to the Bursa. You take these elevators to get to the offices.'

'For peoples,' Yalom said. 'Too much peoples.'

Decker didn't understand but didn't press it. Maybe it was some security thing. The car rode up to the fifteenth floor and they got out. It was quiet and looked similar to Yalom's office in Los Angeles. But unlike the LA diamond center, every door had a *mezuzah* on it.

The *mezuzah*. The symbol of a Jewish establishment. On every single door. Yes, Decker finally realized they were in a *Jewish* country. It made him feel simultaneously strange and at home. Yalom pressed a button to the office and they were buzzed into an anteroom.

The secretary behind the glass partition reminded Decker of Yochie. She had jet-black hair and wore lots of make-up and jewelry. She spoke to Yalom; the old man turned around.

'Yossie's downstairs in the Bursa,' Yalom reported in English. 'He likes make old man go up and down, de *mamzer*.'

Decker told Rina she didn't have to translate.

Taking up almost the entire floor, the Bursa was an open area framed by a northern wall of glass. It held strip after strip of black picnic-sized tables, the surfaces covered with hundreds of squares of calendar paper set into black leather blotters. The tables also were crowned with dozens of scales, loupes, and pincers. Chairs were set on both sides of the tables. The place was crowded, but there was plenty of elbow room to walk down the aisles. Opposite the glass wall was a series of teller booths, some marked OFFICIAL WEIGHING STATION. Above the booths seemed to be a viewing area – maybe an upstairs lounge – framed in smoked glass. A nice place to have a drink or watch TV and still be able to see the action below.

Hanging from the ceiling were television monitors that broadcast rows of numbers. Yalom saw Decker staring at the screens.

Rina translated his words. 'Those are pager numbers. Someone needs you, your number goes up on the monitor.'

She took her eyes off the monitor and studied the vast open space. So many people – sitting, standing, milling around, going from table to table as if mingling at a cocktail party. There was a definite camaraderie. The smiles, the greetings, the pleasant conversation. And of course, the sense that there was business to be done. At any given time, there must have been a hundred jewelers holding loupes to stones.

And what stones they were! *Diamonds!* Thousands of them! Their worth just too staggering to contemplate. Piles spilling carelessly onto blotters, being freely passed from one hand to another. How easy it would be to palm a stone. And no one did. What a sense of trust!

Rina suddenly laughed inwardly at her naïveté.

It wasn't trust that prevented theft, it was all the security. Lots and lots of security – unobtrusive, but a constant presence. She caught Peter's eye. 'It's something else, isn't it? Kind of like a stock exchange only without the suits and ties.'

Decker nodded. It was a good observation. There was little diversity in the population. Most were men and they were all dressed casually – dark pants, white shirt, no tie. Except for the occasional sleek-garbed woman, everyone looked the same. Even the religious seemed to blend in once they took off their long black coats.

His eyes went to the tables. Dozens of men sitting across from one another, opening briefcases and photographer's bags filled with folded blue tissue paper. The valises were attached to metal chains, the chains were anchored around the vendors' waists. The noise level was surprisingly civil. It was easy to hear conversation. Too bad Decker couldn't understand any of it. But he was good at reading body language. He could tell at a glance who was making a deal, who was not.

Rina was wide-eyed. The old man looked at her face, smiled, then whispered something into her ear.

'What?' Decker said.

Rina moved in close. 'He said there's enough wealth in this room to buy all of Israel.'

Decker inched closer to the action, caught prisms of sunlight bouncing off the tabletops. Stones strewn over the blotters of white calendar paper. A young man opened up a shoe sized box stuffed with the blue tissue paper. He unwrapped one of the pieces of paper. A heart-shaped gem winked flirtatiously at Decker.

Yalom caught them staring and said, 'You want see close? Come.' He walked over to a vendor and tapped him on the shoulder. The man looked up, then placed something in Yalom's hand. The old man showed it to Decker. It was a raw stone and had an odd shape – two triangles fused at the base. It also looked like bottle glass.

The old man hefted the diamond and spoke in English. 'Maybe three and half carat. They make two.' He made a slicing motion with his empty hand and spoke in Hebrew to Rina, showing her the stone as he talked.

Rina said, 'The cutter will cleave the diamond at the base where the two triangles meet. That way he'll have two nearly identical gems which will be set for earrings.'

'Tell him it looks like glass. That I'd pass it up without a second glance.'

Yalom nodded to Decker and smiled.

Rina said, 'I think he understood you.'

The old man talked to Rina. 'He says usually the buyers sit on one side of the table, the sellers opposite them. The buyers, even if they have offices, often come down here to see the action. If it's real busy, the buyers will take their "want" lists of what they need to the floor, sit down at a table, and place the list in front of them. The sellers walk down the aisles and look over the lists. If there's a match, it's a *mazel und b'racha* – a luck and a blessing. That means they cut a deal.'

The old man continued to talk.

Rina translated, 'If it's not that busy or if the buyers are occupied with other business, they'll post their lists on the front doors of their offices. The sellers also go floor to floor and read the lists. Anything to strike a deal.'

Yalom cased the room, then spoke again.

Rina said, 'He's says Josef Menkovitz usually sits on the other side of the room. Very far away. He likes people to come to him.'

'Let's go,' Decker said.

Yalom led them through the crowd, Decker's eyes scanning the area as he walked. People all around, the men blending together in a black-and-white tableau. It was the few women who stood out. They dressed sharply in gross contrast to the men. Bold jackets accented with colorful scarves, miniskirts showing lots of good-looking leg, jewelry dangling from ears and from around necks.

The old man pointed to the far corner. The spot had attracted a considerable crowd, lots of white shirts bending over the table. Yalom said, 'Yosef's there.'

A shock of color suddenly drifted away from the sea of white cotton.

It hit him as hard as a sock in the jaw.

Speak to my secretary and I'll get back to you.

So much for the big case that was keeping Milligan in Los Angeles. Decker took a dozen steps backward, pulling Rina with him. Yalom was still walking toward the crowd when he realized he'd lost his companions. He turned around and looked over his shoulder. Decker motioned him back, then pressed them all against the wall.

'What is it?' Rina asked.

'Ask him who that woman is,' Decker said.

'Which woman?'

'The one in the bright blue dress with curly copper-color hair and the big handbag.'

The old man understood. 'Kate Milligan.' He spread his arms wide out. '*Macher* . . . shot big.'

'He means big shot,' Rina answered.

Milligan took a notebook out of her purse and briskly flipped through the pages. Decker said, 'Ask him if he sees her at the Bursa a lot.'

Rina did, then translated Yalom's answer. 'He said it's unusual. But everyone knows who she is because she's a *macher* – a big shot – with VerHauten. You know about VerHauten?'

'Yes, I know about VerHauten. Ask him why he thinks she'd be here talking to Yosef Menkovitz?'

Rina asked the question, then translated Yalom's answer as best she could. 'She wants to see how many stones come from VerHauten . . . I don't know exactly what he means.'

'I think I do,' Decker said. 'Ask him if stones from sources other than VerHauten's pipes have been showing up in the Bursa?'

Rina stared at him. 'Repeat that again, slowly.'

Decker did and Rina translated. It took a few moments, Decker's eyes fixed upon Milligan. She was still thumbing through her notebook. Then she checked her watch.

Yalom's answer deepened Rina's frown. 'I don't know if I'm getting this right. He said something like . . . the stones come from all over. Most come from VerHauten. But some dealers go to Russia and buy stones there.'

The old man continued to talk. Rina knitted her brow as she listened.

She said, 'There are also stones that . . . go around. I think he means float around. People don't ask questions about them.'

Yalom continued talking.

Rina said, 'People are afraid of Milligan. The dealers must buy a certain amount of stones from VerHauten. If it gets back that they are buying diamonds from other places, she can make trouble.'

Decker said, 'Ask him if it's rare to see her on the floor.'

Rina asked the question, then listened to Yalom's answer. 'Yes, it's rare to see her on the floor. She mostly goes to offices or to the lounge upstairs where it's quieter and more private. VerHauten likes privacy.'

'So why is she on the floor?'

The old man shrugged a response.

Milligan moved back into the sea of white shirts.

Yalom talked. Rina said, 'Milligan has dealt with Menkovitz in the past. He's big and VerHauten knows all the big dealers.'

'Does he know Milligan no longer works for VerHauten?'

Rina translated. The old man's eyes grew wide. Decker said, 'Guess he didn't.'

Again, Milligan withdrew from the crowd. She snapped her book shut and walked crisply down the Bursa, all eyes watching the click of her heels.

Decker lurched forward, then pulled back.

Rina said, 'You want to follow her, Peter?'

'I can't. She's met me before and I'm too conspicuous in this country to tail her without her noticing me.'

'Then I'll do—'

'Forget it.'

Rina fished the car keys out of her purse. 'I've got three kids at home, including a baby. I promise I won't do anything dumb. I'll call you later at Mr Yalom's house.'

With that, she jogged to catch up to Milligan. Decker started forward, then bit his lip and let her go.

There was no point in trying to change Rina's mind. She wouldn't listen and it would just create an argument. She'd seen him on stakeouts. Hopefully, she'd picked up a couple of salient tips. And she looked innocuous enough, clad in a simple blue dress and flats, her hair braided and tucked under a blue tam. She looked about as threatening as a bunny rabbit.

Stomach in a knot, Decker took a deep breath and let it out slowly. Why was he so interested in Kate Milligan?

What evidence did he have that she was a player in this case? Then again, what was she *doing* here when she was supposed to be working on a case in Los Angeles? She had told him *specifically* that she'd be in town. Obviously, she had had a change of plans. It could happen.

Decker rubbed his eyes.

The boys were missing and so was Gold; then Milligan popped up from nowhere. And now Rina was on the loose. He would have never involved her if it weren't for the Yalom kids. Goddamn boys. They'd sucked him into it. He cared about the kids just like Rina cared about Honey's kids.

Why was he so concerned?

He knew Rina was at home in the country. In fact, she knew Israel better than either Milligan or he did. She knew what was dangerous and how to avoid it. And Decker did want to know what the woman was up to. Besides, how much possible harm could come from one woman following another?

Don't answer that question, Deck.

Decker continued to rationalize. Rina had told him she wouldn't do anything dumb. She had three kids at home. He knew what Hannah and the boys meant to his wife. He tossed negative thoughts out of his head and decided to believe her promise.

28

The woman had clout. Rina saw her being led by security to the front of the line. And while procedure wasn't suspended, it did seem abbreviated. Milligan left the building in record time while Rina cooled her heels in a line of testy working stiffs. At that point, she had two choices – give up the chase or try her luck at the front with a sob story.

Lucky for her, the Israelis had hearts of gold. Who would dare restrain a mother rushing off to pick up her sick baby from the sitter? Whisked ahead to the front window, Rina turned in the necessary tags and papers, secured her passport, and bolted out the door. She reached the parking lot just in time to see Milligan unlocking the door to a Volvo Sedan parked three rows away from Rina's rental.

Rina smiled. A Volvo 740 was a high ticket out here. The car would be a snap to follow, easily standing out in a country of subcompacts. Quickly, Rina slid into the driver's seat of her diminutive Subaru. She turned on the ignition. The Volvo took off and so did Rina, following Milligan to the on ramp on the *ayalon*. They headed southeast toward Jerusalem.

Safe on the freeway, cruising at a comfortable speed, Rina felt a bit smug as she tailed Milligan. Jerusalem put her on solid ground, since she'd lived in that area for a number of years. True, the City of Gold had changed, grown and modernized, but it was still tiny compared to LA.

Rina turned on the radio, tuning in to Hebrew chatter. A talk show – just as stupid here as it was in the States. She switched to one of the many Arabic stations, hearing the modal octaves of native music. Traditional Arabic songs were a form of storytelling: They could go on for hours. About two minutes was enough for her. She changed the dial. This time she found contemporary rock music. Pearl Jam had made it to Jordan.

After riding for twenty minutes through long stretches of cultivated fields, the mountains hovering in the distance, Rina felt a cooler nip in the air. Ten minutes later, the hills began to close in, the roadway becoming a narrow strand cut through stone. Oncoming traffic was obscured by the numerous bends in the ascending roadway. But that didn't stop the Israelis from leaning on the horn, freely passing vehicles going too slowly for their liking. What's a head-on between friends?

The Israeli drivers were frustrating Rina. One minute she would have the Volvo in plain view; the next moment some obnoxious would-be racer would honk, then pass her at record speed. Fortunately, Milligan didn't appear to be in a hurry.

As the road climbed higher, the mountainside became thick with green and the smell of pine. The last curves upward finally brought a bright wall of golden stone into view. Rocks arranged in Hebrew letters placed in the mountainside. *B'ruchim Habayim leYerushalayim* – Welcome to Jerusalem!

Rina felt her heart race, her body tingle, imbued with

spirituality. And as magically as the aura enveloped her every time she entered the holy city – her own personal *aliya* – so did it drain whenever she left – her personal *yerida*.

Yerida – going down. Israelis who emigrated from the Holy Land were called *Yordim*, because they had declined a level spiritually.

At this moment, Rina couldn't fathom ever leaving. With the shining sun, rays gilding the city, she felt giddy. Everywhere her eye fell on native Jerusalem bedrock. Everything had been fashioned from the amber and rose limestone – the buildings, the sidewalks, even some of the streets. Dispersed among the palette of bronzes, pinks, and reds were the parks, allowing a tinge of greenery to seep through. Beautiful to Rina's eye, even though she knew that she had entered the city through the older, industrial area. So caught up in *being there*, Rina had forgotten *why* she had come. When she brought herself back to earth, the Volvo had disappeared.

Angrily, Rina checked around for the 740. Milligan must have moved quickly even though Weizmann Boulevard was heavily congested. Rina tried to speed up but the artery was just too clogged. Attempting to pass a bus to gain a little visibility, she jerked her head over her shoulder to check for lane clearance. She suddenly spotted the Volvo. It had fallen *behind* her.

She slowed, ignoring the blares of the horns, allowing the 740 to chug ahead. Rina allowed herself a moment to stare at the panoply of people on the sidewalks. Lots and lots of Black Hats. The city kept getting more and more religious because the Religious were the ones reproducing at record-breaking rates. The men in their long, black coats, the women in long skirts and *shaytels* piloting their brood down the walkway. There were modern Israelis in tight jeans and denim jackets, Arabs in kafias and chadors, Coptic priests in flowing gowns and pointed hats, nuns in full habit. The pushcarts, the open-air stands flanking an ultra-modern high-rise *kanyoneet* – the mall.

Rina returned her eyes to the Volvo and not a moment too soon. The 740 hooked a right down HaNasi Ben Zvi – a multi-laned boulevard that provided a good view of the Knesset. As the seat of the Israeli government, the Knesset was architecturally modeled after the Acropolis, the ancient seat of Greek government. Why Jews would deliberately copy Greek architecture was beyond Rina's comprehension. For the past eighteen hundred years, the religion had assiduously celebrated Channukah – a festival commemorating the Jewish overthrow of enforced Hellenic rule.

HaNasi Ben Zvi was a psychological dividing line. East of the boulevard was the heavily populated area of Jerusalem – a nest of apartment buildings and businesses. West of the highway evoked memories of a different time, a quieter time – a few major government structures bleeding into broad stretches of rolling hillsides.

Rina felt her thoughts elsewhere when, abruptly, Milligan turned right onto a side street. The maneuver had been so fast and sharp that Rina missed the turnoff. Retracing her steps, Rina took the car onto a dirt lane. Up ahead, she spied the Volvo bouncing precariously along the road. The potholes were much harder on the 740 than on the Subaru.

The Volvo slowed, pulled over, and parked.

Rina braked and made a U-turn in the middle of the lane, not wanting to pass the Volvo. She took her rental off the road, away from Milligan's line of vision. The Subaru handled remarkably well on the grass. She parked next to a tree, straining to keep an eye on the Volvo from her distant vantage point.

The Volvo sat. Rina sat.

Twenty minutes passed before an old blue Fiat subcompact came by, crawling along the pitted lane until it came to the Volvo. Then it pulled over and parked.

Two men got out – thin young men with lots of curly dark hair. One had a mustache. He knocked on the driver's window of the Volvo and the door opened. Milligan got out of the car, a Chanel purse slung over her shoulder.

The men started talking to her. She appeared uninterested, but she did give a perfunctory nod as she rummaged through her purse. She took out a tube of lipstick, applying a sultry red heavily to thick, cupid-shaped lips.

The men spoke with a great deal of animation. Rina wanted to know what they were talking about. As if it had a life of its own, Rina's hand slowly reached for the car door handle. Next thing she knew, she was outside, creeping and sneaking her way into a private conversation.

Heart racing in her chest, grateful for her flat shoes, she tiptoed from tree to tree until she nested behind a thick tree trunk within hearing distance. Milligan had finished with her lipstick. She dropped it into her purse, zipped the handbag shut, and curtailed Mr Mustache's speech.

'Ibri, I don't *care* about your problems. I care about my investment. If your idea of heroism is gunning down a bus full of schoolchildren, you're with the wrong people. Either you're working for me or you're not. Which is it?'

Ibri, Rina heard. The men were Arabs, ergo, natives,

and that made her nervous. It ruined her advantage over Milligan.

Ibri folded his arms across his chest and took up a defensive posture. 'I work for Mr Donald.'

'Well, Mr Donald works for me,' Milligan snapped back. 'He is my underling, do you understand that?'

Ibri rocked on his feet and said nothing. The other thin man piped in. 'We take you to Mr Donald. He tell you problems.'

Milligan took a peek at her Movado. 'I have a very important business meeting at the American Colonial Inn in Jerusalem. Can you get me to Donald and back in an hour?'

Ibri said, 'I take you to Donald.'

'Yes, I understand, Ibri,' Milligan said through clenched teeth. 'But you must get me back to Jerusalem in an hour.'

'No problem,' Ibri said. 'We take my car. Gamal take the Volvo. We go now.'

Milligan turned her back to the men and went over to the blue Fiat. Ibri opened the passenger door for her, then went around to the driver's seat. Gamal slipped inside the Volvo.

First the Volvo took off, followed by the Fiat, passing Rina's Subaru hidden behind the tree. Rina sprinted to her car and gunned the motor. She caught a glimpse of the distant Fiat, turning onto Keren Kayemet. Rina hit the accelerator, catching up with the Fiat as it merged onto Melech George.

City center.

The Fiat, as well as the Volvo, was headed in the direction of the Old City of Jerusalem – a walled fortress built at the time of the Crusades. The Old City had been the site of conquest after conquest. In the bright sunlight, it was a golden castle complete with crenellations and slits for bows and arrows. Rina hoped the Fiat wasn't actually going into the old City through one of its seven gates. Inside was a labyrinth, with roadways so narrow there was barely enough room for one car to squeeze by. And it was dangerous for her in certain sectors – the Moslem Quarters through the Damascus Gate.

The Volvo turned toward the Damascus Gate, but the Fiat bypassed the old City and continued southeast, passing block-long Liberty Bell Park, heading toward the train station.

Then Rina knew where it was going and she bit her lip in fear. She had been so intent upon keeping her eyes on the Fiat's rear window that she had forgotten a very basic rule. Get the car's license number. And when she looked at the plates, her heart sank. It was rimmed in blue and white checks and held a small, blue Hebrew letter – *chet*.

Chet standing for the ancient city of Hebron.

Hebron.

A city rich in history, a city flowing in blood.

Once Hebron had had a famous yeshiva. But the Arabic city had resented the Jewish scholars. In 1929, when it had become clear that the Jews intended to stay, the Arabs had hit upon a way to rid themselves of the interlopers. They had brutally slaughtered them en masse

Sixty-five years later, a deranged Jewish settler who had made Hebron *his* home had felt betrayed and neglected by his own Jewish government. Adding another deluge of blood to the village, he mowed down twenty-nine Arab men bowed in prayer.

Though Rina knew that Hebron was still a *Jewish Holy*

City, would always be a *Jewish Holy City*, it was time to be realistic. Hebron was no longer *Jewish* and hadn't been for fifty years. It was a typical overcrowded Arab village that bred rage and hatred against Jews. It had become such a hotbed of politics, Rina wasn't sure who was securing its borders – the IDF, the Israeli Police, the Palestinian Police or UN troops.

And here was Rina, driving the Subaru down Derech Hebron – the road to Hebron. She knew she should turn back. A lone woman going to Hebron was sheer suicide. But then again, the area had been quiet for a while since the beefed-up security. And maybe the car wouldn't go all the way to Hebron.

A few more miles.

She rolled up the windows and locked the doors, on her way to enemy territory.

The moment Rina left, Decker knew he was in trouble. He couldn't speak Hebrew and Yalom could barely speak English. When the old man motioned him toward Dalia's father, Decker cursed his stupidity.

A stranger in a strange land – a *ger*.

Yalom bent down to whisper something in Menkovitz's ear. Menkovitz was much older than Yalom, in his late eighties. His arms were thin and bony, sticking out of short white sleeves. But when Menkovitz stood, Decker noticed not only was he taller than the average man, but he sported a sizable gut. Like many old men, Menkovitz was high-waisted, his black pants stretched over his belly and supported by suspenders. He had thin, white hair and a long face specked with liver spots.

After Yalom was done with the whispering act, Menkovitz

looked Decker over, dark eyes not missing a trick. Then with much deliberation, he picked up a shoebox-sized leather case and chained it around his waist. Slowly, he put on his black jacket and walked away.

Yalom followed and so did Decker.

'Where are we going?' Decker asked Yalom.

'*Savlanoot,*' Yalom said. '*Pacien.*'

Decker assumed he meant patience and kept silent. Menkovitz kept his eyes straight on, not even bothering to grace Decker with the merest of courtesy nods. But Decker knew it wasn't out of rudeness, it was out of numbness. Menkovitz had the look – old man going through the motions. They took the elevator back to the fifteenth floor, back to Menkovitz's office. The old man walked into the sally port, the secretary buzzing them through without Menkovitz's uttering a word.

The old man's office was spacious, holding a panoramic view of what Decker assumed was industrial Tel Aviv. He saw factories, smokestacks, warehouses, train tracks, and lots of commercial buildings. The day was clear, the sun was bright, but the mood inside was dim. Menkovitz spoke to Decker in Hebrew. Feeling like a dunce, Decker asked him if he spoke English.

Angrily Menkovitz turned to Yalom and fired off some rapid guttural speech. Yalom fired back a response. Menkovitz waved his hand in the air.

Decker said, 'Excuse me, Mr Menkovitz. If there is a problem, I can come back later with my wife. She speaks Hebrew.'

No one responded.

Decker said, 'Uh, *ani* can come back.' He realized he was speaking with his hands. Something he had never done before. 'Uh, *ani ba—*'

'I understand you,' Menkovitz broke in. 'Don't break your teeth. Sit.' The old man took the chair behind his desk and motioned Yalom and Decker to two office chairs.

Decker sat. 'Thank you.'

Menkovitz said, 'Moshe tells me you are *mishtarah* – police, *nachon*? So what news have you to make an embittered old man feel better.'

Decker said, 'I'm very sorry for your loss.'

Menkovitz's eyes narrowed and homed in on Decker. 'So tell me, Mr Policeman, what the *hell* do you know about loss?'

'Not much.'

'That's right, not much! You are just like all spoiled Americans led by a draft-dodging president. You know nothing of loss because you don't know what is dear. Because America is the land of plenty and everything's cheap. Even life.'

'Not to me,' Decker said. 'That's why I'm here.'

'That's why you here?' Menkovitz gave him a dubious look. 'You here because someone pays for you. A free holiday.'

'I'm here on business,' Decker said, calmly. 'Your daughter's death.'

'That's what you say,' Menkovitz said. 'You lie through your teeth.'

Decker was silent.

Menkovitz rubbed his face. 'When do you ship my Dalia back to me so I can give her decent burial?'

'I'm doing the best I can,' Decker said.

'It's not very good.'

'You're right.' Decker leaned forward. 'It's not very good. The whole thing stinks and again, I'm sorry. I know that doesn't mean much, but it is the truth. I have four kids

344

of my own and there isn't a day that goes by when I don't worry about them.'

Menkovitz was silent, then he sighed and rubbed his eyes. 'I come to Palestine, I fight in '48 and I fight in '56. In '67, I'm too old, they give me civil duty – *haggah*. I watch streets as Jordanian soldiers pour into the city like a *mabul*. You know what is *mabul*?'

'Flood,' Decker said.

'Right. Like flood, they come into the city,' Menkovitz said.

'Much soldiers,' Yalom agreed. 'Like *mabul*.'

'You were scared, Moshe?' Menkovitz asked.

'*Lo*,' Yalom stated curtly. 'After Treblinka...' He waved his hand in the air.

Menkovitz said, 'I was not scared. I am a fighter. But this...' He lowered his head. 'I have no more fighter, Mr Policeman. I just want my daughter home so we can bury her on our land. That is all.'

Decker had no other answer except silence. Then he said. 'We're on the same side, Mr Menkovitz. *Help* me.'

Menkovitz stared at Decker, then said, 'You want some tea? I do. Moshe, *rotzeh teh*.'

'*Betach*,' Yalom answered back.

Menkovitz put in requests over the intercom. Then he turned to Decker and said, 'What do you want to know? Dalia was always a good girl. A little spoiled. That's why she liked America. There it is not a crime to be spoiled. Here people don't like it. She married young. And she married a mean man.'

Yalom spoke up and pointed an accusing finger at Menkovitz. 'She marry man like papa.'

Menkovitz allowed himself a brief smile. 'Yes, Arik was

like me . . . too much like me. He was short-tempered and a *hondler*. Even at times, a *gonif*.'

Decker knew *gonif* meant thief. He raised his eyes.

Menkovitz said, 'You don't think Arik is a thief? Let me tell you something, Mr Policeman. You see Bursa, today. You see all the people. They are *all* thieves. If not thief today, then tomorrow they will be thief. Arik was a tomorrow thief.'

The two old men began to quarrel. Decker suspected the cantankerous routine predated the death of their children. He waited them out.

Finally, Menkovitz said, 'Yalom don't like me calling Arik a thief.' The argument with Moshe seemed to have revived him. 'So ask your questions. That is why you're here.'

Decker said, 'Mr Menkovitz, what were you and Kate Milligan talking about?'

Menkovitz stared at Decker. There was a knock on the door, then it opened.

Teatime. The secretary came in carrying an oversized salver. She set it down on Menkovitz's desk, poured tea, then passed around a plate of finger sandwiches. Menkovitz picked up a sandwich of olive and cream cheese and popped it into his mouth. Yalom chose egg salad. Decker passed the first round.

The secretary smiled at her boss, then kissed the mezuzah, and left. Menkovitz asked, 'Why you want to know about Kate Milligan?'

'She and Arik Yalom weren't on good terms.'

Moshe Yalom sat up in his seat. 'What you mean?'

Decker said, 'The two of them had exchanged a series of angry letters.'

'*Ma?*' Yalom turned to Menkovitz. '*Ani lo mayveen.*'

346

Menkovitz translated. Both men seemed confused.

Decker said, 'I had just spoken to Milligan in the States. She claimed to be working on a big case in Los Angeles that took up a great deal of her time. So I'm surprised she's here.'

'Me, too,' Menkovitz said. 'She don't come to Bursa many times. She don't like Jews.'

Decker paused, remembering how she had told them that diamond cutters werc clannish and gossipy. He had told Marge that she had meant the Jews. 'Why do you think Milligan doesn't like Jews?'

'Because she don't like Jews.' He translated his conversation for Moshe Yalom, then went on. 'She thinks they are dirty thieves. So we are thieves. We are *little* thieves. VerHauten is *big* thief – *anak*. You know what is *anak*? Goliath is *anak*. Og is *anak*.'

'A giant,' Decker said.

'Yes, a giant. VerHauten is giant thief,' Menkovitz continued. 'Like a mix-up Robin the Hood. Steal from the poor, give to the rich.' He shrugged. 'I don't like it, but so what? I'm not in Dachau, I am a happy man.'

'Did she ever have a problem with the Jews specifically?'

Menkovitz shrugged. 'Who knows? Maybe yes, maybe no. Who needs excuse to hate Jews?'

Decker said, 'Why is Milligan here, Mr Menkovitz?'

'She looks at the stones. How many come from VerHauten, how many come from Russia, how many come from other African country.' He hesitated, then said, 'Why was Arik mad at Milligan?'

Decker said, 'According to Milligan, Arik Yalom had become threatening and abusive toward her and toward VerHauten. According to Arik's letters, he was being cheated by VerHauten.'

Menkovitz translated Decker's words to Yalom.

'VerHauten cheat all peoples,' Yalom piped in.

Menkovitz said, 'How was VerHauten cheating Arik?'

'I'm not quite sure,' Decker said. 'Arik had some land-holdings in Angola that he wanted to sell to VerHauten. VerHauten passed.'

'Passed?' Menkovitz asked.

'VerHauten passed up buying the land. They weren't interested.'

'It wasn't good land?'

'It might have been very good land,' Decker said. 'But for whatever reason, VerHauten didn't want to buy it. Then there were a few letters . . . let's see how I can explain this.'

Decker paused while Menkovitz translated to Yalom.

'Let's try this. VerHauten said that the land Arik was trying to sell them wasn't even legally owned by Arik. Do you understand?'

'*Cain, cain*,' Menkovitz said. 'Did he own land?'

'Kate Milligan seems to say no. But I definitely saw land deeds that belonged to Arik. That's why I wondered what you and Kate Milligan were talking about. Maybe she asked you about land deeds?'

'She says nothing about land deed. Only talks about diamonds.' Menkovitz translated for Yalom, then turned quiet.

Decker blew out air. 'Mr Menkovitz. Milligan doesn't work for VerHauten anymore. I know that. And I have a feeling you know that. She's on her own now. Do you understand what I'm saying?'

Menkovitz didn't answer.

'So why would she bother asking you about your diamonds?'

'She still does work for VerHauten.'

'As an international lawyer, not as the director of marketing and sales in Overseas Operations. She wouldn't be asking you questions like that anymore.'

'But she did.'

'Is that all she talked about, Mr Menkovitz? Just diamonds?'

Menkovitz hesitated. 'She's interested in Arik's business. I don't know why. Arik is small time. But she keep asking questions.'

'What did you tell her?'

'I told her I don't know. She should talk to the partner, Shaul Gold.'

'Shaul Gold,' Decker said, mildly. 'Did Ms Milligan ask you some questions about Shaul Gold, sir?'

'Yes, and I wonder why.'

'What kind of questions?'

'Have I seen him? Have I heard from him since the murders? Do I know if he is in Israel?'

'And what do you say?'

'I tell her nothing.' Menkovitz was matter-of-fact. 'I don't like Milligan. I don't like the way she acts. She has power and is bully with it. She would have been a fine Nazi.'

'Why do you think she was asking about Gold?'

'I don't know, I don't even ask. Because if I ask, I could say something wrong.'

Decker said, 'Have you heard from Gold?'

'Why do *you* want to know?'

'He's disappeared from the States. He claims to be looking for your grandsons. I'd just like to know where he is, why he fled from America so suddenly.'

'If he goes to Israel, it isn't fled.'

Decker felt his heartbeat quicken. 'Then he is here, isn't he?'

'He has nothing to do with this terrible thing. He is an honest boy. He loved Dalia.'

'So I heard.'

'You hear but you do not understand.' Menkovitz shook his head. 'Yes, he loved her. But after she marry Arik, there is no funny stuff. She is good girl. He is good boy.'

'Shaul Gold is looking for your grandsons, am I right?'

The room was quiet. Decker didn't wait for an answer. 'Mr Menkovitz, do you know where your grandsons are?'

Again, Menkovitz shook his head.

'But they're here.'

Menkovitz picked up a cucumber sandwich. He put it in his mouth and chewed slowly. 'Take some food. It will help you think.'

Decker thanked him and picked up egg salad, ate it and sipped his tea, making sure he didn't rush anything. Then he said, 'Where are your grandsons, Mr Menkovitz?'

'I don't know.' He turned to Yalom. 'Do you know where they are, Moshe?'

'Just they are here, not *where*.'

Menkovitz said, 'We heard from them maybe two, three days ago. My wife ... she was so happy they are alive. Dovie, the little one, say they are here in Israel. And they are both here in Israel. But they are not together.'

'They split up?' Decker asked.

Menkovitz nodded.

Swell! Decker thought. 'And Shaul is looking for them?'

'Shaul knows the boys are afraid. He thought they come to Israel to hide with us. Shaul knows we help the boys any way we can. Shaul looks for the boys to find out *why* they are afraid. Because Shaul is afraid, too. If he finds out why boys ran away, maybe he finds out who did this terrible thing to my daughter.' He looked at Yalom. 'To our children.'

'Do you know where Shaul Gold is?' Decker asked.

'*Lo*. Shaul says he looks for the boys, then he will call me. I ask Shaully where are you staying, but he won't tell. He says it's better if I don't know. I think he's right.'

Decker noticed that Shaul had become Shaully.

Menkovitz straightened in his seat. 'I wish I could help, but Dov tells me nothing. Shaul tells me nothing.'

'Dov didn't give you *any* idea where he might be staying.'

'*Lo*. Only he and Gil are apart and we should not look for them. I want to, of course, but Dovie says *no, no, no*! Don't look, he will call later.'

Decker allowed himself a pat on the back. He had been the *right* man for this case *because* he was Jewish. Rina had drummed it into him. Every identified Jew alive looked to Israel for sanctuary. The Yalom boys were no exception. And if Honey needed a city of refuge, she and the family were probably here as well. He said, 'Dov hasn't called you yet?'

'Not yet. So I wait.' Menkovitz sipped his tea. 'Yes, I wait. My wife waits. The Yaloms wait. We don't say anything, we just wait. And wait and wait.' His eyes misted. 'I hope he don't wait *too* long. I am an old man. I'd like to see my only grandsons before I die.'

29

As if she didn't know, the sign said it all: Tourists were advised to turn back. If not, they traveled the roads at their own risk.

Rina plowed ahead, tailing the Fiat at a brisk pace.

Congestion eased as they moved out of downtown Jerusalem. The road wound its way out of the city, framed by old Arab homes – big houses with doors and grillwork painted blue to ward off the evil spirits. Flower boxes decorated the balconies, impromptu gardens springing up in empty spots. The hillsides were lush with vegetation. It must have been a wet winter. Farther along, past the old houses, were the newer Israeli developments. Hundreds of attractive-looking apartment houses waffled into the mountainside. Then as fast as they appeared, they faded. Once again, the ground was opened for cultivation.

Rina passed olive groves, citrus groves, and cultivated fields. Here was strong land. Here was fertile land. And here was contested land.

The sun was high, beating downward with unmolested power. The road to Hebron bordered on the Judean Desert and Rina had forgotten how hot the Mediterranean sun could be, even in the tail end of winter. She switched on the air-conditioning.

The road continued to ebb and flow through hilly terrain.

353

Rina kept her eyes not only on the Fiat but on her rearview mirror. Though in hostile territory, Rina was calmed by the slew of army jeeps she had passed – in front of her, behind her. In about ten minutes, she knew she'd hit Bet Lechem – Bethlehem. Once the Christian Arab city had been a sleepy little berg that had catered to Christian tourists wishing to see the Church of the Nativity. It had been full of tiny little shops stocked with religious articles and icons. The stores had done a bang-up business around Christmas and Easter. But when the uprisings had swung into full gear, tours had been canceled. The result? Lots of empty shops.

A few moments later, a large block of Israeli soldiers came into view. Rachel's Tomb. Once visible from the road, it was now blocked by a wall. It was a holy spot for the Jews, especially infertile women. They would go there to beseech God for children, in the same manner that Rachel *Emainu* had beseeched the Almighty thousands of years ago.

Rina felt comforted by the army's presence, by the Uzis the boys held. There were many of them. So young. Dressed in khaki greens, the kids weren't much older than Sammy. Rina briefly flashed on her other life, how it might have been for her boys if she and Yitzy had stayed in Israel. It had been her loneliness that had propelled them back to the States – to Rav Schulman's yeshiva. And just as soon as they had settled in the United States, Rina wished they'd never left Israel. Everything had gone downhill after that.

After incanting a quick prayer, Rina passed through the square blocks of Bet Lechem without incident. It was the same town she had known – open-market fruit and juice stands, cafés with Arab men passing around the hookah, playing long games of backgammon. Rina passed women balancing baskets on their heads as they walked down dusty roads in sandals or bare feet. Their hair was swathed in colorful scarves, their bodies covered with long, intricately embroidered black dresses.

Abruptly, Rina realized that the Fiat had become a dot in the distance. She sped up, the car grunting as it accelerated, hugging the road as it twisted and turned. Once the Fiat was in striking distance, Rina allowed herself to relax.

The hillsides had changed, no longer walls of rock. Instead, the mountains had been terraced, carved into steplike mesas of cultivated lands. This ingenious job of landscaping had been done hundreds of years ago, the barriers of granite and limestone still holding back the forces of Mother Nature with grace and beauty.

The Fiat moved rapidly and so did Rina. They passed the turn off to Efrat, a town that had been mislabeled as a settlement. Settlements to Rina conjured up images of temporary inhabitance – people with backpacks wandering through fields, pitching tents and sleeping on the ground. Efrat was anything but. The town was perched atop the hill and was filled with modern apartment houses and sprawling private homes. It had its own school system, its own libraries, its own stores, and of course, its own synagogues. Rina had lots of American friends who had moved to Efrat to enjoy the fresh air, safety, and open land. Now, with the Arabs set to patrol this land, Rina feared for their safety.

Rina thought about that as she drove farther into the West Bank. The road became not only emptier but decidedly more Arab. For every car she passed with an Israeli license, Rina had passed five with Arab plates. Her rental was a target, as vulnerable as if she were a blip on a radar screen. She rechecked her door locks, glanced in her rearview mirror, scanned the area for signs of an ambush.

Everything appeared quiet. Another oncoming army

jeep passed her in the opposite direction. It gave her courage to continue.

The Fiat was speeding by now. The terraced mountainside had become a blur of rock. When it made the turn into Hebron, the wheels screeched. Rina followed, the air-conditioning blowing full force at her face. But the frosty air did little to relieve the internal heat. Sweat was running down Rina's face, seeping through her clothing. The armpits of her blouse had become darkened stains. Taking the turnoff, Rina slowed as the roadway narrowed to the entrance to the city.

Then things began to move in slow motion, the area growing dense with people as she delved deeper into the village, into the marketplace. Hostile, hateful stares cast upon her, the heat of anger born thousands of years ago and nurtured steadily by blood and revenge. Rina kept her eyes straight ahead, hands clutched to the steering wheel. She wanted to check her doors again, but that would show fear. Fear is always an invitation for trouble.

The city seemed to reproduce before her eyes, the crowd thickening with each second that passed. The marketplace began to close in on her, fruit stands spilling onto the roadway. Donkey-driven carts sided her Subaru, animal and human faces staring into the car's window. Some eyes were curious but most were unfriendly. Rina attempted to act outwardly calm, but inside her heart pounded furiously.

Not an army jeep in sight.

A 'ping' echoed inside her car. The slightest sensation of movement – as if someone had tapped the trunk. A sudden rush of adrenaline shot into her system. Were the tires just spitting out gravel or was someone stoning the car?

The Fiat had slowed to accommodate the heavy traffic of cars, carts, and camels. Rina's Subaru was nudging against the Fiat's back bumper. She was directly behind the car and that wasn't good at all. But where was she to go? She was *trapped* in congestion.

A louder clunk against the trunk of her car, this one heavier, more meaningful. She wanted to turn around but didn't dare. A glance to her right showed she was hemmed in by another donkey cart. Her eyes panned her surroundings, assessing her options. In the distance, a flash of army green.

Another hard clunk against her car.

Rina slid down into her seat, amazed by how calm she was. All those safety drills she had done when she had lived out here years ago. It had all come back.

The Fiat slowed, then hooked over to a small unpaved lane, not much more than a rut in the ground. Rina was not about to follow an Arab car into the isolated hillside. She had eavesdropped on Milligan's conversation, had gotten the Fiat's license plates, had tailed it into Hebron until it headed for the mountains. She had done enough. It was time to go home.

Heart hammering in her chest, Rina did an abrupt U-turn and headed back to Derech Hebron, once again into town. Sweat poured off her forehead as she carefully drove the car back through the marketplace. Everything seemed under control.

Then the deafening blast inside her car! Light flying, stinging her face! Instinctively, Rina ducked, but managed to keep control of the car. A donkey brayed, someone kicked at her car door, the sound of curses hurled in her direction. Through tear-stung eyes, Rina saw a streak of olive pass by.

An *army* jeep!

With finesse worthy of a race-car driver, she twisted and

turned the Subaru, nearly knocking down a fruit stand, until she was tailing the jeep, until a platoon of army green came into view. A half dozen jeeps and dozens of soldiers – men and women in Israeli uniforms armed with Uzis!

Pools clouding her eyes, Rina realized where she *was*! Directly in front of her vision was a limestone building with a dark, cavernous archway for its entry. She had reached *Ma'arat HaMachpelah* – the Tomb of the Patriarchs. The ancient burial place of the holy ancestors. She brought the choking Subaru up a steep gravel hill, then pulled over and parked. Laying her forehead onto the steering wheel, she wiped glass off her hands and buried her face in the crook of her sweat-soaked arms.

She wept aloud.

Decker was trying to remain calm, but wasn't succeeding. Having given up on Rina's return to the Bursa, he went back to the hotel, deciding to wait for her there. But another hour had passed since she had left, two in all, and Decker was downright frantic.

He hadn't any idea where Rina had gone; he hadn't a clue on how to proceed to find her. All he had was the license plate of the Subaru. Decker had called the rental agency and had asked in English if their cars had been equipped with tracking devices. The two people he spoke to hadn't the faintest idea of what he was talking about. He hung up in disgust, his stomach sizzling in its own juices.

The harsh ring of the phone made him jump. He grabbed it and muttered an angry hello.

It was the long-distance operator.

Fuck! Now something was wrong at home. And here he was sick with worry ten thousand miles away.

Thanks to good old fiber optics, the voice on the other

end was familiar and clear. An instant wave of relief came over him. It wasn't his mother-in-law or the baby nurse or Sammy or Jake. It was Marge.

Decker caught his breath and said, 'What *time* is it over there?'

'Two in the morning. What's it over there? About one in the afternoon?'

'About.'

'Yeah, I'm all messed up with the time zones. I called your hotel yesterday – four o'clock in the afternoon my time. Some indignant desk clerk informed me in no uncertain terms that it was two o'clock a.m. over there and she was not going to wake you for anything less than an emergency. I figured I'd call back later. You've been busy?'

'Non stop since we arrived yesterday.' Decker took out his pad and pencil. 'I take it you have some news?'

'First, a quick update on the Honey Klein case. I got a call from a Sturgis in West LA. I told him you were in Israel and he told me you should get a job as a clairvoyant.'

'Honey is here?'

'No one's certain, but Manhattan police think so. Right after Klein's murder, they set up a specialized team to go out to the village – a couple of Jewish cops on the force who could speak Yiddish, including one woman. The men were mute, of course. With the women, it was a different story. While they weren't exactly chatty, some things about Honey did come out. She had been talking for a long time about going to live in Israel. Then, right before Honey left for vacation, one of the neighbors saw a thick envelope sitting in front of Honey's house; the return address was a federal office building. She had asked Honey about it. Honey had replied that she had updated her passports.'

'Interesting,' Decker said. 'Do they have any evidence she was involved in her husband's murder?'

'No evidence. But police have got a motive.'

'Let me guess. Her husband had been abusing her and the children. She wanted to get away, but he wouldn't let her. So she took the kids and fled.'

'You're on the right track, but not quite.' Marge paused. 'You being Jewish and all, Rabbi. Maybe you can explain this to me. Yes, Honey wanted to get away from her husband. She had been asking for a divorce for over a year, but Gershon Klein wanted to stay married. Now this is the part I'm confused about. Apparently, if you're a devout Jew, a wife can't get a divorce if her husband doesn't want it. Is that true?'

'In a nutshell, yes.'

'How's that possible, Pete? We have *laws* in this country. *Equitable* laws.'

Decker was quiet. How could he possibly explain it to Marge when he didn't understand it himself. 'She can get a civil divorce, Marge, but she can't get a religious divorce. Without a religious divorce, a Jewish woman can't remarry.'

There was a long pause over the line. Then Marge said, 'I don't know about you, but that seems imbalanced to me.'

'Me, too,' Decker admitted. 'I think it stinks. Has New York concluded *how* Gershon Klein died?'

'He drowned,' Marge said. 'Rather he *was* drowned.'

'What kind of water was in the lungs?'

'It was fresh water, not seawater. They think he drowned in a bathtub. And they think Honey did it.'

'It would have been hard for Honey to get him into a bathtub,' Decker said. 'Gershon had stopped bathing a while back.'

'Stopped bathing? Why? Now that couldn't be religion.'

'It had nothing to do with religion,' Decker said. 'Sounds like the guy was undergoing a breakdown. Go on.'

Marge said, 'The next part is speculation but I'll run it by you anyway. New York seems to think that Honey had intentions of calling it in as an accident. But she suddenly panicked.'

'I can see that,' Decker said. 'It's one thing to drown your husband in a frenzy of anger. It's another thing to explain away a dead body.'

Marge said, 'New York thinks she dragged the body out of her house—'

'This had to have taken place at night.'

'I would think so. Anyway, she dragged the corpse down to her husband's office and left.'

'The body was shot.'

'Yeah, they figure Honey purposely shot the body, trashed the office to make it look like a robbery, then told everyone that Gershon was out of town in Israel.'

'Then Honey called up Rina,' Decker continued the story. 'She made arrangements to be out of town when the body was discovered.' He became angry. 'She *chose* to stay with a woman whose husband's a cop. Got to give it to her. That took balls.'

'Or some screws loose,' Marge said. 'Honey had to have been stupid to think that someone wouldn't catch on.'

Decker said, 'You know, Margie, dead bodies aren't easy to maneuver. Drowning the guy, then dragging him into a car and up to his office . . . shooting him and tossing the place. That's a lot of physical exertion for one little woman.'

'My thoughts to a tee. She must have had help, Pete. Unfortunately, the police can't finger an accessory.'

'An accessory *before* the fact,' Decker said. 'Someone had to have helped her with the drowning. She couldn't have taken down a grown man by herself.'

'Unless the guy was drugged.'

'Anything in the bloods?'

'Sturgis didn't say anything so I assume the tests were negative. Unless the guy was pumped with some rare poison that didn't show up in a normal chemical profile.'

'Honey had help,' Decker stated as fact.

'Probably. Could have been a member of her community. Maybe even one of her kids . . . the teenaged boy.' Marge was quiet for a moment. 'Didn't you tell me that the kids looked like abused children?'

'I was thinking out loud, but the signs are there.' Decker paused. 'So *they* think Honey drowned him, then shot him in a panic to make it look like a robbery. Something's missing, Marge.'

'Agreed. So all you have to do, Rabbi, is find the woman and ask her a few questions. Shouldn't be too hard. Israel's a very small country. I know because I looked at a map.'

Decker laughed. 'It's bigger in the flesh, Dunn. I'll ask Rina if she has any ideas.'

If I can find her!

Marge said, 'Department said as long as they paid your transatlantic way for the Yalom thing, you should look into Klein, too. Davidson was very excited about the latest developments. He's going to ask Manhattan to kick in for some of your overseas expenses since you're working on their case.'

'Our Loo likes things fiscally sound.'

'Our Loo's a jerk.'

'Has he been giving you a hard time?'

'Not really. Simply because I've been producing.' Marge took a breath. 'Are you ready?'

'Yep.'

'We *finally* found the *airline* tickets for the Yalom boys. They took a flight from LA to Vancouver. Another one from Vancouver to Toronto. Then a third from Toronto to Israel. We finally have confirmation that the boys are in Israel.'

'I'm looking for them as we speak. Nothing so far. But I've only been here a day. Anything else?'

'Yep. I've been doing a little research on our friend Katie Milligan.'

Decker felt himself gripping the receiver. He tried to quell a rush of anxiety, but it was a lost cause. '*What?*'

There was a moment of silence. 'Are you okay, Pete?'

'Yeah, I'm fine. What about Milligan?'

Marge couldn't understand the sudden harsh tone in his voice, but maybe he'd explain himself afterward. 'It seems that Katie made some interesting recent investments for her pension plan. Namely Southwest Mines and West African Consolidated.'

'The companies Arik Yalom had invested in.'

'Pete, she bought Southwest Mines *after* it went bankrupt.'

Decker thought a moment. 'Maybe Milligan was bottom fishing. Or it may be that Milligan had insider's information that the company was going to be picked up and restructured.'

'And just who would pick up the company, Pete?'

'VerHauten.'

'On the nose, Rabbi,' Marge said. 'VerHauten is listed as the majority shareholder of the recently defunct Southwest

Mines with Milligan and Yalom listed as prominent minority shareholders. Would you like to hear some of my theories on what came to pass?'

'Shoot.'

'Milligan was intrigued with Arik's stockholdings. She thought he just might literally be sitting on a diamond mine with all his shares in this Southwest. But there was a glitch.'

'The company was going bust,' Decker said.

'Exactly,' Marge said. 'It takes a heap and a half of capital to mine diamonds. The company simply didn't have the wherewithal to see it through. They made overtures to VerHauten for a buy-out, but Milligan knew they were in big trouble. She told VerHauten to sit on the offer and wait until the company went bust.'

'Which it did.'

'Which allowed both VerHauten and *Milligan* to buy it out at a fraction of its worth.'

'With VerHauten in the picture, Arik's stock could be worth a bundle,' Decker said.

Marge said, 'If VerHauten ever decides to *move* on it. Which is a big if. According to my spies, VerHauten isn't developing Southwest Mines for two reasons. Arik Yalom owns too much of the company, and secondly, VerHauten isn't doing any development right now. It seems to have enough diamonds out of its other pipes. Pete, Arik's stock is worthless as long as VerHauten keeps the land fallow.'

'And so are Milligan's shares of the company.'

Marge said, 'Pete, what if Milligan had insider's info that VerHauten would move if they could get hold of Yalom's and Milligan's shares at a reasonable price? Now Milligan could have afforded to sell cheap. She bought at rock bottom. Arik, on the other hand, didn't buy at the low. He was holding out for more.'

'But the company went bust. A little is better than nothing.'

'Maybe not to Arik. Suppose VerHauten began to lose interest. Milligan grew anxious. She wanted her money and needed Arik out of the picture. She offed him and his wife, figuring it would be easier to deal with the heirs – the boys – than with the parents.'

And suddenly things began to click into place. It was time to lay his news on Marge. 'Milligan's in Israel, Detective. And so is Gold.' He filled her in on the details, conveniently leaving out Rina's foray into policework.

Marge said, 'So Gold's looking for the boys and Milligan's asking about Gold. You gotta wonder why she's searching for him. I tell you, they were in on it together.'

'Maybe, but maybe not. I think she's hunting him down. You want to hear my theory?'

'Shoot.'

'Remember when *you* spoke about the inequality of the partnership. Arik seemed to have so much *more* money than Gold.'

'Yes.'

'Gold claimed Yalom had used Dalia's money when Yalom first started investing in his African schemes. But I say no. I think Yalom wanted Gold to believe that the business wasn't doing so hot when in fact it was doing fine. I think Yalom was draining some *business* money to pay for personal investments.'

Marge stated, 'Then Arik covered his ass by saying the money came from Dalia.'

'Some of that may have been true. But not *all* of it.'

'Only got one quibble with your theory, Pete. Gold's a

sharpie. If Arik was dipping into the till, Gold would have found out real quick.'

'Agreed. I think Gold *did* find out about it. And I think he *allowed* Arik to use business money for personal expenses.'

'Pete, why would he do that?'

'Because Gold was in *love* with Dalia – had been for years.'

'He was willing to be ripped off for love?'

'Why not? Sure as I stand here, I know they had *something* going on. As long as Gold thought that the money Arik pilfered was going for Dalia and the kids, for her house, for household expenses . . . that was okay with him. But eventually Gold found out that Arik was using the money for stock and land purchases in Africa. He hit the roof and demanded payment. And I think Arik capitulated, Marge. I think Arik paid him back.'

'How?'

'By selling him the bulk of his mining investments – things like land deeds and Southwest Mine stock.'

'Then Arik got popped,' Marge said. 'Let's just speculate and say that Milligan popped Arik to get to his land deeds and mining stocks.'

'Right.'

'At this point, we both know it's pure conjecture.'

'Agreed, but let's go with it anyway,' Decker said. 'Because with Milligan being here, hot on Gold's tail, it looks like she's involved in some fashion.'

'True.'

Decker said, 'Say Gold had known that Milligan had designs on Arik's former mines. What Milligan hadn't known was that the assets no longer belonged to Arik. They belonged to Gold.'

'So when Arik was popped, Gold knew his ownership of the assets put him in jeopardy. He asked some questions, then split. Eventually Milligan found out that *Gold* owned the stocks and followed him over to Israel.' Marge paused. 'Took her long enough to figure it out.'

'I don't believe she had even thought about Gold being in the picture until *we* brought it up. Then she must have done some checking. Bingo. She found out that Yalom was no longer the primary shareholder. Gold held the cards now.'

'So Milligan came to Israel *specifically* to get Gold?'

'Why else would she be asking about him and not the boys?'

'So why did the boys run scared?'

'Maybe they're next in line to inherit the stocks.' Decker blew out air. 'I know we've got lots of holes in our theory. But why else would Milligan be asking about *Gold*?'

'I still say they could be in on the murder together and he split on her with his assets. She's hunting him down just like she did Yalom. Where is Milligan now?'

A very *good* question. Anxiety suddenly strangled Decker's chest. The better question was, where the *fuck* was Rina?

'Pete?' Marge said. 'Are you still there?'

'I don't know who Milligan's out to get,' Decker said flatly. 'We've just been throwing out stuff, Marge. Maybe I'm completely off base.'

'Pete, you sound upset. What is it?'

He was silent. He just couldn't confess his stupidity to his partner. He just couldn't tell her that he let Rina tail someone potentially involved in a double murder. 'I'm fine. Look, Marge, I've got some work to do here. And you need your rest—'

'Are you *sure* you're okay, Pete?'

367

Decker whispered, 'I've got to go now. Call you later.'
He hung up the phone, grabbed his coat, and headed for
nowhere.

30

Someone tapped on the driver's window. Rina jerked her head and looked up. A soldier, his young face earnest and full of concern. He was blond with bright blue eyes and strong cheekbones – a heartbreaker. She dried her eyes and gave him a weak smile.

'You . . . hokay, *g'veret*?'

Rina unlocked the door and got out of the car, a dry heat grabbed her body. The soldier was sweating, weighted down by his weapon. She spoke in Hebrew. 'I'm . . . overwhelmed by the spirituality, by the *ruach* of Hashem.'

Upon hearing Rina speak his language fluently, the soldier launched into a tirade. What was she doing out here alone? Was she crazy? Hadn't she read a newspaper for the last year? Didn't she know she was inviting herself to her own funeral? Of course, she was American and that explained everything. What the hell was wrong with these crazy American fanatics? Didn't they know what they were doing to Israel, how they put every soldier – every *Jewish* soldier – in danger with their rhetoric and their stubbornness? Who needed them anyway?

Then the soldier noticed her shot-out window.

Rina listened patiently as the man went ballistic.

Did she expect sympathy for her ordeal? Well, she

369

wasn't going to get anything from him. Nosirree. Not when she not only endangered herself but every single man and woman in the Israeli army. And now that she had arrived here in Hebron, how the hell did she plan to get back? Of course, God would take care. The stock answer to everything. God would take care. Except God wasn't out here, *shvitzing* like a *behaima* – sweating like a beast – watching his rear end every second of his duty, fending off hate-driven terrorists, doing frightening, dangerous work just to guard a bunch of crazies who believed that mass suicide was a virtue.

He stopped abruptly, blew out air, then gingerly traced the bullet hole with his finger. 'It is so incredibly *stupid*, you coming out here. No one comes out here, let alone a woman. Who are you? A terrorist in disguise?'

Rina told him she was not a terrorist.

The man didn't seem comforted, asking *now* what was he going to do with her.

Rina spoke softly and meaningfully. 'I'll wait until one of the jeeps goes back to Jerusalem. I'm very sorry to cause you grief. I showed very bad judgment. I do know what's going on, but I guess old habits are hard to break. I lived here twelve years ago. I remember a much different Israel.'

'A much, *much* different Israel.' The soldier cocked his hip and made eye contact. She smiled at him. It seemed to soften his anger. He said, 'You speak Hebrew very well. How long did you live here?'

'About three years. Back then you could travel the main roads without too much concern. Of course, if you went into the remote areas and passed through the small villages, you always carried a gun. I wish I had a gun now.'

The soldier eyed her suspiciously. 'You should have thought of that before you came out here like an American cowboy.'

'Yes, I should have.' Rina looked at the sky. 'Is the *Ma'arat* open?'

The soldier shifted the Uzi in his arms. 'For the moment, until another incident closes it up.'

'Then I can go in,' Rina said. 'At least do what I came here for.' Her eyes suddenly moistened. 'Who knows? I may never see it again.'

Wearily, the soldier looked over his shoulder at the mausoleum holy to two separate nations. He shook his head as if religion was the root of all evil. 'I need to check your purse before you enter.'

Rina handed him her purse. He dug through it, examining her belongings, checking her passport, then handed it back to her. 'Hokay,' he said in English. 'Hokay, you go. I go with you.'

'Into the *Ma'arah*?' Rina stated in Hebrew. 'But it's guarded. I'll be fine.'

'I still go.'

'You don't trust me,' Rina stated. 'I understand. Then come with me.'

The soldier adjusted the strap of his Uzi. In Hebrew, he told her ladies first.

The Jewish name for Hebron was Kiryat Arbah – *kiryat* meaning 'city' and *arbah* meaning 'four' – because the town held the *Ma'arat HaMachpelah* – the Cave of the Pairs. Specifically, there were four pairs of ancestors interred beneath the memorial in a cave below: Abraham and Sarah, Isaac and Rebecca, Jacob and Leah, and Adam and Eve. The holy spot was also the resting place of the decapitated head of Jacob's brother Esau, sliced off by Chushin, son of Dan. He had garroted his great-uncle after the burial negotiations between Esau and his nephews had broken down. The body had remained outside the walls, but the head had rolled in. After much discussion, the nephews allowed the head to be buried in the cave reserved for their ancestors.

Rina thought about that as she entered the shrine. The mausoleum had undergone many transformations, from a Jewish shrine, to a Christian church, then finally into a large Muslim mosque around the thirteenth century. Rina couldn't imagine why Muslims would want to worship in a shrine that held *Jewish* patriarchs and matriarchs. She realized that Abraham was the father of their religion as well as hers. But the others? They had *nothing* to do with the formation of Islam. But every day, six times a day, the Muslims would do just that. They prayed to Allah with Isaac and Rebecca looking on. Their cenotaphs were in the mosque proper.

Rina did concede that the ancient Muslims deserved proper credit. They had not only kept the shrines in excellent condition, they had embellished them in their own unique style.

It had been said that if the Jews were to dig underneath the memorials and into the cave below, if they were to actually reach the graves of the patriarchs and matriarchs, the messiah would come. After 1967, when Hebron came under Israeli rule, which opened the city to everyone, some Jews started digging. The Arabs immediately put a stop to the desecration of their mosque. The Israeli government supported the residents of the city. The messiah would just have to wait.

It was cool inside, albeit dank and musty. Immediately,

Rina was hit by a cry from an elderly, blind beggar. It was anyone's guess how he had become blind, but Rina knew of an old Arab custom. Some men, after they made their haj to Mecca, felt that nothing else was ever worth seeing. So they purposely blinded themselves. Rina wondered if that's what had happened with this man. He continued to plead, palm stretched outward. Rina fished through her purse and dropped a shekel in a jerky dried hand. The man's bony fingers closed in on the coin.

The guard looked at her with angry eyes that said there was no time for charity. Get a move on.

Rina took a deep breath as she entered the heart of the mausoleum. It smelled like a compost pile of rich, decaying vegetation, as if the shrine echoed God's very words – *for dust thou art and unto dust thou shall return*. Rina walked through the memorial, stopping in front of the shrine for Abraham and Sarah. Something ethereal came over her, a sense of personal history. As if she were looking through her parents' scrapbook. She thought about the Five Books of Moses, specifically *B'raisheet*, the book of Genesis. In a sense, B'raisheet was the scrapbook of the first Jews. These people weren't fairy-tale characters or mythological creatures, they were *real* people. And like all real people, they had lived, they had died.

And Rina was standing at their graves.

Every visit to the cave brought Rina that much closer to her ancestral roots. With a shaking hand, she took a pocket *siddur* from her purse and began to pray. First, she did formal prayer – the *Shemona Esreh*. Then she made her own requests of God. First came the prayer for her family's safety and health. Next came the prayer for the Jewish people. Lastly came the prayer for mankind. She prayed for everyone. She prayed for peace.

When she was done, she put her *siddur* away and turned to the soldier. 'I'm done.'

They both squinted as they came out of the shrine. The soldier wiped his face with the back of his hand and quickly escorted Rina back to her car.

In Hebrew, he said, 'Wait here. I tell the next group going back to Jerusalem to keep an eye on you.' He sighed, his expression street worn and melancholy. 'I'm sorry it has to be this way. I'm sorry it is not the same Israel you once knew. But we all must adjust to reality. If *HaKadosh Baruch Hu* has a better idea than our prime minister, let Him run for office.'

Rina smiled and thanked him.

The soldier ran his boot over the dust of the ground. 'Where are you from in America?'

'Los Angeles.'

'I have a cousin in Los Angeles. Micah Golan. You know him?'

Rina held back a laugh. There were six hundred thousand Jews in LA. 'No, I'm afraid I don't.' She wiped sweat off her forehead. 'It's miserable work out here. Again, I apologize for upsetting you.' Her expression was kind. 'Thank you for taking me inside the *Ma'arah*.'

'I have to take you,' the soldier said, grumpily. 'Who knows who is a terrorist anymore?'

'I'm not a terrorist.'

The soldier closed his eyes, then opened them. 'I see with my own eyes that you're a good woman. Because I followed you in the *Ma'arah*. I saw the tears in your eyes when you prayed, the expression on your face when you *davened Shemona Esreh*. I saw you mouth the words with clarity, with assurance with purpose and meaning. Your posture, your sincerity. It shows through as if you have a window to your heart. You pray to a God of mercy, not to a God of revenge. Many pray here – Arab and Jew. I don't think you're a crazy fanatic. And I don't think you are an Arab spy, either. Many try to pretend to be us to infiltrate. They speak our language, eat kosher food, drink our wine, and love our women. But they *cannot* love our *God*. They may know the motions of prayer, but they don't have the *emotions*.'

The soldier paused.

'Here there has been too much bloodshed caused by small minds. I talk to the settlers, try to tell them that bloodshed and revenge is *their* way, *their* customs, *their* laws. It is not *our* way.' He shook his head. 'I talk too much.'

'You feel deeply.'

'You would too if you did this job. It stinks. I think they're leaving for Jerusalem. I'll introduce you to the group. I don't want you to get hurt. Too many people have already gotten hurt.'

After an hour of walking proved fruitless, Decker returned to the phone calls. First, Menkovitz's office. He had called so many times, the secretary recognized his voice.

'No, your wife has not come back here, Mr Decker. I call you if she comes.'

'She hasn't phoned, maybe left a message?'

'No, sir.'

'Thank you.'

'Thank you.'

Click!

Decker slammed the receiver and cursed out loud.

He tried the police. He tried to explain the situation, but

there was a language barrier. In the end, all he could do was wait.

Three hours! Where the *hell* could she have gone?

Time for the Mideast geography lesson.

Once again, Decker quit pacing long enough to study the road map of the region. It was a big mama thing he'd bought at the overpriced bookstore downstairs. He couldn't believe the prices! They had wanted eleven bucks for a paperback!

He blew out air, tried to remain calm. He leaned over the tabletop, studying the map, retracing the squiggly color-coded lines. *If* Rina had been going one way all this time at roughly sixty miles an hour, she'd be in Amman, Jordan, by now! Or if she went north, she'd be in Lebanon making her way up to Beirut. Cairo looked like it would take much longer.

Disgusted, he crumpled up the map, threw it at the wall, then immediately regretted his impulsive action. He cursed again, then smoothed out the wrinkled road-ways.

His ears perked up. A key being inserted into the slot. Decker jumped up and threw open the door, dragging Rina inside. She took her hand off the doorknob and held it up.

'Wait for the speech until I get the door closed.'

Decker didn't move.

Slowly, Rina freed the key from the slot and closed the door. She leaned against the wall and exhaled, waiting for the onslaught.

Fighting control, Decker said between clenched teeth, 'I don't know whether to hang you or hug you. I vote for hug.'

Decker gripped her so hard, he thought she'd break.

Rina allowed herself to be swaddled by him. His embrace felt so protective. She was determined not to cry and was proud when the tears didn't come. In truth, she had no energy left for weeping.

Decker kissed his wife's forehead. 'There is an invention called a *phone*. Even in Israel.'

'I didn't have any phone cards.'

'What?'

'Phone cards. And I didn't want to stop off at the post office to buy them. Once I got into Jerusalem, I wanted to get back as quickly as possible.'

'Why? What happened? Are you all right?'

'I'm fine, Peter. But I'm hungry. Do you mind ordering up a little room service?'

Decker dropped his arms to his sides and sat down on the bed, smoothing out his mustache with his fingertip. 'I'll be happy to order some food for you. I hope you don't think this is too goyish, but if you do, too bad. I need a drink. A very strong drink!'

'Get a glass of wine for me, too.'

Decker stared at her with wide eyes. 'What the hell happened, Rina?'

'I got caught up in the situation. For future reference, I don't think I'd make a very good cop.'

'My fault. I shouldn't have asked you to do my job. I'm so incredibly stupid sometimes!'

'If we're going to self flagellate, I'm way ahead in the stupidity department.' She smiled at her husband, but knew it wasn't going to assuage his wrath. 'I followed Milligan, Peter. She went to Hebron.'

Decker felt his face afire. 'You followed Milligan into *Hebron*?'

'Yes. And I know it was stupid beyond belief. All I got

377

for my efforts was a shot-out window. But I'm here. I'm safe. Do you want to hear what I found out?'

Decker slapped his forehead. 'I don't fucking *believe* you. How could you do that?'

'I already said I was stupid.'

'No, Rina. *I* was stupid. You were *insane*.'

'I see it's going to be one of *those* interchanges.' She picked up the phone and ordered room service. 'I can't fight on an empty stomach.'

Decker stared at her, then stood up. 'Pack your bags. You're going home.'

'Fine. It wasn't my idea to come out here in the first place.'

Guilt shot through Decker's veins. He sat back down on the bed. He willed himself rational, then quietly asked, 'Who shot at your car? Milligan?'

'I have to think for a moment.' Rina sat next to him. 'I don't *think* it was Milligan. Because at that point, I had already stopped tailing her car. It was probably just a villager consumed with hate.'

She began to recount her ordeal. 'In Jerusalem, Milligan met up with two guys in a Fiat near the Israeli museum. The men were Arabs. One of them was named Ibri – short for Ibrahim. The other was named Gamal.'

'How'd you find that out?'

'I overheard them talking.'

Decker paused. 'I don't think I want to know how that came about.'

'Good idea,' Rina said. 'Ibri was complaining to Milligan about something. She interrupted him, saying if his idea of heroism was blowing up a school bus, he was working for the wrong person. They mentioned a guy named Donald. No last name. Does he mean anything to you?'

'No.'

'Ibri said they worked for Donald, not Milligan. Milligan said that Donald worked for *her*. Then Ibri offered to take Milligan to see Donald. Gamal took Milligan's Volvo into the Old City of Jerusalem. Ibri and Milligan went to Hebron. I stopped following them when the car went up an isolated road. I turned around, planned to go back, then someone shot out the window. Luckily, I caught up with an IDF jeep. I went to the Cave of the Patriarchs—'

'Wasn't that the place where the massacre took place?'

'Yes. But it's pretty secure now.'

'Oh, I feel so much better.'

Rina ignored the sarcasm. 'I left the city with a caravan of army jeeps.'

She took Peter's hand. 'Milligan had to catch an important meeting at the American Colonial Inn. The hotel is in East Jerusalem. Not for Jews, but the place is popular with non-Jewish tourists and reporters. We should check Milligan out. I got the willies when she talked about blowing up a school bus.'

'*What?* You think that's actually in the planning?'

'No, but—'

'Oh *shit*!' Decker began to pace. 'If so, we should call the police immediately.'

'And tell them what?'

'That you overheard a conversation where Milligan talked about blowing up a school bus.'

'Peter, she might have been using strong words to prove a point. If we report it as fact and nothing comes of it, you're going to lose credibility with the police. But I realize we just can't let a comment like that slip away.' She looked at her husband. 'First, tell me who Milligan is and why you're so interested in her.'

Decker started from the beginning, explaining Milligan's career in VerHauten, segueing into her financial involvement in companies also carried by the late Arik Yalom. He recapped his conversation with Marge: how Milligan could make a fortune if VerHauten ever decided to develop Southwest Mines. But Arik Yalom's interest in the company seemed to be a sticking point. Then Yalom was murdered, and Gold and the boys disappeared to Israel. Suddenly Milligan was here, too, asking questions about Shaul Gold.'

'Does Gold actually *own* Arik's portion of Southwest Mine stock?' Rina asked.

'I'm not sure. But that's my assumption.'

'Him and *not* the boys?'

Decker sighed. 'I don't know. Maybe the boys do own it and that's why they fled. But if that was the case, why would Milligan be asking about Gold?'

'Well, she couldn't ask the grandparents about the boys. That would be pretty obvious, right?'

'You're thinking that Milligan's trying to get to the boys via Gold.'

'Isn't it a possibility, especially since Gold is looking for the boys?'

Decker paused. 'You're very bright. So now I don't know who to be worried for first. The boys or a school bus.' He ran his hand over his face. 'What I'd like to know is, who were these men Milligan was talking to?'

'If she's out to get someone ... the boys or Gold ... maybe they were hired help, Peter.'

'These men were hit men?'

'Why not?' Rina asked.

'Because why would a woman of Milligan's smarts and stature travel all the way to Israel – a land I'm sure she

380

doesn't know much about – to murder Gold or the boys. She'd hire out.'

'Maybe that's what she was doing. Maybe she came here to hire some locals to kill them.'

'Unless these men were very good friends of hers, I think she'd be taking a very big chance.'

'Maybe they're not good friends of hers. But maybe Donald is. Donald certainly isn't an Arab name.'

'You're right. Who is this *Donald*?'

The room fell quiet.

Rina laughed, 'Well, we can go to the American Colonial Inn, pull Milligan out of the meeting, and ask her.'

'A fine idea in theory,' Decker said. 'It's the practical application. So much is going on . . . I've got to sort all this out. I don't want to act rashly.'

'Peter, *why* are you here?'

A very good question. It put everything into perspective. 'To find the Yalom boys before someone else does them harm.'

'I think it's a very good idea to investigate Milligan. And we probably should call or go to the police and tell them what I overheard. But if you think the boys are in grave danger, they should be our top priority.'

'Right,' Decker said. 'You're right again. We can't get sidetracked too much. Yes, we'll report what you heard. But I've got to remember why I'm here. Gold is looking for the boys, Milligan's looking for Gold. If I find the boys, I'm betting I'll find Milligan and Gold as well.' He turned to Rina. 'You know this country. Where do you think they'd be?'

'First thought?' She shrugged. 'Well, you mentioned something about Dov wanting to be religious but his father wouldn't let him. Maybe he's hiding in a yeshiva. There are

381

quite a few *ba'alei tchuvah* places in Jerusalem that take in
American boys, no questions asked. And, let's face it. All
those boys in black coats and hats look alike, tough for a
killer to spot him. Plus, it's hard to get inside a yeshiva
unless you know the ropes.'

'You think Gold would know the ropes?'

'Possibly,' Rina said. 'But as an Israeli, he probably
doesn't know too much about *ba'alei tchuvah* yeshivas for
Americans. By this time, the Yalom boys are more
American than Israeli.'

Decker agreed. There was a knock at the door. Immediately, Decker's heart started pumping hard. Maybe
someone had followed Rina back to the hotel. He put his
finger to his lips and quietly got off the bed.

'Peter,' Rina whispered. 'It's probably room service.'

He let out a big laugh. Mr Paranoid! Still, he wasn't
taking any chances. He chained the door before he opened
it and insisted that Rina duck out of sight. Better to feel silly
than sorry.

It was room service – a waiter named Mohammed.
Decker signed the bill but gave the young man a cash tip.
Apparently, it was generous because Mohammed grinned,
sporting a clear view of his gold front tooth.

Rina ritually washed her hands, then bit into her
sandwich. She was ravenous and it was delicious. Decker
sipped his Scotch, noticing that Rina was gulping her wine.
She was more nervous than he had ever seen her. Didn't
stop her intellect. Matter of fact, it heightened it.

She said, 'We really should go to Jerusalem. That's
where the two big *ba'alei tchuvah* yeshivas are. Milligan's
there. And so are the national police headquarters located
at French Hill.'

Decker wiped his mouth. 'Then let's do it.'

Rina finished her sandwich. 'Peter, you said that the boys fled shortly after they came home from school. What caused them to run away? The house hadn't been trashed, had it?'

Decker shook his head no.

'So from the boys' perspectives,' Rina went on, 'they just walked in their front door and saw that their parents weren't home. Why would the boys have taken off?'

Another very good question. If the boys weren't involved, how did they know something was amiss. He said, 'The only thing I can think of is that the parents left them a sign.'

'A sign?'

'A *signal* of some sort.' Decker thought out loud. 'Arik knew that Milligan had a lot to gain if she could get hold of his stocks. Maybe he knew she was capable of doing some pretty ruthless things to further her ambition. So he was worried. He told his sons that if they ever came home and saw such-and-such picture was crooked, or if such-and-such lamp—'

Decker suddenly stopped talking.

'What?' Rina asked.

Decker's eyes were on Rina, but his mind was elsewhere. 'Or if a certain porcelain dog was turned around...' He wagged his finger in the air. 'If you see that damn dog in the open shelf in the entry hall turned around, you go grab the money I left hidden for you in the inside mezuzah, you go grab your passports, and you get out of town immediately!'

His focus returned to Rina.

'There was a porcelain dog sitting in Yalom's entry hall facing backward. It would have been a very easy thing for Arik Yalom to do. Just a simple flick of the wrist on his way out the front door. The boys saw it and fled.'

'They must be terrified.'

'I'm sure they are.' Suddenly, Decker pulled his wife into an embrace. 'I love you so damn much!'

'I like it when you're passionate.'

'That's not passion, baby, that's relief.' Decker blew out air. 'Let's go find the boys.'

Decker opened the door, then turned to his wife. 'By the way. Did I mention that Honey Klein's probably in Israel?'

Rina stopped in her tracks. '*What?* She's *here*? You can't just *drop* that on me, Peter!'

Decker slipped his arm around Rina's shoulder and scooted her out the door. 'Tell you all about it on the ride over to Jerusalem.'

31

Rina looked out to a grove of sunflowers, stalks bending under the weight of their fruit, black faces with golden manes craning their necks toward the sunlight. Her eyes stared out the window, but her mind was on other things. She couldn't believe that Honey Klein had set out to murder her husband. The police and their conclusions just didn't square with the girl Rina had known, the woman and mother who had visited their home.

She faced her husband. 'I'm sorry. I just can't believe it.'

Decker said, 'Honey was trapped. As long as Gershon refused to give her a Jewish divorce – a *get* – she couldn't go on with her life. She couldn't see her way out of the relationship, so she took matters into her own hands.'

'Honey would *not* kill her husband.'

'And why not? Jews aren't immune to abject despair that leads to immoral acts.'

'You think she could live with herself and with her *children*, knowing that she purposely murdered their father?'

'How about if the father was abusing the kids?'

A horn honked from behind, a flash of lights in the rearview mirror. Peter glanced over his shoulder, then looked at the speedometer. 'I'm going over a hundred kilometers. What the hell does he want from me?'

'Just let him pass.'

'Jerk.' Decker pulled to the side and let a red Honda speed by. 'I wish I had my unmarked ... pull out the light and flash the mother. Man, I'd love to give him a ticket.'

'He wasn't, you know.'

'Who wasn't? What are you talking about?'

'Gershon Klein. He wasn't physically abusing the children.'

Decker's attention was still focused on the obnoxious driver. He turned to Rina. 'How do you know?'

Rina blew out air. 'Because I asked her.'

'When was this? Why didn't you tell me?'

'We never had time to talk about it. I was going to tell you, but then Honey disappeared. You were preoccupied with this big murder case. I didn't want to disturb your concentration. I thought about it on the plane ride but you slept the whole way—'

'*You* slept. I didn't sleep a wink. Too busy being serenaded by fifty throat-cracking adolescents singing Crash Test Dummies songs in Spanish.'

'Well, for whatever reason, we didn't talk.'

Decker said, 'You specifically asked Honey if Gershon was abusing the kids?'

'Yes.'

'And what did she say?'

'She said something like ...' Rina sighed. 'Oh boy, here goes. She said she'd kill him if he ever did that—'

'Oh boy is *right*!'

'No, Peter, it wasn't like that. You're taking her words out of context. She went on to say that Gershon had been a good man and a wonderful father—'

'Yeah, she was friggin' in love with the guy. That's why she was trying to divorce him.'

'She was cognizant of his problems. She knew he wasn't ... how did she put it ... he wasn't meant for organized life anymore.'

Decker said, 'The woman did him in, Rina. Trust me on this one.'

Another honk from behind. Decker yanked the wheel to the right and allowed the Camry to pass. 'I'm Jewish and they're pissing me off. I could only imagine what a goy would think.'

'It's a young country.'

'It's in its late forties.'

'That's a country in its teens. And like lots of adolescents we know and love, it has no manners. Give it time.'

'What were we talking about?'

'Gershon Klein.'

'Did Honey happen to mention to you that she was trying to divorce the guy?'

'No—'

'Yeah, she conveniently forgot that.'

'I think one of the kids walked in.'

The car began to balk as it made its climb through the mountains, toward Jerusalem. The air was clean and filled with the tang of pines.

'Peter, does it make sense for Honey to murder Gershon by drowning him in a bathtub?'

'It was probably the most effective weapon she had in the house.'

'Then why would she bother to shoot him, drag him over to his office, then trash the place to make it look like a robbery?'

Decker was quiet. 'I haven't worked that part out yet.'

Another blast from a horn. This time it was a woman who passed him. Equal opportunity rudeness. Decker said, 'Why do they have a stupid law like that on the books?'

Rina turned to him. 'What are you talking about?'

'Why can't a woman file for a Jewish divorce? The law is so damn archaic as well as sexist. It's unfair enough to raise even your underdeveloped feminist hackles.'

The car turned silent.

Decker said, 'I didn't mean it like that.'

'Yes, you did.'

'I didn't mean to be hurtful. I'm sorry.'

'Peter, where is it written that you can't be traditional and a feminist at the same time? One doesn't preclude the other.'

'You're right. I apologize—'

'I know *who* I am and I'm happy. There are still a few *relics* like me who are proud to be full-time mothers.'

'I'm proud of you, Rina. I'm proud of who you are and I wouldn't want you to change for the world.'

He was really *trying*! Biting back a smile, Rina gave him a mock sneer. 'You're just kissing up to me because you're lost in Israel without me.'

Decker was hurt. 'I'm being *sincere*!'

'Sincere, my foot!' Rina held back a laugh. 'Besides, it's not the feminists who look askance at us stay-at-home moms. It's everyone else. Especially the *men*—'

'*What*?'

'Men today have such unreasonable expectations—'

'Is this conversation going to deteriorate into a petty battle of the sexes?'

'It's not *enough* for us poor women to keep house and take care of the kids.' Rina began to tick off her fingers.

'We've also got to be beautiful, charming, sexy, physically fit, good cooks – amend that to *gourmet* chefs—'

'I don't believe I'm hearing—'

'. . . who can make cappuccino. You haven't the faintest idea how to steam milk, have you?'

'You got me there, Rina,' Decker said. 'For your information, lady, I don't drink cappuccino.'

'And we also have to work full time and bring in enough money to pay not only our own way, but also help pay for the kids' clothes, the babysitters, the groceries—'

'Are you *done* yet?'

'Basically.'

'Never once have I asked you to work outside the home. And never once have I asked you to pay bills. So I must be way ahead of these other schmucks you're talking about.'

'Indeed, Peter, you are neither a chauvinist nor a jerk.'

'So how about a little appreciation?'

'You're a saint.'

'I didn't say that! How'd we get on this stupid topic?'

'You were talking about Jewish divorce,' Rina stated. 'It's not the law that's bad, it's the implementation of the law that's the problem. In biblical days, if a husband was recalcitrant, the Rabbis had ways of making him cooperate. They might starve him or beat him until he relented and gave his wife a *get*. Harsh methods weren't considered inhumane acts.'

'You don't think starving or beating a guy is inhumane?'

'He doesn't starve or get beaten if he relents, Peter. He only gets into trouble if he remains unreasonably stubborn. Then the rabbis take action because they feel they are actually doing the man a favor—'

'They're doing him a favor by beating him up? This I've got to hear.'

Rina said, 'Any man who would blindly refuse to give his wife a *get* was under the control of his *yaitzer harah* – his evil impulses. The rabbis considered it appropriate to beat the *yaitzer harah* out of his soul until he came to reason, until he felt the compassion and kindness of his *yaitzer tov* – his goodness.'

'A lot like leeches. You bleed to death but it's good for you.'

'Peter, the process wasn't irreversible. At any time, when the husband saw reason and gave his wife a *get*, the beatings were stopped.'

'They just whopped him until he cried uncle?'

'I'm not a rabbi, so don't take what I say as fact. But I think the process went something like this. They'd ask him if he was going to give his wife a divorce. If he said no, they'd strike him. Then they'd ask him the same question again. If he said no again, they'd strike him again. And so on. Each time, they'd stop to ask him, hoping that the *yaitzer harah* had left his soul and he saw reason.'

Decker didn't speak right away. Then he said, 'And what happened if his *yaitzer harah* refused to leave? What happened if he never saw reason?'

Rina was quiet.

'Rina, did you hear my question? What happened if the guy kept on refusing to give his wife a *get*?'

'Again, I'm no rabbi.'

'I understand. Answer the question to the best of your ability.'

Rina exhaled forcefully. 'I think that if he died during the procedure, it was not considered murder. It was considered the ultimate liberation of his *yaitzer harah*. The man has seen reason through death. His wife was free.'

'Are you saying if he consistently refused, he was beaten to death?'

'You should ask Rabbi Schulman—'

'To the best of your knowledge, darlin'.'

'I think he could be beaten to the point of death. If he was that desperate or vengeful to hold on to his wife, he was possessed.'

'So this whole ritual is kind of like an exorcism?'

'Peter, I don't want to misrepresent the law. Ask Rabbi Schulman.'

Decker reflected upon her words as the Subaru continued its upward path to Jerusalem. The whole approach to divorce seemed not only arcane and unnecessary, but *dangerous*. A frustrated woman, a vindictive man, and no way out. Decker cleared his throat. 'Does it have to be beating or starving the man?'

'What do you mean?'

'Suppose the rabbis...' Again, Decker cleared his throat. 'Can they exorcise the demons by drowning instead?'

'Gershon was shot, Peter.'

'But he died from drowning, Rina. And it makes sense, doesn't it? Because if anyone was possessed, it was Gershon Klein. It wasn't his fault per se, just his *yaitzer harah* acting up—'

'You're making fun of me.'

'I'm trying to make sense out of something that's irrational to me. I'm trying to think like Honey's Rebbe, putting myself in his position. Because that's who she'd run to. The Rebbe probably figured what would it hurt to give him a few minor dunkings. It's better

391

than a beating because it doesn't leave marks—'

'Peter, the main objective of the process wasn't to kill anyone. It was to bring the man to reason.'

'But what if the man is simply *incapable* of reason, Rina?' Decker heard another honk. Instead of pulling over, he pressed the pedal to the metal. The car bucked, then flew upward, jolting them back in their seats.

'What are you doing?' Rina cried out.

Decker said. 'Car doesn't accelerate too well, does it? You like my theory?'

'No.'

'Why? Because you don't want to picture a bunch of holy rabbis methodically drowning a crazy man?'

'Even if you're right, even if they were trying to bring Gershon to reason, I'm sure they didn't *mean* to kill him.'

'But Gershon's still dead all the same. No wonder the great Rebbe didn't want me on the case. He wasn't protecting Honey. He was trying to save his own hide.'

'Maybe he was doing both.'

'One thing is for certain. He was being obstructionist for his own gain. Because he couldn't see beyond the absurdity of what he was doing. Talk about blindly following the letter of the law.'

Rina didn't answer. They drove the next few minutes in heavy silence. Finally, she said, 'I'm very religious, Peter. I accept lots of laws on faith. Even laws that don't make a lot of sense to me. Even so, I am a product of the twentieth century. The way Jewish divorce has been used by some men against their wives is a crime. Resentful husbands basically blackmail the women. They use *gets* as weapons – to obtain better property settlements or better visitation rights . . . to get lower alimony and child-support payments.

It's terrible. Some of the rabbis are very sympathetic to the women's plights.' She paused. 'But others are not.'

'Is anyone *doing* anything about it?'

'Yes, of course. Some of the rabbis are putting clauses in the official Jewish marriage contract – the *ketubah*. They add clauses that state that if the husband refuses to give his wife a Jewish divorce after the civil divorce goes through, he must pay her enormous amounts of money daily until he relents. Unfortunately, the rabbis weren't doing things like that when Honey got married.'

Decker said, 'I don't think money would have been a motivating factor for someone as far gone as Gershon Klein anyway.'

'So maybe the rabbis did what they thought they could do. Maybe they used what halachic means they had available.'

'It's *murder*, Rina!'

'You're judging by American jurisprudence standards.'

'Damn right, I am. They live in the USA not in Israel . . . do they do that in Israel?'

Rina shook her head. 'They just put them in jail.'

'But they don't starve them . . . beat them?'

'No, they can't do that legally.'

'So even here, it's murder.'

Rina didn't speak.

Decker said, 'You don't consider it murder?'

'I consider the whole thing tragic.'

Rina navigated Decker down Jaffa Road – an old main thoroughfare cluttered with people and traffic. Decker wanted to gawk, to take in the parade, but there was work to be done. Sightseeing was for another time and occasion. By the grime collected on the buildings, Decker could tell he was in the old area of town. It wasn't pretty but it wasn't ugly either. Part of the reason was that all the buildings were made from the same colored limestone. The material not only lent a uniformity to the city, but was durable as well.

He and Rina weren't talking much. Their discussion about Honey and divorce had sobered them. His mind was ablaze with images: a crazy man dunked in a bathtub, never fully understanding the gravity of his crime. A wife hopelessly trapped in a loveless, mindless marriage. Children caught in the middle . . .

Rina said, 'I think it's right off Machane Yehudah – the Jewish Marketplace. Turn down the next road and let me see where we're at.'

Decker's attention snapped to the present. 'Where are we going?'

'To Or Torah. It's one of the biggest yeshivas for newcomers. Turn here.'

Decker made a sharp right, the Subaru hugging the cobblestones quite nicely.

Rina said, 'Park anywhere you can just so long as the curb is marked with blue and white stripes. They Denver-boot here. The yeshiva's a couple of blocks. We'll walk. It'll be easier and nice to stretch our legs.'

'How about that solid blue curb?'

'That's okay, too.'

Decker squeezed the car into a tight space. As per instructions from the car rental agency, he crook-locked the gear shift to the wheel and got out of the car. He sprinted around the side and opened the passenger door for Rina.

'A gentleman,' she said.

Decker smiled, helped Rina out of the car, and looked

around. The cobbled street was tiny and had no sidewalks. Many of the cars were parked with their right wheels over the curb onto dirt and their left wheels still in the street. A line of cars doing wheelies.

The neighborhood held what appeared to be apartment houses – square limestone buildings punched with small windows. Laundry hung from the sides. Some of the structures had grass patches in front. Some had window boxes. A small fruit stand was perched on one corner; across the street were a bakery and post office. A background buzz of yelps and shouts permeated the air. Something Decker hadn't heard for a long time. Children in the streets at play.

They started walking.

'You look very upset,' Decker said.

'I am,' Rina said. 'This whole thing with Gershon is just horrible. What's worse is, Honey's probably taking the blame for the village's mistake. The cops think *she* did it. And she's not around to set the record straight.'

'Anything for the Rebbe,' Decker said. 'And to tell you the truth, I'm not crying for her. Even if she didn't murder her husband, she owns some culpability. She knew what was going to happen.'

'I'm sure Honey never dreamed they would actually *kill* Gershon. And I'm sure they didn't mean to kill him. Oh, Peter, the whole thing is just sickening!'

'Yes, it is. But right now, I've got Dov and Gil Yalom to worry about.'

'Poor kids. Peter, how in the world do you deal with so much tragedy?'

'I compartmentalize. Come on. Let's go.'

32

The cell-like stone entry to the yeshiva was cold and dim, the scant illumination provided by a small, square barred window and an uncovered light bulb dangling from the ceiling. The walls were masoned with limestone blocks; the floor was tiled with a travertine-colored crushed rock. The air was damp. Decker could almost smell the spores. He stuck his hands in his pockets and bounced on his feet, eyes darting about.

Rina lagged behind, watching her husband's jumpiness. He was lost, depending on her to trailblaze. She stepped inside the chilly room, her hand reaching up to touch the mezuzah posted on the doorjamb. She kissed her fingertips.

'Are you all right?' she asked.

'I'm with you, I'm fine.'

He waited for his pupils to dilate, then looked around. An empty desk along the right-hand wall; behind it was an open door leading somewhere. He called out a hello, then wondered if hello was the greeting of choice in Israel.

It took a few moments for a young man to come through the door behind the desk, his fingers touching the mezuzah, then his lips, as he came into the room. He was good-looking with solid features and a masculine bone structure, even though his cheeks and chin were hidden by a thick, black beard. He wore a black suit, white shirt, and no tie. Atop his close-cropped head was a black hat. Big brown eyes studied Rina first, then Decker, then climbed back to Rina. It was as if he instinctively knew to whom to talk.

'Yes, can I help you?'

An American accent. Decker was elated. *The man spoke English.* 'You're from the States.'

The man nodded.

'Whereabouts?'

'Omaha, believe it or not. Is there something I can help you with?'

'Yes, as a matter of fact there is. I'm Detective Sergeant Peter Decker from the Los Angeles Police Department.' Decker took out his badge and showed it to the Nebraskan. 'I'm here on official business. I'm looking for two teenaged brothers – Gil and Dov Yalom. Their parents were murdered about a week ago in Los Angeles and they've disappeared. We're trying to find them – just to talk to them.'

The young man studied Decker's badge, then lifted his eyes. 'And you think they're here?'

'I know they're in Israel. I have reason to suspect that the younger boy – Dov – might be hiding out in a yeshiva.'

'In Or Torah specifically?'

Decker said, 'A frightened, young kid alone in a foreign country. A yeshiva is a perfect sanctuary.'

'What does *that* mean?' The man was offended.

'All my husband meant was that the boy may be in trouble. He's probably seeking *Hashem* for guidance.'

'Do you know Dov Yalom?' Decker said.

'Not at all.'

Too fast a response? Decker studied the young man.

'Dov Yalom's parents were murdered. He ran away because someone scared him away. It's imperative that we find him before someone else does.'

'I don't understand.'

'I think the boy's in danger. And frankly, anyone who's keeping him might be in danger as well.'

The man stepped back and folded his arms across his chest. 'Who exactly *are* you two?'

Decker peered into the face. 'Has someone else been asking for Dov Yalom, sir?'

'No.' Again, he spoke too quickly. 'I think I should call the police.'

Decker called his bluff. 'Go ahead. We'll search the place together.'

The man said nothing. He rocked back and forth on his heels. Rina broke into Hebrew. The man answered her back angrily. Decker bit his tongue, as the two of them went at it for a while. In the end, Rina seemed to have won out. The man dropped his arms at his sides and stared at Decker.

'You two are *married*?'

Decker nodded.

'She isn't your partner?'

Decker didn't answer right away. Now he was positive that someone had been here before him. Someone who told this young man that a cop and his female partner were out looking for Dov Yalom. Who? Gold? Milligan? Both knew Marge was Decker's partner.

'No, she isn't my partner. She's translating for me.' Decker rolled his tongue in his cheeks. 'Do you have a name, sir?'

'Moti.' He held out his hand. 'Moti Bernstein.'

'Moti Bernstein from Omaha.' Decker took the hand.

'It's a pleasure to meet you, Moti. Now who told you that I might come over here and poke around.'

'No one told me anything.'

'Then why did you think that this charming young woman who covers her hair was my partner?'

Bernstein didn't answer right away. Then he said, 'Look, I'd like to help you. But there's no Dov Yalom here. Sorry.'

'He might be using an alias.' Decker handed Bernstein a stack of Dov's high school pictures. 'Does this boy look familiar?'

The religious man flipped through the pictures, then handed them back. 'I've never seen this boy.'

'I'd like to look around anyway.'

'You don't believe me?'

'I believe you, Moti,' Decker said. 'But sometimes I see things that no one else sees.'

'You know, parents are really nervous about letting their kids stay here. Israel gets a real bad rap because the foreign newspapers depict it as a much more dangerous place than it is. If I let you poke around, it's going to raise a lot of dander.'

Decker didn't speak right away. 'You're willing to risk a kid's life to keep up an image?'

The tops of Bernstein's cheeks took on a rosy hue. 'I'm just saying I don't recognize the boy in the picture. So what excuse do I have to let you poke around and invade people's privacy?'

Again Decker paused before he spoke, his eyes boring into Bernstein's. 'I thought Judaism has a concept called *pikuach nefesh*. That the saving of a life takes precedence over *everything*!'

Bernstein stared at Decker. 'You learn, Sergeant?'

Decker stared back. '*What?*'

'You know about *pikuach nefesh*, you must have done some learning.' Bernstein dragged his toe over the stone floor. 'See, if you were learning, then *maybe* you'd want to go inside the *bais midrash* to look up something.'

Decker knew the *bais midrash* was the study hall which held the library of reference tomes for the yeshiva students. Most of the students congregated there for classes, lessons, and studying. In effect, Bernstein was giving him an excuse to look over the majority of the boys at the yeshiva.

Decker said, 'I'm studying *B'rachos*. I could use some reference material.'

'Fine, I'll take you to the *bais midrash*. Who am I to deny a scholar?' Bernstein glanced at Rina, then averted his eyes. 'It would be better if you waited here. You might be kind of distracting—'

'I know, I know. I'll wait here.'

Bernstein's eyes fell on Decker's face. 'You don't have a black hat, do you?'

'No. Do I look too goyishe?'

'More like a secular Jew, and that's just as noticeable. You're going to draw attention. Do you want that?'

Decker said, 'It would be better if I blended in.'

Bernstein studied Decker and gave a hopeless shrug. 'You won't blend in. But maybe I can help so you won't stand out so much. Wait here. I'll find you a hat.'

Again, Rina checked her watch, amazed to discover that only ten minutes had passed. She now knew the secret of Einstein's theory of relativity. Endless time had nothing to do with the speed of light or the mass of the object. It had everything to do with standing in a cold room on a bone-chilling floor with nothing to do. Ten minutes translated into ten hours in Comfortable Earth Time.

Nobody had passed through the portals. It was as if the entry was the weigh station of purgatory. Suddenly, the concept of indulgences made sense.

The solitude did give her an unwelcome chance to reflect upon Peter's assessment of Honey Klein and her village, to think about Jewish divorce.

It wasn't that Judaism had an innate antifemale bias. As a matter of fact, the original laws of marriage and divorce were laws of protection for both parties. While it was true that men could file for divorce for reasons as trivial as bad cooking, it was equally true that women could file for many reasons – if the man was unattractive to her, if he didn't fulfill her sexually. Wasn't that the case with Gershon?

The law was on Honey's side. Gershon should have granted her a divorce. And when he didn't, the rabbis did what was in their Jewish legal right to do.

Yet, no matter how she thought about it, Peter was right. It was still murder. She wondered how far Peter would pursue what he suspected.

A little old man walked through the open doors, his overcoat dragging on the floor, his black hat too large and slightly askew. His demeanor suggested disorganization. He had a long white beard and spoke to Rina in a high-pitched voice. His Hebrew was thick with a Moroccan accent.

'No one is here?'

Rina shrugged.

The old man rubbed his hands together. 'You haven't seen anyone?'

Again, Rina shrugged innocence.

'You are waiting for someone?'

'Yes.'

'Your son?'

'My husband.'

The old man took out a card. 'Maybe he would like to give us a small donation.'

The card told Rina he was working for Yeshiva Rev Yosef Caro. He was a *meshulach* – someone who goes around collecting money for an institution or a poor family, then takes a cut of whatever he collects. Most Jews called them *shnorrers*.

The man said, 'You can make a donation, too.'

Rina smiled wearily. 'I have your card. Thank you.'

The man said, 'I go inside. Check the *bait midrash*.'

Bait instead of *bais*. Sephardic pronunciation. Rina told him to go check. The man left.

Another ten minutes crept by. Again, Rina thought about Honey Klein, about Arik and Dalia Yalom. Two boys suddenly orphaned, four other children without a father. Her mind drifted with faraway thoughts, her emotions sinking into a whirlpool of tragedy. Tears had formed in her eyes.

No, this wouldn't do at all.

She went behind the desk, through the door, kissing the mezuzah as she went into a hallway.

Lots of doors muffling noise. The air here was warmer, but a great deal more stale. Gravel-voiced men speaking of the intricacies of Jewish civil law. Rina put her ear to one door, then opened it. Empty – devoid of people but filled with folding chairs, the space inside not much bigger than a walk-in closet. A window had been opened, allowing a tiny draft of fresh air to percolate.

At the end of the hallway was a staircase with tiny stone steps worn smooth by traffic. Rina held the wrought-iron handrail and walked down a flight.

The basement held a communal kitchen and dining hall. Wafting through the air was the smell of onions and garlic sweating with grease. The lunchroom was empty, the doors locked. But heat came through the walls and warmed the bottom layer of air a couple of degrees. That was good, Rina thought. The boys could eat in comfort during the winter months.

She climbed back up two stories. The *bais midrash* was the biggest room on the floor. Even at a distance, Rina could hear the shouting and arguing of boys engaged in learning. The *bais haknesset* – the yeshiva's sanctuary – no doubt occupied the other big room. Rina didn't go inside in case there was a prayer minyan going on. She didn't want to disturb anyone. Checking her watch, she saw that only five minutes had passed. She decided to explore the two floors above.

The upstairs levels were just dorm rooms spilling over with piles of dirty clothes and sweat. Each floor had a small private kitchen and a laundry room – three washers and one dryer each. All of the machines were in use.

Rina climbed back down two flights, debating whether to go inside the *bais midrash*. Maybe Peter would need her help. She knew rationally that Moti Bernstein could translate anything Peter needed to know. Plus a lot of the boys here were American and English-speaking. Still, what if Bernstein chose to misrepresent something? Or there was a snatch of conversation in Hebrew that might be relevant to Peter's case? Only Rina would recognize that.

She went inside.

The din was deafening, the sweat and heat given off by the hundred or so boys hitting her face. The walls were taken up by bookshelves, high dormer windows struggling to let in natural light. The room was made bright by the parallel lines of fluorescent tubing on the ceiling. Through a thick fog of black, Rina could spot Peter across the room, a too-small derby perched over his carrot-colored hair. The hat looked like a candlesnuffer trying to extinguish a flame.

On the left side of the room was a big conference table occupied by a group of twenty boys. The rabbi was giving them a lecture, his deep voice managing to project over the noise. The rest of the room was filled with lecterns and desks. Most of the boys had paired off with their *chavrusas* – their learning partners. The boys shouted at each other, locked in verbal combat. What looked like a hostile interchange was, in fact, just a routine method of learning Talmud.

Rina looked about, sensing that more than a few of the boys were aware of her presence. Some stared hungrily, others gripped their *payis*, as if holding their side curls would ward off their lust.

Decker spotted her and waved. She squeezed her way through black coats and desks, and found her husband.

'Any luck?'

'A blank so far. At least, *I* haven't seen him. How many other yeshivas are there like this one?'

'In Jerusalem there are two others,' Bernstein answered.

Rina felt eyes upon her. The gravel-voiced rabbi who was giving the lecture was glaring at her. 'Maybe I should leave.'

Bernstein nodded vigorously.

'I won't be more than a few minutes, Rina,' Decker said.

Rina took a final glance around the room, espying the little old unkempt man. 'I see the *meshulach* found you, Moti. Boy, are those guys persistent.'

'What *meshulach*?' Bernstein said.

'That little old man who's walking out the door—'

Rina's hand suddenly flew to her chest. 'Peter, catch up with that guy. He doesn't belong.'

, Reacting as a professional – actions first, questions later – Decker took off immediately, breaking through the wall of black clothing, just in time to see the little old man enter the stairwell.

'Hey!' Decker shouted out loud. 'Hey! You!'

The man bolted like a jackrabbit, scaling down the steps in allegro tempo. He hit the door, then fastballed his overcoat into Decker's face. Cursing, Decker peeled it off his eyes and sprinted after him, both of them running into the glare of a blinding, setting sun. Squinting, Decker took off in what he hoped was the right direction, praying that strong rays had slowed the guy's pace.

Through bleached vision, he managed to spot the intruder darting through the streets, into the path of oncoming cars. For just a moment, he froze – a deer caught in the headlights. Then he sped forward, causing several vehicles to screech and swerve on sudden stops.

The moment's hesitation was all Decker needed. He leaped with full stride across the street, narrowing the distance between him and his prey. The man was faster but shorter. Decker used every inch of his long legs to close in. Another few seconds and he knew he'd be in striking distance. Taking a giant step forward, he extended his gorilla arms and shoved the man hard in the back, breaking his rhythm, causing him to trip over his own feet.

Decker leaped to the side as the man fell forward, running past him for several paces. Then he backtracked and jumped on top of the man, his knee pressed into the small of the intruder's back. The man was young, his flailing arms striking wildly. Decker pulled them behind his back.

'Take it easy, buddy. I just want to talk to you.'

The guy was small and slight, his pasted beard falling off his face. Without it, he appeared no older than twenty-five. He was talking rapidly and in gibberish. It took Decker a few moments to realize that, in fact, the man was speaking in a foreign language. People had gathered around, all of them talking to him at the same time.

Well, this was swell, Decker thought. He had literally tackled a man without knowing why and couldn't explain himself to anyone around.

Get yourself out of this one, Deck.

When in doubt, don't talk. Just look official. He flashed his badge and, in a deep, authoritative voice, told everyone to move back.

Not a soul budged. In fact, the crowd began to close the circle around him, people shouting, probably demanding explanations. The man broke into bloodcurdling screams. The crowd moved closer. Sweat began to pour down Decker's face. All he could remember were Rina's words – that they were in a Levantine country. Which at the moment conjured up images of mob rule or, just as bad, a Levantine jail.

Then, like the angel Gabriel, Rina appeared, breathless and wet with perspiration. Moti Bernstein was at her side. She stammered out, 'This guy said he was a *meshulach*, which he isn't. Find out who he is, Peter.'

'I don't think we speak the same language, Rina. First, get the crowd off my back.'

Rina shouted something in Hebrew. It took several orders and a little pushing by Moti Bernstein before the crowd retreated an inch. Then she focused her attention on the man, demanding answers to her questions. The man remained silent.

Decker held the man tightly, 'Moti, search his pockets.'

A quick trip through his garment revealed nothing. In Hebrew, Rina asked him his name.

'*Kus amak!*' he replied.

And then he spat at Rina's face.

Decker felt his head explode. He pushed upward on the man's restrained arm and gripped it hard. 'You got ten seconds before I snap the sucker in two—'

'Noooooo!' The man began to struggle violently. 'No break!'

'Well, look who talks English.' Decker thought quickly. It was only a matter of minutes before the police arrived and the guy would be lost to him. Calmly, he said, 'Rina, ask him what he was doing at the yeshiva? And tell him if I don't like the answer, he's dead meat.'

Rina translated the question. The man turned white but said nothing. Decker knew it was useless questioning him among the masses. He jerked him like a rag doll. 'Let's take a walk back to the yeshiva—'

'No yeshiva!' the man cried out. 'Is bomb there! No yeshiva!'

'You *fuck*!' Decker screamed. 'Moti, run back and evacuate the yeshiva immediately.' Decker gripped the bomber's arms and pushed him forward, dragging him as he went limp. 'Now you're going to show me and the police where you put the bomb, you understand!'

'No good! Fife minoots!'

'It's going to go off in five minutes?'

The man nodded. 'Fife minoots.'

'Jesus Christ!' Decker grabbed the first male he saw – a man in his forties who appeared fit. 'Hold him.'

Decker took off, raced in the direction of the yeshiva, his only concern now saving the boys. Moti had just finished rounding up the boys when Decker stormed into the *bais midrash*. Moti was trying to keep order among panicked boys, but was losing control. Everyone was running toward the stairwell. Moti saw Decker and started shaking.

'Someone has to go upstairs to get the boys in the dorm!'

'Got it!' Decker screamed. 'Single file everyone.' He began pushing boys in an orderly line. 'Move it, but watch your feet. I don't want anyone trampled on. Moti, is there another staircase?'

'No.'

'Then we'll make do with this.' Decker bounded up a flight of steps, then went running down the hallway, shouting the word bomb as he pounded on doors. He fished out about twenty boys and led them to the staircase. He checked his watch.

If the motherfucker was right, he had two and a half minutes to go.

Up the final flight of stairs. Again, shouting to be heard. Three boys emerged from the front rooms. Then to the last room down the hallway. Out came a teenaged boy dressed in yeshiva garb, a small mole under his eye.

Gil Yalom.

Victory, but a pyrrhic one if they all blew to smithereens. Decker grabbed the teenager's hand and led him and the remaining boys to the bottleneck of human flesh, disorganization, and panic slowing things down. Decker knew he was going to have to direct traffic if they were all going to get out of here alive.

Two minutes to go.

To Gil, Decker said, 'I'm police, Gil. I'm here to help. If you run from me, you'll be dead in a week. So wait for me outside!'

Decker broke loose of Gil and pushed his way to the

front, using his wide arms to unclog the drain. He pushed boys, rearranged them, forcing order upon the horror-stricken. Rapidly and orderly – two at a time out the door. He looked up.

The staircase was still half full.

One minute to go.

'Run! Run! Run!' Decker shouted as he and Moti shoved the boys out the door. 'Far away from the building! Run!'

Decker looked up at the staircase again. At the top, behind all the boys, were a dozen rabbis holding Torah scrolls – four large scrolls, two men to a Torah. Decker prayed they wouldn't drop one of them in his sight. That would mean 40 days of daylight fasting ... providing he made it in one piecc.

Decker looked beyond them, at the empty space at the top of the steps.

Thirty seconds.

More and more boys filing into the streets. Moti shouting at them to go farther back. At last, Decker could see Gil Yalom approaching the exit.

The last of the boys!

Behind him a parade of long-coated rabbis. Slowly, the Torahs began to descend the last flight of steps, rabbis walking carefully so they wouldn't drop the holy writings.

Twenty seconds.

Three steps down, another three steps down.

'C'mon! C'mon!' Decker shouted.

Ten seconds.

Another step down.

Five.

And another.

Four.

Another.

Three.

To the front door.

Two.

Decker grabbed the last of the holy scrolls and fled to the streets.

One.

And then nothing.

A huge crowd had gathered. They waited.

Fifteen seconds passed.

And waited.

A minute.

And waited.

Decker shifted the Torah onto his right shoulder and looked at his watch. Another thirty seconds had passed.

A false alarm.

The police arrived, two cars, then another two. They pushed the crowds back. One gentleman was moving toward Decker, who was still holding the Torah. He spoke, Decker didn't understand. Then the man started talking English.

He was with the police, around five-ten, one-eighty with well-developed arms. His complexion was dark, his face was round with fleshy cheeks, and he had a head full of black curls. He was wearing a yarmulke. His English was accented but understandable.

'Who are you?' he repeated.

'You want the long version or the short one?' He looked around. Gil Yalom was standing by himself, wiping his eyes. 'Someone planted a bomb in the yeshiva.'

'Who?' the cop asked.

'I don't know who he is. He's back a couple of blocks. They're holding him for you. I ran back here to get the boys out.'

Three minutes had passed. The yeshiva remained whole.

Decker shifted his weight, realizing he was still holding the Torah. He called a rabbi over and passed him the holy scroll. Once liberated of the heavy article, he rolled his shoulders and looked at the cop. The face was round and he looked to be around thirty-five, with intelligent black eyes.

The man lit a cigarette and blew smoke in Decker's face. 'I hear on my radio. There is no bomber—'

'*What*!'

'He escape. Where he say he put bomb?'

'I think it's in the *bais midrash*.'

'You think? You don't know?'

'He never said where he put it.'

'He never said! A quiet man, this escape bomber.'

Decker stared at the cop, aware that he had zip credibility. 'I gave the bomber over to someone in the crowd, then came back here to help. I told the man to hold him until the police came!'

Moti broke into the conversation. He and the cop spoke for a few moments in Hebrew. The cop turned his attention back to Decker. 'You have some identification on you?'

Decker reached into his jacket pocket and handed a stack of papers to the cop – his passport, his badge, and official papers for the Yalom boys. The cop started to rifle through them, staring at the typed words. He probably spoke some English, but Decker was willing to bet he didn't read it too well. Rina had finally caught up with him, hugged him fiercely.

'Thank God!'

Decker embraced her back. Five minutes had passed and still nothing had happened. He felt like a fool.

The cop took his cigarette out of his mouth. 'Who is this woman?'

'My wife.'

'You always take your wife on your cases . . .' The cop squinted and studied Decker's passport. 'Sergeant Peter Decker, is it?'

He pronounced the word *ser-kee-ant*.

'I don't speak Hebrew,' Decker explained. 'My wife does.'

The cop pocketed Decker's identification. The action gave Decker a sinking feeling in the pit of his stomach. 'We talk later. I make my calls. You wait here.'

'I'm not going anywhere. You have my passport.'

'*B'emet, adoni*. You not go anywhere.'

The cop turned his back, just in time to miss the initial blast from the second floor of the yeshiva. It was followed by an even stronger explosion. Glass rained down, the air heavy with the smell of smoke and fire and panicked screams. Decker pushed Rina's head deep in his chest and shielded his own eyes from the glass. When he looked up, he saw flames licking the sashes of the blown-out windows. Rina was shaking in his arms, sobbing against his chest. Decker looked at the hundreds of black-garbed boys. The children were hugging each other and crying. The rabbis were embracing the Torahs and weeping as well. Moti Bernstein had frozen in panic, tears running down his cheeks. Decker blinked. His own eyes felt as dry as dust.

The cop stared at Decker open-mouthed, his dangling cigarette falling from his lips and onto the ground. In a soft but firm voice, he said, 'Who *are* you?'

Decker's eyes were on Gil Yalom. 'See that boy over there sitting under the olive tree?'

The cop nodded.

'I came here to look for him. His name is Gil Yalom.' Decker pointed to the scorched building. 'I'm looking for his brother, Dov, as well. Rina, can you give this guy a quick rundown for me.'

Rina spoke rapidly. The cop answered her back in equally rapid Hebrew. They spoke for a few minutes. Then the cop crooked a finger in Gil's direction. Slowly, the boy got up, his face a mask of terror.

The cop said, 'We need to talk – all of us.'

Decker said, 'I'm ready.'

33

In the brief car ride over to the police station at French Hill, Rina, placed in the front seat, had learned that the cop was a *mefakeah* – an inspector. His name was Ezra Elhiani; he was thirty-four and a former colonel in the Israeli army. His division had been tanks. Elhiani wore dark slacks and an open-necked white shirt. He smoked like a chimney, sucking his cigarettes down to the butt. The smell was so thick, it was nauseating. Unfortunately for Decker, it was also inviting.

Four years and, like a zombie, the cursed craving refused to die.

Knees to his chest, Decker was pressed into the back-seat, next to Gil Yalom. He tried to make some headway, the first question being, where was his brother, Dov? But no matter how much he stressed urgency, Gil sat motion-less and mute. Decker knew Gil's behavior was a product of shock so he eased up. But his mind kept going, bursting with images.

A director couldn't have staged the scene with more drama. The screaming fire trucks, the wailing ambulances, the racing squads of police cars, frightened boys hugging themselves, hysterical neighbors hugging each other, rab-bis praying in the street, and lots of standers-by offering opinions without foundation. Then the newspeople came.

415

Lucky for Decker he didn't speak Hebrew. He was relieved when Elhiani motioned Rina, Gil Yalom, and him over to the police car.

It was a tiny thing – a white compact with a blue flashing light – an igloo on wheels. He could barely squeeze inside. He opted for the backseat to get to Gil. But it was Rina who got information, such as it was.

At police headquarters, Gil was taken away immediately. Decker and Rina were seated in a tiny windowless cell barely big enough to accommodate the few folding chairs it had. There was a one-way mirror on the wall.

Elhiani came in, lit up, and blew out a plume of smoke that hung in the static air.

Decker said, 'We've got to get Gil Yalom to open up. Find out where his brother is staying. If someone tried to blow him up, someone's going to do the same for Dov.'

Elhiani puffed his cigarette and licked his lips. 'The boy is not talking to anyone right now.'

Decker reminded himself to speak slowly. 'People are going to die unless we find out where his brother is hiding.'

'Your anger will not serve anything, *adoni*.'

Decker took a deep breath. 'I'm not angry, I'm *anxious*. We evacuated just minutes before the building blew up.'

'Nothing blew up,' Elhiani answered evenly. 'Yes, windows popped, and some *sepharim* burned. A pity, but the fire people put the flames out like that.' He snapped his fingers. 'The building still stands and hardly a stone is cracked. Good construction.'

Decker glared at Elhiani.

'Not that you didn't do a *tovah* and a *mitzvah*,' Elhiani said. 'Maybe we give you key to the city and take your picture for newspaper.'

Decker forced himself to unclench his jaw. 'I'm not

interested in accolades, but I do want to find Dov Yalom. I need to talk to Gil.'

'The boy is with doctors. He is in shock and is given sleepy medicines. Your talk with him will have to wait.'

Decker was about to explode, then held back, remembering the ride over. The boy had been stunned with fright. What was the use of pounding him with questions he couldn't process?

'I go through all your official papers,' Elhiani said. 'Everything is in order. Why don't you contact police when you first got here?'

Decker said, 'I just arrived here yesterday.'

Elhiani raised his brow. 'Do you always make such excitement in twenty-four hours?'

'It's a long story.'

Elhiani sucked in smoky poison and took out a pad and a pen. 'Tell me your long story, Sar-kee-ant.'

Decker did just that. Every so often Elhiani would interrupt and ask Rina to translate. After Decker had finished, the room was silent, bathed in suds of nicotine.

Elhiani leaned back in the folding chair. 'Why do you think this bomb is for Yalom and not terrorist act?'

Decker ran his hand over his face. 'That's just it. It was supposed to look like a terrorist act. The only reason *we* know it wasn't random is because we know the history.'

'I'm still not so sure,' Elhiani said. 'Describe to me this mad bomber.'

Rina broke in. 'He came into the yeshiva wearing a long beard and an overcoat. He acted like a *meshulach*. He even gave me a card with the name of the yeshiva he was collecting for.'

'You have the card?'

'In my purse.'

'And where is your purse?'

'You took it,' Rina said.

'Ah,' Elhiani said. 'Please. Continue.'

Rina said, 'I had no reason to suspect he was anything else but a *shnorrer*.'

'But you changed your mind?'

Rina squirmed in her seat as she thought about a soldier's words.

They may know the motions, they don't have the emotions.

'It was the way he kissed the mezuzah.'

Decker looked at her. 'What?'

'When he walked out of the *bais midrash*, he didn't kiss the mezuzah right.'

'You told me to tackle a complete and utter stranger based on the way he kissed the mezuzah?'

'I was right, wasn't I?'

'Please, please.' Elhiani waved his hand. 'Go on, *g'veret.*'

'Peter, rabbis usually touch the mezuzah with the fringes of their tzitzit, then kiss the fringes. Even if they use their fingers, they touch the mezuzah with their fingertips only. This guy covered the mezuzah with his entire hand and kissed his palm. Someone had schooled him, but not quite correctly. And even though he was wearing tzitzit, he didn't use them. Because he didn't know what they were for.'

She threw up her hands.

'What can I say? It's an intangible thing. And I was right.'

Decker thankfully admitted she was.

Elhiani spoke to her in Hebrew. Rina laughed.

Decker asked, 'What'd he say?'

Rina said, 'The moral of the story is listen to your wife.'

'I have a problem,' Elhiani announced.

They waited.

Elhiani said, 'If this is not act of terrorism, if the bombing is to kill Gil Yalom, it is a stupid way to do that. What if Gil was not in *bais midrash*? Then the explosion does nothing to him. And as fact, he wasn't in the *bais midrash*.'

Decker said, 'At any given time during the day, the *bais midrash* holds the majority of the boys. The man was playing the odds.'

'I don't understand playing odds?'

Rina translated.

'Ah,' Elhiani said. 'They want him dead but only ninety percent.'

Decker smiled. 'Mefakeah, someone brutally murdered this boy's parents. The boys fled in fear. I think someone was out to murder Gil. But he didn't want to draw attention to the fact that he was out to get Gil. So he made it look like a random terrorist act. Do you understand what I'm saying?'

'Yes, your English is okay.' Elhiani puffed away. 'And you think your mad bomber will be out to get the other brother?'

'Him or someone else. But yes, I think Dov Yalom, wherever he is, is in danger.'

'It still doesn't make me sense,' Elhiani said. 'To use a bomb. Bomb isn't missile. Bomb doesn't aim and hit target. Bomb just explodes. If you are there, you die. If not, you don't die. Why use something so unperfect? Why not choose to stab him on the street like terrorist usually do?'

Decker said, 'Gil was in hiding. Which means the hit man—'

'Hit man?'

'A hit man is an assassin.' Decker paused, then said, 'Think about it, Mefakeah Elhiani. In order to get Gil, the assassin would have to go inside the yeshiva to find Gil. Then he'd have to get Gil alone. Then he'd have to get close to Gil to stab him or shoot him. He'd have to make sure that the gun didn't make too much noise. Or that Gil didn't scream. Because noise would attract attention. Then he'd have to escape. Wouldn't it be easier to just sneak inside dressed like a rabbi and drop off a small package inside a crowded *bais midrash*, hoping that one of those boys is Gil Yalom.'

Elhiani lit up another smoke and puffed away as he thought. 'It make some sense.'

Decker rubbed his eyes. 'So if they tried this method for Gil, why not for Dov.'

'But fortunately, it didn't work.'

'We were lucky.'

'Whatever the reason, it didn't work.'

Decker said, 'Maybe they don't know that. The bomber escaped. I'm sure he didn't go back to his boss and tell him he messed up. So look what the boss sees. A building with blown-out windows, pandemonium in the streets—'

'What means pandemon—'

Rina translated.

Decker said, 'To the bomber's boss, it looks like success.'

'And who is the bomber's boss?'

Decker remained cagey. 'I'm not sure, Mefakeah. I have my suspects but that's all.'

'Which is suspects?'

Decker and Rina traded looks. Then Decker said, 'There's a woman in Israel named Kate Milligan. She is a well-known lawyer who has worked for the VerHauten Diamond Company for many years. She's big, she's important, and this afternoon my wife tailed her into Hebron. But not before she overheard her talking to two men.'

'Two Arabs. One named Ibri, the other named Gamal.' Rina said, 'Milligan told them that if their idea of heroism was blowing up a school bus, they were working for the wrong person.'

Elhiani's eyes got wide. 'Where do I find this lady?'

'She had a meeting at the American Colonial Inn about two hours ago,' Rina said. 'Maybe she's staying there. I also have license plate numbers for you in my purse. Maybe that will tell you something.'

'That's why I need Gil Yalom. I was hoping Gil could tell me something.'

Elhiani bit his lip. 'But he has been put out. Maybe tomorrow he can talk to both of us.' He picked up the phone and spoke rapid Hebrew. Decker looked to Rina for translation.

'He's having an underling call up the American Colonial Inn.'

'That is right, *g'veret*. Your Hebrew is good.' Elhiani sat back in his chair. 'I still think this bomb is strange. You don't use bomb to kill pacific people.'

'Pacific people?' Decker asked.

Elhiani spoke to Rina. She said, 'He meant specific people.'

Decker continued his argument. But even as he spoke, he recognized the validity of Elhiani's point. Want someone dead, take him out directly. Bombing would have been a clumsy way to kill. The phone buzzed. Elhiani picked it up, then slammed it down.

'Milligan's not there.'

'Why am I not surprised?' Decker said.

I don't know if she was staying there, Peter,' Rina said. 'Only that she had a meeting there. For all I know, she's staying with her pal Donald in Hebron.'

'Yeah, I forgot about him.'

'What?' Elhiani said. 'Who is Donald?'

Rina said, 'The man for whom Ibri and Gamal were working. I think he lives in Hebron.'

A hard pounding at the door echoed through the small chamber. Elhiani frowned, then got up from his seat. He opened the door, revealing an ashen-faced policewoman who spoke using her white-knuckled hands for emphasis. Elhiani punched his fist in his hands. Rina covered her face and muttered an Oh, God.

'What?' Decker said. 'Another building exploded?'

'Not a building.' Rina had tears in her eyes. 'An explosion at Kikar Zion – an open square in the heart of Jerusalem's shopping district. Someone put a bomb in a garbage can. Two dead, fifteen wounded.'

Elhiani turned to them. 'You two can leave your number with me. Now, I have other business.'

Assessing his mood, Decker decided he was tired, famished, and pissed-off in that order. It had taken them two hours to retrieve Rina's purse, another hour to get back to their car. By then night had fallen over the silent city. Two bombings within an hour of one another made people retreat to the safety of their homes. The city was eerie with calm. The curbs once filled with parked cars were empty. Only the Subaru remained alone, sitting like a punished child behind the police ropes.

Decker unlocked the door, and he and Rina dragged

themselves inside the car. He rubbed his eyes and smelled his smoke-drenched clothes.

'I sure wouldn't want to be a bronchiole in Elhiani's lungs.'

Rina gave him a tired laugh.

'Are you hungry?'

'You can eat?'

Decker nodded. ''Fraid so.'

'Sure, let's get something to eat.' Rina paused. 'First let's go back to Tel Aviv. Who knows when the next bomb might go off?'

Decker started the car engine. 'So you buy Elhiani's terrorist bomber.'

Rina sighed. 'Well, someone's bombing the city. Maybe it was random, Peter.'

Decker said, 'Gil Yalom just happened to be in the yeshiva that blew up?'

'Who knows?' Rina said. 'It doesn't matter now. What matters is that, coincidence or not, you saved *lives*.' She felt her eyes watering. 'I'm very proud of you.'

Decker turned off the motor and leaned over the console to hug his wife. 'Thank you. And you should be proud of yourself while you're at it. You spotted the guy.'

'*Baruch Hashem*,' Rina sobbed out.

'*Baruch Hashem*,' Decker repeated.

Rina dried her tears with a tissue from her purse. 'So if this was a random terrorist act, maybe Dov Yalom isn't in danger like you thought.'

'I think he's still in danger.'

'All I'm saying is, maybe we still have time to find him.'

'Well, hope springs eternal confusion or something like that.' Decker started the car and pulled away from the curb. 'You'll have to navigate me back.'

423

Rina gave him a series of directions.

Decker said, 'How about we go back to the hotel and order room service at outrageous prices? Maybe if they find out we're heroes they'll give us a discount.'

'Don't count on it.' Rina looked at her lap. 'A man from the *Jerusalem Examiner* left his card with me. It's an English-language newspaper. He wants to interview you—'

'Publicize my case and let my enemy know what I'm doing? Not a chance.'

Decker turned onto the main thoroughfare to Tel Aviv. The night was black, the road surface barely visible. As the car descended down the mountains, he rode the brake and cursed the poor lighting.

'So what's next?' Rina asked. 'Besides food and a hot bath.'

'We'll have to wait for Gil Yalom to come out of his shock ... whenever that'll be.' Decker pulled to the side, allowing a speeding Fiat to pass him by. Within moments, the car was a red streak in the darkness. Slowly, he accelerated back onto the roadway.

'That driver was obnoxious and you didn't even comment,' Rina said. 'You must be exhausted.'

'You're right about that.'

They rode for a few minutes in silence. Then Rina said, 'Do you want to talk about it?'

'My mind is a bundle of very confused neurons at the moment. Things aren't adding up, Rina. Elhiani kept talking about the stupidity of using a bomb to kill a specific person.'

'For what it's worth, I think you argued your case very well, Peter.'

'Thank you. I appreciate your loyalty. But this isn't about egos. It's about logic. If I were in his shoes, I would have made the same points he made. Bombing is an inexact way to murder.'

'So it was just a coincidence that we were there at the yeshiva?'

'No, not exactly.'

'So it wasn't a coincidence?'

'No, not exactly that, either.' Decker took a deep breath and let it out slowly. 'I think the bomb was meant for Gil but in an inexact way. If they got him, fine. If not, that's fine, too.'

'That sounds really strange.'

'Then this other bomb explodes in the middle of Jerusalem's marketplace. Someone wants all the attention focused here . . . in Jerusalem.'

'Peter, Jerusalem is hot property now. The Arabs want to grab the city and redivide it. We want to keep it united and open to everyone. After all, it is the capital of our country. These terrorists will resort to anything to get their way.'

Decker didn't answer.

'There have always been lots of terrorist acts in Jerusalem,' Rina said.

'I guess I'm thinking like a cop and not like the State Department,' Decker said. 'From my limited perspective, I see it differently. You get a lot of action focused on one spot, it takes attention away from the other spots.'

'I don't understand.'

'Meaning, if you have in mind to bomb something, you want all the bomb experts and all the bomb dogs and all the police and all the other personnel as far away from your target spot as possible.'

Rina was quiet. 'You think these bombings were nothing more than a *diversion* tactic?'

'Possibly.'

'Peter, who are the bombers trying to divert?'

'This is going to sound incredibly arrogant.'

'*You*?'

'Someone knows I'm here, Rina. Someone knows I'm looking for Gil and Dov Yalom. From the minute Moti Bernstein thought you were my partner, I knew that someone had preceded me at the yeshiva.'

'I can explain that,' Rina said. 'There are a few boys in Or Torah whose nonreligious parents aren't happy they're there. Sometimes the parents will go to extremes to bring the kids back. They send over deprogrammers.'

'Moti thought you and I were deprogrammers?'

'He heard a rumor from somewhere that a man and a woman were out to bring home a boy to deprogram. So naturally, he was leery. When you rattled off *pikuach nefesh*, he knew you were legit. He figured deprogrammers wouldn't know that.'

Decker hesitated, then said, 'I know it sounds implausible, but just let me talk this out.'

'Go on.'

'Say someone knows I'm here looking for Gil and Dov. So they bomb Gil's yeshiva to draw my attention to Gil. But they don't really care if they kill Gil or not. What they want is me locked up in Jerusalem. For good measure, they bomb the open square and bring all the bomb experts to Jerusalem as well. It's to throw me off track.'

'Throw you off track from what? What are they diverting you *from*?'

'I don't know.'

'That's a bit of a rub in your theory,' Rina stated.

Decker smiled. 'Look, I'm just talking conjecture. But that's the way Marge and I solve cases. Throw out this theory or that theory. Hopefully, something clicks. Turn on the news, Rina. The more we learn, the better.'

She turned on the radio. News about the bombings, Rina announced. She listened intently and translated. At first, Decker focused on her words. Then his mind began to wander, his attention drawn elsewhere.

He needed to think this out. He needed to talk this out.

He missed Marge.

34

Digital clocks were a pisser when you were stricken with insomnia. The one on Decker's nightstand had a malevolent red face that laughed at him in the dark.

Only five more hours until daylight, sucker. Boy, are you going to feel crappy in the morning.

He began to play games with the LCD dial, guessing how the little illuminated lines would configurate in order to form the next numeral. Soon came some mental calculations. Two-twenty-seven a.m. in Israel would translate into three-twenty-seven yesterday afternoon LA time. Although his body ached with fatigue, his brain simply refused to shut down.

At two-fifty-two a.m., he gave up. Quietly, he climbed out of bed and slipped on a robe. Checking through his jacket, he found his notepad and pen, then went into the bathroom. After shutting the door, he turned on the lights, then lowered the toilet seat. He picked up the phone receiver. The ignominy of it all. Conducting business in the john.

Luck hadn't left him. Marge was in.

'This is weird,' she said. 'I was thinking about you.'

'My vibes are very strong.'

'You sound terrible.'

'I had a tough day. You got a minute?'

'Even two.'

Slowly, he related his ordeal, trying to keep the facts straight while looking at his notebook with bleary eyes. He tried to keep his voice even. Nothing clouded an investigation like emotion. Marge gave him the requisite number of *uh-huhs*, letting him know she was following his train of thought, which was good. Sitting on the can in his bathrobe, his ears ringing, his mind half dead, he wasn't sure if he was making sense.

When he was done, Marge didn't speak right away. Then she said, 'You sound battle-scarred, Rabbi. Maybe you should take a couple of days off.'

'It's not on Davidson's timetable.'

'Pete, even Tug wouldn't argue. You know, I heard something this morning on the news about a bomb going off. But I was listening with half an ear and bombs are always going off somewhere. I'm freaked out.'

'You're not allowed. One of us has to remain sane.' He paused. 'I know I'm running on empty. So what the hell. Keep going until the engine block cracks. Does any of my stuff help you make headway at your end?'

'I do have some news. Nothing dramatic.'

'Thank God.'

'Yeah, thank God is right. You have your pad with you?'

'Yep. Shoot.'

'First, Milligan,' Marge said. 'I've been looking into her finances. Because *if* she's connected to Yalom, it has to be through business. I've been asking myself, what could she be after?'

'Cheap, undeveloped land with diamond potential that she could sell to VerHauten at a great price.'

'Almost. I think she's after cheap, undeveloped land with diamond potential period.'

'She wants to develop it herself?'

'Why share the profits with VerHauten?'

'Where is she going to get the capital to develop a diamond pipe?'

'Let's take it one step at a time,' Marge said. 'First, where is she going to find cheap, undeveloped land with diamond potential? I started checking into diamond companies not associated with VerHauten. I called up your ex-father-in-law, Jack Cohen the lawyer, and he referred me to his broker.'

'Barry "The Deal" Orblatt?'

'You know him?'

'Jack's been investing with him for years.'

'Is he good?'

'Put it this way, Marge. Jack's still working for a living. Did Orblatt tell you anything?'

'Yes, he did. There are a lot of African diamond companies not controlled by VerHauten. Mind you, none of them are big time. But some of them have turned a profit.'

'Are any of them undervalued?'

'That's the trouble. The profitable ones are selling shares at market value. Even the ones that look slightly undervalued are still selling much higher than book value. You know what book value is?'

'The total assets remaining if you liquidated the company.'

'You know your finance. Now the real, real, real *cheap* companies are in fact *not* undervalued. Because they haven't produced a damn thing except red ink.'

'So there is no free lunch.'

'Maybe not superficially. But when you dig deeper, some interesting things pop up.'

'Such as?'

'A little birdie dropped Milligan's tax forms for the last two years in my lap.'

Marge's contact didn't sound like a snitch, more like one of her ex-beaus. Quickly, Decker ran through his mental Rolodex of Marge's formers. 'Ah, the birdie who worked at Health Alliance?'

'You've got a good memory for birdwatching.'

'What did Tweetie-pie tell you?'

'You know, Pete, it's amazing. Feed a computer a Social Security number, it spits back a life history. There is no privacy in the electronic age.'

Decker said, 'Marge, go on. We're long distance.'

'Milligan has been investing heavily in the defunct companies for over *two* years.'

'That's predating Yalom's angry letters to VerHauten.'

'Exactly. But not predating Yalom's purchases in his African companies. Maybe Milligan and Yalom had done some investing together. Because the same companies kept cropping up.'

'Why would Milligan invest with Yalom?' Decker asked. 'What does she need him for?'

'If she was working for VerHauten, she couldn't very well invest in competing companies.'

'He was her front?'

'Maybe,' Marge said. 'Except somewhere down the road, they obviously parted company. Maybe it was over Southwest Mines. Arik bought in when the company was still operable. VerHauten and Milligan bought in when it had gone under. Still, if VerHauten ever decides to mine it, Milligan and whoever owns Arik's shares will make a nice chunk of change.'

'But VerHauten's sitting on it at the moment.'

'Exactly,' Marge said. 'I think she *had* hopes for Southwest Mines, but with Yalom owning so much and VerHauten sitting on it, she decided to move on. Orblatt did some checking around mining stocks and co-op funds. Much to his surprise, he discovered some recent movement upward in these investments. Plus, three of the prominent companies in the mining funds were also in Arik Yalom's portfolio.'

'Did Yalom own large quantities of those stocks?'

'He owned some, but nothing like Southwest. And VerHauten isn't even in the picture. Now even though shares have been changing hands, the price hasn't risen. But the activity indicates something.'

'Interesting.'

'It gets better. These companies are also being heavily traded by the African exchanges with an influx of buy orders coming out of countries like Tunisia, Libya, Algeria, Morocco, and Egypt.'

'Arab countries.' Decker paused. 'They're also North African countries.'

'Exactly,' Marge said. 'I don't know which fact is more significant.'

'Maybe both,' Decker said. 'With oil prices dropping, could be some Arab countries are trying to branch out into diamonds. And why not, Marge? They *are* African countries. The continent is their sphere of influence.'

'Good point,' Marge said.

'Is it the government or individuals who are investing money?'

'That I don't know,' Marge said. 'But it doesn't take a lot of money to buy stock in these companies. They're either bankrupt or moribund. So they're cheap.'

'Why invest in them in the first place?'

'All I can say is, look at Southwest Mines. It has potential. VerHauten's just sitting on it. Maybe Milligan has found other companies with the same potential as Southwest.'

'Any indication?'

'Nothing yet, but it takes a while to get that kind of information.'

Decker said, 'You know, Marge, no matter how much potential the land has, Milligan would still need huge chunks of capital to develop it.'

Marge said, 'You told me that Rina followed Milligan into the occupied territories, right?'

'Yep.'

'So maybe Milligan's on a mission to convince the Arabs to invest with her.'

'Except the territories are inhabited by poor Arabs. And while I don't know my per capita incomes by heart, the countries you've mentioned are also the poorer Arab countries compared to the oil-rich countries like Saudi Arabia or Kuwait.'

'Libya has oil.'

'Libya has been in the doldrums economically since the United States bombed it.'

'Well, all I can tell you is *someone* from those countries is trading in diamond mines.'

Decker heard a knock on the door.

'Peter, are you all right?'

'I'm fine, Rina. Go back to bed.'

'What are you doing in there?'

'Hold on, Marge.' Decker reached over and unlocked the bathroom door. 'I couldn't sleep. I'm talking to Marge.'

Rina was squinting from the light. 'Go back to bed and use the phone there. You can't possibly be comfortable.'

'I'm really fine.'

'Pete, are you there?' Marge said over the line.

'Yeah, I'm still here.'

Marge said, 'Rina knows more about that part of the world than we do. Ask her who the rich people are in Egypt or Libya.'

Decker said, 'I'll put her on the other phone. You can ask her the question yourself.'

Rina said, 'Marge wants to talk to me?'

'Yeah, if you don't mind.'

'I'm up anyway,' Rina said. 'I'll get the extension by the bed.' She crawled back under the covers and picked up the receiver. 'I'm here, Marge.'

'Sorry about this.'

'It's not a problem. What would you like to know?'

'Who are the rich people in Egypt?'

Rina kept her voice low so she wouldn't blast out her husband's ear. 'The usual. Businesspeople, international financiers, ex-royalty, of course. And politicians probably.'

'But the country of Egypt itself,' Decker said. 'It's poor, isn't it?'

'Very poor.'

Marge said, 'So money is probably coming from individuals rather than the government.'

Rina said, 'What's going on?'

Decker quickly brought her up to date. 'We're trying to figure out if these land investments are government sanctioned or just the doings of some private individuals.'

Rina asked, 'What does any of this have to do with the murder of Arik and Dalia Yalom?'

'Yalom owned stock in companies heavily traded in Arab countries,' Marge said.

'Someone killed him for his stock?' Rina asked.

Decker said, 'We don't know. All I can tell you is that Yalom had investments in companies being heavily traded in African exchanges – Egypt, Morocco, Libya, Tunisia—'

'PLO,' Rina said.

'What?' Decker asked.

'PLO,' Rina repeated. 'The PLO's corporate office is in Tunisia. Has been for years.'

Marge said, 'So maybe I'm *right*, Pete. Maybe Milligan did go to the territories to raise capital. Maybe not from the *inhabitants*, but from their *government*, which is essentially the PLO. Aren't they representing the Palestinians in the peace talks?'

'Yes, they are.' Decker grew excited. 'Aren't they and Arafat highly capitalized by rich Arab countries?'

'Not anymore,' Rina said. 'They're broke.'

'Well, so much for my theory,' Marge said.

Rina said, 'They used to be *highly* capitalized. The Soviet Union gave them money. But now there is no more Soviet Union. They used to get money from oil-producing Arab countries. But times change. Libya has never fully recovered from the US bombing. The Gulf War just about did in Iraq economically. The war put a nice dent in Saudi Arabia's economy as well. And it couldn't have come at a worse time for them, with oil prices being depressed. The PLO's cash cows just don't have the disposable income they used to have.'

There was silence across the line.

'Then how does the organization exist?' Marge said.

'As a matter of fact, Arafat was very, very weak until Israel gave him and the PLO power by giving them Gaza and bringing them into the peace talks. If Arafat ever gets a

real government – and it looks like that's a strong possibility – the PLO has been pledged hundreds of millions of
dollars by the US and Europe to get the Palestinian
economy off to a rip-roaring start. Even if *half* that money
comes through, Arafat will have plenty of investment
capital.'

Again no one spoke.

Finally Decker whispered, 'Milligan saw it all coming.
She's been cultivating the PLO for several years. Now
that everything is almost in place, she's making her
move.'

Rina said, 'What move?'

Decker said, 'First, Milligan buys out undercapitalized
land with potential for diamond fields. Then she cultivates
the PLO, betting that *eventually* they'll get a government
and lots of start-up capital for its economy from the
Western countries. Now that Israel and the PLO have
struck some kind of deal, she knows she's in like Flynn.
She's just waiting for someone to sign on the dotted line, so
she can tap into those pledges.'

'If the peace process lasts.'

'Rina, it only has to last long enough for her to raid the
initial investment capital pledged by the Western nations.
Because the woman knows her Western civilization.
Remember her bookcase behind her desk, Marge?'

'Not really.'

'I do,' Decker said. 'Because I thought her choice of
books was rather eclectic. She had a row of books that dealt
with the economies of postwar Japan and Germany.
Meaning, she knew from history how the US and the Allies
poured billions of dollars back into those countries to set
them on their feet. They not only throve, they became
world economic powers.'

437

'I don't see the PLO becoming a world economic power,' Rina said.

'That doesn't *matter*!' Decker said. 'All Milligan cares about is the money that's going to start flowing in. The newly formed territory or country or whatever the hell you want to call it is going to have to set up some businesses if it's going to thrive economically. Why not diamonds, offers Milligan.'

'But why would the Arabs use her as a middleman?' Marge asked. 'Why wouldn't they invest in the land directly?'

'In fact, that's just what they're doing,' Decker said. 'They are investing in the same companies that Milligan is investing in. But this time, Milligan knows they're not going to sit on the land like VerHauten's doing. They're going to try to develop it, paying her for her expertise. So she wins two ways. One, she gets paid as an expert. And two, if they strike it rich, so does she.'

Marge said, 'She has everything to gain and nothing to lose. All she had to do was make her pitch and apparently it worked. Because the Arabs are buying.'

Decker said, 'What do you think, Rina?'

There was a long moment of silence.

Exasperated, Decker finally said, 'What's the problem?'

'I don't know. Something's off.'

'*What* is off?'

'If Milligan's interested only in start-up capital from the PLO, why was she dealing with two local Arabs from Hebron instead of someone high up in the PLO. And who is Donald?'

'Donald?' Marge asked.

'The Hebron Arabs Milligan met with – in secret –

claimed they were working for a man named Donald,' Rina explained. 'Milligan claimed Donald was working for her.'

'Who's Donald?' Marge asked.

'No idea,' Decker said.

Rina said, 'To my untrained eye, it seemed like Milligan and those men were planning something clandestine. Besides, I just don't see the PLO giving something away for nothing.'

'They're not giving away something for nothing,' Decker said. 'They're investing in Milligan's know-how.'

'But Milligan is still setting herself up as queen bee without giving them something tangible.'

'She's giving them something tangible. She's giving the Palestinians, headed by the PLO, the potential to be *big* diamond producers.'

'Potential is not a commodity,' Rina said. 'Besides, you're thinking like a Westerner, Peter.'

'How so?' Marge asked.

'Most of the Arabs in the territories are dirt poor. Sure, they'd love to be rich. But they've never had capital so they don't even know what wealth is. Their prime motivator is *revenge*, not money.'

'Revenge . . .' Decker thought a moment. 'Then suppose Milligan presented the deal not only as an economic boon for the Palestinian government but also as a way to strike out at Israel.'

'The PLO would go for that,' Rina said 'What do you have in mind?'

'She could present the deal like this. If the PLO invested with her, they would control vast amounts of raw diamonds. With that, they could undermine Israel's economy by going into direct competition with the Israeli diamond industry and the Israeli cutters.'

439

'So who would cut *their* stones?' Rina said, 'With the Israelis out, there go the *best* cutters in the world. And VerHauten wouldn't dare deal with the upstarts.'

'They could develop their own cutters,' Marge said. 'A good industry for a fledgling country.'

'A skill like that takes ages to learn,' Rina said. 'And even if they did, the stones would be second-rate. The brilliance of a diamond is as much in the cutting as it is in the raw stone. To get any kind of competitive edge, the Arabs would virtually have to annihilate all the Israeli cutters. Even *they'd* have a hard time doing that.' She paused. 'Unless they're planning to blow up the Bursa.'

Decker heard her words. Then he broke out in a cold sweat.

35

Jet lag was a blessing in disguise. While the country slept, Decker was in high gear, his body fueled by urgency. He cut his conversation with Marge and began raking through his coat.

'Elhiani gave me his card.' Decker pulled something out of his pocket. '*Damn!* It's his work number.'

Rina took the card. 'We've got to start somewhere.' She dialed the digits. It took a long time for someone to answer. Not unusual, considering it was four in the morning. As calmly as she could, Rina related the emergency nature of the call, the necessity to speak to Mefakeah Elhiani directly. A moment later, Rina placed her hand over the receiver.

'I'm on hold.'

Decker covered his face with his hands, then looked up. 'He's going to think I'm crazy, you know. *I'd* think I was crazy. Because what I've got is a house of cards. If there's a glitch in *any* of my suppositions, the whole thing's going to come tumblin' down.'

'What's the alternative? Letting the Bursa blow up?'

'Yeah, you're right. So I'll look like a fool. Better that than . . .' Decker began to pace. 'I hate being here. Out of my element. My investigation completely stymied because I don't know the friggin rules!' He stopped walking and ran

441

his hands through his hair. 'Hell with the self-pity, Deck. First things first. Get hold of Elhiani.'

'I'm trying!' Rina felt her husband's desperation. 'Should I hang up and call back?'

'No.' Decker checked the clock. Four-twelve. 'No, don't hang up. If need be, I'll call from another phone.'

He laughed softly, imagining himself trying to communicate with a night operator without Rina's help.

Rina held up a finger, indicating she was back on the line. The woman on the other end told Rina to go ahead. Through the crack of static, Rina could make out a voice heavy with sleep. She identified herself to Mefakeah Elhiani and told him why she was calling.

Elhiani heard the crisis in her voice. 'Let me talk to your husband.'

Rina handed the phone to Peter. Decker told her to pick up the extension in the bathroom in case he needed help.

'Explain yourself,' Elhiani stated.

Decker told the story, Rina translating when asked to do so. When he was finally done, there was a moment of silence over the line. Decker could picture incredulity on Elhiani's face.

The Mefakeah said, 'You like bombs, Sar-kee-ant?'

Decker took a deep breath. 'I know this sounds farfetched—'

'What is farfetched?'

'*Meshuga*,' Decker said. 'Crazy.'

'*Cain*, it *is* crazy. I would hang you up, but I have news.'

Decker felt his heartbeat quicken. 'What?'

'I take your wife's purse . . . look at the license number. One of them belongs to Khouri family. The father lost a brother and two sons in the massacre at Hebron. Ibrahim Khouri has pledged act of revenge. Your wife talks about

442

blowing up school bus. I get *very* nervous. This sounds like Ibri's act of revenge. But now you talk about blowing up Bursa ... this is act of insanity.'

Decker said, 'Look what happened with Or Torah yeshiva. That was an act of insanity.'

'Not like blowing up Bursa.'

Without emotion, Decker said, 'It's your call, Mefakeah. This is your country. You're in charge.'

The line fell silent. Decker could hear Elhiani breathing hard.

'If this *G'veret* Milligan put bomb in Bursa,' Elhiani said, 'why is it still standing?'

Decker said, 'Maybe she set the timer to go off when there are people inside. The idea is to incapacitate Israel as much as possible.'

'It should blow up today?'

'Maybe.'

'You tell me Milligan is rich lawyer person with power. And this is what she does with free time? She plans acts of terrorism? Why?'

Decker said, 'Greed. If she can destroy the Bursa, she can set up her own diamond center with Palestinian money in the newly formed Palestinian territory.'

'Milligan is terrorist for money?'

'She may have other reasons.' Decker paused. 'Did you ever find out who Donald was?'

'Ah, Donald. The man Ibri works for. No, I not find out yet. Is he terrorist, too?'

'I don't know *who* he is,' Decker said. 'Mefakeah, I called to let you know what I know. Now it's in your hands.'

There was a pause over the line. Elhiani said, 'If, by some *neis*, you are right and Bursa blows up and people die, it is terrible, terrible tragedy that I did not prevent. If you are right and I investigate, there is no tragedy and I am big, big hero. If I investigate and we find nothing, they think I'm crazy for listening to crazy American sar-kee-ant. You give me big headache.'

Decker said, 'I'm giving myself a big headache.'

Elhiani said, 'You call me Ezra. I call you Peter.'

Decker knew this was a turning point. 'Call me Akiva.'

'*B'seder*, Akiva.' Elhiani sighed. 'I call Northern District Headquarters for you. Ask them what they want to do. I tell them you wait downstairs in lobby. Leave it up to them. It's their territory.'

'Fine.'

'I tell them to meet you at your hotel. Some advice to you, Akiva. Take your wife with you. She talks better than you. And she looks better, too.'

In a frantic rush, they dressed and went downstairs into the brightly lit hotel lobby. The front desk was deserted, the couches and chairs empty. In the background was the hum of some kind of generator. The outside picture windows framed twinkling lights set into a backdrop of blackness. Everything was quiet but tense, like an animal crouching for its prey.

Two police cars came fifteen minutes later – uniformed officers who checked their papers and identification. Since Elhiani still retained their passports, the officers from Tel Aviv had to make do with the leavings, confiscating their driver's licenses and Decker's papers as well as his police badge. Stripped of ID, Rina felt naked and faceless, then wondered why. Perhaps it was the realization that she and Peter were actually viewed as suspects. She glanced at her husband. His eyes said nothing, his expression was all work. Too wrapped up in the case to care about indignities.

The cops escorted them into the backseat of the subcompact police car, Decker contorting his body to get inside. Night blanketed the city and the asphalt roads were very dark. But the faint visibility didn't stop the police from racing through neighborhoods, the automobile jumping hurdles whenever it encountered a rut or a bump. Tiny vehicles had tiny shocks.

They reached the Bursa just before five. The boulevard was empty, but the curbway was lined with blue flashing lights. The cop parked the car and opened the back door. Decker got out first, then helped Rina to her feet. He stretched his legs, heard yelping dogs in the background.

Within moments, he and Rina were surrounded by the police both uniformed and nonuniformed. A tall, well-built man in his forties broke through the protective circle. He was fair-complexioned and good-looking. Enter Paul Newman in *Exodus*, Decker thought. Except his clothing was cheap – old suit, an open-necked white shirt, and scuffed oxfords. He puffed away on unfiltered cigarettes. Decker drank in nicotine with craving nostrils.

Mr Exodus was presented with their papers and looked them over intently. Decker wondered if he actually understood them since they were written in legalese English. Finally, Exodus handed them back to the uniformed cop, crushed out his cigarette on the sidewalk, then stuck his hands in his pockets.

'I'm *Sgan Nitzav* Levi Kreiman,' he said, 'Mefakeah Elhiani wasn't too clear over the horn. He mentioned something about a possible bomb threat in the Bursa. Is this just a little hunch of yours or are we all in imminent danger of being blown up?'

Joy of joys, the guy spoke English fluently! Decker could *communicate*! 'I don't know if there is a bomb. And *if* there is a bomb, I don't know when it's been programmed to detonate.'

'So basically you don't know what the hell is flying,' Kreisman said.

'A correct assessment,' Decker said, flatly. 'Maybe I should tell you what I do know.'

'Shouldn't someone be searching the Bursa?' Rina broke in. 'I mean, if there's a bomb, what are we waiting for?'

Kreisman glared at her. 'Who the hell are you?'

'She's my wife,' Decker said. 'I brought her here because I don't speak Hebrew.'

Kreisman turned to her and broke into Hebrew. Rina answered back. They talked for a few minutes until Kreisman returned to English. To Decker, he said, 'I'm explaining to your wife this isn't the Wild West. We have to coordinate an operation like this with Bursa security. And since there aren't any people inside, the safety of everyone involved is the primary concern. It would help a great deal, Detective, if you told me what's going on.'

Decker related the case as concisely and as quickly as he could. But with all the questions and answers, it still took time. When Decker was done, Kreisman patted his breast pocket and took out a pack of cigarettes. Bringing it to his lips, he saw longing on Decker's face. He offered him a smoke.

Without hesitation, Decker took it. Just this one time, he promised himself. Kreisman lit the cigarette for him and Decker inhaled deeply, enjoying the infusion of nicotine into his hungry bloodstream. From the corner of his eye, he saw Rina's face.

'I'm nervous,' he told her.

'I know, Peter. I am, too. I love you.'

Kreisman cleared his throat. Decker smiled. He and

Kreisman smoked, they checked watches, they looked at the sky and at the ground. They asked each other questions. They took notes, then compared the notes they took.

Finally, Kreisman spoke into his walkie-talkie at length. He signed off and said, 'Okay, we'll check it out. We'll go in with Bursa security, but only the public areas – the entry, the lockers, the trading room, the restaurants, etcetera. We'll pass on the individual offices because we don't have keys. You have any ideas where this bomb might be planted?'

'I first saw Milligan at Mr Menkovitz's spot,' Decker said. 'It's the far side of the trading room. It would be easier if I just showed it to you.'

Kreisman tapped his foot. 'I don't know who the hell you are. Why should I let you in with us?'

'Have it your way,' Decker said. 'I'll remain here in the custody of your men.'

Kreisman gave him a sour look. 'You're giving me a headache, you know that?'

'I'm noted for that,' Decker said. '*Nitzav*, you're in charge. I'll do whatever you want.'

'Technically, it's *sgan nitzav*. You just promoted me.' Kreisman cursed under his breath. 'Put your arms up.'

Decker did. Kreisman frisked him very carefully. Afterward, he said, 'I suppose you can't do much harm under my eye.'

'Maybe I'll even do some good.'

'I doubt that,' Kreisman answered. 'All right. Let's go collect stories for our future grandchildren.'

At first glance, the trading room had been transformed into the morgue. It was large and deserted, cold and sterile. It held no life. Lit with fluorescent fixtures, the long rows of vacant tables resembled autopsy slabs. The scales, though small, could have been path scales for weighing small organic tissue or evidence such as bullets. Decker went on to notice the goosenecked lamps, the calibrators, rulers, pincers, cleavers, loupes, microscopes—

The loud barks of the tracking dogs shook the image from his brain. Funny what happens on so little sleep. Security closed around him – Kreisman's men, guards from the Bursa itself – encircling him as if he were an escape risk. Like it or not, Decker knew he was a suspect.

Kreisman said, 'We'll stay here. You point the dogs in the right direction.'

Decker could see clearly over the human wall that surrounded him. The advantage of being six-four in a Mediterranean country. With an extended finger, he indicated Menkovitz's spot. The leader of the bomb squad, suited up in full regalia for the 'just in case' scenario, guided the dogs toward the site.

Decker studied the animals – medium-sized spotted dogs with a decent coat. They had pointed snouts and alert eyes. 'Those aren't retrievers or shepherds. What kind of dogs are those?'

'Canaan hounds,' Kreisman said. ''Bout as close to a dingo as you can get and still be considered domesticated. Smart little suckers.'

Banned from his cigarettes, Kreisman became jumpy. Decker regarded him, bouncing on his feet, hands in and out of his pockets. Decker felt the need for a fix as well. But there was no smoking in the Bursa. Besides, the odor would wreak havoc with the dogs.

Decker kept his eyes on the search. The guide had first taken the dogs to Menkovitz's spot. Yanking on their leashes, the animals sniffed the table and chairs in the vicinity, but nothing appeared to register. The guide then led them around the entire room. It took around twenty minutes for them to canvass the area. Drawing a blank first time out, the handler took them in for a second pass.

Decker asked Kreisman where he was born.

'Dayton, Ohio. I moved to Israel when I was nine, then went back to the States for college. I moved back here about ten years ago.'

Another twenty minutes rolled by. The dogs went around for a third time. Decker watched the animals work. Sometimes it took multiple passes before the dogs could detect a bomb. Sometimes they missed cues. Sometimes they got distracted. As the animals hunted, members of the bomb squad conducted their own visual search, going methodically through the Bursa from table to table.

Decker was feeling more stupid by the moment. But at least it had been Kreisman's call. Mr Exodus was pissed but holding it well. Time announced its passage by the beginnings of daylight. The room-sized picture windows that walled the Bursa had lightened from black to gray. Decker checked his watch. Five after six.

Kreisman spoke on his walkie-talkie. He signed off, then turned to Decker. 'We've cleared the entry area, the front lockers, and the restaurants. If we don't find anything soon, we're going to have to pack it in. People are arriving, waiting to do business with the world.'

'Are you letting them in?' Decker asked.

'Not yet. We've cordoned off the area. But I can't stall them with no good reason. This is their livelihood. This is the country's livelihood. Diamonds are probably Israel's *biggest* industry. The one thing I liked about your theory. If the Arabs wanted to get back at us, it'd be with diamonds. It's the heart of Israel's economy.'

The bomb-squad leader shouted something to Kreisman. Kreisman nodded and shouted something back. To Decker, he said, 'We've cleared this area. I told him to take the dogs to the upstair lounge.' He pointed to a series of smoked windows above the official weighing booths. 'If the dogs don't find anything, we're out of here.'

'Can we go up and watch?' Decker said.

'No,' Kreisman said. 'The lounge is relatively small and has lots of furniture. I don't want to distract the dogs.'

Decker nodded, realizing how much credibility he had lost. He wondered how he had got sidetracked from Yalom to Milligan. Everything had happened so damn fast. From a visit with Tziril and Moshe Yalom to Menkovitz and Milligan at the Bursa. From Milligan in Hebron to a bomb in Gil Yalom's yeshiva.

Gil. He did find Gil and that would certainly help the Yalom case. At least, the trip wasn't a failure. Today, maybe the boy would talk.

Suddenly, Decker's ears perked up. The ambient noise in the Bursa dramatically changed. The dogs were barking. Loud, loud barks. He and Kreisman exchanged glances. The buzz of Kreisman's walkie-talkie. The *look* on his face as he listened to rapid-fire speech emanating from the box.

'Where'd they find it?' Decker asked.

Kreisman waved him off as he spoke back to the bomb-squad leader. Finally, he signed off and began shouting orders in Hebrew. To Decker, he said, 'You got some explaining to do, buddy. But for now you're out of here. My men will take you and your wife to the station house. You wait for me there.'

'Where did they find it?' Decker asked again.

Kreisman glared at him. 'Sure you don't know the answer?'

'No, I don't know,' Decker said. 'I wasn't even in the lounge. Ask Mr Yalom. He's the one who took me around the Bursa.'

To his men, Kreisman said, 'Get him out of here.' He realized he was speaking English, then switched to Hebrew.

In a flash, Decker was surrounded. Slowly, he was guided – even shoved – out of the building. Conversation was flying a mile a minute. If only he could *understand*. Pushed forward by cops, aware that at this point he had no control over his destiny, he decided to roll with the punches. Eventually, someone would tell him what was going on . . . maybe.

He strained to hear words that sounded familiar. He finally recognized one and it was a doozy.

Televizion.

It didn't take a genius to extrapolate. Since it was too early for the invasion of TV news cameras, there had to be only one other logical reason why cops would be talking about the boob tube.

The dogs were searching a lounge. They must have found the bomb in a television set.

Though Decker's case was far from over – Dov was still missing – he couldn't help but feel *victorious*! He slammed his fist into his empty palm and whispered, *yes*!

36

This time Decker passed up the smoke. He sat next to Rina, across from Kreisman, and kept a flat expression while being questioned. Kreisman asked about his case, about Gil and Dov Yalom, about Arik Yalom's schemes and how they dovetailed with Milligan's investments. Then Kreisman zeroed in on Milligan. He asked about Rina's excursion into Hebron, asked her to repeat the conversation she had overheard word for word. He asked about Donald – the mystery man. The lull came after an hour and a half of interviewing. Decker took advantage to formulate his own questions.

'When was the bomb scheduled to go off?'

Kreisman pretended not to hear. The two men had formed a cold truce, but as yet no trust.

'Look, *Sgan Nitzav*,' Decker said, 'I'm working on a case. You're working on a case. I'm gathering information just like you. How about a little interdepartmental co-operation?'

Kreisman scratched his head. 'Let's go back to the bomb at the yeshiva.'

Rina was about to interject something. Decker patted her hand and said, 'Sure. What do you want to know?'

'Let's go over it one more time.'

Rina couldn't help it. 'Why?' She launched into Hebrew.

Kreisman answered her back. It was interesting to Decker's ear. When they spoke English, their tone of voice and manner were distinctly American. Talking in Hebrew, they had both become Israelis – the pauses, the inflections, and the gesticulations of the hands.

Abruptly, Rina folded her hands across her chest. 'Okay, I'll keep my opinions to myself.'

Kreisman said, 'A very good idea.'

Decker was about to speak, but Rina stopped him with a gentle squeeze on the leg.

Kreisman said, 'Detective, you said your *wife* told you to stop this guy whom you didn't know at all.'

'Yes.'

'So you took off after him and you didn't know why.'

'Rina told me he didn't belong. That was reason enough.'

'But you didn't know *why* she suspected him.'

'No.'

'In other words, you blindly listened to your wife.'

'She knows the nuances of this country, of the religion. I don't. I didn't listen to her because she was my wife. I listened to her as one listens to an expert witness.'

Kreisman stared at him. Decker stared back waiting for the pissing contest to be over. He understood Kreisman's suspicions. On the other hand, based on Decker's information, a bomb in the Bursa had been discovered. He knew that was worth a lot.

Kreisman went on, 'So you caught up with this guy.'

'I caught up with the suspect, yes.'

'And he just suddenly blurted out there was a bomb in the yeshiva.'

Decker paused. 'After a little physical prodding, yes.'

'And then you just let him go?'

'Not at all. I handed him over to someone in the crowd, emphasizing the importance of detaining him until the police arrived. He had a firm grasp on him as I handed him over. But the bomber must have been limber and strong. He escaped.'

'Why didn't *you* stay with the suspect and have other people go and help out at the yeshiva?'

Decker said, 'It was a judgment call. I cared more about the boys than about apprehending the suspect.' He bit his mustache. 'Did someone call my captain in Los Angeles?'

'Yes.'

'So you know I'm—'

'We've been told that you were sent over here to find Gil and Dov Yalom. They're wanted for questioning about the deaths of their parents – Arik and Dalia Yalom. That's all good and fine. But it doesn't explain *drek* about your fatal attraction for bombs.'

'Nonfatal attraction. No one died.'

Kreisman glared at him.

Decker said, 'You want to know how I think Milligan got a bomb through security?'

Kreisman studied Decker's face. 'Are you telling me firsthand knowledge or is this conjecture?'

'Conjecture.'

'I don't trust you.'

'Fair enough. Do you want my opinion?'

'I want your opinion,' Rina piped in.

Kreisman glared at her. 'You're trying my patience, Mrs Decker.'

'You have no patience,' Rina shot back. 'Why don't you open your mind a little?'

'You want to visit our jails, *g'veret*?'

'I've been in worse places—'

'Rina . . .' Decker interrupted.

'All right, I won't say another word.'

Kreisman exhaled, then broke into a smile. 'Only in this country. What would happen to her if she spoke that way to your captain?'

Decker shrugged. 'You want my take on the bomb?'

'Go on.'

'Milligan couldn't bring an assembled bomb inside the Bursa,' Decker said. 'Security is too tight.'

'Is this going to get better?'

'Can I just get the thought out?'

'Hurry up.'

'Milligan brought in the explosive bit by bit. Every time she visited the Bursa, she toted in another piece of the bomb. Yalom told me it was rare to see her on the floor itself. Mostly she went to offices or to the trader's lounge where it was quieter to conduct business.'

Decker noticed Kreisman was suddenly listening.

'What do people do in the business lounge? They talk. They relax. They read the papers. They catch a little TV. And you know how lounge TV works. They're communal. So nobody would have looked twice if Milligan got up and adjusted the color or changed the channel.'

The room was quiet.

Decker said, 'Every time she made an adjustment, she dropped off a part of the bomb in the back of the TV set. Yesterday, when she was at the Bursa, I'm betting the TV broke down. So no one thought it was odd when some guy with credentials and a toolbox suddenly showed up to repair it.'

'Security checks people out,' Kreisman said.

'Security takes your passport, checks out your business there, and maybe they run your name inside a computer to

456

make sure you're not a terrorist or a felon. So if your name comes up clean because you're using falsified credentials, how are they going to check that out on the spot?'

'Someone would have checked this guy out at the door.'

'I'm sure someone did. So what did they see? A repairman with his toolbox. I'm sure they went through the toolbox and all they saw was tools. So what's the big deal? If the TV was broken, then a repairman and his tools had legitimate business in the Bursa.'

Kreisman's face darkened. 'Pretending he was fixing the TV, he assembled the bomb on the spot.'

Decker said, 'He probably wasn't even pretending. I'm sure he knew about the workings of a TV set. He also knew bombs as well. How was the bomb rigged?'

Kreisman pursed his lips. 'It was set to detonate as soon as someone turned on the TV.'

'So the repairman hooked the detonator up to the power switch on the television set.'

Kreisman nodded. 'A basic device. Nothing fancy. One that could be assembled in maybe ten, fifteen minutes.'

'How powerful was the bomb?' Decker said.

'It wouldn't have ripped the building from the foundation,' Kreisman stated. 'But potentially it could have done bad damage on the trading floor. The back of the TV was packed with plastiques.'

'Not to mention the psychological damage it would have done,' Rina said. 'It's demoralizing when the impenetrable becomes penetrable.'

Kreisman nodded. 'I can't believe Milligan got past security.'

'She brought in the pieces, bit by bit,' Decker said.

'Besides, she was a trusted and respected person in the business.' He turned to Kreisman. 'Are you bringing her in?'

Kreisman bit his lip, then sighed.

'You can't find her,' Decker said.

'We've checked every goddamn hotel in the country.'

'What about Ibri and Gamal?' Rina said. 'Can't you bring them in for questioning?'

Kreisman ran his hand down his face.

Rina said, 'You can't find them either?'

'They're probably in Jordan,' Kreisman said. 'But since we don't have common extradition laws, we're going to have to get them by other means.'

'Do you think Milligan's in Jordan?'

Kreisman shrugged.

'Has anyone taken responsibility for the bomb?' Rina asked.

'You mean a terrorist group?' Kreisman shook his head. 'Why would anyone acknowledge the bomb? We *caught* it, we *won*, they *lost*. Their mission was a failure. As a matter of fact, if I were Hamas or the PLO or some other terrorist group, and I'd paid Milligan a bundle of money to pull this stunt off, I'd be pretty damn *pissed off* at her. If Milligan's involved, she's not only running from us, but from whoever hired her as well.'

Kreisman rubbed his eyes and leaned back in his chair.

'I can understand why any of the terrorist groups would do this. If they succeed, they have everything to gain. And not much to lose, if they fail. But I can't understand why *Kate Milligan* would do it. Risk everything she had – which was a shitload – to be even more obscenely rich. And don't tell me greed. She might be greedy, but we all know she isn't stupid.'

'Money's a powerful motivator,' Rina said.

'She had money,' Kreisman said.

'Maybe she wanted power,' Decker said. 'Maybe Milligan was tired of being passed over when she felt she deserved to be number one. VerHauten is a male-dominated, family business. She knew she couldn't ever be CEO no matter how hard she worked. She wanted it all.'

'So she did all this to get back at VerHauten?' Kreisman shook his head. 'That's stupid.'

Rina said, 'Well, we exhausted money and power as catalysts. She's not an Arab, so she probably didn't do it for revenge. That leaves only one other prime motivator.'

No one spoke.

Rina smiled. 'Maybe she did it for love, gentlemen. Maybe she was in love with a radical Arab terrorist and did it for him. They've used women in terrorist acts before.'

Decker suddenly sat up. 'I don't think she was in love with an Arab. I think she was in love with a black.'

'*Black?*' Rina said. 'Why do you say that?'

'Not American black. A South African black. Wasn't Mandela a big supporter of the PLO when he was in prison?'

Rina said, 'I think he still is, although I know he's more moderate now. He's met with Israeli officials.'

'I'm not painting Mandela as a villain,' Decker said. 'I'm just saying, when Mandela was in prison, the South African blacks and the Palestinians allied themselves together as exiled, displaced people. Israel was often compared to South Africa—'

'That's not a fair assessment,' Kreisman interrupted.

'I'm reporting the news, *Sgan Nitzav*, not making a value judgment,' Decker said. 'My partner in America and I had discussed the possibility that Arik Yalom had been black-mailing Kate Milligan. Why else would Milligan deal directly with someone as small as Yalom?'

'Go on,' Rina said.

'What could Yalom have had on her that would have screwed her up with VerHauten?' Decker asked. 'We figured maybe she had an affair with a black. Maybe the guy was a Black Muslim to boot. Having an affair with someone like that would have been highly frowned upon in a bastion of white conservatism like VerHauten.'

Kreisman said, 'I don't think VerHauten would have dismissed her services as long as she was doing a good job. Business is business.'

Rina said, 'Maybe while working for VerHauten, Milligan came to some sort of an epiphany. She met a black man, fell deeply in love, and was suddenly full of rage that she couldn't *openly* love him.'

Decker said, 'And opportunity reared its head. Here was a way to get rich and *get* even with VerHauten – the white power structure of South Africa. Not only that, Israel, another oppressor country, would get screwed as well.'

'Do you have a name for this mysterious black man?' Kreisman asked.

'No,' Decker said. 'Just throwing out ideas. Retrospectively dissecting Milligan's mind.'

'A nice theory,' Kreisman said. 'Find a name to go along with it and you might give us something to work with.'

Rina blurted out, 'Donald.'

Decker looked at her.

'And why not?' Rina said.

Decker said, 'Didn't Milligan say that Donald was working for her? That he was her *underling*?'

'Peter,' Rina chided. 'Where is it written that the woman can't have the upper hand in a love relationship?'

'Women always have the upper hand in a love relationship,' Kreisman said, dryly.

'Well, not *always*,' Rina said.

There was a pause. Then Kreisman and Decker said in unison, *'Always.'*

37

Without thinking, Rina leaned against the heavy glass door, butting it open with her shoulder.

'What are you doing? I'll get that.' Decker held open the door. 'Chivalry isn't totally dead.'

He stepped aside and let Rina enter the hotel lobby first. It was filled with casually dressed tourists, bellhops, management personnel, and lots of kids garbed in bathing wear. Wearily, Rina trudged up to the front desk and checked for messages. Nothing. She slung her purse over her shoulder and slipped her arm around Peter. 'I'm hungry.'

'I'm tired of room service,' Decker said. 'Let's just eat downstairs.'

'Fine. Do you want to eat meat or dairy?'

'Up to you.'

'I'll opt for dairy,' Rina said. 'The thought of eating fleisch on three hours of sleep churns my stomach. Besides, I'm in the mood for onion soup.'

Descending a flight of stairs, they walked into a patio restaurant, replete with white wicker tables and chairs shaded by a lattice roof of blooming vines. The sun was out, the air smelled freshly washed. Children and pool noises chirped in the background. They were seated in a cozy corner, the table dressed with white linen and scented roses. A busboy came over, filled their crystal water glasses, and presented them with a basket of crusty olive and onion bread. Decker took a slice and topped it with a generous amount of sweet butter.

'This is nice,' he said.

'Let's pretend we're on vacation.' Rina took some bread and picked at the onions. 'How about a moratorium on work?'

'Great.' Decker polished off his bread and took another slice.

A raven-haired waitress presented them with menus which they studied for a few minutes. Decker put his down, then said, 'How were the kids when you spoke to them?'

'Surprised that we were awake at three in the morning. The family was on its way out to dinner courtesy of my parents.'

'Where?'

'Kosher Kanton. The boys were in the mood for sweet and sour chicken.'

The waitress came, took their orders, and left. Decker said, 'How's the baby?'

'In a great mood. Although Nora told me that Hannah does say "Mama" a lot.'

'Uh-oh.'

'No big deal.' Rina looked up. 'We've only been away for two days. We should be home soon.'

'Rina, if you want to go back, I can manage on my own. Lord knows you eased my way. I can take it from here.'

Rina bit her lip. 'I would except I can't get Honey Klein and her kids off my mind.'

'We could look for Honey, too,' Decker said. 'Depends how long you want to stay here.'

'I want to go home,' Rina admitted. 'I'm exhausted and I miss the kids. But I also want resolution. I'm torn.'

'Well, right now we're not going anywhere. We don't have our passports.'

'When do you think we'll get them back?'

'I'm sure you could get yours back anytime you wanted. As for me, they may take longer to check me out.'

'You're going in for questioning this afternoon?' Rina asked.

'Looks that way. Kreisman isn't done with me.'

'He doesn't trust you.'

'I know. Frankly, I don't blame him. I'm here for a couple of days and all sorts of bombs start exploding—'

'Peter, you saved the Bursa from blowing up. You're a hero!'

'I'll let you in on a clue, Rina. Police are suspicious of heroes.'

'What does he want with you?'

'To go over my case, bit by bit. Frankly, I welcome some fresh input. My main concern right now is finding Dov Yalom. But I sure wouldn't mind finding Milligan as well.'

'What about Shaul Gold?'

'Yeah, I forgot about him. Where the hell is Gold in all of this? And why was Milligan looking for him?'

Rina paused. 'Peter, I have a thought.'

'Shoot.'

'What if Yalom found out about Milligan's plan to blow up the Bursa? Wouldn't that be a reason to want him dead?'

Decker waited a beat. 'Absolutely.'

'Suppose Milligan thought that maybe Yalom had told his sons . . . or possibly Gold . . . about the terrorist plan.

465

Couldn't that be the reason why Milligan was looking for Gold . . . or the boys?'

'Absolutely.'

'So maybe that was the reason why Milligan was dealing with Yalom directly. Maybe he was blackmailing her over the Bursa plan.'

'But you can't blackmail someone for something that hasn't happened.'

'Maybe she murdered him so she could make it happen. And maybe Arik's sons found out about it and that's why they ran.'

Decker ran his tongue in his cheek. 'There's one way to find out. While I'm at the police station, I have a job for you if you're interested.'

'What?'

'Find Gil Yalom . . . talk to him.'

'Talk to him about what?'

'See if you can get him to tell you what's going on.'

'How do I do that?'

Decker shrugged. 'It's intangible. Each person's different.' He paused. 'Hell, even if you can't get him to talk about the case, just go visit him. Give him some sympathy. The kid's parents were murdered, he's scared shitless. He's a sensitive kid, Rina. Did I tell you about the poetry he wrote? Full of longing and hope for a better world.'

'That's so sad.'

'Last night he was in terrible shock. Maybe he's been that way since his parents were murdered. It was Dov who had made the phone calls to his cousin and grandparents. Find Gil. If for no other reason than to tell him he's got people on his side.'

Rina nodded. 'How?'

'You might try calling up the Yaloms. They might know which hospital Gil was admitted to. They might tell you.'

'They'd tell you as well as me. After all, you were the hero yesterday. You're in today's paper, you know.'

'I am?'

'The *Jerusalem Examiner* here. Someone showed me a copy while you were with Kreisman in the Bursa. Apparently, you were here with your wife *on vacation*, and you just happened to be visiting Or Torah Yeshiva. Suddenly you noticed a suspicious man.' Rina sang out. 'Duh-da-duh-duh.'

'I never talked to any reporter.'

'Then someone talked for you. They didn't quote you. So maybe they got the story from Moti Bernstein.'

'We're here on vacation, huh?'

'Must be true,' Rina said. 'I read it in the papers.'

Decker frowned. 'Maybe the Yaloms consider me a hero. Or maybe they'll blame me for the bomb in the yeshiva, that my investigation put their grandson at risk. If I were you, I'd call them up acting as a concerned citizen. They like you. You speak their language. You're not an outsider like I am.'

'And if they don't tell me anything?'

'Then do legwork. Check out the hospitals in Jerusalem.'

'Just go in real casual and ask patient information for Gil Yalom?'

'That sounds simple, but sometimes simple works.'

After an hour's worth of searching, Rina was certain that Gil wasn't at Bikur Cholim, Hadassah, or Shaarey Zedek. Which meant he was at one of the smaller Jerusalem hospitals if he hadn't been transferred out of the city. She checked her map against her list, and started with the closest address – in Emeq Refa'im just off the railroad tracks. Rina remembered the area as residential. Any hospital there was probably small, just a step up from a neighborhood clinic.

She started the Subaru's engine and took off, wearing the car's shot-out window like a battle scar. She followed the road through a short business district. At a major intersection filled with stoplights, she turned left and continued, riding on a half-paved, two-lane road lined with apartment houses. When she got to the railroad tracks, the road ended. On her right stood a multistoried stone and glass building completely at odds with its surroundings. She parked the car, got out, and went inside.

The lobby was spacious and flooded with light, the white marble floors gleaming in the sun's rays. At the door, a guard checked Rina's purse. She stepped inside, spotted an information booth, then hesitated. Behind the desk was a guard as well as a young woman in a white uniform. She had a pixie face surrounded by short black hair. Two sets of eyes looked at Rina, then peered with suspicion.

Hospital personnel wasn't usually leery. The bombing had scared everyone to heightened awareness.

The best approach?

Rina lowered her eyes and put a slump in her walk. She approached the pixie woman whose name tag said Orly. Rina spoke in Hebrew. 'My friend had a terrible miscarriage. I'm here to visit her.'

Orly spoke with efficiency. 'The name?'

'Sarah Yardin,' Rina said. 'Yardin spelled like the winery.'

Orly consulted her computer. 'There is no Yardin here.'

Rina scratched the scarf covering her hair. 'Are you sure—'

'Of course I'm sure.'

'Can you check again?'

Orly said, '*G'veret*, I don't need to check again. There is no Yardin in the hospital.'

'Maybe they accidentally listed her under Sarah.'

Orly sighed. 'There is no one here listed under Sarah.'

'Can you just check one more—'

'*G'veret*—'

'She is my good friend. She was so excited about the baby. The miscarriage was just terrible. I need to see her.'

The guard rolled his eyes.

Rina pressed on. 'Once more? Please?'

Orly punched the name back into the computer. 'There is no Yardin here.' She turned the terminal around to show a list of names beginning with the Hebrew letter *yod*. 'You can see for yourself.'

No Yardin, but a Yalom ... room 346. Rina looked upset. 'How can that be?'

'I don't know, *g'veret*.'

'Thank you,' Rina said, meekly.

'What's to thank me? I didn't do anything.'

Rina went back to the car, took off her scarf, and unpinned her hair. Layers of black satin fell down her back. To change her look even further, she untucked her blouse and hiked up her skirt. The final touch was the shades – Peter's aviator glasses. They were too big for her face, but it gave her the look she wanted.

She studied her reflection in the window of her car – a righteous woman posing as a floozy. She wondered if Tamar felt that way when she was picked up by her father-in-law, Judah.

Coming back into the hospital lobby, she presented her purse for a second time to the same guard. First time out, he didn't notice her. This time, he did. As he rifled through her purse, his eyes were on her legs.

No wonder terrorists used women.

She went inside the hospital and studied Orly and her henchman from a distance. The woman was good, doing paperwork but constantly scanning the lobby. Rina waited. A young man with flowers came up to Orly's desk. At the same time, the guard had strolled over to the bathroom.

An opportunity not to be lost! Rina took a deep breath and walked briskly over to the elevators. She was fast, but not fast enough.

Orly shouted at her to come over.

Rina turned around and lowered her shades slightly. She spoke in rapid English. 'Areyoutalkin'tome?'

Orly seemed perplexed. She attempted to speak English. 'You get badge first.'

'I've already got my badge,' Rina fired out in a high voice. 'I was here yesterday and I still have it in my purse.' She pulled out a piece of paper, held it up for a split second, and pushed the elevator button. 'I didn't want to wear it 'cause it punches holes in the clothes, you know. I hate that. But if you really want me to wear it, I can do it. Like if it's really important to you.'

The young man tapped his foot impatiently. Orly asked him if he understood her. The young man shook his head. The elevator dinged. Rina held the door and stepped in. 'See ya.'

The doors closed and that was that. Once inside, Rina lowered her skirt, folded her hair into a bun. She tucked in her blouse and got out on the third floor. Immediately, she saw the guard down the hallway, posted in front of a room.

With feigned confidence, she went up to him, opting to keep the shades because it made her look official.

'Police,' Rina said, in Hebrew. 'I need to speak to the boy – Gil Yalom.'

'ID.'

Now what? Rina fished through her purse. Hoping the guard couldn't read English, she brought out her rental-car contract. 'My official papers to interview him.'

The guard said, 'This is in English.'

Rina appeared exasperated. 'Of course they're in English. I'm the liaison between the American and Israeli police departments. Bomb division. Northwest – Tel Aviv. *Sgan Nitzav* Kreisman's office. You heard what happened this morning at the Bursa, didn't you?'

The guard's cheeks took on a blush.

'Ach!' Rina said. 'You haven't heard. No wonder you don't know what's going on.' She snatched the rental-car contract out of his hands. 'These papers allow me to interview Gil Yalom and search his car. He has a Subaru. See here?' Rina showed him the contract. 'Subaru. This is the model number and the license plates. Can't go around searching cars without knowing which cars to search.'

She shoved the contract back in her purse and snapped it shut. 'I'm pressed for time. *Shalom.*'

The guard let her pass.

She stepped inside the room. Her heart sank. Another guard posted on the inside. He sat up when he saw Rina, started coming toward her, blocking her view of Gil Yalom as well as Moshe and Tziril Yalom, who were keeping vigil by their grandson's bedside.

'I have papers.' Once again, Rina took out the contract. The guard grabbed them and read.

'Nice,' the guard said in accented English. 'You rent a Subaru.' He grabbed her arm. 'You're under arrest.'

471

Tziril Yalom stood and came to her defense. 'Are you crazy! Let her go. I know her. She is a very nice young lady.'

The guard continued to hold Rina. 'My strict orders were not to let anyone in here other than relatives. Orders are orders—'

'Orders are orders? So this is the Third Reich?' Tziril came up to him and whacked him on the shoulder. 'I tell you I know this young woman. She came here to help. Let her go!'

'Only relatives, *g'veret*. Sorry, but—'

'She is my illegitimate daughter,' Moshe Yalom announced.

All eyes fell upon him.

'It happens to the best of us.' Yalom shrugged. 'Just ask anyone at the Bursa. I took her there yesterday and introduced everyone to her as my daughter.'

The guard laughed. 'You expect me to believe that?'

'Yes, I do,' Yalom said gravely.

The guard continued to hold Rina, but looked at Moshe. 'Then why didn't you say that in the first place?'

'I should embarrass my wife by making such an announcement out loud?' Yalom retorted. 'Let her go. She is a relative.'

Reluctantly, the guard released Rina's arm.

Rina shook off her indignity. 'Thank you.' She took off her glasses, went over to Gil Yalom's bedside and hugged Tziril. 'Thank you.'

'I should thank you,' the woman said. 'Moti Bernstein told us what your husband did yesterday at the yeshiva.' Tziril hugged her again. 'You married a very brave man.'

Rina swallowed dryly. 'Mrs Yalom, he sent me here because he was concerned about Gil.'

'You need to talk to him, don't you?' Tziril said.

Rina nodded.

Grandmother looked at grandson. Rina studied Gil. Peter had told her that Gil had been in a state of shock. But the teenager Rina saw was alert. He stared at her for a long time, intense eyes sizing up her worth. Rina smiled at him, but it failed to elicit a response.

Finally, Tziril spoke, 'Gil, this woman is here to help. You need to tell her what you know.'

Gil didn't answer.

'Gil—'

'I heard, *Savta*,' Gil whispered.

Rina sat by his bedside. Gil was more young man than boy. His full beard had yet to come in completely, but patches of stubble shadowed his lip and cheeks. His cheeks were gaunt, his eyes tired. Rina waited a moment, then tried another smile. He still didn't smile back, but this time it got a response.

Gil looked at his grandparents and spoke Hebrew. 'I need to be alone with her.'

Moshe Yalom stood and said, 'I can use a cup of coffee.' He took his wife's hand and they walked out the door. Gil watched them leave, then turned his eyes to Rina. In English, he said, 'My *savta* tells me you're the cop's wife? The one who saved the yeshiva.'

Rina nodded. The boy's voice was low and soft. Rina could tell the guard was straining to hear.

'How'd he know I was there?'

'Luck. We were searching all the *ba'alei tchuvah* yeshivas. Actually, we were looking to find Dov. We were told he'd been *frum* a while back.'

'Yeah, my dad took care of that one real quick.'

The sarcasm was dripping. Rina kept her voice soft, 'Is

473

that why you sent your grandparents out? You didn't want them to hear negative things about your father?'

Gil didn't respond, just peered at her. Then he said, 'Am I going to be extradited to LA?'

'I don't know if extradited is the right word. Sergeant Decker was sent here to take you and your brother back to Los Angeles.'

Gil looked at the ceiling. 'In a way, it's a relief. I shouldn't have left in the first place. But in a panic you make bad decisions.'

'Why didn't you go to the police?'

'I had reasons.'

Rina moved closer and spoke softly. 'Your dad warned you off with the porcelain dogs.'

'Not my dad, my mom—' Gil stopped talking. His eyes widened. 'Shit, you know everything, don't you?' He waited a beat. 'You know, your husband almost had me killed by finding me. They were following him to get to me.'

'By *they*, do you mean Milligan's men?'

Gil whitened at the mention of her name. 'They were using your husband to find me. He played perfectly into their plans. Is he stupid or what?'

Rina knew it had been the reverse. Milligan had located Gil before they had. She had planted the bomb in the yeshiva in order to draw Decker there and away from her intended target – the Bursa. But she played along. 'Milligan was out for you because you knew too much.'

Gil nodded.

'We know a lot, too, Gil,' Rina told him. 'We know about the stocks and land deeds in Angola that your father owned. We know Milligan wanted those assets and your father wouldn't sell them to her at the price she wanted. So she had your parents killed, figuring you two boys might be easier to deal with. But you two escaped before she had her chance. She came here looking to find you.'

The boy looked down and said nothing.

'Honestly, we're not as stupid as you think,' Rina said. 'Do you know where your brother is? My husband's really worried about him.'

'He's safe. But he's homesick, too. Not that either of us have much of a home anymore.'

Tears began to roll down Gil's cheeks. He quickly wiped them away. 'You don't know as much as you think.'

'So fill me in.'

The room fell silent. Gil whispered and spoke to the ceiling. 'Bastard was sleeping with her. She had him totally bagged, the stupid *fuck*!' He lowered his head. 'Excuse my language.'

'S'right.'

Gil rubbed his eyes, slumped in his bed. 'Dov and I used to do bullshit work at the office. Dad *made* us do it. "Turn you two boys into men." What a total crock! Anyway ... you hang around a place long enough, you hear things. Whether you want to hear them or not.'

Rina said, 'Your father was going to sell Milligan his assets?'

'He was going to *give* them to her! *Anything* to keep her on her back!' He covered his face, then let his hand drop slowly. 'He stretched it out too long. She lost patience, the bitch.'

Rina thought a moment. Was the exchange of all those hostile letters just a front? 'He was going to *give* Milligan his stocks and land deeds?'

'Yeah, can you believe that bastard?' Gil said. 'Only problem was, half of the shit wasn't *his* to give away. My uncle made him transfer it to my mom a while back.'

'Your uncle?'

'Uncle Shaul,' Gil said. 'My dad's partner. We called him Uncle. Shaul was going to sue my dad, because my dad bought some of his assets with business money. Shaul caught him monkeying with the books. Dad realized he was up shit's creek, could have done time. So he transferred a little over half the assets into my mom's name.'

'Why didn't Shaul keep the assets for himself?'

'I don't know. Why don't you ask him?'

'We know he's here in Israel. Do you know where he is specifically?'

'No. Wish I did. Shaul's a good guy. Rough but straight. He was around a lot, especially when my dad was out of town. Which was all the time. Used to take us out to dinner. My mom liked him. He liked my mom. Who didn't like my mom? She was a wonderful . . .'

Again, the boy's eyes welled up with tears. He made a quick swipe at his face.

'Do you know what happened when Milligan found out your dad didn't own all the assets?'

'Not totally. But once at work I accidentally picked up the extension. She was yelling at my dad that he was a traitor. My dad was pleading, just *begging* her for another chance he was so hot for her. God, it was *pathetic*. But she wouldn't have it or him. She totally blew him off.'

Gil bit his nail.

'Dov and I thought it was *finally* over.'

'When was this?'

'A year ago, maybe longer. But it wasn't over. Maybe a month or two after I overheard her blow him off, Dov overheard my dad talking to Milligan . . . again. Dov said that Dad sounded real up about something . . . money opportunities in the Mideast if the Palestinians ever got their own state. Dov said Dad did most of the talking. Milligan just listened.'

Gil looked at Rina.

'Dad went yo-yo after that. For a year, he was lunatic. One minute he was on top of the world, saying he was going to make it big enough to buy out all of Israel. The next minute he'd be paranoid, sure someone was out to get him.'

'Did you believe him?'

'That someone was out to get him?' Gil shook his head. 'Not really. But my mom was real worried.'

'She felt he was in danger?'

'Mostly she felt he was coking again. Dad used to do a lot of coke. The way he was acting, it sure looked like he was having a relapse. She felt that under the influence, he might be doing some stupid things. And you can't do stupid things in diamonds. Because the business is dangerous enough just being what it is – all cash and stones. Dealers have been gunned down in broad daylight. *She* was the one who told us to get out immediately if we saw the dogs turned around. I don't think she ever trusted my dad.'

'She knew about the affair?'

Gil looked pained. 'Probably She never said anything.'

'When did you first notice the porcelain dogs had been turned around?'

'As soon as we came home from school,' Gil said. 'They're right in the open.' His breathing became audible. 'We panicked. We knew it was bad. Mom had special money for us put aside—'

'In the mezuzah?'

'God, you do know everything!'

'How many Jewish families post a mezuzah on the inside of the door?'

'Yeah, you would notice that. *If* you were Jewish.' Gil

paused. 'Anyway, Mom told us not to take my car, that we might be followed. We just grabbed the money, grabbed our passports, and walked down to the shopping center. We took a bus to the airport – several buses. We already had about a half-dozen flight plans mapped out. Bought some tickets and . . .'

Again, Gil looked up at the ceiling.

'I have never been so fucking scared in my entire *life*! Not even when your husband pulled me out of the yeshiva. As much as I want to die and start over, you know . . . I know I can't. Mom wouldn't have wanted that.' He paused. 'God, I *loved* her.'

The boy broke into unrestrained sobs. Rina reached out for him and he fell into her arms, hugged her tightly.

'I gotta take care of my brother,' he wept. 'I'm almost a man, but I'm such a goddamn kid.'

'Gil,' Rina said softly. 'That's what family is for. You have grandparents who love you. You have an aunt in Los Angeles who loves you, too.'

The boy broke from Rina's embrace and wiped his eyes. 'Yeah, we can probably stay with her until we both graduate. Their house isn't as big—'

'I'm sure that's not a problem.'

Gil smiled through tears.

Rina said, 'Gil, we need to talk to your brother.'

'I know. But I've gotta talk to him first. There are complications.'

'What kind of complications?'

'I can't say. Besides, he might not agree to it. He's in real bad shape. Super-scared of Milligan. Especially after we found out about my parents in the mountains. Milligan's vicious. I know she set my parents up.'

'You know that for a fact?'

478

'No . . . I mean, my dad was always doing *secret* meetings with her – obviously. He didn't want my mom to know . . . even though she *did* know. Dov and I could understand how my dad fell into the trap. We couldn't understand why my *mom* would. Only thing we could figure out is . . .' He lowered his head. 'She must have known we were due home from school soon. She must have left the house to get Milligan or her men away . . . to protect us. Why else would she have gone with my dad to the mountains?'

He looked at Rina.

'You know where Milligan is?'

'No. But she's a wanted woman, Gil. *Everyone's* looking for her. Israeli police, my husband and the American police. Even people who she thought were on her side.'

'What does that mean?'

'We think Milligan may have been behind some terrorist acts in Israel.'

'The bomb in my yeshiva?'

'And other things. But her plans went awry. We think the people she worked with may want to find her as well. Please, Gil. Tell me where your brother is.'

The teen covered his face, then dropped his hands, and blew out air. 'I wish I knew who to trust.' The boy shook his head. 'You'll just have to wait.'

Rina bit her lip.

'You're pissed at me,' Gil said.

'No, of course not.' Rina took the boy's hand and squeezed it. 'I'm just concerned about Dov. You know, even if you don't tell me, your grandparents have a right—'

Rina stopped talking.

The one person she and Peter hadn't had time to visit. 'He's with your other grandmother, isn't he? That's why she's not here with you.'

Gil closed his eyes and flopped back on his pillow.

Rina patted his hands. 'Don't fret, Gil. You didn't tell me. I guessed.'

38

An hour's nap and Decker felt much better. He showered, shaved, then dressed, automatically reaching for a non-existent shoulder harness. He was still brooding over his nakedness when his phone rang. He picked up the receiver.

'I need to talk to you. Please.'

A female voice – familiar.

'Where are you?' Decker played along.

'Downstairs,' she said. 'I'd like to come up to your room. Make this as private as possible.'

The light bulb went off. Honey Klein. Decker said, 'Fine.' He gave her his room number. A minute later, he answered a knock.

Had Decker not heard the voice, he wouldn't have recognized the person. While in Decker's home, Honey had dressed modestly in keeping with Orthodox tradition – a dress below her knees with long sleeves – and her hair had always been covered. But judging from the way she looked, Decker knew that something inside of her had snapped. Only the face was visible among the drapery of black that swathed her body. A gaunt face with sunken eyes ringed with dark shadows. She looked more like a nun in habit than any Orthodox Jewish woman Decker had known.

She looked around the hotel room, then zeroed in on Decker with tired eyes. 'Where's Rina?'

'She's not here.'

Sitting down on the bed, Honey blew out air. 'I read this morning about what you did at the yeshiva – a real mitzvah. I'm happy for Rina that she remarried such a *tzaddik* – such a righteous man.'

There was pain in her voice.

'The article said you two originally came here for vacation. I know you and Rina hadn't *planned* on any vacation. Now I know *you're* here because of your case. But with Rina? I was wondering if she came here to look for me.'

'She did indeed. She was very concerned about you and the children.'

'That's Rina. A *tzedeikess* for a *tzaddik*. She's a good woman. I could take lessons in *middos* from her.' Honey looked at Decker. 'I can't hide anymore, Akiva. Not that I couldn't have done it physically . . . you wouldn't have recognized me, right?'

'Not at all.'

'I can't hide mentally. I can't do that to my children. I'm here to bring resolution to the mess I created. What do you want to do with me?'

'The authorities want to ask you some questions, Honey.'

'Ask.'

'It would be better if we conducted the interview in America.'

Honey's shoulders slumped. 'It wasn't supposed to work out like this.' Tears formed in her eyes. 'All I wanted was a second chance. It wasn't . . .'

Decker waited.

'Nothing can help me,' Honey whispered. 'It was all my fault. The Rebbe told me to be patient with Gershon.' She

482

looked at him. 'I ran out of patience, Akiva. I simply . . . gave up. You should never, *ever* give up.'

'You stuck with Gershon a long time, Honey.'

She swiped at wet eyes with the back of her hands. 'I know you won't believe me, but I had nothing to do with his death.'

'I believe you,' Decker said. 'But for your *own* protection, I suggest you don't talk to me without a lawyer. Because I am a sworn officer of the law. And if you say something incriminating, I could use it against you.'

Honey nodded. 'But I can talk to you if I want?'

Decker buried his hands. 'Please don't. Wait until you're back in New York.'

'But I want to explain it to you. I was trying to divorce Gershon—'

'Honey—'

'He refused to give me a *get*. I was *stuck*. It wasn't supposed to work out like that. I didn't . . .'

'I know,' Decker said. 'You went to the Rebbe for help, didn't you?'

Honey was quiet, her eyes far-away. 'It's too bad you and Rina didn't know Gershon when I first married him. He was . . . *wonderful*! Handsome and kind . . . a wonderful father.'

She closed her eyes and opened them.

'The changes happened so subtly. I blinked . . . and the next thing I knew I was married to a stranger. Looking back, I wonder if it wasn't something organic – a tumor or a mental breakdown. Because a person doesn't change just like that.'

She adjusted the black scarf that covered every inch of her hair.

'It was so subtle. First it was the davening all day. Then it was him becoming a Nazir. It was only when he started in on the children that I knew it was hopeless. Preaching to them. He'd sit them down and preach to them for hours, screaming at them if they moved a muscle or squirmed or blinked.'

She licked her lips.

'He'd make them wear sackcloth when he sermonized. Then, when he started making them fast once a week, I knew I had . . . do you know what kind of mental damage he did? *Baruch Hashem*, the Rebbe was there to neutralize him.'

'Why didn't you just leave him, Honey?'

'He swore he'd see me dead before he'd give me a *get*. The Rebbe tried to get a dispensation . . . you can divorce a crazy person. Unfortunately, Gershon was rational in his fanaticism. If you talked to him, he could answer you back. He was coherent . . . but he wasn't.'

'Did the Rebbe talk to him?'

'Of course!' Honey said. 'Everyone could see what was happening to him. They all did what they could to try to make Gershon see reason.'

'But he wouldn't listen to reason. His *yaitzer harah* had invaded his *yaitzer tov*.'

Honey broke into tears and nodded.

Decker said, 'No one meant any harm, only to get Gershon's *yaitzer tov* back.'

'So you *do* understand.'

'Of course.' Decker spoke very softly. 'The Rebbe had no choice. He did what he had to do. What he was allowed to do halachically, what he was permitted by Jewish law.'

Honey's head shot up. 'What? *What* are you suggesting?'

Her voice had turned cold. She wasn't about to incriminate her beloved leader.

'Honey,' Decker said. 'You may not verbalize what happened. But I *know* what happened. I know it was probably an accident. But that doesn't mean it's not murder. Keeping quiet to protect individuals isn't going to help anyone.'

Honey hesitated, then said, 'Let me put it this way. I know that some . . . people in my town were going to talk to Gershon, try to convince him to give me a *get*.'

There was a long stretch of silence.

'That's why I came out to Los Angeles. So people could talk to Gershon alone.'

'And that's why you're here using a false passport?'

'Akiva, I knew that if it didn't work, Gershon would be furious. I didn't care for *me*. But I feared for the kids. I knew I would have to go far away. That's why I bothered with forged passports.'

Decker sat beside her. 'Honey, listen to me. Because what I'm saying is from the heart. I'm sorry for all your tragedy. Because this really is a *tragedy*. But I think the best way to deal with it is to face it head-on. You get yourself a lawyer, get great legal representation for the Rebbe—'

'He had nothing to do with this!' Honey snapped.

'Okay, okay,' Decker backed off. 'Okay, we'll just stick to you. You get yourself a lawyer and you work out your case with him. Where are the kids?'

'Safe.'

'Here?'

'Yes. With people who love them and can care for them. I don't have to bring them back to America with me, do I?'

'You want to leave them here . . . alone?'

'They're not alone here, Akiva.' Honey blinked and regarded Decker's face. 'They are with three million brothers and sisters. That's an awfully big family.'

'If that's what you want, fine.'

'That's what I want.' Honey looked down at her lap and straightened her skirt. 'It's funny. Originally, I moved with Gershon to the village as a refuge against the outside world. But there's no escaping evil. It comes at you in many forms. It took me time to realize my strength. And now, like Jacob, I'm ready to wrestle with the *Ish*. You're right. I have to face whatever is in store for me head-on.' She stood. 'Where do I go from here?'

'I'll get you an official escort back to the States, Honey. Manhattan police will detain you for questioning. Once in America, you hire yourself a good lawyer.'

'I didn't kill Gershon.'

'I know you didn't.'

'Thank you, Akiva. Thank you for believing me.'

Kreisman bit into an overstuffed pita. From the smell, Decker figured it was bologna with mustard. He sipped his coffee and waited for the interview to commence. The *sgan nitzav* was chewing slowly. Decker wondered if it was on purpose. A waiting game.

But he didn't mind. In fact, the silence was a welcome respite, a chance for him to digest his thoughts. Honey was now in official hands. He couldn't get her face off his mind, the plaintive way she had looked at him as she was led away by a gentle-looking Israeli policewoman. Honey's expression had been agony and anguish. And though anguish wasn't a viable excuse for murder, he sincerely hoped that things might work out for her. Then Rina had called him, describing her conversation with Gil Yalom. He recalled the crack in her voice as she recounted how the teenager had cried in her arms.

Too much pain. So let Kreisman take his time with his

damn sandwich. The *sgan nitzav* gave a final swallow and wiped his mouth with a napkin.

'I got word to be nice to you. That isn't easy for me. Especially because I don't fully trust you.'

Decker waited.

'Actually someone called from the prime minister's office. Some bigwig wants to thank you publicly.'

'You can take my place.'

'Fuck you, Decker. I don't need to ride the coattails of your glory.'

'Kreisman, I'm not interested in glory. All I want is to collect my suspects, go back home, and sleep for a day.'

'Well, if you're looking for Milligan or Ibrahim Khouri or Gamal Shabazz, you can stop. They're gone. However, our detectives did pick up some interesting information from some of the residents of the town.'

'People actually *talked* to you?'

'We have ways and I don't mean *physical* ways.' Kreisman rubbed his thumb against his fingertips. 'Works like a charm.'

'Who's Donald?'

'Donald Haas. He isn't a Black Muslim, but he is a South African black and a very radical one at that. He's far left of the ANC and has been responsible for the deaths of at least a dozen people. Some were white, but some were moderate blacks who publicly opposed Haas's known philosophy of white extermination. The guy did ten years in jail, got sprung shortly after they liberated Nelson Mandela.'

'And what's the connection between him and Kate Milligan?'

'Pussy connection. They were lovers.'

'Longtime lovers?'

'Who knows? Guess Haas had no problem justifying his

inconsistency. A fuck is a fuck. What I don't get is why a woman like Milligan would go for him? What could she *see* in him?'

Decker thought about what Rina had told him. How Milligan had slept with Yalom – a Jew whom she probably despised – to get what she wanted. 'Maybe she saw a pit bull who could implement her plans.'

'That could be.'

Decker studied his thoughts, recalling his conversation with Marge. Perhaps they had been right all along. Yalom had originally gotten Milligan's attention by blackmail. Perhaps she and Haas had been longtime forbidden lovers. Had her plan worked, had she been able to raid Palestinian start-up capital, she would have set them both up for life. He said, 'Then again, Kreisman, you can't explain love.'

'Love.' Kreisman made a face. 'Milligan's a cold bitch. She doesn't have a heart, Decker. She's just got a pump.'

'Where is Donald Haas? Is he gone as well?'

Kreisman nodded. 'They all must have slipped over the Jordanian border last night. From Jordan, they could move freely about the Arab countries without worrying about us tailing them. But that doesn't mean we're giving up. We have ways of finding people even in hostile countries.'

'Is the PLO helping at all? Because Milligan's stunt must be an embarrassment to them now.'

'Not helping, not hindering, so far as we can tell. Yeah, Milligan's an embarrassment to Arafat. Every time someone in any of the Arab organizations fucks up, it lessens his chance of becoming king of Palestine.'

Kreisman waved his hand in the air.

'Yeah, we're still hunting, but your part in all of this is over. You got the Yalom boys. Take them home and let us do our job.'

'Sounds good. I'll need my papers back.'

Kreisman stood. 'I'll get them for you. Maybe we'll meet again down the line.'

'Maybe,' Decker said. 'But I hope not.'

Kreisman smiled. 'You're blunt.'

'I speak my mind.'

'I can see that. You'd make a good Israeli.'

Part III
America

39

Marge said to Decker, 'You look great! Are you sure you didn't go there on vacation?'

Decker put his feet up on his desk. Man, he'd missed her. True, he had had Rina, and she'd been great. But he had worked with her only out of necessity. He valued their marriage vows as bonds of intimacy. Rina was his life partner, not his business associate.

But now he was back in the groove and, happily, so was Rina. She was thrilled to get home to the baby and the boys. Decker had wondered when she had hugged the kids if her mind hadn't been on Honey Klein's loneliness.

'You know, Dunn,' Decker went on, 'I bet I'm the only religious Jew who went to Israel and missed the Wailing Wall. That's how dedicated to work I was. Only sightseeing I did was accompanying Rina to her late husband's grave. You can imagine how much fun that was for me.'

'Then why'd you do it?'

'I did it for Jake and Sam. I sure as hell wouldn't want my kids to forget about me. I can't let my boys forget about their father.'

'You're a good guy, Pete.'

'Tell that to Davidson. You believe that son of a bitch

giving me a hard time about my expense account? Asking me about all those phone calls to New York? I brought in Honey Klein. What's the asshole going on about?'

'He's an asshole, Pete. But you did make a few personal calls.'

'I talked to my half brother, Marge, but that was strictly business. I had to explain to him why Rina wasn't coming out.'

Marge smiled. 'Not that I care but you talked to him for two hours.'

'I'm meticulous.' Decker swung his feet to the floor and sat up. 'If he doesn't like it, fuck him!'

Marge said, 'I got a call from the DA's office. The office is prepared to go ahead and indict Milligan on two counts of first degree murder based on the evidence – the statement of the Yalom boys, the papers in Yalom's box, and lastly, evidence pulled by the Israeli police. Do you know what that's referring to?'

'Yes, I do. They got some statements from some Hebron residents. They also did some hunting and searching. They found receipts made out to Milligan for tools, parts, and chemicals that could have been used in the making of plastiques.'

'She kept receipts?'

'She was a businesswoman. They were deductible.'

Marge broke into laughter.

'Along the way, they found one real damning piece of paper. A written statement attributed to a guy named Mohammed Husseini, a former bigwig in the PLO. The note expressed sorrow over the terrible tragedy in the Bursa and condemned all acts of violence. It went on to suggest that the Arabs and Jews work together to build a bigger and more comprehensive diamond exchange in the new state of Palestine. One that would be internationally recognized as the top in the field of diamonds.'

Marge laughed incredulously. 'I can't believe such . . . oh God, I know I'm going to pronounce this wrong . . . chutzpah?'

'Very good,' Decker said. 'Incidentally, the statement was not only written in *English* – Husseini speaks only Arabic – but was in Milligan's handwriting.'

Marge stopped talking for a moment. 'Wonder who actually pulled the trigger on the parents?'

'We asked the boys about that,' Decker said. 'They seem certain it was Milligan's doing. Gil told us that his father and Milligan often had secret meetings.'

'Then what lured Dalia to the mountains?'

'Gil thought that maybe his mother went willingly to get the gunmen away from their house. Because she knew her sons would soon be coming home from school.'

'She was protecting her offspring.'

'It's a basic thing,' Decker said. 'We may never know the truth unless we get Milligan. And frankly, I don't think that's likely. According to Israeli intelligence, she and her friend Donald Haas have the means to bury themselves for a long time. He's got lots of friends in Arab countries. And she made lots of contingency plans. She owns places in Libya, Iraq, and Syria.'

'The countries that invested heavily in the diamond stocks.'

'Right. For all we know, she still may be calling some shots from wherever she is. And if the Palestinians ever get their own state, she'll be a queen. Israel won't be able to touch her. And she'd be a hero among the terrorists, the woman who almost destroyed Israel's biggest industry. You want to know the irony of the whole thing?'

'What?'

'She got the idea from Arik Yalom. Not the blowing up the Bursa part. But the idea of setting up competition in the industry, using Palestinian money as capital. Yalom probably felt his knowledge of diamonds was going to be indispensable to her. So he was probably walking around feeling pretty damn secure.'

'Or maybe not. Didn't Gil say he wavered between euphoria and paranoia?'

'Yeah, you're right. Could be he knew Milligan wasn't trustworthy no matter how much he felt she needed him.'

'Or maybe he found out about Haas. Found out that Milligan was just using him.' Marge paused. 'You know, she didn't *have* to use him once he gave her the idea. Why bother killing him?'

Decker shrugged. 'Maybe Arik found out about Milligan's plan to blow up the Bursa. He might have been in love with her, he might have been greedy, but doing something like that ... I don't see even a schmuck like Arik going along with destroying his homeland.'

'So why didn't he just say something to security?'

'Maybe he tried to reason with Milligan first. That would have been a big mistake.' Decker took a deep breath and let it out. 'Milligan is a formidable enemy.'

'Think we'll ever get our hands on her?' Marge asked.

'Truthfully?' Decker shook his head. 'Not a chance.'

A grin on her face and a baby in her arms, Rina greeted Decker at the doorway. 'Can you believe it! Hannah's *walking*! She's only ten months old!'

Decker grabbed the baby from Rina. 'Ten months old and walking! Does that mean we're going to have to put all the breakables up another notch?'

'Looks that way.' Rina kissed Hannah's cheek. 'She waited for us to come home before she took her first steps. I know it was a conscious decision.'

'Absolutely.' Decker handed the baby back to Rina. 'Where are the boys?'

'Preparing the horse for the ride.'

'Oh, that's right.' Decker frowned. 'I did promise to take them, didn't I?'

'What's wrong?'

'I wanted to make a couple of calls first.'

'They'll wait. Who're you calling?'

'New York,' Decker said. 'The detective in charge of Honey Klein's case had left by the time I called. They gave me his home phone number. His wife told me to call around now.'

Hannah squirmed in Rina's arms. Gently, she lowered the baby to her feet. 'What's happening with that?'

'They're investigating the murder, but they're a ways off from any indictment.'

'Is Honey a suspect?'

'Their prime suspect. But they don't have any evidence to back up their suspicions. The cops have gone out to the village at least a half dozen times and come back empty. They're hitting walls.'

'Peter, maybe she really didn't know what was going on. Maybe she left without knowing any details.'

'I don't think she knew details, but she knew what was going on. Otherwise, why would she bother with the false passports? And, Rina, she admitted that, in her absence, she knew that some people were going to try to *convince* Gershon to give her a *get*. What does that sound like to you?'

Rina didn't answer.

497

'Then when you add the fact that the Rebbe didn't want me looking into Honey's disappearance . . . it doesn't look good for her. But that doesn't mean they'll get an indictment.'

Rina followed Hannah around the living room. 'Nobody meant for him to die.'

Decker tailed after his wife and daughter. He picked Hannah up by her waist and swung her under his knees.

'This is all too sad to contemplate,' Rina said.

'Yes, it is. Sometimes life is very sad.' He smiled softly and placed Hannah on top of his shoulders. 'I guess I don't have to tell you that.'

Rina sighed and sat down. 'So what should Honey have done?'

'You're asking for my opinion?' Decker said.

'Yes.'

'She should have gotten a civil divorce and gone on with her life.'

'What kind of life would she have had without a Jewish divorce?'

'So she's better off now, knowing that in some way she's responsible for murdering her husband?'

'No, you're right. She's not better off.' Rina was quiet. 'Sometimes you simply make the wrong decision.'

'I feel sorry for Honey,' Decker said. 'From the bottom of my heart, I feel very *bad* for her. But, Rina, she didn't make the *wrong* decision. Unfortunately, she made a *bad* decision.' He lowered Hannah to the ground. 'I think she needs to be changed. My shoulders feels a little too warm and a little too moist. You want me to do it?'

'I'll do it.' Rina scooped up the toddler. 'Thank God for babies. They keep you honest.'

* * *

Decker pressed the button; Yochie buzzed him into the anteroom. She seemed happy to be back at work, her eyes bright, her smile genuine. In gross contrast to Shaul Gold, who appeared a moment later. It had been over a month since Decker had seen the dealer. Gold's face was worn and drawn. He looked like he had dropped ten pounds.

'I would have thought you had lost your taste for diamonds, Sergeant,' he said.

'Just goes to show you,' Decker said.

'Come,' Gold said. 'We'll talk in my office.'

They walked down the hallway into the once shared office, now taken over completely by Gold. It was sunny and bright, the walls having been newly painted, the windows recently washed of LA's smog and soot. Gold's desk was almost entirely devoid of frills, holding mostly the tools of the trade – a microscope, a loupe, a pincer, and a scale. The exception was a sterling-silver double frame holding two pictures – an old one of Dalia Yalom, and a recent one of him sided by the two Yalom boys, hands around each other's shoulders and waists. Gil looked the same, but Decker noticed that Dov was wearing a yarmulke.

Decker picked the picture up. 'Who took this?'

'Orit. At a backyard barbecue. It lacked joy, but life goes on.'

'So you still see the boys?'

'They work here once a week,' Gold said. 'After the day is done, I take them to dinner if they want. It's nice.' Gold pursed his lips. 'When the time's right, I teach them how to cut stones. It's too bad Arik never did it. He was a top cutter. I'm just a peasant. But I do what I can to keep on the tradition. For Dalia's sake.'

'How are they doing?'

'They cope.' Gold shrugged. 'They like living with their aunt and uncle. Dov is close to his cousin, Sharona. I suppose they do as nicely as can be expected.' He paused. 'I'll show you stones if that's really why you came.'

'It isn't really why I came.'

Gold sat behind his desk and clasped his hands. 'So what do you want from me now?'

Decker reached in his pocket and pulled out a week-old news item from the overseas edition of the *Jerusalem Examiner*. Rina subscribed to the paper. Only way he would ever have found it. He handed it to Gold.

The bald man took it, studied it, then read aloud. ' "Two single shots to the head ... motive was robbery." ' He clucked his tongue, then handed the article back to Decker. 'The diamond business can be very dangerous. All cash and stones. You are asking for trouble if you carry such goods in a corrupt country like Syria. They are all cutthroats. A woman as smart as Milligan...' Again he clucked his tongue. 'She should know better.'

'I think she did know better,' Decker said. 'Milligan's death was a professional hit. Two shots to the head, right next to one another. The guy must have been trained as a sniper – a *tzalaf*.'

Gold's expression was flat. 'I'm surprised it didn't make the papers here. Milligan was quite well known. But then again, in Syria, it isn't easy to get information.'

The room fell silent.

'Where were you a week ago, Mr Gold?'

'I was in Israel.'

'Business?'

'No. My heart is too heavy to do business. I visit the

families – the Yaloms and the Menkovitzes. I give them words of comfort.' He hung his head. 'It is big tragedy.'

Decker said, 'I pulled out my notes from when I first interviewed you in your apartment, Mr Gold. Didn't you say you fought on the Golan Heights?'

'In '67 and '73. Seventy-three was very tough – a hard-fought victory because of the lateness of the Israeli air force. But we made it. Stick together in times of crisis.'

'You're familiar with Syrian territory.'

'I know the Golan. I fought wars there. But I've never been in Syrian territory. It is suicide for any Israeli – any Jew – to be in Syria. Too bad. I would like to go to Damascus. Did you know it is the oldest city in the world?'

Decker stared at him. 'Yes, Syria is a dangerous place for Jews. All I can say is you must have really liked Dalia to take a chance like that.'

'I don't take chances, Sergeant,' Gold said. 'Arik was the risk taker. I'm the stick-in-the-mud, remember?'

Decker didn't answer.

'No, I don't take risks,' Gold said. 'But I do what I have to do.'

Again, nobody spoke.

'You are a religious man, Sergeant?' Gold asked.

'At times.'

Gold smiled. 'I like that answer. Me too. At times, I am very religious. Do you learn at all?'

'When I get the chance.'

'You have heard about the *arey miklat*, maybe?'

'The city of refuge,' Decker said.

'The city of refuge,' Gold repeated. 'If an offender murders one of your own—'

'A relative, Mr Gold. And it has to be a murder by *accident*.'

Gold paused. 'Yes, you are the scholar. It is a relative and it is by accident. But anyway, if the offender takes one of your own, and you are so angry, so full of rage that you get revenge, the law makes exception and you do not get capital punishment for this offense of his murder.'

'You do get punished,' Decker said.

'Maybe you get whipped, I don't remember. But you don't get capital punishment.'

'Unless the offender makes it into one of the cities of refuge. Then you're not allowed to kill him.'

'This is true.' Gold stared at Decker. 'Sometimes people think they make it to a city of refuge. Sometimes they think they do, but they don't. Because there is no city of refuge if the crime is purposeful. Nowhere on earth. Nowhere under God's heaven. The person may think he – or she – is safe. But this is a falsehood.'

'Especially if the chaser is an expert sniper who can hit the head of a nail from five kilometers.'

Gold smiled. 'You take good notes.'

'Not so hard to do,' Decker said. 'Sneak into Syria using his expert knowledge of the Golan Heights and do a couple of pops.'

Gold said, 'You think it would be easy, you do it.'

Decker said, 'You must have loved Dalia very much. You spoke of her as one of your own just a moment ago.'

Gold rubbed his hands. 'A long time ago, there was a little boy of five who escaped Nazis by skin of the teeth. The boy had parents, the boy had a brother. The boy was not taken by Nazis because he was hiding when they came to the door. They simply missed him. But the boy remembered very good the look on mother's face when the Nazis

502

took away family, especially part when they took away younger brother from the mother. It was terrible, you understand?'

Decker nodded.

'Good. I thought you would understand. I remember you tell me that you were in war for America, right?'

'Right.'

'See, I have a memory, too.'

'What happened to the little boy?'

'Somehow he made it through the war. He was very young so he doesn't have much memory. But he made it. Then somehow he goes to Palestine and grows up into young man. And Palestine becomes Israel. Young man becomes an Israeli. At last, he has family of sorts. So many now had big family called Israel because so many lost all family in the war.'

Gold licked his lips.

'One day, the young man sees a list in the paper. There are many lists, he reads them all. But this is a very important list. It tells him he still has a mother. She did not die like father and the brother. She still lives. He feels joy in his heart. He finds mother.'

There was a pause.

'You cannot go backward,' Gold said. 'The man sees mother but she is not the same. She is very scared. She never goes out of house. She has remarried a man very rich who is older than she. For protection. The young man is worried. He is worried that if he comes back to his mother's life, her new husband may not want him. And the new husband may not want *her*. And the young man does not want to see mother in any more pain.

'So they make deal. They don't tell husband. The young man moves close to be with mother, the young man helps mother when she gets pregnant. The young man even baby-sits the new little girl. And they grow close, the young man and the baby. They grow so close that young man learns trade of her father.'

'And the husband still doesn't know?'

'No, he still does not know. And neither did the little girl. Never! The man was just a friend.

'Then . . .' Gold swallowed hard. 'Then one day the little girl is murdered. And the young man, who is now older man, goes to see his mother, to comfort her in her pain. And what does he see? He sees in her eyes that same look when they took his first, younger brother away.'

Gold clenched his fists.

'We still hunt Nazis, Detective. Because there are things in this world that are so bad that there is no city of refuge. There is just no sanctuary for pure evil, you understand?'

'I understand,' Decker said. 'But I don't agree. I believe in a system of justice.'

'And I just believe in justice.' Gold stood. 'Anything else, Detective?'

Decker stood. 'No. Nothing else.'

More Thrilling Fiction from Headline:

FAYE KELLERMAN

GRIEVOUS SIN

"WIFE OF THE MORE FAMOUS
JONATHAN BUT...HIS PEER" *TIME OUT*

Minutes after Sergeant Peter Decker witnesses his wife give
birth to their first child his policeman's instinct tells him
something's wrong, something the doctors are not telling him.
He is right, and in the midst of his wife's trauma he begins to
suspect something else is awry in the hospital. The
disappearance of a new-born baby, together with that of the
nurse in charge of the post-natal unit, confirms once again that
Decker's instincts were correct – but this time *he* is the
professional best qualified to deal with the potentially tragic
crisis, a task to which he takes with a vengeance.

The early signs look bad – the missing nurse's burnt-out car,
together with some charred remains, are found in a remote
ravine. But as Decker and his partner Marge delve deeper, they
start to uncover the network of family tragedy and betrayal that
led to the frantic kidnapping of an innocent baby girl.

"Faye Kellerman creates powerful, unhingeing characters and
her narrative leaves you sweaty-palmed" *Jewish Chronicle*

Don't miss Faye Kellerman's previous novels *Milk and Honey*, *Day of
Atonement* and *False Prophet*, also available from Headline Feature:
"Painfully touching as well as taut with suspense" *Mystery Scene*;
"A marvellous melange of complex family feuds...satisfying
denouement" *Scotsman*; "Tautly exciting" *Los Angeles Times*;
"The most refreshing mystery couple around" *People*

FICTION/THRILLER   0 7472 4118 X

A selection of bestsellers from Headline

HARD EVIDENCE	John T Lescroart	£5.99 ☐
TWICE BURNED	Kit Craig	£5.99 ☐
CAULDRON	Larry Bond	£5.99 ☐
BLACK WOLF	Philip Caveney	£5.99 ☐
ILL WIND	Gary Gottesfield	£5.99 ☐
THE BOMB SHIP	Peter Tonkin	£5.99 ☐
SKINNER'S RULES	Quintin Jardine	£4.99 ☐
COLD CALL	Dianne Pugh	£4.99 ☐
TELL ME NO SECRETS	Joy Fielding	£4.99 ☐
GRIEVOUS SIN	Faye Kellerman	£4.99 ☐
TORSO	John Peyton Cooke	£4.99 ☐
THE WINTER OF THE WOLF	R A MacAvoy	£4.50 ☐

All Headline books are available at your local bookshop or newsagent, or can be ordered direct from the publisher. Just tick the titles you want and fill in the form below. Prices and availability subject to change without notice.

Headline Book Publishing, Cash Sales Department, Bookpoint, 39 Milton Park, Abingdon, OXON, OX14 4TD, UK. If you have a credit card you may order by telephone – 0235 400400.

Please enclose a cheque or postal order made payable to Bookpoint Ltd to the value of the cover price and allow the following for postage and packing:
UK & BFPO: £1.00 for the first book, 50p for the second book and 30p for each additional book ordered up to a maximum charge of £3.00.
OVERSEAS & EIRE: £2.00 for the first book, £1.00 for the second book and 50p for each additional book.

Name ....

Address ....

....

....

If you would prefer to pay by credit card, please complete:
Please debit my Visa/Access/Diner's Card/American Express (delete as applicable) card no:

Signature .... Expiry Date ....